FOR HIRE

"How do I know you're really a starship captain—that you're hiring me to fly, and not"—Tee blushed furiously—"for sex?" She waved her gun at him, and he resisted the potent urge to cover his privates. Never in his life had he seen anything like this pistol-toting pixie, her chin jutting out, her eyes accusing him of unspeakable perversions.

Think fast, he told himself. *Act like a seasoned space veteran, not a guy four years out of Arizona State.* "Now that you bring it up, how do I know you're really a pilot? For all I know, you're just another good-for-nothing drifter, lying your way aboard my ship for the chance at a hot meal and a clean bunk. However, I need a pilot and you need a job. We have no choice but to trust each other. But if that isn't going to be a possibility, Tee, let me know now—because that's the only way it's going to work."

She peered at the row of shops and sleazy bars, doubt saturating her features, then she shifted her attention back to him. In her eyes sparked a glimmer of wonder—the look she'd given him when they first met. He tamped down on the unexpected rush of pleasure he found in that gaze. "So," he prompted, "what will it be?"

She stowed her pistol. "It appears I will trust you, Earth-dweller."

"Good. And just so there's no misunderstanding about my personal life"—he caught her by the arm, bringing his mouth close to one perfectly formed little ear—"when I want sex, I don't have to buy it."

THE
STAR
Prince

SUSAN
GRANT

LOVE SPELL   NEW YORK CITY

A LOVE SPELL BOOK®

November 2001

Published by

Dorchester Publishing Co., Inc.
276 Fifth Avenue
New York, NY 10001

ISBN 0-505-52457-0

Visit us on the web at www.dorchesterpub.com.

For my critique partner Theresa Ragan, who squeezed my hand throughout the entire, mostly excruciating, birth of this book. Thank you for being there every step of the way. You are a talented writer with a giving, generous soul and you deserve all the success that comes your way.

ACKNOWLEDGMENTS

As always, I owe much to many wonderful people: Chris Keeslar and everyone at Dorchester Publishing, cover artist John Ennis, Romance Writers of America, Laurie Gold, Carolyn Stahl, Laura Novak, Pamela Fryer, the Lollies, Catherine Asaro, the paranormal romance listserve, the staff at Harley Davidson motorcycles in Rocklin, California, Joey Febres, West Coast Taekwondo, Jesse Crowder, Susan Wiggs, Chris and Carolyn Gilson, every one of my treasured readers, and last but never least, my children Connor and Courtney, who make it all worthwhile. Thank you all.

THE STAR Prince

Chapter One

"He's not drunk, Captain; he's dead."

"Yeah, yeah. We found him like this last week—
and the week before. He's no more dead now than
he was then." Ian Hamilton pushed past his mechanic and the stragglers milling around the bar. His
pilot—his only pilot, and the third he'd hired since
taking command of the *Sun Devil*—was slumped
forward. Not surprisingly, Carn still occupied the
perch he'd chosen the night before, when Ian had
joined him and the rest of the crew for what was—
for Ian—a rare drink. Now blotches of early-
morning sunlight spread over the pilot's uniform
and the gritty floor, heating the already muggy air.

Ian dragged his arm across his forehead as he
pushed toward the bar. The unrelenting tropical
weather was another reason in a long list of why
Donavan's Blunder, although a bustling crossroads,

11

was arguably the sorriest stopover in the frontier. No worthless lump of space scum was going to keep him here an extra day.

"Move back," he growled irritably at the onlookers pressing in on him from all sides. His eyes must have indicated how close he was to the edge of wringing someone's neck, because no one could stumble backward fast enough.

Ian grabbed Carn's thick shoulders and gave the man a hard shake. "You've overstayed your shore leave, Mr. Carn. Get up." But the pilot's forehead remained on the greasy table, his motionless fingers clamped around an empty shot glass. "Move your sorry butt—*now*—or you're relieved of duty."

Judging by the grumbling of the crowd, firing the drunk was a worthy threat, one expected of a starship captain. "Any of you happen to know how to fly?" he asked. A chorus of apologetic murmurs gave him the answer he expected. Starpilots were scarce in the frontier.

Ian exchanged glances with Quin, the stocky young mechanic who had dragged him off the *Sun Devil*. Quin gave him an I-knew-this-would-happen frown. Their original pilot had drunk himself into oblivion as soon as they arrived in the frontier, the farthest and barely civilized reaches of the galaxy. Ian had sent him home. Unfortunately, the next pilot he hired turned out to be an alcoholic, too. Now pilot number three was following in the others' wobbly footsteps.

But, unreliable or not, he needed Carn. There wasn't time to hunt for another pilot. When the king of the galaxy sent you, an Earth guy, on a mission, the outcome of which was possibly critical to the future of the galaxy, you kept on schedule and finished the job. Especially when that king was your stepfather—a concept Ian doubted he would ever take for granted.

Rom B'kah was a king of kings, the hero ruler of the conservative, staunchly pacifistic *Vash Nadah*, and not even his tradition defying seven-year-old marriage to Ian's mother, Jas, had diminished him in his people's eyes.

Ian suspected that the driving reason behind the *Vash*'s acceptance of the marriage was the fact that their beloved king was sterile. The most advanced medical intervention hadn't been able to reverse the effects of radiation poisoning that Rom had suffered during space combat many years ago, and so there was no need to worry about potentially unsuitable heirs produced with a non-*Vash* wife. Or so the *Vash* had thought.

Rom had broken tradition again, however. He'd chosen Ian as heir—over several eager, genetically qualified young princes in line for the throne—and the decision had left more than a few galactic royals unhappy. "By blood and ability, no Earth dweller has the right being crown prince," some whispered in the halls of the Great Council. All they'd need for proof was word that Ian had gotten himself stuck on Donavan's blunder, marooned by a sloshed, judgment-challenged boozer.

"Sober him up," he ordered Quin. "Nothing short of a gallon of *tock* poured down his throat is going to get him back to the ship."

"It'll take more than that, sir." Quin grabbed a fistful of Carn's blond hair and tipped his head back.

Ian winced. The pilot's face was puffy and tinged a decidedly unheathy blue. His brownish gold eyes were glazed and unseeing, and spittle leaked from the corner of his mouth, which was still curled into the idiotic grin he'd been wearing when Ian left him and the rest of the crew last night.

Ian drove the fingers of both hands through his hair. "Beautiful, just beautiful." His starpilot had drunk himself to death.

He tossed two credits to the bartender. "Call someone about the body. And you might as well put the word out; the *Sun Devil* needs a pilot, a qualified one."

It dismayed him how quickly frustration blunted his pity for Carn, but now wasn't the time for soul searching. After an Earth month in the frontier, he'd met with a year's worth of setbacks—ship malfunctions and pilot problems. *They weren't accidents*. His neck tingled. His years spent submerged in the *Vash* culture had taught him to trust his senses, and that instinct now warned him that someone wanted to thwart his mission.

"Tie up the loose ends and return to the ship,"

he told Quin before shoving outside, past the canvas flap that served as a door.

Steamy heat throbbed up from the pavement in the still-deserted marketplace. A poor excuse for a breeze stirred up the odors of stale liquor and urine. Action started late on this disreputable planet and went on all night. Now, most of the inhabitants were either sleeping in their bunks aboard hundreds of trader vessels docked near the outskirts of the city. Or they were in the bed of a pleasure servant: a woman specially trained and authorized to sell her body for sex.

Ian hoped everyone was enjoying themselves, because his life lately made the average monk look like a party animal. He had become the consummate prince; his behavior was impeccable, his adherence to *Vash* ways beyond reproach. It was the only way to earn the honor his stepfather had bestowed upon him.

He'd studied galactic history and *Vash* religion until he could quote passages from the Treatise of Trade as confidently as most members of the Great Council. Slowly, he was gaining the respect and trust of the tradition-loving *Vash*; although the recent troubles at home could very well drag him back to square one.

Since first contact, public opinion polls on Earth had consistently showed high approval ratings for the *Vash*. Earth liked being part of an intergalactic Trade Federation. But not anymore, apparently, thanks to U.S. Senator Charlie Randall's "Earth First" crusade. The campaign's central theme that Earth was better off as a sovereign planet was attracting followers like a magnet dragged through iron shavings.

"The *Vash* Federation is woven like an ancient quilt," Rom had once told Ian, "a tight center and tattered edges. If the fringe unravels, we will fall apart."

Ian truly believed in his stepfather's conviction that peace depended on a strong, benevolent galaxy-wide government. If Earth pulled out of the Federation, the move might entice other frontier worlds to do the same, setting off a dangerous chain reaction and undermining the stability of the entire galaxy. Yet, that view was, and would always be, tempered by loyalty to his home planet. He wanted what was best for Earth. He wanted to continue his stepfather's legacy and keep the galaxy at peace. Somehow, he had to bridge his two worlds without sacrificing the needs of either.

Which is why, when Rom asked him to go to the frontier and see if the unrest had spread, he'd grabbed hold of the chance. In exchange for the answers he promised to bring back, Rom had given him the *Sun Devil*, a crew of loyal, experienced, merchant-class spacefarers, and his own valued bodyguard. But the mission was more to Ian than a covert scouting foray, more than a way to prove himself to the skeptical *Vash*; this was his chance to demonstrate his worth to Rom, a man he'd come to admire—and love, in many ways—more than his own father.

Only, so far, things were not going well.

Ian put on his Ray•Bans, brushed his hand over the laser pistol in his holster, and started back to the *Sun Devil* to mull over his latest fiasco.

"Captain!" Halfway across the plaza Rom's bodyguard intercepted him, an incongruously named, six-foot-eight hulk of rippling muscle. "Muffin is an old-fashioned name," the big man always explained patiently, if a little defensively, to English speakers like Ian, insisting that "Muffin" personified the essence of rugged masculinity on his homeworld, not a sugary breakfast treat.

"I guess you heard about Carn," Ian said.

"If you can't die a warrior, you might as well die happy."

Ian managed a smile. "True." He appreciated Muffin's tactful attempt to lift his spirits. Although Carn had been a pain in the rear, he had been a member of their small crew, and they'd all feel his passing. "Did he have a family?"

"None that he mentioned. I don't think anyone will miss the guy."

Except me, Ian thought wryly. A rookie space captain marooned on a remote frontier outpost with a cantankerous crew, one of the finest ships in the galaxy—and no one to fly her.

* * *

A backdrop of stars whirled slowly behind a wheel of ruby, emerald, and platinum. Distance made the bejeweled disk appear as tiny as a child's toy, but the structure was as large and populous as a city.

"Rotation synchronized," Tee'ah Dar stated when the spin of the cargo freighter she piloted matched that of the space station ahead.

As expected, Mistraal Control issued final approach instructions via the comm. "Cleared to dock, *Prosper*. Bay Alpha-eight."

"Copy. Alpha-eight." Tee'ah's hands tightened around the control yoke. *You were born for this*, her thoughts sang out.

If she were truly the pious princess she was raised to be, the dutiful daughter her parents thought she was, she'd be in bed, sleeping. But with her hands wrapped around the controls of a cargo freighter, she wasn't the king's sweet and sheltered daughter; she was six hundred million standard tons of lightspeed-strong, molecular-hardened alloy, screaming toward a docking bay that looked too small to hold her. In her imagination, her breaths hissed with hydraulics, her heartbeat with mechanical whirs and clicks. She *was* the gargantuan starship she piloted, her nearly impenetrable trillidium skin shielding a crew of thirty, ten of whom looked on with experience-forged scrutiny as she decelerated the *Prosper*, gliding it into its assigned bay.

There was a gentle rumbling of metal sliding over cushioned guards, and a muffled, soul-satisfying thunk as the great ship settled into place. Soundlessly the bay's external hatches closed, sealing and pressurizing the compartment where the ship now rested from the vacuum of space. *Yes.*

The crew applauded, and for once she allowed the warmth of pride to flood her. Docking the ship on her own was an achievement symbolizing the culmination of a year's worth of clandestine visits to the *Prosper*, a ship used to haul goods between the moon-based mining stations and her home planet, Mistraal, one of the eight *Vash Nadah* homeworlds. Sure, Captain Riss had greeted her request for flying lessons with polite incredulity, particularly after she'd beseeched him to keep her identity a secret—she was a royal woman, after all, and the Dars' only daughter. But once she proved she had the talent to be an intersystem cargo pilot, hard work earned her a coveted pair of pilot wings and a crew's respect, a regard infinitely more satisfying than that given to a cloistered *Vash Nadah* princess.

"Well done." Riss extended his arm across what would be an unbridgeable distance at the palace and clasped her hand in a congratulatory squeeze.

She responded with the self-deprecating retort expected of a space jockey when complimented. "It's a testament to your teaching abilities that no one's now wiping us off the walls of the spaceport."

An outer hatch whooshed open. She expected to see the usual cargo handler or two, there to confirm the load of goods. Instead, four uniformed royal guards strode into the cockpit, followed by a tall, broad-shouldered man with coppery dark blond hair exactly the same shade as hers.

"Father." The blood drained from her head. She gripped the armrests on her chair to steady herself.

Captain Riss snapped to attention. "Behold, the king! Welcome to the *Prosper*, my lord," he said, and fell to one knee. The rest of the crew reacted with similarly respectful, albeit shocked, shows of respect. The cargo crew was civilian, not military, and kings rarely, if ever, boarded mining freighters. But Joren Dar gave the men little more than a cursory wave. His blue travel cape slapped at his boots as he climbed the gangway to where Tee'ah sat.

Her hands fumbled with her harnesses. Finally free of her seat, she stood, facing him. "Greetings, Father."

He spoke in a low, ominous tone, so that no one else would hear. "I would not have thought that you, Tee'ah, would have deceived me in such a"—he waved his hand around the cockpit—"blatant manner."

His golden eyes chilled her with his disappointment and disapproval. Tee'ah fought a watery feeling in the pit of her stomach. "I know it means little now," she replied in an equally hushed tone, "but I intended to tell you everything." She squeezed her clasped hands together until her pulse throbbed in her fingertips. "But I thought you would take the news better once I'd officially earned my wings."

His eyes flicked to the silver intersystem cargo pilot wings she wore over her left breast. Embroidered in metallic thread onto her rich indigo-hued flight suit, the emblem was a replica of the genuine pair she kept in a box in her bedchamber and treasured above all else. "I've had the wings only a month," she whispered, hoping her achievement would prove to her father how much she desired personal freedom.

Or were you merely longing to spark in him a bit of pride in your accomplishments?

His frown deepened. She cursed herself for thinking that such a tradition-defying feat would win her father's praise. She should have told him sooner where she disappeared to three nights a week. She should have informed him before he figured it out on his own or, worse, learned of her exploits from someone else.

Joren Dar turned his attention to Captain Riss, who waited uneasily for further instructions. He'd risked his career by teaching her to pilot his ship, all because he'd understood when she confessed that her yearning to fly, to be free, flared so hot it burned. He mustn't take the blame that was hers alone.

"Why was I was not informed that my daughter was spending her nights flying your ship?"

"I asked him not to," Tee'ah said before Riss had the chance to answer her father.

21

The captain compressed his lips and made a small sound in the back of his throat.

"He did not understand that what I requested of him was against your wishes," she went on.

"My lord—" Riss attempted. "I—"

"Well, perhaps he did, Father, but know this: I sought out the *Prosper* because of Captain Riss. He's the best in the fleet. He's professional, knowledgeable. He's ensured my protection from my first day aboard this ship. The only place I'd have been safer was in my bed."

Riss's mouth quirked and he stared hard at the alloy flooring, clearly fighting a smile. Evidently he'd given up the struggle to get a word in edgewise.

His yielding to her persistence was not lost on the king, and that was the point she had hoped to make. At times, though only over small issues, even her father fell victim to her cajoling. "If anyone is to blame for my presence here," she said, her voice pleading and low, "it's me."

Joren scrutinized the beleaguered captain. Riss lifted his eyes. Strangely, an understanding of sorts flickered between the men. "I will see you in my chambers tomorrow, Captain."

Then he gently but firmly took Tee'ah by the elbow. "And you, daughter, I will see in my chambers *now*."

The shuttle ride back to the surface was excruciatingly long. On her lap, Tee'ah clutched the satchel containing the handmaiden's dress and cloak she'd used to disguise herself when traveling back and forth to the spaceport while her family slept. Her father's hands were spread on his knees, his muscular arms braced, his eyes downcast. His expression was guarded, making it difficult to tell what he was thinking, although she had her suspicions as to what occupied his thoughts.

Within a few weeks, her marriage contract would be signed and she'd be officially promised to Prince Ché Vedla, a man she'd met only once, when they were both children. One standard year from the day the promise took effect, they would marry, a union arranged with good intentions, but little regard for her personal wishes. Marriages among *Vash Nadah* royalty were part of a complicated, ongoing stabilizing of power shared by the eight ruling families. They were political alliances, not love matches, although the *Vash* culture emphasized the importance of good relations between a husband and wife. Eventually her union with Prince Ché could be a pleasant one, if he'd matured from the overconfident royal brat she remembered.

But the extraordinary events of the past few years—her uncle Rom's startlingly unconventional marriage to an equally unconventional Earth woman, and then, more recently, Tee'ah's own daring spaceflights—revealed choices she'd never imagined, much less contemplated. She was less certain than ever that the path so carefully prepared for her was the one she should take.

Susan Grant

Upon their arrival at the palace, Tee'ah walked with her father to his private chambers. The ancient polished white stone walls and floor she normally admired now struck her as featureless and cold.

Her mother met them. Her eyes were swollen, as if she'd been crying. Tee'ah embraced her, whispering, "I'm sorry."

But was she? After all, it wasn't as if she'd run off to a lover, knowing she was about to become engaged—*that* would have been unforgivable and symptomatic of a weak character. She'd only learned to fly. What was so terribly wrong with that?

Joren regarded her for long moments. Tightening his features was a loving father's complicated mix of emotions. "You have responsibilities, Tee'ah. Maintaining a trade, like flying, drains time and energy away from those obligations. And then, of course, there is the issue of propriety to consider."

Stiffly, she stepped out of the circle of her mother's familiar warmth and sweet scent. "But after I marry, if Prince Ché agrees—"

"Don't pursue this. The Vedlas will not approve. You cannot fly."

You cannot fly.

There. With three words, he'd ended her dream. Apparently the king's renowned mercy and open-mindedness didn't extend to his daughter.

The sensation of suffocation was so real it felt as if a vise squeezed her lungs. Her hand crept to her throat, her fingers trembling. *Breathe.*

Oblivious to her grief, her father paced in front of her. " 'The welfare of all comes before the desires of an individual,' " he quoted from the Treatise of Trade, the holiest document of their people. "Recite the rest of that passage, Tee'ah. Feel the words; *feel* what it means to be *Vash Nadah*."

He halted, waiting. She took a breath, her hands fisted at her sides. Then, at the king's command, she recited the words she'd memorized too long ago to have a recollection of doing so: " 'Eleven thousand years ago the Dark Years engulfed us. Technological evolution outpaced spiritual evolution; societies that had existed for eons crumbled; disease, endless famine, and fear caused by selfish warring kingdoms spurred a complete collapse of civilization. Warlords renounced spirituality and condemned sexuality. Weapons of unimaginable destruction were created and perfected by those without conscience, and used by those who embraced cruelty and worshiped soulless power.' " She took a shuddering breath. " 'Eight great warriors banded together to vanquish the evil. Peace for all time, they vowed when the Great Mother's light dawned once more. Praised be the Eight.' " Flatly she finished, "A reading from the Treatise of Trade."

Her father nodded. "The blood of the Eight flows through your veins, Tee'ah. That brings responsibilities, obligations that others cannot imagine. We, the eight royal families, must lead through sacrifice and example."

She shifted her gaze to the window. Outside was the endless savanna, a vista she'd often gazed at with longing. Whenever she'd needed to breathe, whenever she feared she'd suffocate in her scrupulously sheltered, relentlessly comfortable life.

The long grasses were completely flattened, meaning a *Tjhu'nami* was fast approaching. The orbital weather stations predicted that one of the dry windstorms that periodically scoured Mistraal would hit by morning, bringing wind velocities exceeding eight hundred standard galactic knots.

Using all her senses, she concentrated. She could feel, but couldn't quite hear, a steady rumbling—the receding tide of air before a distant massive wave.

She turned to her father. "To be honest, I'm afraid," she said.

He shook his head. "Afraid? Of the *Tjhu'nami?*"

Not once in her twenty-three standard years had she waited out the terrifying storms anywhere but ensconced with her family in the noisy communal dining hall. But a greater fear gripped her. "No, Father. Of losing *myself.*" She pressed her knotted hands under her chin. "I barely remember meeting the Vedlas. Now I'm to join them on a distant planet I've never visited . . . where custom will keep me rooted for the rest of my life. It frightens me."

But her confession only bemused her parents. "Ah, child," her mother said, placing a warm hand on her cheek. "Your husband's family will love you, as we love you."

26

Her mother's tender maternal caress showed Tee'ah that she believed what she told her. "Before long you will settle in, and you will feel with them what you feel here, with us."

And that, Tee'ah thought, was exactly what she feared.

With her thumb, her mother wiped a rare tear from Tee'ah's cheek. "Your father and I will see you in the dining hall this evening," she said gently. "Change your clothing and join us there. We will tell stories and wait out the storm. Just like always."

"Yes. Like always, Mother," she whispered.

Tee'ah bowed her head respectfully and returned to her own chamber. A floor-to-ceiling window dominated one wall. She pressed her forehead to the cold surface, her hands spread on the glass-composite pane, and watched the coming storm from the safety of her bedroom, unable to escape the parallels to her own situation.

She could stay as she was and be safe. Ché Vedla was considered by many to be one of the most promising young princes of her generation. With him she'd look forward to a luxurious—but anonymous—existence as a powerful man's wife. But if she left the palace, she'd face the unknown head-on.

She thought of her aunt from Earth. "Too many people never go after what they truly want out of life," Jas once told her. When Tee'ah had asked why not, Jas had replied, "Because it's easier not to."

Only now did Tee'ah truly understand what her

aunt meant. The paths forged on one's own were the most difficult to travel. If she tried to make her own way, she might fail, spectacularly so, and hurt those she loved in the process. Or she might achieve everything of which she'd dreamed. But if she stayed here, she'd never find out, would she?

She walked away from the window. Wrung her hands. Walked back.

Outside, ocher plains stretched to the distant, gently bowed horizon, now smudged by blowing dust. The *Tjhu'nami*. When the dangerous winds arrived, no one would attempt flights in or out of Dar City. What if she were to leave tonight? Steal a star-speeder. Palace security wouldn't risk going after her until the gale subsided to a safe level. Leaving just before the storm hit would give her a full standard day's head start, would it not?

She wrung her hands harder. The plan was too rushed. She needed more time to think it over. There would be another storm later in the season. But if she were forbidden to fly, her piloting skills would have deteriorated by then, reducing her chances of success.

She dropped her hands. If she was going to leave, it had to be tonight—*if* she could find a starspeeder and *if* the confusion of the *Tjhu'nami* indeed cloaked her departure.

So many "ifs." Doubt swamped her.

Her family didn't deserve the pain her sudden departure would bring them. But if she stayed on in a culture that treated her as if she had no free will, no control over her destiny, no *choices*, she'd soon be as dry and empty as a seed husk in the autumn winds. Her body would live to a ripe old age, yes, but her spirit would be dead long before that.

Go. Follow your dreams. Yes, before they were lost to her forever. Her blood surged. This time when she turned away from the window, it was to gather the items she needed to facilitate her escape.

Chapter Two

Tee'ah used the waning hours before the storm to work on the mechanics of her plan. She'd packed a small satchel with money credits and a few shirts and pairs of pants of her brother's, taken from his quarters after she was sure he and his family had left for the dining hall. She'd requisitioned his laser pistol, too. He wouldn't mind, she reasoned, once he realized she'd need the weapon for protection. The letter she'd written her parents—a heartbreaking task—would not appear on their private comm channel until after she'd gone.

The familiar sound of falling shields, thunderous explosions rumbling through the palace, signaled the imminent approach of the *Tjhu'nami*. Designed as protection against the storm, the clear barriers slammed shut automatically over all windows when the wind reached a predetermined velocity. When the last of the shields' resounding booms faded, Tee'ah opened her bedroom door. She yanked the bill of her cargo pilot cap over her forehead and peered into a suddenly silent, deserted corridor. The ragged tufts tickling her jaw were all that remained after chopping off her thick, thigh-length hair.

The wind bombarded the shields, harder now. Her ears popped with the oscillating atmospheric pressure.

She clutched the doorjamb, unable to force herself forward—or back—caught between her future and her past, between a crazy wish and common sense. Her uneven breathing became a roar in her ears, amplifying her self-doubt, threatening her resolve. But if she wanted to escape to freedom and independence, she'd have to overcome her childish fears, starting with her terror of the storm.

Go. She grabbed her satchel and propelled herself into a full-fledged run through a labyrinth of white polished-stone corridors she knew by heart. Her cargo pilot coverall allowed her a freedom of movement she'd never experienced in the ankle-length gowns she'd worn all her life. Her lungs burned, her legs tightened, but the exertion brought her joy, as if her body were a fresh-from-the-shipyard starship experiencing light speed for the first time.

She skidded to a brisk walk as she entered the mezzanine of Mistraal's spaceport. Cool, dry air and the resonance of the enormous chamber snapped her into instant alertness. From under her pilot cap, she gazed at the dust-glazed sky reflected in an immense but graceful passenger shuttle, newly arrived from the orbital space-city, and packed with hundreds of passengers eager to arrive before the storm.

Slashes of early-evening sunlight fanned over the marble floor, illuminating the travelers exiting the shuttle. *Great Mother.* She recognized half the people milling about—palace staff and workers . . . and several members of her father's Security Council.

Praying she looked nothing like a princess, she rolled her shoulders back, swinging her arms in the cocky, casual stride used by the intersystem cargo pilots she'd always admired. And envied. Perspiration trickled down one cheek. Her flight suit clung to her damp skin as she pushed forward against the tide of travelers.

Faster. You must launch before the storm hits.

Eyes downcast, she left the mezzanine behind, walking as swiftly as she could without actually running. A locked door separated the shuttle bay from the passenger area. She shoved her left palm into a hand reader. The receptacle beeped and displayed ACCESS DENIED.

She steadied herself with a deep breath and again wedged her hand into the reader. STAND BY. An amber light blinked while the unit attempted to reconcile her sweaty, tense palm with what it "thought" her hand was supposed to look like.

Heartbeats ticked by. Tee'ah swore under her breath.

CHECKING . . . CHECKING . . .

You'll never see your family again. Heavens, she loved her parents, her brothers, their wives and children. If she ran away she'd cause them untold pain and worry. The muscles in her arm contracted and her fingers stiffened.

CHECKING . . . CHECKING . . .

She forcibly relaxed her hand, tamping down on her upsurge of guilt. She had to keep her mind clear, her thoughts rational. She mustn't allow regret to distract her.

VERIFICATION COMPLETED.

The door slid open. Her breath hissed out. She dashed into the vast hangar, her boots thudding against the silver alloy flooring in lonely echoes. The area where the starspeeders were docked was predictably deserted. When she'd accessed the computer in her bedchamber, she'd noted that only gates six and seven were scheduled to have a vessel occupying the bay. One . . . two . . . three: she counted the gates as she ran. All were vacant. Her stomach quivered with the unwelcome vision of finding six and seven empty, too.

Four . . . five . . . *There!* She gave a silent cheer. The ship she'd had her eye on was safely docked at bay six to wait out the storm. It was the break she'd counted on.

The starspeeder was small, built for a crew of four. But its oversize engines and sleek fuselage made it fast. She would need that speed to put distance between her and the soldiers her father would inevitably set on her trail—by tomorrow, she figured. She did a quick mental calculation: the stored food and water on the ship, a week's worth for each of its four pilots, would keep her alive during the journey to the frontier.

She eased her hand into her right pocket. Her fingertips brushed the cool, impersonal cylinder of her borrowed laser pistol as she stepped inside the ship's darkened interior. By the heavens, someone was sitting in the cockpit—at the controls.

She almost groaned aloud. The last thing she'd anticipated was leaving behind a witness. Raising her pistol, she moved out of the shadows. "Get up," she said, her voice calm, in fact miraculously so.

The pilot spun around in his chair. His throat bobbed when he saw her weapon, but his hand slid toward the flashing red light that was a direct link to Mistraal's planetary security.

"Touch the comm and you're space dust."

A flush rose in his face and his hand retreated. Nonetheless, she aimed at his head, praying he didn't call her bluff and make her use the thing. She'd never shot at anything, certainly not a live person, as if she'd actually ever try. Even if she did, she'd no doubt miss and rip a hole in the hull and heaven knew what else, blowing her chance to take the ship.

"Stand up . . . slowly." Her heart thumped harder in her chest, but somehow she kept her hands steady. "Set your pistol on the comm panel and back away."

The young lieutenant bristled. "Why would I need a pistol doing postflight checklists in the cockpit of an empty intersystem merchant vessel—a *docked* empty merchant vessel?"

"I said *move it*!" She advanced on him.

He shot to his feet. "Lady Tee'ah!"

Sweet heaven. She hadn't recognized him, but that didn't mean he didn't recognize her; there were a lot fewer princesses on Mistraal than cargo pilots.

"Honored lady—" From where he stood, he peered under her cap and grimaced. "What happened?"

She forced a scowl. "Bad hair day." He blinked in confusion. "Go," she snapped before he had the chance to respond.

He backed up, hands raised. "You'll need a pilot to fly her."

"*I'm* flying her."

That threw him. But he recovered swiftly. "Without departure codes you'll never get clearance out of here."

Tee'ah admired his clever efforts to stay aboard to keep the speeder from being stolen. Men like him had made the Dars one of the most respected of the eight royal families. "I have the codes," she said quietly. "And you, Lieutenant, have one standard-minute to clear the bay. Them I'm firing the thrusters."

Exhaling, he climbed down the gangway from the cockpit to the cabin. The muzzle of her pistol matched his progress along the bulkhead leading to the exit hatch. He looked positively forlorn. She gentled her tone. "I left a note of explanation. You won't be blamed."

The pilot shrugged dejectedly. She thought of Captain Riss and prayed that her father's famed benevolence extended to both him and this young lieutenant.

She clutched the pistol in her sweaty hands, waiting for the pilot's measured steps to take him farther into the empty, cavernous docking bay. The instant he was safely away from the ship, she smacked her palm onto the door panel. The starspeeder's hatch snapped shut with a hiss of air. From the viewscreen, she snatched one last glimpse of the displaced pilot staring at her from the safety of the spaceport before he dashed away to find help.

She jumped into the pilot's chair, buckled in, and flipped on the thrusters. The starspeeder shuddered as she turned the craft within the confines of the docking bay. Clearing the hangar, she aimed the ship's nose at the sky and pulled the control stick to her chest, shoving the thrusters forward with her other hand. Acceleration slammed her into her seat as she soared skyward.

The storm had intensified more swiftly than she'd anticipated. Bone-shaking turbulence dislodged her cap, and roiling clouds of dust scoured the forward viewscreen. The airborne particles made the engines whine. Her pulse skipped erratically as her deep fear of the *Tjhu'nami* threatened to overwhelm her. But as the pale orange sky dimmed into indigo and then the black of space, and stars took the place of the setting sun, the rough air eased. Only then did she tip her head back against the headrest and allow herself a single soft, triumphant laugh. She was free.

"Talk about dropping off the face of the Earth!"

Bleary-eyed from a string of restless nights, Ian slouched in his command chair on the *Sun Devil*, waiting for his twin sister to finish berating him from the viewscreen attached to his right armrest. His boots propped on a box of produce destined for the ship's galley, he pondered the benefits of ancient technology that allowed the *Vash* to communicate with minimal lag times over vast interstellar distances. Then he weighed those benefits against the grinding reality of being light years from Earth and pestered by his sister, real time.

"Ian, do you have any idea how hard it's been trying to get hold of you? Mom said you were in the frontier, but didn't know where. This is *so* not like you, Mr. Goody-two-shoes."

"Hey, I called, didn't I?"

She snorted. "Mentally, I'd already tossed your ashes into the wind."

"I'm undercover, Ilana. No one can reach me. Remember?"

"Was I supposed to?" She appeared unconvincingly apologetic as she smoothed her bangs away from her forehead. On anyone else, the tangled bleached-blond hair would look like a mop. On her, it looked good, and probably fit her life as a young, single filmmaker living in Santa Monica, California.

"I needed to ask you a few questions," he said, "but it sounds like you have something for me." Ilana had once said that his eagerness to devote his life to the greater good was as pointless and boring as her dating only one guy at a time. But her love for Rom B'kah was one thing they had in common, and she acted as Ian's eyes and ears on Earth, keeping him updated on public opinion regarding the Federation.

"Well, the Neanderthals are at it again."

"Earth First?"

"Yes. Two anti-Federation rallies—one a couple of weeks ago at the U.N., the other last weekend in Washington."

"No protests overseas?"

"No. Not yet."

He rolled the tension out of his shoulders. Because he and his mother had unprecedented positions in their society, a high-ranking Earth official instigating a bid for independence was bound to attract *Vash* attention. What member of the Great Council would approve of a prince from a rogue planet?

"Don't let it get you down, Ian. I have good news,

too. Randall's on his way to the frontier. A little fact-finding tour, he's calling it."

"No kidding." Adrenaline rushed through him, and he dropped his feet to the floor. Finally, something was going his way. "Have you got anything recorded?"

"A press conference. Ready?"

"Yes. Play it."

Charles Randall appeared on the viewscreen. Dressed in a crisp flightsuit with a NASA emblem, the senator posed comfortably before an array of viewscreens that were clearly part of a new starship. Ironic, Ian thought as he waved Muffin over; the Federation's biggest critic was enjoying himself on a spaceship cut from a *Vash* pattern with *Vash*-donated parts.

Muffin settled into the adjacent chair. The recording was in English, of which the man had a limited command. He could use a Basic English translator—a high-tech, palm-sized device that transformed speech to text—but he preferred observing body language, which he said he often found more useful than verbal cues.

"Senator," a correspondent asked once Randall was done rhapsodizing about his upcoming adventure. "How do you reconcile your harsh accusations regarding the *Vash* with their actions over the past seven years? In exchange for an ordinary trade agreement, they've given us cures for cancer and AIDS, and medical science enabling us to heal newly damaged spinal cords. Yet you say we're better off without them?"

Randall ran a hand over his silver hair, cut in a short military style buzz. "The *Vash* have indeed been generous with us," he acknowledged. "Light-speed capable spacecraft, cures for devastating diseases; the list goes on and on. But at what cost to us? They've absorbed us completely into their empire." His piercing blue eyes narrowed. "If that doesn't frighten you, it should. The arrangement you call an ordinary trade agreement is the proverbial deal with the devil. We sold our souls for some fancy tech. This may not be what some of you want to hear, but it's reality, folks. It's time we faced it, took action and looked out for our own interests. That's why I'm going to the frontier. For you, for me, for all of us. I want to see what has happened to other planets who have made deals with the *Vash*. And I want to see what actions will be most favorable for our peoples in the years to come. I expect that detaching ourselves from the Federation is the only way to get what we need. Remember, Earth must come first."

A few journalists cheered.

"Great," Ian muttered to himself. Their eagerness to swallow Randall's sugar pill of sovereignty showed their naiveté in galactic history. Independent, power-hungry worlds caused instability; only unity would keep the peace.

"What's your itinerary, Senator?"

"Planet Grüma will serve as my base camp for the month. From there I'll launch several side trips."

Ian drummed his fingers on his thighs. "Grüma." The rural planet was home to the frontier's lively but mostly harmless black market. "I wonder what facts he thinks he'll find there?"

"We can easily find out," Muffin said. "It's close, a day's ride. Maybe two."

Ian scowled. "It might as well be in another dimension without a pilot to fly us there."

When Ilana reappeared on the viewscreen, she searched his face and grinned. "All right. You're going after him?"

"You better believe, I am."

"Hot damn! Ian Hamilton's going to kick some butt. *Tae-kwon-do*! Make Randall eat his propaganda, would you?"

He replied dryly, "The *Vash* crown prince duking it out with a U.S. senator? Yeah, that'd go a long way toward helping interstellar relations."

"You know, maybe it would."

Muffin chuckled, and Ian glared at him.

Ilana lifted her hands. "I know, you don't have to tell me. You prefer the thinking man's approach; diplomacy is paramount; 'make love not war,' the *Vash Nadah* creed. Hey, it worked for most of eleven thousand years, right?" She leaned toward the viewscreen. "But sometimes, you just have to kick a little ass."

Ian pushed his tongue against the inside of his

cheek. Ilana recognized the warning sign and smiled sweetly. "All I'm saying is that you have a black belt—put it to use for once in your life."

"On a different subject," he interjected. "Thanks for the heads-up on Randall."

"Anytime," she said, softer.

He reached for the viewscreen, then dropped his hand. "I owe you big time. And don't tell Rom *or* Mom that I called. I want to take care of this myself."

"Okay." She blew him a kiss. "Be careful out there," she murmured, then she signed off.

Rom had approved a mission for Ian to see what was happening in the frontier, not to chase after an Earth senator. "Quin," he called over his shoulder. "When you have a chance, redo the encryption on our comm."

"But, sir," Quin said, "it was done before we left Sienna. Lord B'kah's chief mechanic is an expert in the security field."

"That's the point. Rom knows the codes." As long as there was a way for the king to find him, the umbilical cord was still attached. This was something he wanted to achieve on his own. "We're about to take a little detour. It's best no one knows about it but us."

The ship felt suddenly claustrophobic. Ian pushed himself off the chair and tiredly tucked his shirt into his jeans. "I'm heading out for awhile," he told the men. "Call me on the comm if any pilots come knocking on our door, begging for work." He checked his utility belt for his laser pistol and sunglasses, then left in search of a likely establishment for a glass of iced *tock*. The licorice-tasting beverage passed for coffee everywhere but Earth.

Not much happened on Blunder before mid afternoon. He'd use the quiet hours to reformulate his strategy now that it appeared his nemesis was coming to him. But as soon as the streets filled at sunset, he vowed to find someone capable of flying him off this stinking rock.

There was a decided swagger in Tee'ah's stiff, too-long-on-a-ship gait as she strode down the gangway of her starspeeder. The air on Donavan's Blunder was thick, almost suffocating, and the sun's intense heat seared through the fabric of her brother's unseasonable black shirt and pants. She would have been far more comfortable in her flight suit, but with the Dar fleet likely on her tail, armed with the description of her clothing the lieutenant would have given them, she couldn't risk being recognized.

She donned her cap, now stripped of its wing-shaped emblem, and ducked under the shadow of the speeder. Her boots crunched on the hard, bleached dirt as she took in the bustling spaceport, marveling at the sheer volume of people. The scents of dust, food, and decay, the thunder of ships roaring overhead and merchants shouting, slammed into her, making her senses whirl wondrously. Filling her lungs with hot, rocket fume-laden air, she tasted freedom with every breath.

"Donavan's Blunder," she said on an exhalation. The name was legendary, conjuring images of danger and adventure. Her uncle, Romlijhian B'kah, a legend in his own right, once dismissed Blunder as a rather notorious but necessary stop on the far-flung trade routes of the frontier. But to her, a woman raised within the custodial elegance of a *Vash* castle, the port was exotic, exciting. Glamorous. How far she'd veered from her ordained path, a destiny she'd never questioned until her uncle married Jasmine Hamilton, the most fascinating individual she'd ever known. The woman flew starspeeders and acted as freely as her ruler husband.

A starcruiser roared overhead, reminding Tee'ah quite starkly that as soon as the storm passed, her father would have dispatched his security forces to find her. Certainly one contingent would have been sent to search the major ports in the frontier, and if they hadn't already searched Donavan's Blunder, they certainly would soon. This was no time to act like an awestruck tourist.

She tugged her cap over her eyes and set her jaw. Fighting dizziness and the beginnings of a headache triggered by sensory overload, she left the speeder behind, limping across the plaza to the crowded market, where she was sure to find a cloaker. The crew of the *Prosper* had often talked about their travels. From those tales of adventure Tee'ah had learned about obtaining the illegal services of a cloaker, a specialist who could "disguise" a vessel by hacking in and scrambling the identifying codes it transmitted when queried by space controllers or other ships. As long as her ship was virtually screaming *I'm a stolen speeder piloted by a runaway princess*, she had a star-berry blossom's chance in winter of making it off Blunder without her father's knowledge. A cloaker would change all that, allowing her to traverse the galaxy as just another run-of-the-mill ship.

Heat rose from the dirt. Ahead, a row of ramshackle buildings undulated like palace banners in the morning breeze. As she neared, the illusion solidified into tents with frayed canvas flaps for doors. Although a lot of money flowed in and out of the port, it wasn't apparent in the area's architecture. She suspected that those who profited here funneled their illegally gained wealth off planet to where it would be safe from thievery and *Vash* seizures.

She chose the nearest tent. Pushing past a musty tarp she walked inside, blinking as her eyes adjusted to the stuffy interior dimly lit by laser candles. A man who looked as though he hadn't slept in weeks lowered the cup from which he'd been drinking. "Yes, lad?" His breath held the sharp scent of liquor.

"Can you tell me where I can find a cloaker?" she whispered.

He pointed unsteadily with his cup. "That way." Clear liquid sloshed onto the dusty floor. "Second shop from the end."

"Thanks." She exchanged the oppressive heat of the tent for the sharp glare of the sun-baked street. She infused her steps with confidence she didn't quite feel, but she was stared at nonetheless; strangers were noticed on the Blunder.

Some in the mostly male crowd looked mean, their eyes hard. Others showed signs of disease—pockmarks, bowed limbs, or colds with coughs and reddened noses—none of which she had seen before. If advanced medical technology reached all corners of the galaxy, as the *Vash* Federation claimed, then why was it not evident here?

A wisp of a breeze teased the tarnished wind chimes dangling from the beamed ceiling of a café. The delicate melody lingered and seemed out of place. Longingly she gazed at a glass of iced *tock* in the sole patron's hand. Then a glint of silver dragged her attention to the man's face. He was wearing mirrored eye-shaders! No one wore shaders anymore. They hadn't been popular for thousands of years, not since the advent of optic implants. But they somehow fit the trader, right down to his fair skin and odd-colored dark hair, a rich nut brown.

Tee'ah slowed, curiosity overcoming her. The exotic stranger noticed, warily twisting around on his stool. He glanced over his shaders with greenish eyes as brilliant as gems. An Earth dweller! Just seeing someone from the provincial and stubbornly independent frontier world, close enough to touch, was thrilling proof that she was far, far from home.

The man gave her a brief nod, the kind one traveler might give another, and then went back to his *tock*. Almost reluctantly she resumed her pace, leaving the café behind.

"What do we have here?" she heard someone say.

She jerked her attention up from the dusty street. A lanky merchant with intense, intelligent eyes scrutinized her from the shade of an awning. "A genuine intersystem cargo pilot cap you're wearing there," he noted. "Minus the emblem. Where's the rest of your pretty uniform?"

Unease fluttered in her belly, and instinct urged her to run. Pride kept her from doing so. She dismissed her admirer with a nod but he caught up to her, matching her strides.

She halted with one hand on the tent flap to the cloaker's shop. "I have business to attend to," she said crisply.

He peered under the brim of her cap and his eyes sparked with surprise. Whether it was because he had discovered she was female, or that she had the classic features of her class, she wasn't sure, but he didn't ask the question she saw on his face.

"Well, the plot thickens," he murmured. "Nice ship you have there. Looks fast."

"She is that." With wistful pride, Tee'ah glanced backward over her shoulder. The distant speeder's fuselage glowed painfully bright in the sun. "Sublight–speed at only twenty-five percent thrust."

"Impressive. Bet you'd like to keep her."

Her heart stopped. "What?"

He handed her his palmtop. His gaze was cool, discerning, as if he knew what she was all about. She forced herself to focus on the series of numbers and letters scrolling across the screen, a code identifying her ship as a Dar speeder without clearance to be this far from home.

"Stole her, did you? From the Dars." He broke into a laugh when the rest of the blood no doubt drained from her face. Then he waved at the dozens of ships docked on all sides. "Not to worry; half the ships here arrive with owners other than those who were intended."

Somehow she kept the quivers in her belly from reaching her hand as she returned his palmtop. "What do you want?"

"A little business."

"Who are you?"

"I'm your cloaker."

"But . . ." Stupidly she peered into the empty interior of the tent.

"It's a quiet day. I was out combing for extra work. You simply beat me back to the store." The merchant lifted the tent flap and waved one arm with a flourish. "After you, my lady." With a shrug, she went in.

The shop smelled like tobacco and stale incense.

Half-hidden behind an array of computers was a desk littered with surprisingly sophisticated hardware. The cloaker pulled out a chair and sat, leaving her standing. "I'll be happy to fix your hot little speeder," he said. "But I'll require insurance."

"What? I require cloaking, nothing more."

"You're wearing the cap of an intersystem cargo pilot, but you're in the frontier, way out of the usual neighborhood, correct? Not to mention that at first sight you look purebred *Vash* ... but you can't be because you're standing here talking to me about a Dar speeder that ain't supposed to be here." He slammed his palmtop onto the desk separating them. "Someone's going to come after your ship eventually. If I'm still on board working when they do, they'll fine me to oblivion. I'll need insurance for that—and to steer them off your trail should they ask about you." He paused, regarding her. "They *are* going to ask about you, aren't they?"

She studied the sunlight creating patterns on the floor. It seemed the cost of her freedom was rising. "How much?"

"Fourteen thousand credits."

She gave a strangled cough. "Fourteen?" That was most of what she had with her. "Ten thousand," she shot back, her belly twisting from nerves. She desperately needed the cloaker. But she needed her credits, too. "That's all I'll spend."

He plopped his arms over his chest. "Thirteen-five and not a credit lower. As a special favor I'll throw in my expert subterfuge, which is me convincing anyone who asks—at my own risk—that you're not here. Long gone. Off planet. Got it?" His eyes narrowed. "You're dealing with the Dars here. *Vash* royalty. They'll want back what's theirs."

"There are other cloakers on Blunder." She swallowed tightly, then headed for the exit, praying she was right.

"Twelve, then," she heard him say. "You won't get it any lower. Not under these circumstances."

He was right. She wasn't in possession of just any ship; she'd taken a top-of-the-line Dar starspeeder. Other cloakers might not want to risk the wrath of a *Vash* royal family by altering such a vessel, no matter how much money she was willing to pay.

She let out a breath and turned around. "All right. Twelve thousand credits."

"For six thousand more I'll resync your thrusters."

She almost snorted. "Do I look like I'm made of credits?"

"As a matter of fact, you do." He propped his elbows on the table and leaned forward. "Ever think of putting those looks to use? I mean, grow your hair a bit, a bath, a clean gown maybe. No one would know you weren't genuine." He used his tongue to wet his lips. "Traders would pay good money, real good money, to buy sex with a pleasure servant who looked like a *Vash* virgin."

Her cheeks flamed.

"I could help get you started, and—"

"No. Thanks." Swallowing, her throat suddenly dry, she whispered tightly, "Just fix the ship."

She backed out the door into the sun-baked plaza. A cruiser landed at the docks, making the ground rumble beneath her boots. Slumping against one of the poles holding up the awning, she pressed her sleeve to her cheeks, blotting rivulets of sweat and what likely remained of her blush of embarrassment.

The tent creaked: then the cloaker eased past her carrying a sack bulging with clinking hardware. "Three standard hours," he called over his shoulder. His facial expression was benign, as if his offer to help sell her body hadn't occurred at all.

Maybe he hadn't meant anything by it. It was a business proposition and nothing else. Men here were merely cruder than what she was used to, and she couldn't expect them to keep their conversations within the boundaries of accepted etiquette. Before long—she hoped—such encounters would no longer mortify her.

Faintly, wind chimes tinkled in another weak breeze. She peered across the plaza to the café. Her stomach gave a little flip; the Earth dweller was sitting in the same place, appearing almost forlorn, his hands curled protectively around his *tock*. She'd bet he didn't care much for *Vash* rules, she mused wistfully. He was independent, unconventional, maybe dangerous, too. He symbolized all that she had run away from home to find.

Speculatively, she studied him. She had time to

kill, didn't she? Three hours. And she was thirsty, too. Besides, the café afforded an uninterrupted view of her speeder.

She swiped off her cap, then shoved it into her back pocket. Where she'd worn the hat, her hair was molded to her scalp. But the bottom strands were beginning to curl, exposing her ears to the harsh sun. She attempted to tidy up, using her fingers as a comb—then stopped herself, hands in midair. Heavens, what did it matter what she looked like? In fact, she thought wryly, the more she resembled the other grubby traders around here, the better. Less chance of being recognized, for one thing.

She scrubbed her scalp until her hair stood on end, then smiled as she crossed the plaza with deliciously full strides. She was a free woman now, a soon-to-be galactic explorer. Joining the foreign trader for a frosty glass of *tock* would merely be the first nibble of adventure before she devoured the full feast.

Chapter Three

"A pleasant day to you!"

At the sound of the too-cheery female voice, Ian slid his hands off the bar and pushed himself upright. The last thing he needed was another solicitation from one of Blunder's overenthusiastic pleasure servants. The women were independent contractors who profited from consensual sex, but he didn't partake of their services—unlike every other trader on this godforsaken rock, it seemed. Even if he did, he doubted a around of brainless, bought-and-paid-for sex would keep him from steeping himself in misery over the knowledge that Senator Randall was on Grüma, and he was stuck here.

"Find someone else," he snapped, turning around. "I'm not interested."

The sweet-faced sprite gawking at him took a step

back. The wounded look in her wide gold eyes made him feel like a total jerk.

"Sorry," he said quickly. "I thought you were . . . someone else."

"No offense taken." She chose the stool to his left, smoothing her dusty black pants as if she were dressed in a gown and not baggy clothes that could have been borrowed from an older brother. A tell-tale bulge in her right pocket hinted at a laser pistol. Yet everything else about her indicated a cultivated upbringing—her impeccable posture, the way she clasped her hands primly atop the bar. He couldn't figure out the hairstyle, though. A few red-blond strands clung to her ears and jaw. The rest was spiky and looked as if it'd been hacked away with a machete. A dull machete. Distantly, he hoped he never found himself sitting in her barber's chair.

"I saw you, didn't I?" he asked. "About an hour ago. You were wearing a cap."

"Yes." Proudly she added, "You nodded at me."

"Right . . ." He folded his arms over his chest and drummed his fingers on his biceps.

She contemplated him in wonder, then shyly averted her gaze. Fidgeting, she appeared to be searching for words to fill the silence. Finally she said, "I imagine the *tock*'s quite good here."

He suppressed a smile. He had no idea where the cute pixie hailed from, but she was proving damned near worth her weight in gold in entertainment value. A whole minute had passed since he'd last dwelled on where—or how—he was going to find another pilot.

"Had worse to drink," he admitted. "But it sure beats the company." He jerked his thumb toward the bartender, who gave a shuddering snore, startling himself half-awake. Immediately the man started asking questions—and then giving himself muttered answers.

The pixie tipped her head to the side and whispered out of the corner of her mouth, "I believe he's seen the back end of one too many freighters."

Ian laughed. The girl's sense of humor was a welcome bonus on a day in which he felt about as light-hearted as a half-ton pickup. "Bartender! Bring the lady a . . ." He shot her a questioning glance.

"*Tock*. Iced, if you please."

The bartender started awake, grunted, then unsteadily made his way to the chiller, chatting to himself all the way there. Mumbling, he opened the door and withdrew one frosty mug. Frozen water vapor rose in white streamers, evaporating instantly in the hot air. In a display of unexpected agility, he filled the glass with *tock* and slid it along the bar.

Ian caught the mug and handed it to his new companion. Then he propped his chin on his palm and studied her as she sipped from it. "So . . . what's a nice girl like you doing in a place like this?"

A smile lit her face. "An Earth expression! That's where you're from, is it not?"

"They call Blunder the crossroads of the galaxy," he said carefully.

The ends of her mouth lifted in a cryptic smile. Then she raised her glass. He watched her take a long, thirsty drink. She hadn't answered his question, he thought. But neither had he answered hers.

Companionably, they people-watched in silence. But his eyes kept going back to her. She pretended not to notice, but he knew she was aware of his scrutiny by the color that crept into her cheeks. For a crazy instant, he pictured himself back in Tempe, Arizona, and they'd just met in one of the places near the campus. He hadn't thought of his college days in ages, and when he had, it was because he missed football and burgers, not the simple, taken-for-granted freedom of taking a woman out on a date. But it was easy to imagine bringing this woman along on a road trip to the canyon. His Harley. The open road. Her slender arms wrapped around his waist—

"*Crat!*" she coughed out, nearly spilling her drink.

Crat was the Basic equivalent of "shit." His hand over his pistol, Ian followed her fearful gaze to the docks, where one of the local merchants was arguing with a dozen soldiers in crisp silver-trimmed blue uniforms and shiny black boots. *Vash Nadah* elite guard. The medium-sized cruiser he'd seen land a short while ago sat nearby. More soldiers were tramping down the boarding ramp.

Ian regarded the woman with heightened interest.

"Dar security forces. On Blunder. What brings them so far from home, I wonder?"

Wild-eyed, the sprite swung her attention to him. "They'll see me," she said fervently. "They'll take me back." Her chest rose and fell in increasingly deep breaths.

"Listen, if you're in some kind of trouble, maybe I can help. I—"

"No." She shut her eyes as if praying, then whirled around to watch the scene unfolding on the docks. The focus of the argument appeared to be centered on a sleek speeder parked behind them. Several groups of soldiers broke off from the gathering and strode across the plaza, heading their way. The curious crowd of bedraggled traders and merchants parted to let the big men pass.

"Your eye-shaders!" The woman snatched Ian's sunglasses off his face, shoving them on before he had the chance to react. She bumped her stool closer to his. "Put your arms around me."

He hesitated for a heartbeat. He didn't like to jump into situations blind. On the frontier—anywhere—it was an easy way to end up dead.

"Please," she beseeched him.

Wordlessly he drew her to him. She was quivering. Instinctively he tightened his arms around her.

The soldiers made their way through the shops; others walked through the bars, asking questions, their weapons in their holsters. Apparently they didn't consider their quarry dangerous. But when a pair of officers veered their way, Ian felt the woman go rigid.

"Greetings, Earth dwellers," the robust officer called to them.

The woman lifted her head. "Greetings!"

"My apologies for disturbing you. We're gathering information on some stolen goods. I'm in search of a tall woman, looks *Vash*, has short hair. She's wearing a blue flight suit—or was the last time she was seen. Have you seen her?"

They shook their heads and chorused, "No."

Clearly taken with the prospect of chatting with exotic Earthfolk, the officer leaned casually on the bar while his partner peered behind barrels and rooted through a pile of trash, before trying in vain to question the semiconscious bartender, who'd added more imaginary friends to his somnolent dialogue.

Waiting for his partner to finish, the officer lifted the visor of his helmet and dabbed at his forehead. "Hot weather, this."

Before Ian could answer, the pixie chimed in. "On Earth, Ah-ree-zona is worse." She kissed Ian on the cheek. "Is it not?"

Ian gaped at her.

The officer winced in understanding. "With all due respect to the B'kah's Queen Jasmine, I'll not be taking any trips to Earth anytime soon."

Apparently satisfied that what they were searching

for was not in the café, the men bade them good day and departed.

Immediately, the girl scooted away from Ian. Her eyes darted skyward at the telltale high-pitched whine of speeder thrusters. Her jaw clenched and unclenched, as if she was fighting hard to control her emotions. A screech rattled their glasses as the sleek vessel—the one the Dar security men had been arguing over—soared overhead so low that the bar's stools danced across the patchwork flooring. Then the speeder streaked across the sky and disappeared on the horizon.

"There goes my ride," she whispered.

"And look—there go those Dar soldiers, back to their cruiser. That's what you wanted, right?"

"Yes." She dragged her attention back to him. "Thank you for . . . your help."

"I aim to please, ma'am." He plucked his sunglasses off her nose. "Obviously they were looking for you. So what'd you do? Or *not* do?"

She blinked at him in the bright sunshine but gave no answer. Somehow he hadn't expected she would. Blunder was a place for secrets, and this pixie evidently had more than her share. Her appearance alone was enough to pique his curiosity. She had the classic sculpted features of *Vash* royalty—high cheekbones, a long, perfectly formed nose, and pale gold eyes that tipped up at each end—but she was more animated, more *genuine* than any of the wife

59

candidates he'd met at court on Rom's home world of Sienna.

That was because she wasn't a royal, he quickly assured himself. *Vash* princesses rarely left their homeworlds. And when they did, they didn't come to places like Donavan's Blunder. The idea was inconceivable. The protocol that kept *Vash Nadah* women cloistered dated back to the years before and during the Great War, a period of anarchy when the protective measures were necessary. Eleven thousand years later, the galaxy was stable and safe. Yet the customs restricting royal women remained. Strange that the religion binding the galaxy together was based on a feminine entity, the Great Mother, when the highest-ranking women in the eight royal families spent their lives in the shadows.

Thoughtful, he sipped his *tock* and studied the young woman next to him. Plenty of upper-class merchants carried *Vash Nadah* blood, so this one must have royalty as her ancestors.

"Everything I had was in that ship," she said glumly. "Now I'm stuck on Donavan's Blunder with a really bad haircut, a quarter of the credits I came with. And these"—she sighed—"are my only clothes."

She sagged forward on the bar, supporting her chin with her hands. "I don't think it can get any worse than this."

Ian lowered his drink. "I've had a pretty lousy day myself."

They shared lingering commiserating grins.

He asked, "Buy you another *tock?*"

"No. This calls for something stronger." She pounded her fist on the counter. "Bartender—Mandarian whiskey!"

The old spacehand came to life, reaching under the bar for a dusty red bottle and uncorking it.

The woman tossed a few credits on the table. "Order yourself some spirits—what's your name, anyway?"

"Ian."

Her expression tightened in alarm before her eyes narrowed in concentration. She scrutinized him as if she thought she knew him—or hoped she didn't. "Ian . . . ?"

"Ian Stone," he finished for her, using the alias he'd chosen for his surname.

"Ah." She swallowed. "Ian. Your given name is common on Earth, is it not?"

He smiled innocently. "Very."

She relaxed and shook her head. "What will you have, Ian Stone? I'm buying."

He chuckled. "I'll stick with *tock*, but thanks."

She grabbed the cup the bartender handed her and tossed the contents into her mouth. Her breath exited in a wheeze and her golden eyes filled with tears. "Great Mother," she whispered hoarsely. Her dark-lashed eyes focused, then unfocused. "Another," she huffed.

"I don't think you want another. Mandarian whiskey is potent stuff. If you're not used to it—"

"Who says I'm not used to it? Why, I drink all the time, every day, morning and night. I brush my teeth with the stuff. Yes, that's what I do. No one keeps me from my whiskey!"

Anger blazed in her eyes. "I've followed orders my entire life. No more." She shoved more credits across the bar. "Your glasses are too small," she informed the bartender. "Hand me the bottle."

He shifted his watery eyes to Ian, his brows raised questioningly. Ian shook his head ever so slightly, and the man wedged the cork into the bottle.

"Hey!" The pixie swiped for the whiskey, snatching it from the barman's gnarled fingers. "I paid for it, didn't I?" Her hand was unsteady as she poured another glass.

Ian groaned, folding his arms across his chest. Well, he knew what he was doing this afternoon: baby-sitting. With this heat, that liquor, and the girl's obvious low tolerance for the stuff, she was going to be feeling pretty low, pretty fast.

"Quite good, this Menerian—Manarian—this *whiskey*." She hiccuped. " 'S'cuse me."

"What's your name, pixie?"

She tilted her head at the Earth word. She seemed to be having a tough time focusing on his face. "Tee—" She clamped her mouth shut. "Just Tee."

"Tell me your story, 'Just Tee.' You say you lost your ship. Who'd you work for? The Federation merchants?"

"Had my own ship." Her lips compressed into a resolute line. "It's all right. I'm not afraid of hard work. Someone will need a pilot."

Ian grabbed her upper arm. "You mean you *fly?*"

She wedged a wrinkled cap out of her trousers and fit it on her head. Above the brim was the faint outline of a pair of wings. "There. See?"

He gave a whoop of delight. "An intersystem cargo pilot—with no speeder!"

She frowned at him with accusing eyes. "Thought you were s'posed to be making me feel better."

"I am . . . I mean, I can. That is, if you're interested."

As she watched him with skepticism, he rummaged through his front pocket and dug out Carn's old pilot wings, placing them on the table. "The job's yours if you want it. What do you say, Miss Tee?"

The wings glinted in the hazy sunshine. Her hand crept forward, her long fingers at last closing reverently around the pin. She lifted her gaze to his and smiled. Then her eyes rolled back, and she passed out.

"Tee?"

Ian took off his sunglasses. In the lull between departing ships, a puff of wind ruffled the woman's hair, accentuating the stillness of the rest of her.

She had to be joking, he thought. No one passed out after two drinks. Did they?

"Hey, kid," he called.

She remained facedown on the counter, her forehead resting on her knuckles. *Like Carn.* Fear squeezed his gut. Even if she was an experienced drinker, the toxicity of frontier brews varied tremendously. She had drunk only two glasses, but the percentage of alcohol to her body weight could be dangerously high. And Mandarian whiskey was notorious for the quickness with which it was metabolized. The girl might not have known that.

He gave her shoulder a shake. Her head lolled to the side, exposing her slender throat—and her pulse. Relief rippled through him.

"Come on, I was enjoying the conversation," he said, massaging the back of her neck. Her smooth skin was damp from perspiration and warm to the touch. Sighing, she flexed her fingers, using her hands as a pillow. Her lips curved into a blissful smile, but her eyes remained closed.

Ian gave a quick, pained laugh. "I can't believe this is happening. Thirty seconds in my employ and she's already unconscious."

The bartender jolted awake, snuffling and scratching his scalp.

"Like every other pilot I've hired," Ian told him, as if he or anyone on this miserable rock cared. He downed the rest of his *tock*, wishing for once that he'd chosen a stronger drink. "I feel like Bill Murray in *Groundhog Day*."

The bartender blinked uncomprehendingly.

"An old Earth movie," Ian explained, though it

was probably futile. "This guy wakes up to the same day over and over. He's trapped until he finally learns from his mistakes." Watching the ice melt in the bottom of his glass, he scowled. "Tell me I'm not doomed to hire one liquor-loving space jockey after another."

The thought was downright depressing. He'd never prove to the *Vash*—to Rom—that he had what it took to rule the galaxy if he couldn't even master the basics of commanding a starship, including hiring and maintaining a crew. He'd best turn things around, right here, right now.

"On your feet, Miss Tee," he said briskly. "I have an appointment on Grüma I'd like to keep." He wrapped his arms around her waist and lifted her away from the counter. It took a moment to untangle her long legs from the stool. Dragging her away from the bar, he supported her with one arm hooked around her waist. Her legs wobbled under her weight, indicating the extent to which the liquor was mucking up her system. How she'd survived in the frontier with such a low tolerance for alcohol, he had no idea.

"Wait, Earth dweller," the bartender called out.

Ian turned around, Tee heavy in his arms. The bartender's yellow-brown eyes were watery, but a new glint suggested he was more alert than before.

"Watch your back," the man rasped.

"Why?" Ian asked carefully. "Is someone following me?"

The bartender coughed into his hand.

"Who is it, old man? Who's after me?"

The man waved vaguely across the outdoor bar toward the docks.

Unease trickled down Ian's spine. "This isn't helping my paranoia any," he muttered, scanning the crowd.

But the bartender's moment of lucidity—if that's even what it was—had ended. He took a soiled rag from his pocket and began wiping the countertop, contentedly engaged in another one of his solitary conversations.

Despite the iffy source, Ian decided to consider the warning valid. He'd brief the crew and launch as soon as he could get this pilot sobered up.

He urged her to walk faster. "After listening to what that old spacehand just said, I think it's time we got the hell out of Dodge."

The girl's eyes opened to slits. "Hmm?" She lifted her head, clutching the wings he'd given her to her chest.

"Sorry. I slip into English sometimes," he said. "Welcome back. We're on the way to the ship."

Her eyes flew open, and she dug her heels into the dirt. "To where?"

"My ship. I hired you, remember?"

She pulled away from him and clumsily fished out her pistol.

Ian's hands shot up. "Put that away!"

She scrutinized her weapon with some consternation, as if trying to remember what to do with it. Then she dropped her right arm, pointing the deadly laser south. Her speech was a bit slurred. "Not so fast. How do I know you're really a starship captain—that you're hiring me to fly, and not for"— she blushed furiously—"for sex?"

She waved the gun at his waist, and he resisted the potent urge to cover his balls. Never in his life had he seen anything like this pistol-toting pixie, her chin jutting out, her eyes accusing him of unspeakable perversions.

Think fast, he told himself. He forced an expression of serene calm to his face, a skill he'd learned from Rom. "Now that you bring it up, how do I know you're really a pilot?"

Clasping his hands behind his back, as if he were a seasoned space veteran with decades of space travel under his belt instead of an Earth guy four years out of Arizona State, he walked in a circle around her. . . .

Slowly . . .

. . . forcing her to turn in order to follow his deliberate and thorough inspection.

"For all I know, you're just another good-for-nothing space drifter," he said, "lying your way aboard my ship for the chance at a hot meal and a clean bunk."

That threw her. Her mouth worked, but nothing came out.

"Or a thief," he went on, "waiting until my crew

and I are asleep tonight to steal us blind—"

"I'm a pilot! My wings were in that speeder."

"Which is?"

"Gone," she replied glumly, wobbling on her feet.

"My point exactly. I have no proof you're who you claim you are, other than what you've told me. You feel the same about me, obviously." He stopped, facing her. Warily she watched him. "I need a pilot and you need a job. We have no choice but to trust each other. But if that isn't going to be a possibility, Tee, let me know now, because it's the only way this is going to work." That, and her staying sober.

She peered at the row of shops and sleazy bars. Doubt saturated her features. Then she shifted her attention to him, artlessly examining him from his hair to his boots and back again. In her eyes sparked a glimmer of wonder—the look she'd given him when they had first met.

He tamped down on the unexpected rush of pleasure he found in that gaze. "So," he prompted, "what will it be?"

Weaving slightly, she stowed her pistol. "It appears I shall trust you, Earth dweller."

"Good. And just so there's no misunderstanding about my personal life"—he caught her by the arm, bringing his mouth close to one perfectly formed little ear—"when I want sex, I don't have to buy it."

Her eyes widened, and then she blushed, deeper than before. He'd meant the statement as fact, not as a boast, but her irresistible reaction left him in no hurry to explain.

"Now let's go." Ian took Tee by the elbow and pulled her along the road leading to where the ship was docked. Harsh sunlight glinted off the tiny beads of sweat on her golden skin, illuminating her angelic face. Unexpectedly, something inside him softened.

But then she hit him with another demand. "What about my money?" she asked.

"It's in your left pants pocket. I paid the bartender—left him the bottle, though. The last thing I need is whiskey on board, with your partiality to the stuff—"

Her boot heels skidded to a halt on the gravel.

He ground his teeth together. "Now what?"

"I mean my salary." She screwed up her face, trying hard to focus on him. "I'm a starpilot. I require starpilot wages."

"You're an intersystem cargo pilot. There's a difference." Yet she'd made it all the way to Blunder from wherever she'd come from, proving that her skills went beyond short planet-to-planet cargo runs.

Ian thought of what he'd paid Carn and raised it ten credits. Mostly out of desperation—and with the fervent hope that this newest stick-monkey would last more than a few weeks. "Sixty each standard week. Plus benefits: room, board, medical—"

"Two hundred credits."

"I'm not paying you two hundred a week!"

69

Her eyes snapped in challenge from within the shadow of the cap half hiding that . . . hairdo. "Do you need a pilot or not?"

"Do you need a ship or not?"

She didn't flinch. "I'll agree to one-fifty."

"One hundred." He supposed he was nuts to risk losing what appeared to be a qualified pilot over the question of a few credits, but if he didn't act from a position of strength from the beginning, as captain he'd never squeeze a worthwhile day's work out of this drunk. "Take it or leave it."

She glanced at the empty place where her vessel had been parked before being whisked away by Dar security. A look of profound pain flickered across her expressive face, chased by obvious indecision in the way she clenched her jaw. Her blatant inner battle heightened his curiosity about her, but he forced himself to wait in silence for her answer.

"I shall take it," she said in a quiet voice.

He snatched her by the hand before she changed her mind—again. But the sudden move caused her to trip over her boots. He caught her before she fell, wrapping his arm around her waist. "I'm sobering you up with hot *tock* even if it takes me all day— which I hope it doesn't, because you, my friend, are flying me to Grüma, come hell or high water."

Chapter Four

Ahead, the long fuselage of his ship gleamed pale silver. "There she is," Ian said. "The *Sun Devil*."

"She's . . . beautiful," Tee murmured. Genuine longing softened her features. He'd seen that expression before on his mother's face when she reminisced about her days as an Air Force fighter pilot.

Quin and Muffin met them at the bottom of the gangway. Quin's eyes twinkled. "It's not like you to bring home *company*," he said, while Muffin squinted at the woman, studying her.

"She's not company. This is Tee, our new pilot. Tee, meet Muffin, chief security officer. And Quin, ship's mechanic."

"Nice to meet you." She stuck out her hand. Thrown off balance, she grabbed onto Ian. "Whoa."

Quin's smile froze with incredulity. "She's drunk!"

"Right. Let's get her sobered up. I want to launch as soon as possible." Hastily he swept Tee past the two men and up the gangway. After a moment's silence, Ian heard two pairs of boots thumping on the alloy flooring behind him.

"We've been through three pilots already," Quin called after him. "Now here you are with another stray."

Ian didn't have to turn around to guess the expression contorting the man's face.

Muffin was typically good-humored. "Reminds me a bit of my sister and the way she collects lost ketta-cats."

"I can deal with ketta-cats. It's good-for-nothing pilots I have no stomach for," Quin grumbled.

Through the forward cargo hold they went, down the central corridor and past the crew quarters, while Quin ranted about starpilots and their general unreliability and mental instability.

"This way." Ian planted his hands on Tee's hips and boosted her up the gangway to the galley. Haltingly, she climbed to the upper deck, stumbling over the top rung. She giggled, then slapped her hand over her mouth as if the sound had startled and embarrassed her.

Ian guided her into the galley, settling her onto a seat next to the table. Crushed by her cap, short locks of hair clung to her temples and flushed cheeks. He shook off the oddest urge to smooth the strands off her skin.

Muffin lumbered into the galley. Ian told him, "One of the locals, a bartender, said I should watch my back."

"Did he elaborate?"

"Unfortunately no. He wasn't exactly stable in the mental department, either."

Muffin frowned. "Let's launch as soon as possible."

"Agreed."

Quin marched past. "I'll get the *tock* started." Glowering, he slammed a kettle on the ion-burner.

The last two members of Ian's crew, Gredda and Push, the cargo handlers, peered into the galley from the corridor. Ian made another around of introductions.

Dressed in a brown leather sleeveless jerkin with studded straps crisscrossing over a tight woolen chemise, Gredda looked like a mythical Viking queen. She crossed her impressive arms over equally impressive breasts, her skin glistening with grease smudges and perspiration from a long session loading cargo. "A female flyer this time," she said approvingly.

Tee acknowledged Gredda with a smile that quickly faded. Much paler now, she lifted an unsteady hand to her cap and plucked it off her head.

Quin stared. "By the heavens, what happened to her hair?"

Tee's expression could have frozen plasma fuel. "Do you have a problem with the way I look?"

Quin sized her up. "What if I do? I doubt looks matter much in the places you frequent."

Ian whistled softly as the two exchanged heated glares.

When Quin returned to the stove, Tee sank into obvious misery. She was perspiring, even in the cooler air, and a greenish pallor bleached her face. Ian had experienced the morning-afters of enough fraternity parties to know how she was feeling. Mandarian whiskey meant a quick buzz and a killer hangover.

"Drink up," he coaxed, handing her cup of *tock*. I REFUSE TO ENGAGE IN A BATTLE OF WITS WITH AN UNARMED PERSON, the mug read. He hadn't chosen it deliberately, but it seemed somehow appropriate. Although, he had to admit that Tee had done a hell of a job negotiating her salary, despite her inebriated condition.

She lifted the cup, sniffed at the liquid, then lowered it. Her voice quavered. "I—I need your lavatory."

Ian plucked her off the bench, steering her toward the lav in the corridor. She waved him away, and the door hissed closed. Waiting for her to exit, he leaned against the bulkhead, folding his arms over his chest.

Quin stepped in front of him, hands spread. "Captain, listen, save us all a bit of trouble and haul her back to the nearest drinking hold. Another pilot will come along."

"Another pilot is *not* going to come along, Quin."

Quin's attention swerved to Muffin. "Didn't you say *you* fly?"

Muffin's fists closed and the sinewy muscles in his

neck flexed. "I flew a combat mission in the war. It was part of a raid to free Queen Jasmine. The young lad I was paired with took a shot in the abdomen. I got him off Brevdah Three, but"—regret darkened his eyes—"he bled to death during our escape. I haven't wanted to pilot a craft since. You wouldn't want me to try now."

From inside the lavatory came the swish of water in the hygiene sink. Then Tee emerged, her choppy hair slicked back from her pale forehead, her baggy clothes hanging in wrinkled folds, making her appear more gaunt than slender. Grayish shadows under her eyes added to her air of fragility, turning the once-enchanting pixie into a forlorn waif.

She passed them, her gait faltering but still proud as she made her way back to the galley.

Ian spoke in undertones, preempting his mechanic's protest. "She'll have to do, Quin. Randall's on Grüma, and we're going after him."

Quin's jaw moved back and forth, a sure indication that he was pondering their predicament.

Ian jerked his thumb toward the galley. The pixie was definitely a sight, dressed in her dusty old clothes, her short red-gold hair sprouting in all directions. But something inside him lightened inexplicably every time he looked at her. "Now that she's purged her system, we'll fill her with *tock*."

Referring to Tee as if she were another bulky piece of shipboard equipment appeared to comfort the mechanic. "All right, Captain. After launch, I'll allow her some downtime to bring her back to maximum efficiency."

"That's it, Quin," Ian said with a smile. "Now we're talking."

After a prolonged private conversation with his men, the handsome Earth dweller returned to the galley. Tee'ah gave a small moan as the room tilted.

"When was the last time you had a meal?" he asked.

"It's been awhile. Sometime yesterday, I think."

"Quin," he called out. "Don't we have some leftover stew in the chiller?"

"No!" Tee'ah's belly contracted at the mere thought of congealed stew, no matter how delicious it might be once heated. "But thank you," she added quickly, trying to blunt the initial sharpness of her tone with a smile. The last thing she wanted was to rebuff the Earth dweller's kindness; he might listen to that foul-tempered troll Quin and toss her off the ship. She'd lost her starspeeder and most of her credits. If she didn't soon shake off the aftereffects of the whiskey she'd boasted about drinking all the time, she'd lose this job, too. If that happened, her dreams of a new life were over. Broke and unemployed, a woman's chances of surviving in the frontier diminished to nearly zero.

No matter what, she must stay on this ship.

In that case, she'd better know who her captain was. Ian Stone's similarities to Ian Hamilton were numerous and striking. Her stomach flip-flopped with the mere thought of being on the same starship as Rom's handpicked heir. From all reports the crown prince was an unfailing devotee of *Vash* custom, a model heir. If he were to find out who she was, he'd certainly order her to return home. Her personal desires would mean no more to him than they had to her father. She was ungrateful, disobedient; she'd run from an arranged marriage and shamed her parents in the process.

Regret lay heavy in her chest, and perhaps it always would. Humiliating her family wasn't what she'd set out to accomplish, but sadly it was what would come of her actions.

Woozy with nausea and exhaustion, she listened carefully to Ian's conversations with his crew: discussions of mundane shipboard matters, the goods stored in the cargo hold, ordinary trader lingo. She noted that the Earth dweller needed a shave, and that his wavy dark brown hair brushed the bottom of his neck, a length longer than *Vash* standards. His jeans and eye-shaders completed the image of a dangerous and handsome space rogue. She couldn't fathom his being the crown prince. He was so marvelously alien; nothing about his behavior reflected the courtly manners and rigid tradition of a *Vash* castle.

Anxiety and the natural stimulant in *tock* made her pulse race. Her empty stomach worsened the effect. In fact, hunger was likely the reason the liquor had played havoc with her system in the first place. So were shock, lack of sleep, and physical exhaustion from pushing the starspeeder and her body to the limit. While drunkenness couldn't be so readily shrugged off, exhaustion and hunger could be overcome.

She set her mug on the table. "On second thought, I think I will have something to eat. Something light, if you don't mind."

Quin dropped a few slices of lar-bread onto a plate. Tee'ah bypassed the jar of sticky jam he offered and forced herself to eat the flatbread plain. When she was sure the bread would stay down, she drank what was left in her mug. This time Ian refilled it, while his acid-tongued ogre of a mechanic paced behind her, his impatient footsteps thundering in Tee'ah's aching head, his skeptical gaze boring into her back. Slowly the fog dulling her senses began to retreat like dust from Mistraal's skies after a *Tjhu'nami*'s passage.

Time elapsed. A few hours, she guessed. Ian scrutinized the Earth-made chronograph on his wrist and then her. "So. When do you think you might be able to fly me off this rock?" Brows raised, he gave her a long, questioning, intensely appraising stare.

A sense of purpose swept through her, the desire to surpass Ian's expectations and those of the crew. This was her chance to prove, if only to herself, that she was more than a coddled princess, more than a woman whose identity would be defined by the accomplishments of a future mate.

"I'm ready now," she said, and stood. Lightheadedness swept through her. She gulped a few breaths and gripped the edge of the table to steady herself.

Quin balked. "She'll kill us all!"

Only you, bonehead, if I get half a chance. Summoning her remaining dignity, she lurched into the corridor, followed by the two men.

Ian caught her elbow. "Is that true, Tee? Are you going to kill us all?" He regarded her with an irritatingly amused smile. "I'm afraid I'll have to dock your pay for every life lost."

Perhaps she might have chuckled at his teasing had the stakes not been so high. She yanked her damp cap over her hair. "I intend to fly this ship safely and to your satisfaction."

"Good. But the cockpit's this way." And with that, his grin turned devilish, and he steered her in the opposite direction.

The *Sun Devil*'s cockpit was smaller than the cargo freighter she was used to, but she'd managed all right with the starspeeder, a smaller ship. A sweeping forward-viewscreen framed a vista of brown hills below a pallid sky. Below the screen was the pilot's station, a panel with state-of-the-art instrumentation, as on the *Prosper*. The indicator lights winked invitingly, illuminating the black composite of the control yoke. Her fingers twitched in anticipation of gripping it.

Ian sat in his captain's chair. "All hands to launch

stations." Gredda, Push, Muffin, and Quin took their seats.

At Ian's firm command, Tee buckled herself into the snugly comfortable pilot's seat. Her empty stomach and bone-deep tiredness made it difficult to resist the craving to lie down and sleep for an entire standard year. But she willed away her sluggishness and shook her head, blinking.

The voices around her hushed. Slowly she became aware of the crew's doubtful gazes, particularly Quin's.

She wrapped her dust-streaked hands around the control yoke. "Strap in." Her lips drew back in an evil smile. *"Tight."*

There was a chorus of clicking harnesses. Then the scuffling ceased as the crew awaited her next order. To her delight, Quin looked decidedly paler.

She used the ship's computer to guide her through the unfamiliar prelaunch checklist display: prompts scrolling past on the viewscreen.

"Pilot ready, Captain," she said upon completing the last step in the procedure.

Ian folded his hands over his stomach. "Commence launch."

That he was calm with her at the controls of his craft infused her with confidence. She tapped the comm icon and told Blunder's port controller they were ready.

"Cleared to depart, *Sun Devil*."

She heard the sound of straps being yanked extra

tight. Then a deep rumbling gave way to a satisfying surge of power. A force several times that of normal gravity pressed her into her seat. Her queasiness surged. She took deep breaths to control her nausea until the ship was out of the atmosphere and in its assigned space-lane routing, where the forces of acceleration eased. She was grateful the *Sun Devil* had a gravity generator, making the shipboard environment feel normal. If she had to contend with weightlessness, as she had on the starspeeder, she'd have long since lost her last meal.

She used everything she had to concentrate on Ian's instructions to take the ship through a short jump to hyperspace, where greater than light-speeds could be achieved through physics she battled to comprehend. Only after they'd dropped back into normal space did she have a free moment to grin at the silent crew.

Gredda gave her a respectful nod. The others attempted weak smiles. But the Earth dweller's eyes simply gleamed. She'd gotten him off Donavan's Blunder, and that was what he wanted.

Exhaling, she relaxed a fraction and returned her attention to her viewscreens and the planet Grüma ahead. Maybe this wasn't exactly what she'd had in mind, but by the looks of it, she'd found herself a job.

Chapter Five

Gann Truelénne dismissed the escort assigned to him; he preferred to navigate the maze of corridors in the palace himself. His travel cloak whipped around his legs as his strides carried him into the heart of the largest personal residence in the galaxy. To his left and right massive columns soared to the ceiling, the space between them open to a vast desert. He breathed deeply. With Sienna's two suns now below the horizon and the palace heat shields lowered for the night, the B'kah homeworld felt almost habitable, a term not generally used to describe any of the eight *Vash Nadah* home planets. But it had been so long since Gann had trodden upon anything but the deck of his starship, the *Quillie*, that he swore he felt the polished-stone floor rolling beneath his boots.

"Welcome back," a voice boomed from the distant end of the passageway.

Gann squared his shoulders. Ahead, the king awaited him, his tall, muscled frame illuminated by the laser candlelight flooding the hall. Romlijhian B'kah was the undisputed ruler of all known worlds, a direct descendant of Romjha, a warrior of almost mythical greatness credited with saving civilization from extinction over eleven thousand years before. A hero in his own right, Rom was a statesman, a decorated soldier, and a devoted husband. But to Gann, his most fitting title would always be *friend*.

Gann halted and snapped his fist over his chest, dipping his head in a bow. "You summoned me, my lord."

Rom's eyes sparked with amusement. "Ah, such formality."

Gann slowly raised his head. "I thought it was better to be safe. It's been two years since I last saw you in the flesh; your rank may have finally gone to your head."

"My one-too-many-times-battered head?" Rom asked dryly. When Gann grinned and pretended to search for a tactful answer, his friend laughed heartily. "Ah, my friend, it's good to see you."

They came together in a spirited embrace. Then, hands clasping each other's shoulders, they moved apart, a thousand shared memories in their eyes.

Finally Gann let his hands fall to his sides. "You

83

didn't bring me here simply because you missed me."

"Not entirely." Rom's tired smile was maddeningly enigmatic. Without further comment he waved toward an open set of double doors and led Gann through a vast chamber, where a floor of Siennan marble reflected lavish tapestries and pieces of furniture—all ancient and priceless—encircling a saltwater fountain stocked with rare sea creatures. Such grandeur was breathtaking to those viewing the palace for the first time, but such trappings of wealth and power did not intimidate Gann. He'd grown up amid this wonderland. His father was a member of the previous king's elite guard, as was his father's father, and the thousands of years of Truelénne men who came before him. The loyalty Gann felt for Rom and his family went beyond friendship, beyond the years they'd served on the same starship during Rom's exile. It was bred in his bones.

The men walked silently. Gann studied his uncharacteristically subdued friend, wondering suddenly if this mysterious summons translated to a family emergency. "How is Jas?"

Rom's eyes lit up at the mention of his Earthborn wife. "Very well. She looks forward to seeing you. In fact she's chilling several bottles of Red Rocket Ale as we speak."

Gann had hoped as much; he found the Earth beverage delicious. And he wasn't alone. Beer was swiftly becoming a sought-after libation across the galaxy, making Jas's longtime friend, Dan Brady, creator of this royal favorite brand, one of Earth's wealthiest businessmen.

Gann made another bid to determine the root of Rom's concern. Rom was close to his children-by-marriage, and treated them as if they were of his own blood. "Ian and Ilana—I trust they are well?"

"Yes." Rom leveled him with a perceptive, if somewhat worried gaze. "All are healthy, thank the Great Mother. But you are correct in assuming the reason I brought you here is not a *Vash Nadah* matter. In fact, it's quite personal. A predicament of lost and found, you might say. *Found*, I pray, with your help."

A surge of anticipation quickened Gann's pulse. Life had lacked a certain . . . *spark* since he and Rom had parted ways upon his friend's ascension to the galaxy's throne. Whatever Rom required of him now, it was bound to be good and, he hoped, exactly what he needed to lift him from his doldrums of late. Though he couldn't help wondering why a king with an immense army and security forces trained in covert operations at his disposal would need an aging warrior's help.

His curiosity soared higher as he trailed Rom to where soft music emanated from a sitting area hidden behind a screen. Here the walls were whitewashed and plain, the tile floor strewn with cushions, all glowing in the light of Sienna's three pockmarked moons framed in an enormous skylight. Mementos from Rom and Jas's travels, along with framed holo-images of their families, graced shelves and ledges clearly installed for that purpose, making obvious the intimacy of the couple who lived there.

A stab of longing blindsided him as an image blossomed in his mind's eye of a private retreat like this, shelves stacked with holo-images of a wife, children. He frowned, then cleared his throat. Family life was for other men; that was the way of it. Serving the B'kah was his calling, a choice he'd made long ago, duty over personal wishes, if not consciously then by birth. Why, then, had regret tainted where only pride dwelled before?

Because the tedium of your life is chipping away at your sanity, that's why.

Stiffly, he clasped his hands behind his back. It was blasted obvious that he needed this mission. This *adventure*. He hoped it was good.

"Gann!" A woman's accented singsong voice mercifully dragged his thoughts outward.

Clutching three frosty bottles in her hands, Jas breezed into the room. Immediately her presence lifted his spirits; her energy and zest for life were contagious. She stretched up on her toes to kiss him on the cheek in the overt display of affection characteristic of Earth dwellers, as her exotic black hair, common on her homeworld if nowhere else, swung over her shoulders.

He pressed one hand to her back and returned

the kiss, on her cheek, Earth-style. Then she stepped back to gaze at him. Smooth and elegant in her simple white gown, she looked every inch Rom's queen, though he knew she still flew as an active starpilot in Sienna's space wing. "I bet you could use a beer," she said.

He grimaced. "I could use ten."

"Yeah, I know the feeling." Delight shone in her eyes. The bottles were passed around and conversation filled the cozy room. "Like old times," Jas said after a bit, grinning up at him before exchanging a deeply affectionate glance with Rom.

When the couple's eyes met, their smiles slowly faded.

Rom set his bottle on a nearby table. "It's time I explained why I summoned you here."

Gann dipped his head. "I await your orders."

As custom dictated, the men waited until Jas sat before they, too, settled onto the carpet, arranging plump cushions for comfort. Gann leaned against his pillow and crossed one long, boot-clad leg over the other.

"Few know the frontier better than you," Rom began. Gann's muscles thrummed as they did during a rousing game of Bajha, the sword game played to hone instinct and the senses and fought in the dark. He'd looked forward to a possible extended stay planetside, but running a personal mission for Rom, particularly in the remote and unpredictable frontier, sounded far more intriguing. "Out with it,

B'kah. What particularly corrupt and misguided soul would you like me to apprehend? Or is it a cache of stolen personal objects that requires my expert interception?" Grinning eagerly, he tipped his bottle for a swig.

Jas sighed. "Our niece ran away. We're sending you after her."

Gann almost choked on his swallow of beer. Jas's intense expression indicated she was not joking, and the expectancy bolstering him drained away. Valiantly he attempted to keep his disappointment from his voice. "I'm to fetch a runaway princess?"

"Yes. Tee'ah Dar, Joren and Di's daughter. Joren thought—*prayed*—she was here." She pressed her lips together. "If only she had come here . . ."

"Jas," Rom said gently, taking her fingers in his.

Her voice was fervent and low. "God, she must have been so unhappy. I wish she'd told me. I might have been able to help her, to intercede with her parents, to offer alternatives to . . . this." She sighed. "I met Tee'ah right before the war, seven years ago, when Rom and I were living in the Dar palace. Unlike us, Joren and Di maintain the old traditions. They raised Tee'ah in seclusion." She squeezed her husband's hand. "Rom and I are working to change the customs that have outgrown their usefulness, like the ones keeping women like Tee'ah so isolated."

"But all this must be done slowly," Rom said. "Or we'll aggravate the mistrust and resentment that is not so well hidden by some members of the Great Council."

Jas continued. "I kept in touch with Tee'ah, but only occasionally—via viewscreen, never in person. I gave her advice and encouragement, solicited or not, just as I do with my daughter Ilana. But there's a huge cultural difference between a royal *Vash* female confined to a palace and a career-minded young woman living in California, and I failed to account for that. I filled her head with ideas . . . with possibilities. Now she's headed into danger she's little prepared for. I can't help feeling responsible."

Gann set his empty bottle on the floor. With a silent sigh, he resigned himself to the nursemaid duty it seemed he was acquiring. What the B'kah asked of him, the B'kah received. Such was his duty, and honor allowed him no alternative. Moreover, he didn't like the idea of an innocent *Vash* princess in the clutches of disreputable frontier primitives any more than her family did. "I only glimpsed her briefly—seven years ago. What does she look like now?"

Jas handed him a holo-image. The princess, a grown woman, gazed innocently back at him, her posture erect, her long red-gold hair woven ornately in the traditional way atop her head.

Cradling the picture in his palms, he admitted, "Frankly I cannot fathom her, or any *Vash* princess, for that matter, running away, much less going to

89

the frontier. You're certain she went there voluntarily?"

"Quite." His skepticism had brought a smile to Rom's lips. "She stole a starspeeder, threatened a lieutenant at gunpoint, and launched in the middle of a *Tjhu'nami*."

Gann whistled, taking a second glance at the holo-image.

Jas said, "Joren's men found her starspeeder on Donavan's Blunder . . . with a cloaker already on board. The cloaker said she'd traded her speeder for another and had already left the planet. Who knows if he was telling the truth? Security saw no sign of her, other than the ship."

"Any communication from her?" Gann asked.

Rom took the holo-image he handed back. "Yesterday her parents received a short message via a multiple-channel encrypted relay. This was in addition to the note she left them before she departed. In both, she said she was safe, that she'd gone voluntarily, and that they mustn't worry. They assume the message was genuine, but they can't, of course, authenticate the note or tell where it originated . . . or when it was sent. Dar intelligence is working on it." Rom pressed his fingertips together and leaned forward. "There's something else. Ian's in the frontier, too. But he's undercover. I've tried, but I can't reach him. My messages to him . . . bounce."

Gann stared. "Ian's undercover?" This plot was

becoming more incredible and more convoluted with each passing minute.

"Not that Ian would know Tee'ah if he saw her," Jas put in, evidently missing Gann's reaction to her husband's statement. "Because of custom, she stayed behind at the palace when the rest of the family traveled here for the wedding. I think she saw holo-images of the ceremony, but Ian's appearance has changed considerably in seven years. So has hers. I doubt they'd recognize each other."

Gann cleared his throat. "I believe I'm missing something here. Why is Ian undercover?"

"Because I don't want the Great Council to know he's there," Rom explained.

"I see," Gann said, although he didn't.

Rom's sharp glance demanded his discretion. "I'm in somewhat of a quandary regarding the frontier. All I can tell you, so as not to place Ian in danger, is that I require his frontiersman's perspective to guide me in future decisions on the matter." Rom appeared to choose his next words with care. "Our realm is growing, changing. We're settling new worlds farther and farther from the heart of our kingdom. Ian will be the first ruler with direct family ties to both the frontier and the Great Council. People on both sides will look to him for leadership. Yet there are still those who don't see the wisdom of Ian's someday taking the throne. I . . . want to give him the chance to prove them wrong."

Rom fell silent before he smiled tiredly and

added, "But you must find our wayward princess."

Gann assured him, "I'll have her home before her bed grows cold. Hunk of bread."

"Hunk of bread?" Jas appeared baffled.

"It's one of your Earth-dweller expressions, is it not? Used to describe the ease of a particular task?"

Her lips quirked. "You mean piece of cake."

"Yes, yes, that's the one. A princess in the frontier will stand out like an iceberg in the desert. I'll have her back to the palace in no time. Piece of cake."

Jas and Rom walked with him to where the screen separated the sitting area from the larger chamber. Embracing his friends in turn, he bade them farewell. Then he swept his travel cloak around himself and strode from the room.

Chapter Six

"I know she overslept, Quin. But seeing that she got us off Blunder and onto Grüma—and we lived through it, I'd say she earned her time in the bunk. But Randall's already gone, and I want to follow him. The only way we're going to do that is if she's rested."

Sprawled on her stomach, Tee'ah woke to voices in the corridor outside her quarters. The bedsheets were twisted around her bare thighs, pinning her legs in place, and her head hurt too much to move, so she lay there, listening.

The *Sun Devil* was on Grüma now, and the thrusters were shut down. It was quiet except for the whispery hum of the air recyclers and the men's voices.

"A round-trip to Barésh is no quick jaunt." Recognizing Quin's voice, she winced into her pillow.

"Tee can fly, I'll give her that. But taking a new pilot deep into new territory when we hardly know her . . . ? I don't know, Captain. I don't like it. And her drinking—"

"Oh, she won't be drinking; I guarantee that," she heard Ian reply before he lowered his voice. She lifted her head, straining to hear. "I'm not about to let her go anywhere unsupervised. I'll watch her myself, if I have to."

Heavens. They thought she was wild and reckless and not to be trusted. What a difference from how she'd been viewed by others—and herself—for most of her life.

"With Randall a day ahead of us, I don't see that we have a choice. *Tee!* Are you alive in there?"

With that came a horrible knocking on her door. She moaned and rolled onto her back, untangling her legs from the sheets. She didn't have to pretend to be a shiftless pilot. She felt like one from her throbbing head to her sore feet.

"Tee! You're on duty. Rise and shine."

"I'm trying." Her first attempt at speech came out as a raspy croak. Clearing her dry throat, she tried again. "One moment." She hunted for clothes in the mess she'd left upon finding her bed and collapsing into it. Cleaning droids at the palace scoured her chamber daily, while handmaidens returned everything she used to its proper place, leaving her room faultlessly clean. A neat chamber had never been a reflection of her own preferences, but of those who looked after her. At that, she smiled. It seemed untidiness was rather liberating—and it was a far safer vice than Mandarian whiskey.

She left her brother's shirt hanging loose over her trousers and limped to the door. Ian stood in the entry, a mug held in each hand. Steam rising from the exotic cups brought with it a tantalizing nutty smell. One mug was painted with Earth runes: SHOOT FOR THE STARS—RED ROCKET ALE. The other sported a montage of clothed black-and-white rodents with big around ears and the letters: DISNEY WORLD—CHICAGO.

"Good morning," her employer said pleasantly, looking her over as if searching for signs of the continued hangover she hoped to hide. Why did people drink if this was the consequence? "Sleep well?"

"Quite well. Thank you." Awkwardly she attempted to tidy her uneven, spiky hair, then gave up and dropped her hands.

His expression was one of gentle amusement as he offered her the rodent mug. "Coffee. Try it. It beats *tock* hands down."

She moved aside to allow him into her cramped quarters. He wore an outer garment cut in a foreign style and constructed of black leather. It was unsnapped to his waist, revealing a plain white, close-fitting shirt that drew her attention to his firm, athletic build.

"I apologize for oversleeping," she said. "I usually never do. Of course there are quite a few things I've done lately that I don't do, like stumbling out of bars drunk." He looked a bit skeptical, and she couldn't blame him. She had told him she drank all the time . . . and guzzled all that whiskey. "I shall set two alarm chimes from now on."

"Quin can be your backup, I suppose."

She laughed. "That's all the incentive I need to wake on time."

After a moment Ian's grin faded. "All right, pilot. We have to talk."

Her pulse sped up. "I figured that. Please, have a seat . . . if you can find one."

The silver fastenings on his hip-length outer garment glinted as he contemplated the snarled sheets and blanket spilling onto the floor, the boot she'd left sitting on the bedside table, and the soiled socks draped over the bunk's metal footboard. After a moment, stymied, he offered her the mug of coffee again.

She accepted it with a quiet thanks, then clutching the delicious-smelling hot beverage in her hands, unable to come up with anything else to say, she simply stared in fascination as he moved aside her other boot and sat on the edge of the bunk. He wasn't overly tall, yet he seemed to fill the room with his presence. There was something about him, something she couldn't define but that nonetheless attracted her. Charisma, self-assurance. But as she'd discovered since coming aboard the *Sun Devil*, his confidence with his crew stopped blessedly short of arrogance. She was all too used to that particular trait in the royal men she'd met at court.

"All right, Tee, let's talk. About that little incident on Blunder—what can you tell me about that?"

The ache behind her eyes began to throb. "With Dar security?"

"Yes." He observed her as he sipped his coffee.

She fought the mighty urge to fidget under his scrutiny. "What would you like to know?"

Something flickered in his eyes, but she couldn't tell whether it was annoyance or amusement. "Did you steal that starspeeder?"

"I borrowed it."

"Ah."

"Long-term," she qualified.

"I see."

Maybe he did, but she had the feeling he wouldn't stop asking questions until she had satisfied his curiosity. She didn't dare tell the truth. On the other hand, she was a horrible liar, and she wouldn't feel comfortable wholly deceiving the man who'd helped her escape her father's guards. She'd best come up with a version of the truth, a background that paralleled her own.

"I worked as a pilot on Mistraal, the Dar homeworld." It felt strange, mentioning that fact so casually, as if the Dars were merely employers, not flesh and blood. "I wanted to fly, but my family wanted me to marry. Had I agreed, I'm sure I would have lost the last of what little freedom I had. The speeder was my only way off planet." She willed him to understand the hopelessness that drove her to such a desperate measure.

"Didn't you think the Dars would miss their ship?"

Her cheeks burned. "Well. They have it back now."

"True."

"I intended to keep it only until I saved enough for a down payment on a vessel of my own. I would have returned it. Eventually." Nervously she tried the contents of her mug, more out of a desire to appear relaxed than to quench her thirst. But the beverage tasted heavenly, and she brought the mug to her lips for another drink.

Ian leaned forward, balancing his forearms on his thighs. "Did you talk at length to anyone on Blunder besides me and the bartender?"

"Only the cloaker I hired. The only way Dar security would know that I boarded your ship is if the cloaker saw me go with you and Dar security forced it out of him."

"Forced?" Ian gave a quick laugh. "He'd volunteer the information in a heartbeat if it meant reducing his fine."

Tee'ah felt her heart jump. "I had to give him thousands of credits as insurance against those fines. I don't think he's one to want to help the authorities." She prayed that was so.

Ian shoved one hand through his hair. His misgivings regarding rescuing her were evident in the shadows under his eyes. She felt bad. He'd saved her; he didn't deserve the risk she was bringing him. The least she could do was make him feel comfortable about keeping her aboard his ship. "All right," she said. "Let's assume the cloaker talked, then. And with a few judicious bribes and maybe a few threats, Dar security used what they learned from him to find out which ship belonged to you, the Earth dweller. We didn't file destination coordinates with the space controller, correct?" She took a steadying breath. "So the only data available to them would have been our initial routing. Even if they retrieved, deciphered, and downloaded our routing, without knowing our destination they'd have lost us when we jumped to hyperspace."

Ian nodded, as if he agreed with her reasoning. "I've already had a look around the city," he said. "There were no Dars."

"Then the cloaker held his tongue, yes?"

"I hope so." Her employer tipped his mug toward his mouth and drained the contents. Then he set the cup on the floor between his boots. When he focused on her, his gaze was penetrating. His voice was low. "As part of my crew, you're going to see and do some things you don't understand. The less you know, the better, if you know what I mean."

Tee'ah wasn't sure she did, but she nodded nonetheless.

"I sell Earth goods on the black market. That

99

means I go where I want, see whom I want, and stay as long or short as I want. I don't make a lot of money, but enough to afford a few luxuries and to support my ship and crew."

He searched her face for shock, perhaps, or distaste. But that's not what Tee'ah felt at all. She envied his life of independence and freedom.

"If the Trade police wanted to," he continued, "they could easily fine me out of business. Or arrest me. So I make it a point not to attract their attention."

"I don't care to attract anyone's attention, either."

He considered her statement. "That's true. You're on the run."

She gulped her coffee and scalded her throat.

He paused, then shrugged. "Well, so are half the people in the frontier I suppose." He gave her a curious look. "I saw the way the soldiers acted when they combed the bars on Blunder looking for you. They were friendly. More importantly, they had their pistols in their holsters. Right away I knew you weren't dangerous." He regarded her steadily. "But what *are* you, Tee?"

Her reluctance to explain sat between them like a *Tjhu'nami* shield, thick and silent. It was clear that he sensed her hesitation. Compassion filled his greenish-gray eyes. Curiosity, too. Which unnerved her. If she were careless in what she revealed about herself, he'd grow more suspicious than he already was. And she couldn't afford that, couldn't risk the chance of anyone—especially a black-market merchant—discovering who she was. She'd eluded her father's men last time, but there was no guarantee she'd escape the next. After the sometimes terrifying yet exhilarating days since leaving home, she was certain that she never wanted to be trapped in the sheltered isolation of her old life again.

With that in mind, she chose the frankest reply of all. "I'm not what I was."

He kept silent, as if hoping she'd volunteer more. She didn't. But neither did he. Perhaps he recognized that pressing her for information would lead to questions about his own activities. Perhaps there were other reasons.

He regarded her for a moment longer before he stepped into the corridor. "By the way, I need you ready to fly."

"Again?" She'd already figured that going back to bed wouldn't be possible, but another flight so soon after the last? She gritted her teeth against her aching head. "Of course, Captain, To where?"

"To Barésh. Have you been there?"

"No. I have never heard of it."

"That makes two of us. A respectable portion of the galaxy's trillidium is taken out of the Baréshti Mines, from what I'm told." He hesitated, as if gauging what to tell her. "I learned this morning that my competitor is headed there. I want to find out why he's interested in the place."

"When do we leave?"

He must have sensed the anticipation in her tone as well as her fatigue. He replied with a slightly apologetic smile. "This afternoon. Quin's working on some repairs—today the environmental control system's giving us trouble. Tomorrow, who knows?" he added irritably. "So get finished dressing and get something to eat."

She stopped him before he left the room. "Is there a market nearby?"

"Yes. About a mile away."

"Excellent. I need to go shopping."

"I see." He scrutinized her. "For what, exactly?"

She fought an evil urge to say, "Whiskey." Instead she pointed to her stained, ill-fitting outfit. "I need new uniforms, extra clothing, and a way to replace the toiletries I left on my ship."

"Understood. I'll take you after breakfast."

She stared at him as he stood and strode away, uncertain what she had gotten herself into. The Earth dweller was an enigma, like no one she'd ever known or been exposed to. Certainly he was up to no good. Danger and excitement were a way of life for him.

And it appeared she was going along for the ride.

"Is this the way you treat your best repo pilot?" a woman shouted. "Wait. I'm your *only* repo pilot. I want what you owe me. Now. Every last blasted credit!"

Gann Truelénne stood in the shadows outside a

faded tent in a row of seedy shops on Donavan's Blunder. He'd journeyed here immediately after leaving Rom and Jas on Sienna, intent on questioning the cloaker who had tried to help Princess Tee'ah camouflage her speeder. But from within the tent, an argument raged.

"Lara, there's no money left to recover your ship. None. Dar security fined me into oblivion. But I'll make good on what I owe you; I swear it. Give me more time."

" 'Give' you?" The woman spat the words with contempt. "I don't give anything to anyone. Not even you, Eston. You know that." The female's voice turned sullen. "I needed the credits to pay the landing fees on that disgusting rock, Kabasten. If it weren't for you, I wouldn't have been there. Now they've impounded my ship! Damn it, Eston, it's the only thing I have, and you know it."

Gann detected a slight thickening in the woman's voice. "Where am I supposed to go?" she asked. "Would you tell me? How am I supposed to make a living now? Damn you, Eston!"

Something heavy crashed to the floor and shattered. Gann winced.

"Lara—"

"The next one will hit the target; I swear it," the female said in a hiss. "All this has happened because you helped that spoiled little *Vash Nadah*. How could you? After all you know about them!"

Against his better judgment, Gann pushed aside

the tent flap and walked in. Broken pottery crunched under his boots. "Good day to you." Smiling, he glanced around the disorganized tent, looking for hints, items of clothing, anything that might indicate that the princess had been there.

"*Vash* scum."

The woman, Lara, had directed her remark at him. Her honey brown eyes full of fire, her chest heaving, Lara glared at him. Her voice was low and venomous. "I despise the *Vash*. Every . . . last . . . one."

Her ferocity caught Gann off guard. At forty-five standard years, he'd seen his share of the darker side of life; he'd fought in an unpopular, protracted war—the only conflict since the inception of the *Vash Nadah*—and subsequently accompanied its instigator, Rom B'kah, into exile. Gann was no stranger to bitterness and anger in all their forms. But never had he seen hatred displayed with such intensity and passion as that expressed by this woman. Which was truly saddening, for apart from her animosity she was fascinating to behold. What a waste that such a beauty could be filled with such ill will.

From nearby, the cloaker's cheery voice shattered the awkwardness in the room. "Good day to you, sir," he sang out, his expression eager. "Do you need your ship cloaked, perhaps?"

"Let's just say that I need your expertise."

"Expertise, my eye." The woman's mouth dipped

in a sneer as she looked him over from head to boots. Stripped naked, he doubted he would have felt more exposed to her scrutiny.

She leaned against one of the support poles, her arms folded over her chest. Although her skin was as smooth as a twenty-year-old girl's, her eyes looked eighty. He'd place her age somewhere in between—mid-thirties, he guessed, a good decade younger than himself. Her black one-piece outfit was utilitarian and unisex, like her tawny neck-length hair, a contrast to the dainty jewelry sparkling on her ears and wrists. "So . . . the *Vash Nadah* didn't extort enough credits from Eston their first time," she taunted. "They had to send you back for more. That's why you're here, isn't it? Admit it, *Vash*."

Gann decided to ignore the moody little fireball. To his mild amusement, he saw that it infuriated her. "The *Vash* woman you were fined for helping is a runaway," he told the cloaker. "Her family fears for her welfare, and sent me here on their behalf so that they may be reunited with her swiftly and safely. I'm not here to punish you or to coerce you, but to reward you."

The woman choked out a laugh.

"Generously," Gann said, as if he hadn't heard. "*If* you cooperate and give me information leading to where I can find the woman." One by one he laid currency cards on the cloaker's desk until the equivalent of five thousand credits fanned out over the alloy top.

105

Shoulders held stiffly, the woman named Lara walked to a small ion-burner and poured a cup of *tock*. An intricately patterned silver band slid down her wrist. The workmanship was exquisite and matched the braided ring adorning her left ear. She sipped silently, her slender back toward him. "Don't waste your time, Eston," she snarled. "I'd trust a desert snake before I'd trust a *Vash Nadah*."

Eston cast her a pleading glance before he regarded Gann with interest. "I may be able to help you," he said, and waggled his eyebrows pointedly at the credits.

"Excellent." Gann allocated a thousand more to his cause. There were times when Rom's bottomless fortune came in handy, he thought. "You told Dar security that the woman disappeared off planet while you labored aboard her speeder. Is that true?"

"Don't you dare accuse us of lying." The woman's voice squeezed out past her gritted teeth. She strode to the tent flap and shoved it open, allowing a steamy, sickly-smelling breeze to seep inside. "You don't belong in the frontier. None of you *Vash* do. Get out!"

"Lara, please," Eston beseeched her.

Great Mother, how could he have pitied himself over being sent on a mission to retrieve a petulant princess? Things could be much worse: he could be a bankrupt cloaker, like Eston, stuck with Miss Sunshine here for company. "I don't believe your partner feels the same as you," he drawled.

The woman's mouth tightened. She had very expressive eyes, Gann noted. In them, it was very easy to see every detail of his own painful demise, should she get her hands on him.

"Eston?" Gann prompted.

The cloaker's mouth slid into a winning smile, revealing teeth that were surprisingly white and straight. "I told the truth. The *Vash* woman did go off planet," he said. "For ten thousand credits more, I might know exactly how you can find her."

Chapter Seven

While Tee ate breakfast and the crew prepared for the flight, Ian climbed down to the cargo hold, his place of choice when he needed to think.

"Lights," he said. Held by a protective brace for space travel, his vintage 1990 Harley-Davidson Softtail glinted in the crisp illumination. He wheeled the hog to the rear of the hold where he stored his tools, then tried to lose himself in the mindless tasks of tinkering, tightening, and polishing.

You should have let her go, gotten yourself another pilot.

Yeah, but he also needed to follow Randall.

Now he was stuck with a pilot with a shaky past when he most required reliability in his crew and the ability to stay focused on his mission. He'd gone to Tee's quarters fully intending to tell her that her position was temporary, that he intended to let her

108

go as soon as he found another flyer. But somehow she'd plowed him under; that crazy mix of bravado, naivete, and grace under fire she exuded, it had totally snowed him. He'd stood there like a moron and let her wheedle him into letting her keep her job long-term. It wasn't like the dependable Ian that everyone back home knew: the responsible son, the summa cum laude finance major, the guy his sister called Mr. Goody-two-shoes.

The pilot didn't have a clue as to her effect on him—which was a good thing, because he hadn't figured it out himself. No woman had ever affected him this way.

It was a moot point, anyway. It wasn't as if he could have any relationship with this girl. Not only was she his pilot, but she had a shaky history and was a non-royal—and his *Vash* opponents in the Great Council were watching his every move, waiting for him to make just one misstep. No, Ian would marry the woman chosen for him. That was all he could do. He owed that much to Rom and his mother.

As for his attraction to Tee, it was likely tied in to the *Vash* belief that certain people had a mental and emotional affinity of thought. When such people paired up, their thoughts resonated, creating an immediate and powerful attraction. Which pretty much described what he felt with Tee. He couldn't stop thinking about the way she smelled, or the feel of her skin. Or the way she moved, and her humor and quick mind—the whole package.

Lust; that's all it was.

His lips drew tight over his clenched teeth. He'd long prided himself on his ability to control his sexual urges. Sure he had them, had a lot of them. He'd slept with his share of women, but always within the context of a relationship, never as a mindless fling or one-night stand. It wasn't easy taking that route, in fact it had damned near killed him a couple of times, but he'd dedicated his life to being everything his biological father was not. He'd been celibate for over five years now. Within the teachings of the *Vash Nadah* he had found the strength and guidance he needed to hold himself to his own high standards. Which was why this fascination with the pixie was as startling to him as it was inappropriate.

He opened a storage shelf and looked for a can of motor oil while his thoughts reeled back to his childhood in Arizona. He'd grown up watching his mother deal with his father's adultery. Whether Jas's loyalty went too far, or she'd ignored much of her husband's behavior to keep the family intact, Ian could only guess, but by the time he reached manhood, he'd concluded that only those with despicably weak characters let testosterone guide their actions.

He shoved an opener into a can of oil, releasing a spray of viscous brown liquid. *Great.* Frowning, he grabbed a rag, wiped his hands, and slam-dunked the rag into the sterilizer. Maybe the pilot would prove herself undependable, like her predecessors. Dereliction of duty would make it easier to dismiss her . . . unless her pursuers solved his problem and got to her first.

Gann laid five thousand credits on the cloaker's desk. "Tell me where the woman went," he said. "And with whom." As he added the remaining five thousand, he saw Lara staring in amazement at the prodigious stack of credits now on the table.

Eston was much more at ease. "I saw her sharing drinks with an Earth dweller at old Garjha's bar. Then she went off with the man."

"Tell me about the Earth dweller," Gann said.

"Young fellow. Odd-colored hair." Eston grimaced. "Brown, like so many of them have. In case you're wondering, he didn't file destination coordinates with the port controller. I wish he had. Your little *Vash* owes me for my troubles; I'd have liked to know where she was headed."

Gann mulled that over. "By now the ship could be anywhere."

Eston smiled. "You'll need a tracker to find them."

Gann contemplated the cloaker. What the man said regarding hiring a tracker was true. He hadn't been in the frontier in years, and not this far out for years beyond that. He needed someone who knew the territory. "I'm willing to pay good wages. If the

111

hunt is successful, I'll throw in a bonus. Do you have someone in mind, someone good?"

Eston smiled triumphantly. "She's the best there is."

At the same time it dawned on Gann, the woman in question realized whom Eston meant. She made a small choking noise. Her hand opened, releasing the tent flap she'd been holding in hopes that Gann would leave. "Eston," she said in a hiss. "What are you doing?"

The man crossed the tent and took her by the hand, steering her to a private corner, but not out of Gann's hearing range. "Lara, your ship's impounded. I don't have enough to get her out—even with what the *Vash* gave me. If you want your ship back, go with the *Vash* on his."

Something akin to fear quenched the fire in her golden brown eyes. "Go to hell."

Gann turned his back on the pair as they continued to argue in hushed tones. A pot of *tock* in the corner was nearly full. But he decided against pouring himself a cup. The couple obviously had few supplies left in the wake of the stiff fines they'd paid for cloaking a stolen Dar starspeeder. He decided to wait in silence.

Finally Eston pushed the sullen woman toward him. "Lara Ros, master tracker. She'll take you where you need to go."

The woman's eyes were steely and cold. "I am going with you only so that I may recover my ship."

Her voice caught on those words, as if that ship meant more to her than any person. "My bonus will equal the fine I'll have to pay."

Gann's doubts surged. This Lara's attitude was as rotten as year-old oster eggs. He hoped it didn't interfere with her ability to do a job, because he had no time to waste hunting for another tracker. "I'll pay you what you need to free your ship—once the woman is in my custody." He clasped his hands behind his back. "I'll wait while you gather your things."

She scowled at Eston as she walked past, her demeanor proud but unyielding. The cloaker smiled. "Tell me all about it when you get back."

"Yeah, right." The tent flap whooshed closed.

Only then did it hit Gann that he was stuck with Miss Sunshine. By the heavens, he thought, this voyage was going to prove very long indeed.

"I'll stand for no more sleeping past your assigned rest period, Tee. Every one of the six crewmembers aboard this ship carries his own weight." Admonishing Tee'ah as she sat in the pilot's chair, Quin leaned toward her.

She reared back, but the headrest stopped her from retreating as far as she'd like. After he'd spoken to her, Ian vanished to who-knew-where, Muffin headed into town, while Gredda and Push drank *tock* in the galley and went over files listing what goods were in the cargo hold. That had left Tee'ah alone with Quin, who delightedly used the time to lecture her on the ship's rules and her duties, which he said included taking her turn in the galley to cook meals when her number came up—something she prayed wouldn't be soon. She had never prepared a meal in her life. While cooking her own food was something she'd expected, and even looked forward to, dinner for six was something she'd never anticipated. Her sympathies went out to the crew.

Quin pursed his lips, scrutinizing her. "I hope that liquor you like to guzzle hasn't eaten all your brain cells, because you'll need a few for this." He shoved a palmtop computer into her hands. "Here—your shipboard systems manual." He tapped the palmtop with work-worn fingers. "You've done all right so far. But like I told the captain today—if you fly rough, I'm not fixing whatever you break without it first being docked from your pay. Got it?"

"Yes. I do," Tee'ah replied. Her tone was cool but not cold. As a professional starpilot she refused, no matter how much the man baited her, to bicker with her mechanic, wrench-wielding demon that he was.

She was thankful when Quin skulked off without further provocation. With the palmtop nestled in her hands, she relaxed against the contoured pilot's chair. *Her* chair. She could grow used to the sound of that, she thought as she accessed the data stored on the little computer and began studying the lengthy shipboard systems manual.

But, as she waited for Ian to come back to take her to Grüma's marketplace, her attention drifted to the miles of sunlit, forested hills outside the ship's forward viewscreen. True, viewscreens in late-model starships weren't transparent and displayed only what the computer "saw," but it was obvious the day was lovely. The idea of being closed inside smothered her with a sensation of claustrophobia. She'd spent too much of her life gazing longingly out of windows; it was her time to be on the outside. She'd await Ian there.

She checked her hip pocket for credits, her laser pistol, and the personal comm unit Ian required her to carry. Across the cockpit, Quin crouched on his knees. His head was buried in an open panel underneath the comm station and tools glinted near his boots. The mechanic had been working since they'd landed, muttering about "bad luck" and "suspicious damage." She doubted that cutting short her studying of the ship's systems would make his mood any worse. "I will see you later, Quin."

As she rushed down the gangway from the cockpit, Ian exited the cargo hold. "Ready?" he asked.

His words were interrupted by a shout: "Tee! Halt!" Quin clambered down the gangway. Red-faced, he looked as if he was ready to vent all the outrage in his rancorous little soul. "You're confined to the ship."

"She's on probation," Ian corrected. "Not confinement."

"But, sir. I thought you said we had to keep an eye on her."

"*I'll* keep an eye on her. I'm taking her to the market."

"Quin's worried about the remaining quantity of functional brain cells in my head," Tee said dryly.

The mechanic scowled at her. "Do me a favor, starpilot; don't go losing any more today." He hoisted himself up the gangway and stomped back to his repairs.

After watching him go, Ian turned and dropped a cap and a pair of eye-shaders into Tee'ah's hands. "A makeshift disguise," he said.

The crown of the cap was decorated with Earth runes: A.S.U., and a mean-looking little red man with horns and a tail. "Thank you. Is this Quin? It rather reminds me of him."

To her delight, her employer laughed. "Meet the Sun Devil, the Arizona State University mascot and my ship's namesake." He seemed to search for a suitable English-to-Basic translation. "A.S.U. is where I received my higher education on Earth."

Tee touched her fingertips to the emblem on the cap. Earth and its inhabitants symbolized all she hoped for in her new life: unconventionality and brash independence. "It will be an honor to wear it," she said. Proudly, she wedged the hat onto her wretched hair—or what was left of it—and led the way down the entry ramp.

She walked with Ian along a dirt path leading

away from the ship. The breeze held a slight chill, but it was sweet with the scent of sun-warmed pine and mild enough to warrant leaving off the thermal-control sewn into the inside lining of her brother's shirt. Inhaling, she angled her face into the sun, an intense blue-white pearl so different from Mistraal's oversized golden star. The sunshine complimented the hues of the lavender sky and a forest of conifers that was broken only by frothy streams and a few outcroppings of bald rocks.

Ian spoke companionably as they walked, picking up pebbles occasionally and tossing them into the dense undergrowth lining the trail. "So. You and Quin aren't best friends yet."

She rolled her eyes. "If he could inventory and keep track of my brain cells, he would."

"The truth is, I need you, Tee, and he knows it. We've lost three pilots to alcohol. And don't for-get—you were drunk when I hired you."

"I don't drink . . . that much." *I don't drink at all,* she longed to tell him. But she had a questionable past to maintain.

"Carn used to say that, too. Then he killed him-self with the stuff."

Her hand flew to the wings on her chest. Likely they'd belonged to her predecessor. The thought made the hair on the back of her neck stand on end. "I'm sorry," she said.

His casual shrug belied deeper feelings on the subject. "Between us, I'm sure we can think of some recreational activities that don't include alcohol."

He bent over to scoop up more pebbles. As she stared at his strong back and tight backside, outrageously wanton and explicit thoughts overtook her. *When I want sex, I don't have to buy it.*

"Well"—she blushed hard—"I am open to sampling new and varied methods of enjoyment."

But how new and how varied? She wasn't sure. She was a virgin, yes, but she'd received instruction in the art of lovemaking from her toddler years. As a female *Vash* she'd been part of discussions, done reading, heard comparisons of techniques by experienced teachers. All her questions had been answered honestly and completely, or she'd been given the appropriate literature. Her brothers, on the other hand, had accumulated actual physical experience as teenagers with the palace courtesans. They'd been taught skills designed to bring their future wives pleasure, to ultimately strengthen each of their marriages.

The foundation of society is family. Sexuality enhances spirituality, said the Treatise of Trade. It was an integral part of her culture, and her faith. Tee'ah had expected to be a virgin on her wedding day, now that the marriage was off, there was no requirement to remain untouched. Was there?

Oblivious to her speculation, Ian shrugged off his black leather outer garment and anchored it over one shoulder with his index finger. The short-sleeved shirt he wore beneath was tight enough to

glimpse the flexing of his stomach muscles as he strode beside her. The end of a thin gold chain disappeared into his shirt. Otherwise, he wore no skin jewelry, which was so fashionable of late, and no other adornment. And no *Vash* signet ring, she noted—another sign that she wasn't keeping company with the one Earth dweller she needed to avoid at all cost. She couldn't imagine the crown prince being without the trappings of his rank.

She steered the conversation back toward safer ground. "What will we find at the marketplace?"

"Just about anything you'd want—most of it illegal as heck." He acted as if he assumed she'd seen the like before. Perhaps she hadn't yet, but in a month or two, she'd undoubtedly be a veteran of such emporiums of unauthorized merchandise.

"Are the goods dangerous, then?"

He smiled. "No. Only hard to come by. Especially Earth beer, salt, coffee"—he rubbed his faded indigo pants—"and blue jeans."

"I would think, since Grüma is so close to Earth, that those products would be easy to find."

"Not when the Trade Federation ships them directly from Earth to the central galaxy, bypassing the frontier. By the time the products are transported back here and offered for sale—if they ever are—the price is beyond the average person's reach."

He didn't sound enamored of the Federation. She wondered what he'd think if he knew who he'd hired—one of the daughters of its heads.

The path toward Grüma's largest city took them into a thick grove of trees. A cool, damp hush enveloped them, the air soaked with the scent of ferns and pine.

"We're almost there," Ian said. She could hear the sounds of urban life ahead, though she could still see no signs of it. "Stay close in case your Dar friends show up. I've got pressing business to take care of later; it wouldn't do to lose you now."

She focused her eyes on the sun-dappled path before them. Ian might not want to lose her, but if her father committed fully to bringing her home, Tee'ah wondered if there would be anything Ian could do to stop him.

Chapter Eight

The streets of downtown Grüma radiated outward from a central plaza teeming with people: men, women, and even a few children. All had lighter complexions than Tee'ah, as well as the pale blond hair and brown eyes common to the merchant class. Tee'ah hoped her Earth-dweller facade was convincing enough. There wasn't much she could do about her golden skin, but eye-shaders hid her pale irises, and only a few bits of her trademark *Vash* coppery dark-blond hair stuck out from under her cap.

As she walked across the plaza with Ian, no one gave them more than a glance. Anticipation quickened her steps. She'd never had the opportunity to be anonymous, to bargain with a vendor who wasn't fearful about insulting a princess by asking too high a price for inferior merchandise. When she'd visited the market outside the palace gates on Mistraal, it was in the protective company of her handmaidens or her parents and their usual entourage. Here, someone might actually attempt to cheat her. Her spirits soared. Let them try!

In a move that would have been completely out of character for her in her days as royalty, she grabbed Ian's arm, just above the elbow, and tugged him forward. "Come, Earth dweller. Let us see what bargains await."

He laughed, his boots crunching heavily on the gravel.

The merchants carried the usual items: produce, roasting meats, sundries. The spicy-sweet scent of countless unidentified products filled the air. As she browsed, he examined the crowd and shops, as if he were doing a little window-shopping of his own—though for people, she suspected, not merchandise.

The crowd surged toward a street show just getting under way. Onlookers clucked their tongues appreciatively as an artisan released a flock of rainbow-colored bubble-bots into the air. With a wandlike controller, he sent commands to microscopic computers contained in the bubbles' liquid skin, changing the diaphanous, iridescent orbs into different creatures and flowers and a variety of floating figures, from entwined lovers to children playing.

Ian admired the show unfolding above their heads. "We don't have anything like this on Earth. Not yet, anyway."

"I've seen similar demonstrations"—*at the palace,*

she almost said—"but none performed with such skill and creativity."

One by one the bubbles coalesced into nano-computer–rich droplets and fell into a widemouthed beaker the man held on his head. All around them shoppers applauded and clicked their tongues appreciatively.

Ian's comm beeped. He took it out of his pocket and brought the mouthpiece to his lips. "Stone here."

"Look left."

Ian's head turned, and she followed his gaze to where Muffin towered above the crowd. The big man grinned, stowing his comm as he strode toward them. When he caught up to them, he jerked his thumb toward a group of starships docked in a clearing. "The crew of that cargo-runner told me they saw Randall and his men in a pub the night before last."

Ian looked interested. "What did they say?"

"That Randall's looking forward to doing business."

Ian made a disdainful noise. "I imagine he is."

As the men lagged behind, deep in conversation, Tee'ah focused on the purpose of her visit to the market, forcing herself to shop quickly and efficiently, sensing Ian was suddenly impatient to return to the ship. She found three high-necked, one-piece, all-weather outfits in a rich bluish gray that could double as both her flight uniform and off-duty clothing; a lightweight, short thermal-controllable coat; socks; undergarments; and two nightshirts. With those purchases in several sacks, she stopped in front of a stand displaying soaps and incense, oils, and assorted medicines.

"I have everything you need." the young vendor called in a husky voice. She scrutinized Tee-ah's cap, her butchered hair and dirty clothes, but tactfully displayed no distaste. "Whatever is your desire . . . or his"—with an overt smile of approval, she gestured somewhere behind Tee'ah—"you will find it here."

Tee'ah looked over her shoulder, expecting to see Ian, but a tall man, dressed warmly and well, watched her from a stand across the street that was selling fire-cooked meats. The fur-trimmed hood he wore shadowed his features, but she sensed from him an intense, pointed regard. Considering her appearance, she couldn't believe attraction was the cause of his interest, though the Grüman vendor seemed to think otherwise.

So engrossed was the cloaked gentleman with her that he didn't notice at first that the cook was trying to hand him a paper-wrapped skewer. Finally, the vendor tugged on his sleeve and the tall man turned away . . . but not before Tee'ah glimpsed his eyes.

They were gold, like hers.

Her mouth went dry. He was *Vash Nadah*.

She fought the urge to bolt to where Ian and Muffin stood, several shops away, talking. Instead she forced herself to watch the man and ascertain his intentions. If he'd come here to "rescue" her and bring her home, would he not have acted already?

The *Vash* paid for his purchase with a gloved hand. Then, by some miracle, he walked off purposefully, as if he were late for an appointment. Perhaps he was only part *Vash*. Or he could be an expatriate, like her, desirous of a less restrictive life.

Regardless, he wasn't a Dar guard here to force her to go home.

She let out a shaky breath. Shutting her eyes, she composed herself, then turned back to the stand. "I require hair dye," she said emphatically.

The female vendor uncovered a row of little boxes. "I have the very latest from the outer worlds. Clay-roll," she declared, struggling with the pronunciation.

Tee'ah admired the exotic Earth products, particularly fascinated by the dark colors: black, rich browns, russet and auburn. *Clairol*, the labels said in almost illegible runes.

"May I have a translation of the instruction manual?" she asked.

"You won't need it," the Grüman merchant replied. "Simply mix the contents of the vials and massage it into your hair, like soap. When the shade is to your liking, rinse with water."

The procedure was primitive compared to DNA-based hair dye, which altered hair strands on the molecular level.

Tee'ah was beginning to like primitive.

Plunking her bags on the ground, she said, "I'll take the brown, please." She needed a better disguise, and a new darker hair shade would be the ideal camouflage. With eye-shaders on, she'd be able to pass for an Earth dweller, as she had in Ian's arms on Donavan's Blunder.

After selecting several cakes of scented soap, mouth cleanser, and menstruation protectors, she let her fingers drift over a selection of little cubes decorated with a holographic floral pattern. "What lovely boxes."

"Twenty credits," the vendor cajoled. "No one sells blockers for less."

"Blockers?"

"Birth-blockers, yes."

Tee'ah felt the blood drain from her face, then rush back in a heated blush. The woman smiled knowingly, as if she knew a great secret Tee'ah did not. Though the vendor was barely past her mid-teens, she seemed much older and wiser. Tee'ah envied the young woman's feminine self-awareness, her apparent worldliness. If only it were possible to fling off innocence like an old coat. "Of course; birth-blockers," she replied in an airy tone that didn't quite work. Cheap, easy, and reliable, birth-blockers were the most popular method of birth control for the merchant class. But that was as far as her knowledge went. She hadn't been taught more, since it was expected she'd remain a virgin until she married and thereafter go right to work producing royal heirs.

But her life's path had changed. *She'd* changed it.

She was a free woman now. Self-reliant. Open-minded. Women such as herself chose lovers where and when they pleased.

Did they not?

Her mouth went dry. She glanced wildly to where Ian and Muffin chatted outside a neighboring shop. Ian's coat was again hooked on his finger and tossed over his shoulder. The fingertips of his other hand were wedged into the back pocket of his jeans. When he briefly tipped his face toward the sky, the thought of his sun-warmed lips on hers sent a languorous tremor of desire coursing through Tee'ah.

"Which one do you fancy?" the vendor coaxed.

Tee'ah spun her gaze back to the girl. "Which who?"

"Which *cube?*"

Tee'ah gathered her wits. Heavens, she was behaving like a ketta-cat in heat. She didn't know if it was because she was free to act on her impulses for the first time in her life, or because she'd developed a yen for Earth dwellers—Ian Stone in particular.

"This one will do." She stared at her own hand pushing a brightly colored cube across the table, as if someone else had taken control of her body and the real Tee'ah was trapped inside her, gaping at her actions with abject fascination.

Lovemaking would be the ultimate demonstration of rebellion. Once she lost her virginity, she could never go back to her family.

But simply purchasing birth blockers didn't mean she was going to use them. Yet. "I'll take the hair dye and soap, too," she said in a hoarse voice.

She haggled briefly and indifferently with the vendor, as bargaining was expected, but enjoyed it less than she'd expected. She was still feeling too odd. Then she fished her credits out of her pocket.

Tee'ah's self-consciousness apparently had not been lost on the vendor. The girl pulled up her sleeve, her gaze both wise and understanding. On the underside of her slender arm was a tiny skin patch. "Wear it for one menstrual cycle, then remove," she whispered. "It will provide protection against pregnancy for up to a year." Smiling, she added, "For full effectiveness, you must first wait forty-eight standard hours."

"Yes, of course." Tee'ah snatched the shopping bag from the young woman's hand. She whirled away from the stall and bumped into Ian, who had come up behind her sometime during the transaction.

He caught her by the shoulders to keep her from stumbling. "Find everything you need?" he asked.

Her heart pounded a drumroll of disbelief, and she forced herself to look up at him. "Actually, a bit more than I'd intended."

He regarded her, his expression uncomprehending. She was glad he didn't ask what she meant, because she wasn't sure if she could explain it herself.

"But all at a marvelous price," she said. Then she brushed past him so that he would not see the blush she feared was making its way up her neck. "Good thing, too," she called over her shoulder. "The wages you pay me certainly don't go very far." At home, such brashness would certainly have been frowned upon.

Ian only laughed. He caught up to her. "Prove your worth to me, and maybe I'll give you more."

"I got you here to Grüma, didn't I?"

"Beginner's luck."

"Bah! Talent and skill, and don't ever forget it, Captain Stone." She pretended to scowl at Muffin, who watched their exchange with interest. "That means you, too."

The man raised two plate-sized hands. "Any pilot who doesn't turn me into a smoking crater wins my thankful admiration. I'd keep her happy, Captain," he advised.

"After all," she continued, "a happy pilot means a happy captain."

"Does it now?" The corners of Ian's eyes crinkled. Although his weariness was obvious, he appeared to be enjoying the banter as much as she.

The two men took most of her packages for the trek back to the ship. Once back in the woods surrounding the city, coolness washed over Tee'ah, and a deep hush thickened the air, broken only by occasional birdsong. But the path was stained with patches of bright sunlight. Days on Grüma were a third longer than Mistraal's, creating a noon hour that seemed to last forever.

Ian buried one hand in his coat pocket as he

walked alongside her. "If what you said was true, 'a happy pilot means a happy captain,' then that leaves me no choice but to ensure your job satisfaction. I'm at your service, ma'am," he said.

She remembered the one sack she hadn't let either of the men take; it had the birth-blockers inside. What if she told this man that her job satisfaction hinged on taking him as a lover? A slow, hot flush crept up her neck. She was far from ready to admit such a thing, let alone fully accept the idea herself. But the seeds of possibility had sprouted.

A princess should be seen and not smelled.

As Tee'ah stood in front of the mirror in her quarters, her fingers submerged knuckle-deep in gooey hair, she failed to see the humor in her joke. Nor could she decide what she liked least about *Clay-roll*, the muddy stains it left on her forehead and temples, or the wretched odor.

But she needed to disguise herself, a point driven home during the disturbing encounter with the cloaked *Vash* in the market. As long as the possibility existed that she'd encounter her own kind, she had to take steps to avoid recognition.

She lathered her scalp and sneezed until her eyes watered. It was difficult to believe Earth dwellers chose to use such disagreeable products when more advanced techniques were available. Perhaps they clung to antiquated practices to preserve their culture—not unlike the *Vash Nadah*, she thought wryly, who insisted on safeguarding their women from the outside world as if the horrific war that drove them to do so raged yesterday, instead of eleven thousand years ago.

She peered at the viewscreen on the wall. Quin would soon be finished with his repairs to the ship. Then they'd eat a quick meal before the launch. As she rinsed her hair in the sink, Tee'ah hoped the dying process was complete; she'd worn the substance for barely an hour.

Bracing herself, she lifted her head. Her hair stood up in tufts, dark tufts, but not at all the shade she'd expected.

"Dear heaven," she murmured. Her hair was green.

"Tee!" Push's voice came over the ship's comm. "If you want to eat before we launch for Barésh, you need to do it now."

"I am coming." She squeezed her eyes shut. Her hair was the color of the algae-topped mud puddles that collected under the vast indoor gardens at her father's palace. And it smelled worse. Hastily she shampooed again, but the sweet-scented cleanser was no match for the tang of residual chemicals, reminiscent of rotten eggs. Nor did it alter the brownish-green tint to her hair.

Crat. Why hadn't she insisted that the merchant include instructions? Her stupid error echoed every stumble she'd taken so far since leaving Mistraal. First her entire escape was witnessed. Then her starspeeder was confiscated on her first stopover in the frontier—with all her possessions aboard. And her one attempt to alleviate her misery had turned into a drunken escapade that ended with her coming aboard the *Sun Devil*—the one bright spot, she conceded, in a black hole of blunders.

She let out a long, weary breath and forced herself to face the woman in the mirror. Each one of her mistakes could have ended her dreams of freedom. But they hadn't. Nor would her slime-hued hacked-off locks, she vowed. The way she saw it, the chances of Dar security spotting her in a search had just diminished another stress-reducing iota.

Vigorously, she towel-dried her hair and tried to scrub the spots of brown from her forehead. Her hair looked somewhat better after she combed it off her forehead, but the fuzzy ends curled as they dried. She pressed them down, but they sprang up again. Defeated, she threw down her hands and dashed to the galley.

The noise and laughter pouring from the chamber spurred memories of the bustle of the dining hall in which she'd taken her meals with her family. It seemed she would not be able to stop missing them as easily as she'd cut her ties. Clutching her hands together, she waited for the heaviness in her chest to pass. Then she skulked through the hatch, hoping the crew was too engrossed in their meal to notice her hair.

Ian calmly folded his napkin and stood. It was a

show of respect practiced by all *Vash Nadah* males when a woman entered a room, but not one she'd expected from an Earth dweller. Before she could ponder his behavior, conversation ceased. A few spoons clanked into bowls and Quin began choking. Gredda pounded him on the back.

"Her hair . . ." he sputtered.

Tee'ah was unable to resist the opportunity to torture the man. "I do have an extra box of hair color in my quarters. I planned to save it for a later date. However, perhaps I shall reserve it for you, my dear mechanic, should you decide to join me on the"—she winked—"wild side."

Red-faced, Quin wheezed something at her. Gredda and the others chuckled appreciatively.

As he pulled out her chair and seated her, Ian appeared thoroughly entertained. "Nice 'do," he said.

"I'd been wanting to try something different."

"It is that."

Smiling, she turned her attention to her meal. His gaze was totally without censure. Perhaps it meant that she was one step closer to being accepted as a member of his crew, green hair and all.

Chapter Nine

Gann found Lara in the *Quillie*'s cockpit. She must not have heard him drop down from the ladder, for she remained as still as a statue, her petite dancer's body nestled in the pilot's chair as she stared out the enormous curving viewscreen at the bow. They were traveling at many times light speed, and had been for most of the day, racing toward Padma Eight, a boisterous little planet known for its cargo operation and where, according to Lara, pilots went looking when they needed a job. Gann hoped Princess Tee'ah would be one of them.

Lara brought her hands to her eyes and rubbed.

Noticing, Gann said, "You've been on duty long enough, Lara."

At the sound of his voice, she went rigid, but she did not turn around.

"It's my turn to watch the computer fly the ship," he added.

"My shift's not over," she returned coldly.

"It's been eight hours."

"I'll take eight more, then."

"You're a workaholic."

"Actually," she said, glancing at him with hollow, haunted eyes, "I'm an insomniac. You might as well go back to sleep, because I won't be able to."

He thought of suggesting a few mutually enjoyable activities that would certainly tire her, but he held his tongue. "So take a sleep-inducer. In eight hours I want you back here, on tracking duty, refreshed and ready to go."

"Bah. No drugs. That's a *Vash* weakness." Her tone was cold, but stopped short of overt disrespect.

"I said you're relieved of duty, Ros. Go to bed. That's an order."

"Fine." She stood with her back to him as her fingertips tapped over the navigation computer. "We're on course, on schedule. I show atmospheric entry on Padma Eight in sixteen-point-two standard hours." Without looking up, she pushed past him. "I'll be back in eight."

Gann folded his arms across his chest. He had been raised to celebrate and appreciate the differences between men and women, but Lara was unlike any female he'd ever encountered. She was devoid of warmth, of softness, of anything he remotely associated with femininity.

And it roused his curiosity.

"All right, Miss Sunshine, what is it about me, or maybe men in general, that's so blasted distasteful to you?"

She turned. Her face conveyed an air of fragility, but the muscles flexing beneath the skin of her slender limbs indicated endurance and strength. Dim, bluish light illuminated the cockpit, bleaching her tawny complexion. "You have no idea, do you?"

"Why don't you enlighten me?"

The cavernous chamber in which they stood rang with mechanical emptiness, but it didn't come close to matching the desolation in her eyes. "This conversation falls outside the parameters of my job description. You hired me to track for you, not to be your friend."

"True," he replied.

"You pay me, I get my ship back. Then we go our separate ways. It's that simple. Don't ask for more than that, because you won't get it."

"You left out one very important element of your job description," Gann said.

"Did I?" Her proud stance faltered almost imperceptibly, but he was trained in such subtle clues and so he did not miss the change. He'd intended to tease her for leaving out any mention of finding the princess—the reason he'd hired her in the first place—but seeing the uncertainty tightening her features, he changed his mind.

Had Eston somehow implied to Lara that Gann might require more from her than tracking? Sex, perhaps? Though he couldn't imagine the cloaker being able to order her to give her body against her will. Sexual servitude was illegal and reviled by the *Vash Nadah* and merchant class alike, but rumors of it still abounded in the outermost reaches of the frontier.

"I was going to tease you," he said gently. "First you find the princess, then you get paid, then you get your ship back. It's *that* simple."

Her expression was as cold and as impenetrable as stone.

His hands folded over his chest, Gann looked out at the stars. "She could be anywhere by now," he said quietly, conjuring the young princess as she appeared in the holo-image, placing her in his mind's eye in the raw and dangerous worlds he remembered from his years in the frontier. "Her honor is at stake. It's my sworn duty to protect that honor."

"Her honor," the woman scoffed. "You mean her virginity, don't you?"

Her smirk threw him. It was clear she didn't share his courtly views of the princess. "It is my duty—and my wish—to defend her. She is a woman, and thus deserving of the highest respect."

"A treasure to be valued and protected," she finished for him.

"Yes, like you. Like all women. Beautiful and precious."

She glanced up sharply. "Please. Save your bad poetry for where it'll do you some good." She walked to the gangway leading from the cockpit.

He didn't understand how he'd insulted her with what he considered to be the greatest compliment: his awareness and appreciation of her femininity. "I adhere to the warrior's code. I trust you'll grow accustomed to my views by the end of the voyage," he called after her.

"I doubt that," she replied, turning. "As for finding your precious princess—believe me, *Vash*, nothing will please me more. In fact, I will now use my break to determine the best way to speed the process along."

Determination gleaming in her eyes, she pulled herself up the gangway and disappeared into the corridor leading to her quarters.

During the journey to Barésh, Tee'ah's confidence in her flying ability soared as her fear of being rounded up by her father's guards diminished. Driven, like a man possessed, Ian kept her—and the entire crew—to a grueling schedule, requiring her to be on duty almost constantly at the controls of the *Sun Devil*. Her hopes of getting to know the Earth dweller better succumbed to a string of long days and too-short nights—not to mention an almost complete lack of time alone with him.

Shortly before the scheduled arrival on Barésh, Tee'ah's alarm chime woke her from a deep dreamless sleep. Struggling out of bed she stumbled into the baggy flightsuit she'd borrowed from Push. She alternated between it, her new clothes from Grüma, and her brother's clothes. The handfuls of cold water she splashed onto her face would have to keep her functioning until she could get her hands on a good, dark, steaming cup of Earth coffee. Not only did the stuff taste like heaven, it did a far better job of waking her than the *tock* she was used to.

After a quick stop in the galley to pour herself a cup of Earth-brew from the pot Ian had already prepared, she hurried down the corridor. Only Ian, Muffin, and a grouchy-looking Quin awaited her in the dimly illuminated cockpit.

She sat in her piloting chair, snapped her coffee cup into its spill-proof holder, strapped in, and went to work. Her hands, now accustomed to the prelaunch routine, skimmed over the glowing, touch-activated control panel, her fingers flying as she entered arrival information into the computer.

Then she said, "I've sent our request for docking to Barésh control." She fought back a yawn. "I don't know what time of day it is where we're landing, but I hope someone's awake enough to clear us."

"Doesn't matter." Ian snapped his safety harness into the receptacle between his knees. "We're docking no matter what."

A few tousled locks of dark brown hair flopped

over his forehead, and faint lines of weariness were etched on either side of his mouth. But counteracting his fatigue was tension.

Strange. As she understood it, they were chasing after a competitor of his named Randall. But sometimes Ian acted as if the fate of the entire galaxy depended on this mission. Perhaps there was more to it than he let on. She found it odd that no one in the crew had spoken about selling the goods in the cargo hold. They'd told her they were traders, but she was beginning to have her doubts.

Gredda marched into the cockpit, her thick gleaming blond braid draped over one bare shoulder. "I am ready," she announced, sounding entirely too chipper for the early hour. Push, the assistant cargo handler, stumbled in after her and took his seat. While they buckled in, Tee'ah finished loading the data the ship's navigation computer needed to guide the *Sun Devil* to the colonized asteroid's surface. Most of the time, she flew arrivals by hand, for the pleasure of it as well as skill-honing practice. Tonight, due to fatigue and the hundreds of smaller deadly asteroids in the area, she'd decided to let the automatic flyer do the job. A tired pilot's best friend, she'd heard Mistraal's cargo pilots call it.

A trail of green lights danced across the control panel before her. She sat up straight. "We're cleared to dock."

The front viewscreen showed nothing but a star-filled void; it was deceptively empty. However, three-dimensional, temperature enhanced images on her instruments warned of innumerable asteroids ahead.

A mining colony in the middle of an asteroid field . . . The ore that was gleaned from the rock here was obviously deemed more important than human life and safety.

The huge space-boulders tumbled past, a few, like the one they'd just passed had glinting lights: mining colonies attached to their surfaces like glittering ticks. Just as she reached for her cooling cup of coffee, Tee'ah felt an odd vibration from somewhere under her seat. The *Sun Devil* banked right and several items not secured properly skidded off a shelf and clattered to the floor. She grabbed hold of the control yoke, then a sharp jolt set off a klaxon, telling her what she already knew: the computer was no longer steering the ship through the asteroids. *She* was.

"Hang on," she shouted.

Her heart drummed a staccato beat, but her hands held the controls, and the ship, steady. Guided by the images on her instruments, she chose which way to turn to avoid the asteroids, though she didn't weave between them as precisely as the computer might have.

She thought of the day she'd docked the cargo freighter on Mistraal. Captain Riss had been there, ready to offer her instruction—or take over if need be. Tonight there was no one watching over her. Only her skill could get the ship safely past danger.

Her stomach squeezed tightly. *Concentrate.*

At last the flight path smoothed out, and she made the transition from asteroid dodging to final approach. Moments later, she docked in their assigned spot, an enclosed berth connected by a pressurized tube leading into an immense habitation dome. Barésh.

Slumping back in her seat, she blew a stream of air out of her mouth. "Well, then," she told Ian. "Docking complete."

Quin muttered a silent prayer of thanks and unbuckled from his seat. Then Gredda and Push thumped a few thankful, hearty pats on her back before they left to check for bounced-around goods in the cargo bay.

Ian's gray-green eyes glowed. "I could use a crowbar to pry my hands from these armrests. But that was some flying, Ace."

She smiled with pleasure at his compliment. "The appropriate starpilot response would be—it was nothing."

"No." His voice softened a fraction. "You're really something."

They regarded each other in the star-drenched shadows. Reflected in Ian's eyes was a capable and adventurous woman—*not* a too-often-reproached king's daughter who had laughed too hard, talked too much, and escaped into daydreams always more vivid than her life. No, in the Earth dweller's gaze she saw only her marvelous transformation.

Princess Tee'ah Dar had disappeared. Pilot Tee was here to stay.

While the pixie busied herself with after-landing checks, Ian sat up, elbows on his knees, and ran his fingers through his hair. They'd narrowly missed plowing head-on into that asteroid!

God, he must be crazy, hiring someone he knew so little about. Sure, he had confidence in his instincts, in his abilities to pick good people to work for him . . . but that gut wrenching ride through those asteroids had made him wonder for a brief moment if in Tee's case he trusted himself too much. He'd pictured his mother weeping at his funeral, and Rom B'kah standing by her side, secretly thankful that his stepson had died before he could assume the throne to the galaxy—since it was obvious the boy couldn't even staff his ship with a competent pilot.

But Tee had come through for him beautifully. Her quick and accurate recovery to what might have been a fatal malfunction had kept him and his crew alive. And for that Ian was grateful.

He pushed himself off his command chair and joined Quin, who was hunched over a viewscreen, studying maintenance readouts on what was quickly turning out to be their lemon of a starship. "What happened *this time?*" he asked the mechanic with a baleful look.

"I don't know."

Ian stared at him for a long moment. "That inspires confidence."

"I'm at my wits' end, too, Captain. Automatic flight guidance systems go out; that's not unheard of. It's why we always have someone posted at the controls. But we should have gotten a warning before the whole thing went belly up; there are alarms built in for just that purpose."

"And even in the case of a breakdown, shouldn't the backup system take over automatically?"

Quin spread his hands. "Yes. Which tells me there's a software problem. But I've done a diagnostic, and the computer says there are no malfunctions."

"Maybe the computer is wrong." Ian thought of the frustrating breakdowns they'd suffered over the past few weeks, and the muscles in his jaw tightened. How much bad luck could one crew have? "Work on it."

"Will do, Captain."

Ian grabbed his jacket, then called out to his crew, "Tee, Muffin, you're with me. As standard, we'll check in every hour."

Tee turned around in her chair. "I'm going?"

Ian wasn't sure what had prompted him to take her, so he answered nonchalantly. "I believe that's what I said."

Her wide gold eyes sparkled with excitement. She appeared as surprised as he was, asking her to come along. He supposed the decision wasn't all that strange; his reasons for having her join them fell somewhere between enjoying her company and not wanting her too long out of his sight. He didn't know her all that well, he reminded himself. "I always take an extra crewmember, and everyone else is busy," he said, then shrugged on his jacket. "Bring your pistol."

A brownish mist discolored the rarefied atmosphere of the asteroid colony's immense habitation dome. "Something we don't want to think too hard about breathing," Muffin muttered as they made the rounds of the ships in residence, all huge cargo vessels but for one late-model starspeeder similar to the one Tee had lost.

"Randall's ship's not here," Ian said. He'd expected as much. The senator had beat him here by two days, and he'd said that his side trips would be short. But Randall's absence didn't irk him as much as he'd thought. As long as the man was traipsing around the frontier, he couldn't cheer on his anti-Federation pals on Earth. "It looks like we'll have to chase him right back to Grüma," he said with an apologetic glance in Tee's direction. "But let's take a look around the city first."

But "city" didn't come close to describing what met them beyond the docks. Cesspool would have been a far better description. The thin air smelled of overworked heavy equipment, burning tobacco—or similar—and something putrid, like sewage. With a sinking feeling, Ian saw why Randall had come here. This place would be an embarrassment to the *Vash*.

The buildings were different in appearance from anything he'd seen on Earth, let alone any of the *Vash* worlds he'd visited. They reminded him of squat, upside-down ice cream cones constructed of a material that resembled amber—though logically couldn't be—and wrapped in ribbons of pale silver trillidium with glittering, pointy-tipped roofs. The architecture made it obvious that someone once cared about this colony. Now all it did was give the squalid city a strange and ludicrous facade as false as expensive lace on some junkie prostitute.

Passersby reeked of body odor, indicating hygiene wasn't high on their list of priorities. Hard lives had etched premature lines in their faces. Many wore primitive mining gear and showed evidence of disease and injury. Others had missing limbs and ill-stitched scars.

Tee broke the party's shocked silence. "I thought we—I thought the *Vash* eradicated poverty and sickness after the Dark Years."

"The *Vash* think they did, too."

"Ignorance is no excuse. Why hasn't anyone done anything about this?"

Her passion on the subject startled Ian. He found

himself again wondering where she came from, what her background was beyond the little history she'd already revealed to him. "I take it you haven't seen conditions like this anywhere else in your travels?" he asked.

"Never," she answered to his relief. "The Trade Federation is an enlightened society. Everyone is educated; no one goes hungry." She cleared her throat. "Or so I always thought."

"Me, too." He wedged his fingers in the pockets of his jeans, wondering how much he could tell her and not compromise his mission. "The crown prince is from Earth. I have the strong feeling he's going to force the central galaxy to acknowledge what lies beyond its borders." And I had better do it soon, Ian thought, before Earth and the rest of the frontier grow too disgusted with the *Vash* federation's apparent double standard. They'd pull out en masse.

Perspiration glittered on Tee's forehead. He wondered if he appeared as discouraged as she did as she watched docile groups of miners board the lifts that descended into the bowels of the asteroid.

"I would think there'd be signs of rebellion," she almost whispered. "But there are none."

She was right. Not even a mild protest such as graffiti was evident anywhere. "I suspect they're too busy trying to survive to spare energy for a revolt." The miners' plight reminded him of what had existed in North Korea for the better part of a century before its people finally booted their dictator and demanded reunification with South Korea.

They walked, passing a pair of eating establishments half-hidden behind a trash receptacle. A klaxon sounded and a surge of miners emptied out of the lifts.

"Shift change," Muffin surmised.

The off-duty miners jostled them as they swarmed past. Muffin towered above the crowd, but Ian didn't depend on the man's size; he checked continuously to ensure that Tee was still close by. The miners all around stank even worse than the others who had passed him, and Ian gagged, his eyes watering from the stench. The flood of people was tough to struggle against, but he managed to keep his place.

The workers crisscrossed in front of him, pushing toward an area housing what looked like several video arcades overflowing with patrons eager to spend their few credits on an escape from real life in banks of virtual reality booths. For a price, buyers could spend time in smart-suits that stimulated their nervous systems into "feeling" what they chose to watch on special screens, from tropical vacations and ancient battles to simulated sex. Baréshtis appeared to be as crazy about the technology as Earth people were. Of all the wonders his home planet had inherited from the *Vash*, V.R. had made the most impact on popular culture. And if the inhabitants of this asteroid hellhole considered computer games the only escape from their hopeless existence, he wondered what that said about Earth.

Ian had seen enough. "Let's get out of here," he said, turning to find Tee and Muffin. His heart froze. Tee was no longer behind him. "Tee. Where's Tee?" he called to his bodyguard.

The color drained from Muffin's face as he craned his neck, scanning the light brown heads of the miners milling all around. Nowhere was there a green-haired sprite wearing an ASU baseball cap.

Ian grabbed his personal comm, the stench of the miners' tightly packed bodies all around him made it an effort to breathe. "Tee, Ian here," he called. "Where are you?"

There came no answer. He tried again. Nothing.

"Let's backtrack," Muffin said, shoving close to him.

"Agreed." They pushed against the tide of incoming miners, calling for their pilot, but only a sea of misery-hardened eyes answered them.

Chapter Ten

It took Tee'ah a few disbelieving seconds to realize she'd become separated from Ian and Muffin, swept away by the tide of miners. Instinctively she caught herself before calling out for them. Better to not broadcast the fact that she was now lost and alone. She reached for her comm, but it wasn't in her pocket. Fortunately, her laser pistol was.

Within the length of several arcades, she gave up searching for her comrades. Too many people blocked her line of sight. She pushed her eyeshaders farther up the bridge of her nose. What would Ian and Muffin do? Turn back; she was certain of it. She spun on her heel and headed toward the docks. Infusing her stride with feigned confidence, she aimed to deter any possible predators, as she had on Donavan's Blunder. But the Baréshtis mostly ignored her, too overburdened to allocate energy for curiosity.

Since she'd fled from the palace, her own concerns had dominated her thoughts. Now they seemed incredibly trivial. It wasn't the barrenness of the mining outpost, the indigence, the disease or proliferation of what she suspected was hallucinogenic drug-use that disturbed her most: it was the lack of hope she sensed in the hearts of these people. She'd experienced hopelessness on a far smaller scale. But she'd escaped it. These people hadn't that luxury.

To her left, she noticed a tall figure keeping pace with her. Kept at a distance by a mass of bodies, a man in a pale gray hooded cloak flickered in and out of view like moonlight between trees.

Her chest tightened. His luxurious cloak was a different color than that of the *Vash* gentleman she'd glimpsed on Grüma, but her senses prickled. He had the same look about him.

She ducked into an elevated doorway of a bustling arcade from where she could watch the street. A thin, very young woman regarded her from inside. Her blouse was see-through enough for Tee'ah to notice her breasts and nipples were plumped with ornate body art—tattoos and metallic implants. Tee'ah suspected that the scarcity of pleasure servants entitled her to charge high fees for sexual services, allowing her such vanities in addition to buying food.

Her study of the young pleasure servant was cut short as Tee'ah looked back over her shoulder. The hooded man was heading toward the doorway into which she'd ducked. Balling her left hand in a fist, Tee'ah made an abrupt about-face and pushed into the arcade. Her pursuer was right on her heels. She tried to run, but the crowd pressed in all around her.

"Tee'ah, stop," a voice called. "I want to talk to you." The voice was deep and sweetened by the educated burr of a full-blooded *Vash*. One that knew her name.

She made a sound of dismay and dove forward. She'd barely gotten a taste of freedom, and she wasn't about to give it up so soon.

"Tee'ah. Stop." Her pursuer grabbed her upper arm, spinning her toward him so fast that her eyeshaders clattered to the floor. Almost instantly, they were crushed by the boots of one of the arcade's customers.

"Let go!" Her plea was drowned by the thunder of voices.

The man tugged off his hood, revealing *Vash*-gold eyes and hair the color of Mistraal sunshine. "Tsk, tsk," he said, smiling. "The entire family is talking about you."

"Dear heaven," she gasped. Her ex-betrothed's younger brother's face was painfully familiar after all the holo-recordings their families had exchanged.

Her thoughts spun wildly. Klark Vedla's ambition and brash behavior were often frowned upon at her father's palace, although many of the same critics admired him for being an impassioned supporter of his older brother, Ché—the prince she was supposed to have married. But never would Tee'ah have guessed that Klark was devoted enough—or smart enough—to find her in a trash-littered virtual reality arcade on a poverty-stricken asteroid at the farthest edge of settled space.

"How did you know I was here?" she demanded.

"I've been following you since Donavan's Blunder."

Klark was on Blunder? Tee'ah scoured her memory for anything she might have seen or heard that would substantiate that claim. Then she remembered the hooded man in the market on Grüma. He'd been following her, indeed.

He must have guessed that she'd made the connection. "So, you did see me that day," he said smugly.

She took a step backward. "What a surprise that we bumped into each other. Small galaxy, yes? My apologies for running off, but I'm needed at my ship—"

The man's hand shot out, and his fingers clamped around her upper arm. Her heart lurched and her mouth went dry. Her free hand inched toward her pistol. "Forget it, Klark. I'm not coming with you. I'm not going home."

"Relax," he said. "I'm not here to apprehend you. I'm not supposed to be here myself. So let's keep this little meeting from the family—agreed?"

Tee'ah stared at him. "Ché didn't send you?"

"None of this is about you, princess—as hard as that is to believe."

She bristled. His implication that she was self-centered hit a nerve. She'd struggled with that doubt since leaving home. "Then what are you doing here?"

He took her by the arm and pushed her toward the bar. "We're two vagabonds far from home. Let us share our experiences over a drink."

"I don't want a drink." She didn't have time for one, either. Ian would be frantic by now. Or furious.

Klark waved away her protest as if she were a bug with no opinions or desires of her own, and he pulled a floating tray between them. Amazed by the absurdity of the situation, she watched him take a flask and two thimble-sized glasses from his cloak, filling them with a pink-tinged liquid. "Join me in sampling a liqueur created from one of the rarest fruits in the galaxy. It is from a planet with the briefest of summers. When the snow melts, the starberry bushes bloom."

Tee'ah almost growled. She teetered at the precipice of losing her dreams, and Klark acted as if she were paying a social call.

He held the glasses to the light. "The flowers are extremely fragile and fall with the first flurries of autumn. The ripe berries must be picked immediately, else within days they'll be buried under hundreds of standard feet of snow. This makes star-berry liqueur the most precious of drinks. It is—"

"I know what it is!"

"Then you know it must be shared in the traditional way." Klark dipped a finger into his glass and rubbed his glistening fingertip along her bottom lip before she was able to block his arm. Reflexively, she licked at it, tasting the tart sweetness left behind. Star-berry liqueur was a rare and special treat to be shared by lovers. Or potential lovers. By anointing Tee'ah's lips with the precious liquid, knowing that they had no past except for her intended engagement to his brother, he'd all but called her a whore.

"You, Klark Vedla, are unforgivably rude."

"And you"—he took in her fuzzy green-brown hair, her dusty boots, and everything in between— "are an aberration. You aren't good enough for my brother. No, Ché deserves better. He deserves more." His expression darkened, and his fingers squeezed her arm. "Far more than the subordinate role Romlijhian B'kah is inclined to give him."

Tee'ah plunged her hand into her pocket and pushed her laser pistol hard against the fabric. "Let me go, Vedla, or I'll put a crater between your eyes."

To her shock, he complied, immediately. Her legs trembled with adrenaline. She'd never dreamed she was capable of such audacity.

Klark's neck muscles corded, and he sucked in a deep breath. "My apologies. My temper will prove to be my undoing yet." He drew the wobbling tray between them. "Here. Finish your drink."

She fought the explosion of her own temper. "It's said that blessings sometimes come of unpleasant circumstances. Now I see why." She gritted her teeth. "We were never officially promised, Ché and I. And I'm truly sorry if my leaving insulted him. But at least now I'll never have to endure having you as a brother-in-law."

She left him standing by the floating tray. Suddenly lightheaded, she ducked through the crowd, but the Baréshtis jostled her, slowing her progress. A floating sensation enveloped her body in a vague pleasantness at odds with her near panic. Star-berry liqueur was notoriously potent, but this was ridiculous.

She pushed onward.

Her knees nearly buckled at the sound of Ian's voice coming from near the front exit. The young pleasure servant Tee'ah had seen earlier was talking to him, and he was gesturing wildly. Struggling forward, Tee'ah cried, "Ian!" above the clamor of music and voices. The woman accepted some credits from Ian, then pointed him in the right direction before she melted into the crowd.

By the time Tee'ah stumbled into the Earth dweller's arms, her head was spinning. She wrapped her arms around his waist and buried her face against his chest, breathing in his scent. At first she clutched him out of fear, then for comfort, and finally for pleasure.

He seemed to sense the change and caught her by the shoulders, moving her back. "Thank God." He appeared as sharply relieved as she felt. "Muffin, I've got her!" he called.

The big security chief joined them within seconds. Steadying herself, Tee'ah tried to work saliva into her mouth, but her tongue felt numb, like it had after that first glass of Mandarian whiskey. "Lesh—let's get out of here."

Disbelief and then reluctant acceptance clouded Ian's eyes. "Ah, Tee." His voice thickened with pity. "You can't keep out of the bars, can you?"

Something warm unfurled within her at his genuine concern. "I wasn't drinking." She hiccuped and pressed her hand over her mouth. "Not intentionally."

Muffin snorted.

"Denial, we call that on Earth," Ian muttered.

She tried to look over her shoulder, and it knocked her off-balance. Ian wrapped his arm around her waist. She leaned on him far more than was necessary, but he didn't seem to mind. "I know what you're thinking, but it's not what . . . what it seems. Someone bought me a drink I didn't want."

"Yeah. And they made you drink it, too."

She wanted to howl. Salvaging her reputation meant explaining what had really happened. But if she did, she risked having to say who Klark Vedla was and how she knew him. She didn't want Ian and the crew to view her as irresponsible; nor did she want her two lives to collide. Her ensuing indecision was almost physically painful.

They burst out of the arcade onto the street. When she saw that Klark was not waiting there, her chest ached with relief so sharp it hurt. She took his disappearance as a sign that she should keep the incident to herself. The prince was part of a life she wasn't ready to reveal, and now it looked as if she wouldn't yet have to. Perhaps all Klark had wanted to do was get her drunk, humiliating her in front of her employer and thereby avenge her jilting of his brother. That made sense, did it not? She tried to concentrate, but her speculation blurred in a liquor-induced haze.

"We'll get right to work getting you sobered up," Ian said, all business again. "Muffin, you get the *tock* ready, and Tee, you shower up and get something to eat. We're launching for Grüma as soon as you're able."

She gave a silent groan. Wonderful, she thought dazedly. Here we go again.

They completed the return journey to Grüma with no ship malfunctions. Ian liked Tee's reasoning that the computer was behaving itself only because it feared the consequences of further mischief. Her joking explanation was as good as any Quin had come up with so far and was one he suspected had paralleled her own outlook since she'd gotten tipsy on Barésh. Aside from remaining acutely apologetic about losing his extra pair of sunglasses, she avoided all mention of the incident. Yet here he was, bringing her to a bar on her first night back on Grüma. He needed his head examined.

"Randall's here," Muffin said as they emerged from the woods.

Anticipation buoyed Ian. Tonight he'd finally meet the man he'd chased halfway across the frontier. The local merchants had told him that Randall liked to eat dinner out and socialize in the town's pubs afterward. Ian would be waiting for him when he did.

"What is the Earth word for that . . . ground car?" Tee peered in fascination at the jeep Randall and his men had left parked outside a restaurant.

Ian smiled. Like the curious crowd milling around the Army-issue vehicle, sniffing at the quaint scents of fossil fuel and rubber tires, she'd probably never seen a plain old everyday automobile. "It's a jeep."

"Ah." She repeated the word as if savoring the sound. He'd long since learned that the pixie worshipped anything to do with his home planet.

The last of Grüma's three moons settled below the horizon, plunging the downtown strip of eateries and bars into shadow. The planet's major city was a lonely swath of civilization cut into a continent-sized forest, a fact made more apparent as the darkness deepened. Jumbo-sized insects with veined wings and tiny bat-like creatures crisscrossed a sky glowing with trillions of stars, but stranger still were some of the revelers in the rowdy pubs.

With Push on watch back at the *Sun Devil*, Ian led the remainder of his crew across the street. "We'll wait for Randall next door," he told them. As badly as he wanted to know how the U.S. senator had learned about Barésh, Ian was determined to take things slowly. He wanted to get a feel for the man and gain his trust before he revealed his identity. Diplomacy would keep the galaxy at peace. In this modern age of interstellar politics, threats and aggression were as barbaric as Roman Empire gladiator matches. He hoped the senator understood that.

A waitress clad in an ivory pantsuit and matching knee-length hair met them at the door of the pub. "A table by the window," Ian said, slipping a fair amount of credits into her palm. "That one," he said, pointing to the window closest to the adjacent restaurant, from where laughter and the scent of roasting meat drifted in the night air.

The waitress shooed away a table of drunks so Ian and the crew could sit. He thought they'd protest the incident, but money was plentiful on Grüma and bars abounded, so the revelers merely grumbled good-naturedly and stumbled out through the doors leading into the chilly night air.

Tee appeared utterly unaware of the attentive

gazes she received from men at nearby tables, interest that waned the instant she swiped his ball cap off her head and combed her fingers through her freshly touched-up clumps of mud-green hair. Ian watched with misgiving as the whiskey-loving pixie settled her shapely and very distracting rear end on the stool next to him. Fortunately, Quin took the seat to her right. Ian forced himself to relax. She was surrounded. If she wanted to drink herself into oblivion, she was going to find it damned hard with her hands held behind her back.

His fingers flexed involuntarily as an image exploded in his mind . . . of Tee warm and eager in his arms, her mouth opening under his as he kissed her, holding her clasped hands at the small of her back.

A bolt of heat in his groin yanked him out of the vivid fantasy and back to reality in the smoky bar.

". . . And at least the bartender seems semi-coherent, does he not? *Hello*," Tee called to him after he didn't answer. "Ian?"

He became aware of his surroundings as if surfacing from a deep dive. Tee gave him a decidedly flirtatious grin. With her smelly hair, she reminded him of the cartoon character Pèpé Le Pew, the debonair little French skunk whose amorous intent was handicapped by his total unawareness of the effect his odor had on those around him.

"You were light years away, Ian." She smiled and tapped two perfectly formed fingertips on his knee.

His body reacted as powerfully as if she'd placed her hand directly over his . . .

He groaned. "I need a drink." *You don't drink.* "I do now," he argued.

Quin stared at him. "Captain?"

Tee laughed. "He's pretending to be that bartender on Donavan's Blunder."

Only he hadn't been pretending.

"Now that's a depressing thought," he said aloud to Tee's obvious delight.

"That's exactly what he was like!"

He frowned at his folded hands as she relayed the rest of the story to Gredda, Muffin, and Quin. "You should have seen it—the bartender would have conversations with himself. Sometimes in several different voices."

Gredda shrugged. "One would never get lonely that way."

It wasn't a crime to think about Tee, he supposed, as long as he took it no further. And he wouldn't. If a wife hadn't already been chosen for him in his absence, one would be soon. *Vash Nadah* marriages were alliances, not love matches—at first, anyway. The right spouse was essential for acceptance into his adopted culture.

"Here you are." The waitress set bowls of shimmer crackers and croppers on the counter in front of them. The crew each scooped up handfuls of croppers, the crispy little question marks that took the place of peanuts in bars across the galaxy. They were spiced with something savory instead of salted, but were as addictive as potato chips. The shimmer crackers, on the other hand, were bland. Ian couldn't understand why everyone liked them; they were nothing more than flashy junk food.

Tee dusted crumbs from her hands. "I need something to wash down these croppers. A glass of mogmelon wine will do."

"Tee," Quin and Ian chorused in warning.

She spread her hands. "What?"

Quin rolled his eyes. "Do the words Mandarian whiskey ring a bell?"

A faint blush stained her cheeks. "I'm not going to get drunk, for heaven's sake. I'm on duty." She glanced knowingly at where Randall's group had been seated in the restaurant next door. "Am I not?"

No one argued with her, especially not Ian. His attention was drawn to the senator. Then a question dawned on him: How had she known who they were watching? Or had the look simply been a coincidence? Maybe one of the others had shown her a picture of Randall. He was being too paranoid.

The waitress took their orders. Ian kept silent as Tee requested her glass of wine. He wanted to be able to trust her—with alcohol and everything else. The longer she worked on his ship, the more involved she became in his mission. Unwittingly, for now. But she deserved to know the truth eventually.

Muffin chuckled. "Why not have the entire bottle, Tee? I'm sure the captain will carry you off to bed like he did on Blunder."

Ian frowned at the bodyguard. "Figuratively speaking."

"No kidding," Tee said, imitating Ian's accent. "Had I ended up in your bed, Earth dweller, I would have remembered it."

The crew burst into delighted laughter. Even Quin slammed his hands on the table, spilling croppers onto its faded holographic surface. Tee realized belatedly what she'd said and looked as if she wanted to crawl under the table. Ian leaned toward her, his mouth close to her ear. The few locks of greenish hair that brushed over his lips were surprisingly silky. "I would have remembered it, too."

Her eyes widened. Immediately, she clutched her hands together, squeezing her fingers tightly atop the table. Warning bells sounded in his head. He was playing a dangerous game: she was on the run and he had . . . obligations. He had no business flirting with her. But a small, selfish part of him was glad to see she was unsettled by his remark.

"Well," she murmured. "I am glad to hear that." The glow-globe on the table illuminated the pulse under her jaw, spreading fingers of light across the fabric of her flightsuit, beneath which her breasts rose and fell with slow, even breaths. Those breaths would quicken as he moved inside her, her tender kisses turning passionate, her arms tightening around him as he brought her to an intense, drawn-out climax. . . .

God almighty. What was he doing—torturing himself?

Fully and painfully aroused by the erotic image he'd conjured, Ian jerked his attention back to the holographic tabletop. It seemed the pixie was as hazardous to him sober as she was drunk.

The waitress returned with their drinks. Then, thankfully, someone started a around of the All-Folk Chain; a galactic version of karaoke, where individual verses were made up and then sung by volunteers from the audience who came up to the stage and usually made fools of themselves.

"Now, the next port after this we'll make
is known as Donavan's Blunder.
But blunder there we'll only do
if we drink our livers asunder."

Ian had heard far worse. He chuckled and wrapped his hands around his mug of rapidly cooling *tock*, his attention on Randall's party in the restaurant next door. They'd ordered ale, a dark strong ale, instead of juice or *tock*, he noted happily. Alcohol would loosen the Earth group's tongues nicely.

He kept his attention on his quarry next door, trying not to discern Tee's voice from the rest of his crew's, trying not to listen for the sound of her laughter, or smile at her surprisingly dry, self-deprecating humor. But her scent filled his nostrils, yet another chink in his armor, the discipline that had been his strength for all his life.

Anyone who smelled like peroxide would be distracting . . . right?

"Your turn, Captain!" he heard the pixie call out.

Ian slid around in his seat. Push was smiling; Gredda, too. But Tee was standing, one arm extended, her hand palm up and her eyes aglow with what could only be trouble.

Ian said warily, "I almost hate to ask—my turn for what?"

Tee wriggled her fingers. "The All-Folk Chain, what else?" She snatched his hand, and the feel of her warm skin sent a wave of heat up his arm. He planted his boots on the floor to keep his balance on the stool, but deftly she used his legs for leverage and tugged him to his feet.

Applause erupted. That was when Ian noticed every person in the unruly crowd had turned to face him, laughing and clapping. The singer onstage was pointing to him with a handheld voice amplifier. "Here, Earth dweller!" he called out from the platform.

"Earth dweller, Earth dweller," the audience began to chant.

"Go," Tee cajoled, her eyes twinkling. "They like you."

Ian looked to the rest of his crew for help. Only

Quin appeared worried. The others were evidently delighted by the prospect of him making a total fool of himself. He aimed a help-me-out glare in Muffin's direction.

The huge man was dismayingly weak in his defense. "The captain can't sing, you know," was all he said.

"We shall cheer for him anyway," Tee rebutted.

"And whistle, even," Gredda added.

Ian almost laughed at the Valkarian warrior woman's earnest face. "You, whistle, Gredda? Tempting, but forget it. We're here to size up our competition, not to provide the evening's entertainment." He tried to sit down but Tee held fast to his hand.

"Earth dweller, Earth dweller . . ."

Ian gave the cheering crowd a Queen-Elizabeth wave. "In your dreams," he said in English.

Tee shook her head. "You are a trader, yes? Then you must think of this as an opportunity, not an ordeal. 'Trade is a matter of trust,' " she recited. " 'With trust comes reciprocation, and with reciprocation, profit.' "

He gaped at her. She'd quoted directly from the Treatise of Trade, the holiest document of the *Vash Nadah*. Ian recognized the passage only because he'd spent so much of the past seven years memorizing the ponderous and ancient teachings. The *Vash Nadah* peppered their conversations with such quotes, finding phrases to fit every situation. But a

167

merchant-class woman using excerpts in everyday conversation? He wouldn't have expected it.

"You came here to trade, yes?" she went on. "If you sing, they will like you. If the other traders like you, they will buy from you, no matter where you're from."

"Earth dweller, Earth dweller," the chants continued.

"And if they buy your goods," she added with a partner-in-crime wink, "then perhaps you'll raise my salary."

He chuckled as he caught Senator Randall glancing over from the restaurant next door. "I just might do that." Her ploy was ingenious in ways she couldn't imagine. Participating in this silly bar game would guarantee anonymity for his initial meeting with the man. Who'd ever expect to find the disputed heir to the galaxy in the frontier, singing the Chain in a bar filled with drunken black-marketeers?

He gave a longsuffering sigh. "All right, Miss Tee. A captain's got to do what a captain's got to do, but"—he brought his mouth to her ear—"don't think you won't pay for this later."

Leaving her thoroughly flustered, he walked to the stage and snatched the microphone from the man who'd preceded him. With the slim high-tech rod anchored in his hand, he stared out at the audience—shadowy, unfamiliar faces all, but for his crew standing in the left rear of the bar. *All you do is continue more or less from where the last participant left off,"* he recalled Gredda once telling him.

"Okay," he said into the mike.

At that single English word, the crowd went wild, stomping and cheering, and he tried to forget that he couldn't sing. Encouraged by their enthusiasm and by the fact that they were drunk and he was sober, Ian recalled the lyrics of a verse he'd heard earlier and altered them to suit the idea that popped into his head. Using the tapping of his boot on the wooden floor for rhythm, he belted out a song that came out sounding more far more like old Earth rap than folksy:

> *"Donavan's Blunder is the place to come*
> *if to trade you're more than willing.*
> *But keep your pilots away from whiskey*
> *or their minds you will be killing."*

Tee tried to appear affronted, but her eyes sparkled as he floundered through another verse. Then, unexpectedly, three men walked into the pub: Randall and his cronies.

Ian swore. Instead of being able to coolly observe the men from the shadows until he was ready to introduce himself, he was standing front-and-center on a stage in the middle of the bar.

Beautiful.

Hawk-faced, silver-haired, tall and blue-eyed, U.S. Senator Charlie Randall drew the attention of every patron in the bar. The conversation ebbed as everyone gave him a curious glance. But no one on Grüma remained surprised for long, and the noise resumed immediately.

"You must think of this as an opportunity, not an ordeal." Tee's words echoed inside him. Yeah. He ought to turn the tables on Randall, get him onstage while he returned to his seat. Then he'd be able to see how the senator acted under pressure. Rom B'kah often said that there was nothing like a little stress to bring out an individual's true colors.

An oddly appropriate song sprang into Ian's mind. This time he sang in English:

> *"Yankee Doodle went to Grüma,*
> *A-riding on a pony.*
> *Tucked some coffee in his jeans*
> *and called it macaroni."*

Randall swung his silver-haired head in Ian's direction. Narrowing his eyes, he regarded Ian with a stare that would have intimidated anyone not already used to similar looks from powerful men. He'd gotten more than a few from the more intrigue-prone and distrustful *Vash Nadah* royals, so Ian didn't flinch.

> *"Yankee Doodle keep it up,*
> *Yankee Doodle dandy.*
> *You're the new Earth dweller on the block*
> *And feet-first in my territory."*

Okay, so the rhyme sucked eggs, but his goal was to put Randall on the spot, not win a talent contest. Ian grinned and aimed the mike at Randall. The crowd roared and again began to chant, "Earth dweller, Earth dweller."

The senator glanced around helplessly. His followers visibly recoiled. Then a merchant at a nearby table tugged impatiently on Randall's sleeve, gesturing to the stage. Another gave him a nudge.

Shoulders sagging with the inevitability of it all, the senator marched to the front of the bar. His blue eyes were more penetrating in person than they were on television. "You're American," he said, snatching the mike from Ian's hand.

"Yep."

"You're also a pain in the ass. You owe me a drink after this, young man."

Ian shrugged then returned to his table where his cheering crew waited.

"You can't sing," Tee said.

"I never said I could."

"Ah, but you were wonderful!"

With her face flushed with happiness, her beauty radiating from deep within, she came across as utterly sweet and unspoiled . . . and more out of place in the frontier than ever. He fought the impulsive urge to wrap his arm around her waist and draw her close, not only to shield her from the undisciplined mob, but to feel her warm and soft against him. Luckily, Randall's singing brought him back from

171

the edge of doing something entirely inappropriate.

The senator had a reasonable grasp of Basic, and the crowd guffawed good-naturedly at his mangled version of a common jingle. When he relinquished the stage to the next participant, with his two companions in tow, he strode to where Ian stood. "Where's my drink, kid?"

Ian tossed Quin some credits and dispatched the man for a around of ale. A few extra chairs were pulled up and the entire group sat together.

Ian stuck out his hand. "Stone," was all he said. His hair was longer than he usually wore it and he purposefully sported a few days' worth of stubble. He doubted the senator would recognize him.

"Senator Charlie Randall," the man said as they shook hands.

"A U.S. senator in this godforsaken place? What brings you here?"

"Fact-finding," he replied in English to Ian's Basic. He leaned over the table and lowered his voice. "I've seen things that would curl your hair."

Barésh. "Yeah? Like what?"

Smugly, the man spread his suntanned hands on the table. In an open-necked powder-blue polo shirt, the prominent American senator looked more likely to play a few rounds of golf than turn the balance of the galaxy on its ear. "All isn't as it seems in the *Vash* Empire," he said cryptically. Then he smiled, drawing out the moment, enjoying Ian's patent interest. "That is what I was told, now I've seen it for myself. Let's just say I intend to bring home with me a little enlightenment regarding that fact."

Like hell you will. Ian was certain Rom B'kah knew nothing of Barésh. He'd never stand for such conditions. On the other hand, if places like Barésh existed without Rom's knowledge, it in essence proved Randall's point that the Federation didn't care about the frontier. Until Ian could show that the *Vash* were committed to changing what was wrong, he had to keep Randall from taking the news home. Just how he was going to do that he had yet to figure out. But he would. Without Rom's help. This was his chance to show that he could take a delicate and potentially disastrous situation and turn it around.

"Sounds intriguing," Ian said casually. "Tell me more."

"Over our drinks." Randall waved a hand at his companions. "This here's Mike Gruber, assistant secretary of commerce. And Bud Lucarelli and Tom Dowdy, secret service."

Ian introduced Gredda, Muffin, and Tee, pointedly switching the language from English to Basic, allowing his crew to participate in the conversation. There was another around of handshaking when Quin returned to the table with a small cask of ale and mugs. Then the two groups made smalltalk.

Ian ignored the glass of ale Quin placed in front of him. Tee, he noticed, did the same. In fact, her original flute of mog-melon wine was still two-thirds full. Maybe the pixie was learning, after all.

Susan Grant

"How long have you been out here, Stone?" Randall asked.

"Awhile. I sell Earth products. Business is good."

"Excellent. I'd like to see more young people seeking their fortunes in the frontier. We're the home team out here, you know. Earth." He wrinkled his nose at Tee. "What's that you're drinking, young lady? It smells like hard-boiled eggs."

The senator's thick accent made his words tough to understand, but everyone in Ian's party knew to what he'd referred. Quin choked back a laugh, while Muffin tried hard not to smile. Tee shot them a warning glare, then curved both hands around her glass of wine. "It's only mog-melon wine. Perhaps the odor is coming from that group over there," she suggested.

The senator and his cohorts glanced at the particularly grubby collection of traders sitting behind them, and Ian was pleased to see them nod. Good. He didn't want any of his crew arousing suspicions.

But Randall wasn't done scrutinizing Tee. He refocused on her, his blue eyes intense and searching. She shrank back before appearing to catch herself. "Are you a *Vash Nadah?*" he asked warily.

"Her, *Vash?*" Ian chuckled. "She's a space drifter, through and through." He said it to protect Tee, though he was far from convinced it was the truth.

"Yes. That's me. Scum of the galaxy." To Ian's dismay, Tee lifted her flute to her lips and downed the contents in two deep swallows.

174

Quin chimed in. "You should have seen her the day we hired her. Had enough Mandarian whiskey in her blood to pickle a hydro-farm of Danjo shoe-beets."

Eyes watering, Tee clasped her hands tightly atop the table and nodded. "More likely two hydro-farms."

Randall laughed and relaxed in his chair. "That certainly doesn't sound like your typical *Vash*. I've never seen a more self-righteous, gloom-and-doom spouting people in all my life."

Tee's knuckles turned white.

Ian said tightly, "For someone who's spent a career fighting against the erosion of civil rights, don't you think that's a mighty big generalization?" Immediately he felt Tee's eyes on him, and he wanted to kick himself for jumping in to defend the *Vash* when he was supposed to be making friends with Randall.

The senator appeared unrepentant. "There are always exceptions. But overall I don't trust them. They want the frontier under their thumb. But there's a brighter future for Earth if we remain independent of that control. We have more than enough resources to survive. We don't need *Vash* rule." His face came alive with passion. "I envision a future where the frontier thrives independently of the *Vash* Federation."

"What about that war the galaxy almost didn't survive ten thousand years ago?"

"Eleven," Tee corrected absently.

"Right," Ian said, almost smiling. "Eleven." He'd wanted to hide his expert grasp of galactic history, and being corrected by a ragged-looking space drifter fed perfectly into his ploy. "Wasn't that brought about because all the worlds and systems broke into warring factions? A few got their hands on some bad-ass weaponry and"—Ian mimicked the sound of an explosion—"it was almost 'game over' for civilization. I don't particularly like the idea of heading down that road again, do you? Not after everything's been stable for so long."

He realized that Tee was watching him in shock. He gave her a quick smile to reassure her. What was wrong? Didn't she agree with him? Swallowing hard, she lowered her eyes to her tightly clenched hands.

"There must be a way we can stay part of the Federation for protection and still hang onto our identity as a planet." Ian was operating without a script now. Rom hadn't cleared him to negotiate; the king of the galaxy hadn't even cleared him to talk to Randall. But he wouldn't have chosen Ian as his successor if he didn't believe he could think creatively and independently.

"Romlijhian B'kah chose his stepson as the next king," he said to Randall. "Talk about having friends in high places . . . Don't you think it'd be better to be part of the Federation than opposed to it?"

"There's more to it than just influence—or the

lack thereof," the senator argued. "The *Vash* don't view the frontier—or us—as they do the central area of their empire. We're beneath their regard." The senator glanced at Tee, as if he were still unsure of her. Then he lowered his voice. "I have proof. I've seen the darker side, Stone—poverty, disease, and apathy. My associate took me to Sorak Seven, Lanat, Barésh."

Ian glanced up sharply. Muffin frowned. Randall had an associate? Whom was he working with?

"Those worlds are nothing more to the *Vash* than distant slave pits," Randall continued. "I saw primitive medical care, substandard housing, hungry and overworked populations. The galaxy isn't the Shangri-La they claim it is," he said. "Earth needs to know that."

Yeah, Ian thought grimly, so do the *Vash*.

"What's happened to those planets could happen to us," Randall concluded, "unless we assert ourselves."

Ian stiffened. He was within a hair's-breadth of telling Randall who he was, right here, right now, so they could roll up their sleeves and hash out possible solutions instead of chatting over glasses of ale. But instinct told him to proceed with caution.

"What kind of proof do you have?"

Randall called up a schedule on his wrist-gauntlet computer. "My ship's docked by the old fortress in the hills. I'll be reviewing the information I've gathered over the next several weeks. Stop by for a beer before I leave for Washington."

"Thanks. I'll do that." In the meantime, Ian was going to find out who Randall's associate was. That person was obviously behind the senator's discovery of the inexcusably ignored fringe worlds—and Ian needed to know his or her intent.

Randall lifted his mug and tipped another swig of ale into his mouth. "Rotten stuff," he said, slamming his mug down. "No wonder our beer's taking the galaxy by storm." He stood, grabbing his jacket, and gave Ian a friendly salute before heading with his men outside to his jeep.

Gredda glared after him. Quin blew a stream of air out his mouth, while Muffin gazed thoughtfully at his drink. Tee hiccuped softly.

"Excuse me," she said, patting her chest.

Ian eyed Tee's empty glass and groaned. He was dealing with a powerful U.S. senator who believed Earth was better off opposing a Federation that had maintained peace for eleven thousand years. As if that wasn't bad enough, the man was spreading the word while playing tourist on a trip arranged by a mysterious partner. Convincing Randall that he was better off working with the *Vash* rather than against them was going to be one hell of a job. Though at the moment, Ian thought wryly, his greatest challenge lay in escorting his pilot out of the bar and back to the ship before she was tempted to order another drink.

Chapter Eleven

Quin, Muffin, and Gredda expressed interest in staying longer, but Ian insisted that Tee'ah leave with him. The small flashlight he aimed at the mossy ground beneath their boots enclosed them in a soft glowing circle, but the thick, damp darkness of the forest pressed in all around them, as if attempting to snuff out their light.

Instinctively, Tee'ah moved closer. "I'm not drunk," she informed him.

"I know."

They continued to walk in awkward silence. "I always hiccup from drinking too fast," she insisted. "Milk, fruit juice, or alcohol."

The ends of his mouth quirked in an almost-smile. "I'll remember that."

Again, he became quiet. It was something else, then, that was bothering him. She gave him an uneasy glance. Tonight he'd demonstrated a disturbing level of knowledge and insight into her people. A shiver skittered down her spine.

If Ian Stone was Ian Hamilton, the *Vash* heir, as she'd first feared, then she had to find that out before he found out about her. "I know you told me not to ask questions, but when the entire crew knows what is going on except me, it gets a bit frustrating. Surely I've proven my loyalty. I feel I have a right to know more about the man we're following."

"You have, and you do," he replied. Then he lightly took her by the elbow and led her deeper into the forest. "This way," he said softly.

Was he the *Vash* heir? She found herself wondering. What other explanation could there be? There seemed to be too many coincidences for any other conclusion. And here was her opportunity to find out.

"What were you curious about?" he asked mildly.

She decided to be blunt. "How it is that you, an Earth dweller, are so concerned about the state of the *Vash* federation?"

Ian tensed, or was she imagining it?

She plunged ahead with her spontaneous interrogation. "You seem to have a good knowledge of galactic politics. That's unusual for a black-market trader, is it not?"

"Not anymore than a whiskey-swigging ex-cargo

pilot spouting off entire passages from the Treatise of Trade."

All right, so she'd stupidly revealed her own knowledge of galactic politics. It didn't mean she had to divulge anything else—her real name, her age, where she grew up, who her father was. She loved discussions about politics, and finding out more about Ian was important, but she mustn't let herself become so absorbed that she gave away too much. Hastily, she explained, "My father made sure I received a good religious education."

"Ah." Ian was silent for a few moments before he spoke again. "This hunger for independence on Earth's part bothers me because it's so sudden."

"Odd that your homeworld would just now balk at *Vash* rule almost seven years after signing the Treatise of Trade," she said.

"And even stranger coming after the selection of that Hamilton guy as the next crown prince," Ian added. He seemed eager to continue the discussion, which was strange if he had something to hide. Perhaps he didn't. Perhaps he wasn't Ian Hamilton, as she'd worried. Perhaps he was only a black market trader without anyone in his crew with whom he could discuss such ideas. That, Tee'ah could relate to. She'd often felt the same—alone in the company of her peers—with her brothers' wives, like a corked bottle.

"I cannot blame your Earth for feeling resentful," she said. "After an entire history celebrating your uniqueness in the universe, you now find yourselves relegated to a somewhat trivial role in an already established civilization, yes?"

"Yes." He cast her an admiring gaze. "I suspect that's the essence of what bothers men like Randall. We're still adjusting and getting used to the idea of being contacted by an extraterrestrial race—even though scientists claim we may all share common ancestry. But casting away all that's been established by the Federation . . . ?" He took a breath. "It's the wrong solution. And yet if the *Vash* want to keep the frontier loyal, they'll have to do something about Barésh—and soon."

Tee'ah shook her head. A black-marketeer with a sense of social responsibility was a concept almost as farfetched as the idea of the crown prince wandering about the frontier.

Still, if only more *Vash Nadah* shared Ian's views, then perhaps the frontier and the Federation wouldn't be teetering at the edge of divorce. Well, either way, she was no longer involved. She might enjoy discussing such problems, but she was no longer a noble who could do much about anything on such a grand scale. She was out for herself.

"When Randall returns to Earth, will we follow him?" she asked hopefully.

Ian ducked as a low flying night mammal whizzed past his head. "I'll follow him across the galaxy if I have to."

"That's a lot of worlds to visit."

His teeth glowed in the faint light. "And a lot of flying, too. You'd better keep working hard or I'll have you replaced."

"Replaced?" She huffed. But his playful smile was contagious. "Is that what you meant when you said I'd pay for making you do the All-folk Chain?"

"I don't think you want to know what I had in mind," he said. A delicious shiver coursed through her. She wondered if he'd meant to use such a suggestive tone. She found herself fervently hoping that he had.

Nervously, she moistened her lower lip. She wanted to place his arms around her, guide his lips to hers. She wanted to feel him inside her body, sharing intimacy as lovers did, something she'd never contemplated with any other man.

"But," he quipped, "your suggestion does have its merits. It'll be in your best interest to behave, as tough as that may be."

"No whiskey?"

"Definitely no whiskey."

She laughed, delighted by the repartee. One minute they were immersed in a deeply philosophical, political discussion, the next they were teasing each other about nothing of consequence. She'd never before met a man with whom she could enjoy both.

"Well." She was dying to know what he'd had in mind regarding her "payment" to him, but she suddenly felt too shy to ask. "You'd be a fool to let me go; you'll never find another like me."

His smile faded, and he slowed to a stop. Gossamer-winged creatures floated in the halo of light at his feet. Quietly, he said, "I'm beginning to think you're right."

They stood there, inches apart in the middle of the damp, hushed woods, their faces shadowed, their breaths puffs of mist. Then he lifted his hand to her cheek, four warm fingertips resting on the sensitive skin under her jaw. Her breath stopped, and her heart thundered so loud that she feared he'd hear it. As his dark, searching eyes held her enthralled, he slid his fingers into her hair.

Then she hiccuped. "Excuse me."

His smile reappeared. His palm stroked over her cheek, no longer the tentative first touch of a lover, but a casually affectionate pat. The fairy-like moths fled into the darkness along with her hopes for a kiss.

"It sure is a cold one tonight," he said lightly. "We'd best get you back to the ship before you catch a chill."

His caress had left her anything but cold. "Sure."

Minus the usual guiding hand on her elbow, he resumed his stride. Practically jogging to keep up with him, she cursed her ineptness. *Sweet heaven.* She had much to learn in this game of seduction. And one thing was certain. Whatever future steps needed to be taken, it was clear she was going to have to take them first.

Long after he saw Tee to bed and the others had returned from their night out, Ian sat sprawled in the pilot's chair, his legs propped on the navigation console, his fingers laced over his stomach. The ship was dark, and silent but for the hum of normal shipboard equipment. Yet sleep eluded him.

Still dressed in his jeans and flannel shirt, he stared out the viewscreen at the stars. Light years away were his mother and stepfather, to whom he was impatient to relay the news of his recent discoveries. But before he sent an encrypted message back to Sienna, he wanted to learn more about Randall, and now his associate. The senator had very legitimate and understandable concerns—Ian saw that after visiting Barésh—but if Randall and others on Earth didn't grasp the lesson of the galaxy's violent history, the need to stick together, then Ian had better find something else, something tangible, to keep Earth within the *Vash* fold.

But what?

He closed his eyes, his mind racing.

God, he'd almost kissed her.

He dropped his feet to the floor and sat up, his arms draped over his thighs. He'd known Tee for less than a month and she'd turned him to jelly. He knew nothing about her, other than what she wanted him to learn—a fabricated history, he was sure.

What was she hiding from him? And why?

I don't think you want to know what I had in mind. Had he actually said that to her? *Criminey.* He dropped his face into his hands. The temptation would pass as long as he didn't act on it.

She would have let you.

He groaned. Then he lifted his head. Starlight soaked the cockpit in an ice-blue glow, an illumination so faint that he almost didn't see the hesitant, wraithlike shadow moving off his left side. Then he inhaled the faint odor of rotten eggs.

He shot straight up in the chair. "How long have you been there?"

"Only a moment." Tee pressed her hand over her chest. "My apologies. I didn't know you were here."

"I couldn't sleep."

"Neither could I."

He rubbed his eyes. "I've been thinking about Randall's associate and how to find out who he—or she—is." That was a partial truth, at least.

"What did you decide?"

"Grüma isn't all that big. We'll look for him the old-fashioned way."

Pensive, Tee walked to the enormous curving viewscreen at the bow of the *Sun Devil*. She raised her arms above her head and arched her back. "Look at all the stars. Without city lights it's almost as if you can see them all." The sleeves of her nightshirt slipped down her slender arms. On the underside of her right arm something caught the light.

It was a birth-blocker patch! Ian clenched his jaw and looked away.

He'd assumed she was innocent. But of course she wasn't. When he'd found her she'd been living in the frontier. No one here remained innocent for long.

Her obvious and not-unexpected worldliness wasn't what bothered him; it was that she had been made love to by—and would make love to—other men. Men other than him. "Lucky bastards," he muttered in English.

She lowered her arms, smoothing her palms down her sleeves. "Sorry—what was that?"

"Have a seat. We can watch the stars."

"Or we can count them to make us sleepy." She smiled. "We need to get our rest while we can. I suspect that in the coming days there will be much to keep us awake."

Ian contemplated Tee's entirely too-kissable mouth. "Yeah," he said. That was exactly what he was afraid of.

On Padma Eight, Gann followed the leads Lara gave him, observing and often questioning throngs of permanent residents, starpilot students and instructors, as well as traders who arrived daily from the farthest reaches of the frontier. Lara's decision to come to Padma Eight was an excellent one; if the Dar princess was keeping company with an Earth dweller, there were plenty here, risk-loving entrepreneurs taking advantage of the business opportunities the unrestrained frontier offered.

His long hours seemed to suit Lara just fine. Though sociable by nature and upbringing, Gann was willing to leave Miss Sunshine to her eternal brooding. But not tonight. A nagging sense of loneliness combined with the fruitlessness of his mission had left him in need of cheering. His sulky starpilot was going to join him for dinner and conversation, even if it killed her.

He marched into the cockpit, where she was curled up in the pilot's chair, her fingers deftly weaving together a cluster of silver threadlike strands. Her incessant jewelry making. It seemed a frivolous pastime for such a cool, remote woman.

"Dinner's ready," he said.

She glanced up. As always, he saw something intense and unknown flash in her eyes before she blinked it away. It was as if, when surprised, she surfaced from a deep, dark place, a place that he had no desire to frequent if the pain she thought she was hiding was any indication of its nature.

"I already ate," she stated.

"That was lunch. This is dinner."

She returned her concentration to her silver-weaving. "Fraternization isn't covered in my contract."

He snorted.

She tried a different tack. "I'm not hungry."

"Then come; simply sit with me. I could use the company."

"That's what bars are for."

He straightened, spreading one hand over his heart. "I prefer your company any day over what I'd find in a bar."

She lowered her weaving and regarded him with unconvinced fawn-colored eyes. "Then you must frequent some pretty pitiful dives, Mr. Truelénne."

He laughed.

She frowned. "What?"

"You made a joke," he said with a surprising degree of triumph. "At your own expense, but a joke nonetheless. And I'll bet the rest of that bottled-up chat is ready to burst a seam. If for health reasons only, why not share a little of your word stockpile with a lonely spacehand?"

One corner of her mouth quirked, he thought, but he couldn't be certain. His humor always seemed to startle her. It was as if no one had ever dared to tease her.

Maybe no one else had.

To his pleasure, she put away her weaving. "I don't talk much," she admitted in a softer voice.

An insistent yowl interrupted him before he could reply.

"*Crat.* The ketta-cat." Lara jumped off the chair and scrambled down the gangway to the front hatch, where a thin, scarred ketta-cat waited.

It ran to her, gurgling, rubbing its side against her

189

calves. She shifted her weight from foot to foot, but didn't reach down to stroke the ketta-cat. It mewed loudly.

"I thought I told you to leave," she said, nudging it gently with her leg. "It's been following me all over town. Then today it trailed me here." She spread her hands. "Go. There's no home for you here."

"Let it be," Gann said. "I'll bring out our leftovers later."

"And then it will think it can stay. Good-bye," she told the ketta-cat. But the pitiful creature continued to rub itself around and in between her legs, its fur swishing against the plush sea green fabric of her pants.

Lara stood still, her arms limp at her sides. She appeared utterly baffled by the cat's unconditional love. Gann was equally mystified by her apparent inability to accept affection of any sort. For that his heart went out to her—not in pity, but in stark admiration. To be so emotionally crippled, she must have survived something horrific. But instead of living the rest of her life cowering in the shadows, a victim of circumstance, she'd learned to be a repo pilot and a tracker.

"Dinner's getting cold," he said.

"I'll warm it." She appeared to jump at the chance to avoid the ketta-cat. Without another word, she left Gann and the stray alone on the entry ramp.

The creature watched her go. Then it lifted its

mournful silver-green eyes to Gann and mewed.

"Dinner? Sure, why not?" he replied. "You're a lot more talkative than my partner there." He scooped up the ketta-cat with one hand. "Now, how about we go see if any of it rubs off on her?"

When Lara walked out of the galley holding a crock of stew in her hands, Gann was already waiting for her, his booted feet crossed at the ankle, his fingers laced over his stomach. The ketta-cat darted out from under the chair and began rubbing itself against her legs. She set the crock so firmly on the table that he expected the cookware to break. One of Lara's bracelets jarred loose, and he caught it before it rolled off the edge.

He noticed she said nothing about the ketta-cat. She sat and held out her hand. "I'll take the bracelet," she said.

He studied the delicate bauble before giving it back to her. "It's a lovely piece," he admitted. "You're very good."

Her expression vacillated between annoyance and pleasure as she ladled stew into her bowl and then Gann's, belatedly, as if it were an afterthought. "I've woven silver for years."

"You're always wearing different pieces. Where do you keep them all?"

"I don't. I pull them apart and begin again."

"Hmm," he said between bites of stew. "That fits."

She raised a brow. "Is that supposed to mean anything?"

"It fits your personality." He tore off a hunk of bread and used it to soak up broth. "You don't appear to be attached to anyone or anything."

She sputtered. "If this is your idea of conversation, I—"

"Lara." He spread his hands. "I am trying to get to know you, for no reason other than that I want to."

She contemplated him for a long moment, her gaze searching, as if she were truly seeing him for the first time since they'd struck up their odd partnership. Using his heightened instincts, honed from years of training and practice, he sensed the wounded soul within her.

"I don't mind solitude," she said, then went back to eating with pointed concentration.

His ruefulness of late invaded him. "I don't, either. It's why I chose this life. I've long and willingly put my personal wishes aside for my duty. Yet, with each passing year, I become more aware of what I lack in my life."

He noticed that she'd stopped eating. "And what is that?" she almost whispered, searching his face.

"Someone with whom I can bare my soul."

Reflected in her eyes, he saw his own desperate loneliness. He blinked. "No family?" he inquired after several minutes of silence ticked by.

"No."

"Husband?"

She began eating again, in earnest. "*No.*"

"A lover, then?"

Her outraged eyes gave him the answer he wanted. "Ah. Where Eston fit into your life, I wasn't sure, other than that he's responsible for losing your precious ship."

"Don't remind me, *Vash.*" For the first time, he detected a trace of teasing in her tone. Was that the first step in her softening armor? Perhaps it was. And maybe that meant there was more to come. If he could make her laugh, lovemaking couldn't be far behind. He smiled. A night of pleasure would do this woman a world of good.

As only he could give it.

Chapter Twelve

"Now aim like you mean it!" Gredda called to Tee'ah.

Eyes narrowed, arms extended, Tee'ah held her laser pistol in front of her. Frost-covered grass in the field behind the *Sun Devil* caught the rising sun's first rays, and a breeze numbed her ears and fingers. Concentrating, she waited until threadlike crosshairs centered on her target—a produce box sitting on a tree stump. Then she pressed the trigger. The shrubs behind and several paces to the left of the stump exploded.

"Dear heaven," Tee'ah groaned, lowering the pistol. "Not again."

Gredda grabbed a fire extinguisher and drowned the flames. "That was better, Tee. But you need to practice."

Tee'ah wiped her forearm across her forehead. "I

will." She'd been working on improving her previously nonexistent marksmanship all week. During that time she'd hit Gredda's boxes only twice. But she was determined to hone her skill with a pistol. Now that they were hunting for Randall's associate, such skills were critical for her to prove she was an indispensable member of Ian's crew.

She and Gredda pocketed their weapons and returned to the ship.

Quin met Tee'ah in the galley. The expression of delight he wore on his face made her instantly suspicious. She poured a mug of coffee and did her best to ignore it.

"I've divvied up chores for the week and *you* drew galley duty."

Coffee sloshed out of her mug. Hastily she mopped it off the counter.

"You look like you just swallowed an oster egg," he said "Don't tell me you can't cook."

Nerves tightened her neck muscles. Cooking was a basic skill most people knew how to perform. But she hadn't been raised like "most people." She'd never once entered the kitchens in the palace; the thought of doing so had never crossed her mind. Now, if she were to confess that she didn't know how to prepare a simple meal, it might raise unwanted suspicions about her background. "As I recall, you voiced similar doubts about my flying abilities—and look, I kept you alive."

He brought his index finger and thumb together. "Barely."

"Then I suggest you go on a dietary fast." Perhaps the entire crew would have to do so, she thought as she looked around the small room. Surrounding her was a bank of ion-burners, a chiller, an atomic oven, and shelves of computer-categorized food supplies. It was a vastly more intimidating array than the instrumentation she used to pilot the ship. Swallowing hard, Tee'ah strode to the galley computer, opened the viewscreen, logged on, and spent some time familiarizing herself with the stored data. There was a long list of basic supplies, all requiring creativity if she were to create and then cook a meal with them.

Although she considered herself reasonably inventive, she might fare better if she were able to purchase fresh ingredients from the merchants in town, sticking to those food items that looked reasonably familiar, taking into account the differences in produce of foreign worlds. The market . . . fresh air . . . shopping unimpeded by an entourage—the idea appealed to her.

"There's hardly enough here to put together a proper meal," she said with feigned annoyance, closing the viewscreen. "I'll need credits to purchase supplies at the market."

As if he'd anticipated such a request, Quin handed her several currency cards of various denominations. "Remember," he said in his overprotective-father voice, "this is to be used for food only. Not for any recreational beverages you might be tempted to purchase on the way there or back."

"No 'recreational beverages'? Oh, Quin, please." She threw up her hands. "With such limits placed upon me, how am I supposed to prepare my famous whiskey-soaked Mandarian chicken?"

"We've had our fill of whiskey-soaked fowl on this ship," he shot back, his tone warming.

She grinned. "Not the least of them pilots, eh?"

Ian walked into the galley. He glanced from Quin to Tee'ah and back again. "Don't tell me she's torturing you again?" he asked his mechanic.

Tee'ah beat Quin to a reply. "I've drawn galley duty. And now Quin's worried that I'll spend all the credits he's given me to shop in the first bar I see."

Ian poured coffee into a mug, this one decorated with tiny conifer trees and a cheerful red-nosed man sporting an abundance of white facial hair and a long, floppy red hat. Sipping, he studied her thoughtfully. "I don't know. Barring a few notable instances, I'm beginning to think you're all talk."

"Meaning?"

"I don't think you're half as wild as you'd have us believe." His playful grin invited her to challenge his allegation. "Or . . . are you?"

She sniffed, tugging on her sleeves. Then she gave him a coy look. "Well, I don't dare cause trouble with that threat of yours hanging over my head."

"Threat?" Quin asked. "What threat?"

Ian's eyes dared her to reveal the details of their private conversation in the woods the night they'd spoken to Randall in the bar. Her heart raced with the exhilaration of flirting so openly with someone to whom she was so very much attracted, and she snatched the chance to continue the dalliance.

"The captain said he'd make me pay," she told Quin out of the corner of her mouth. "But when I asked him what he meant, he said he didn't think I'd want to know." She paused for effect. "I've spent many a night since pondering those words."

Ian's eyes turned a deeper green, as they had that night before he'd almost kissed her.

"Captain." Push's voice shattered the moment. The cargo handler waited in the hatchway. There was a black smudge on one cheek, and his fingers sported matching stains. "You ought to take her out, Captain. And don't be gentle or nothing . . . I think she'll go as fast and hard as you want."

Tee'ah wanted to sink into the alloy flooring. Was she so obvious in her feelings for Ian?

"I wasn't planning on taking her this morning," Ian replied matter-of-factly, as if Tee'ah weren't cringing next to him, her face hot with embarrassment. "But I will if you think I should."

Push nodded, wiping his dirty hands on a rag. "I do."

"You do?" Tee'ah managed. Her own opinion didn't matter, apparently.

Maddeningly blasé, Ian set his empty mug on the

table. "All right. Afterward I'll let you know what I think. She might need tweaking."

"Tweaking?" Tee'ah coughed out.

"Yeah." Ian shrugged.

She couldn't believe he would talk about her in such a cavalier manner. She wanted to be made love to—not *tweaked*, or whatever Ian had called it, the results of which he apparently had no qualms about sharing with the crew.

Ian explained, "Push is helping me repair my Harley."

She felt her heart stop. "Your two-wheeled Earth transport?"

He nodded and finished discussing with Push the various mechanical components that concerned him, while Quin listened in with interest.

Heavens. She shifted from one foot to the other, the heat in her cheeks receding rapidly, leaving behind an intense feeling of foolishness. He'd been referring to his Earth vehicle the entire time, the noisy, primitive, fossil fuel–burning Earth curiosity he stored in the cargo bay and rode during rare hours of free time. He hadn't been talking about— or thinking about—her. Never around any man had she acted like such a self-centered, vacuous idiot.

She collected her wits. "I'm going to the market."

"I'll give you a lift," Ian said.

She went over his statement in her mind. Reasonably certain that there were no double meanings hidden within, she asked hopefully, "On the two-wheeled Earth transport?"

"If you don't mind riding with me."

Heavens, no. Her shopping excursion was looking better with every passing minute. "Not at all," she said.

Ian followed her into the corridor leading to the forward entry hatch. "You'll need a helmet and jacket."

Once dressed in the leather garment he provided her, she carried his extra helmet to the gangway. At the bottom stood the transport—the Harley—a hulking example of primitive machinery propped upright on a metal leg. Glinting silver and black, the transport seemed to bring ancient history to life.

Anticipation pulsed through her. "What a glorious day," she said, inhaling the scents of sun-warmed leather and fossil fuel, grease and dusty, dry dirt.

As Ian tugged on his gloves, she donned her helmet and lowered the visor after only a few seconds of fumbling.

Ian boarded first, holding the vehicle steady with his feet as she threw her leg over the seat and hopped on behind him, sliding about a bit on her rear until she felt centered on the wide saddle.

He peeked over one broad, leather-clad shoulder. "Put your arms around me and hold on tight."

Tentatively she wrapped her arms around his waist. Her pulse sped up, this time because of their physical closeness rather than the anticipation of the ride.

"Ready?" he asked.

She tightened her arms around him. "Ready."

The thunder of the vehicle's engine startled her. She hugged him tighter and the side of her helmet brushed against his back. Then they lurched forward, jerked, stopped.

Ian swore. "Damned clutch," he muttered in nearly unintelligible English.

She lifted her head. "Has the vehicle malfunctioned?"

"Hold on a moment."

Happy to comply, she settled against his back, her hands flat on his belly. His stomach muscles flexed, pushing at her palms as he shifted his body weight to adjust something on the transport's handlebars.

Finally he asked once more, "Ready?"

"Ready," she murmured in bliss.

Smoothly the motorcycle rolled forward, crunching over the dirt-packed landing pad and onto the adjacent wide, flat market road used by local ground and hover cars. But the thoroughfare was empty, only sunshine and trees before them.

When they reached the market, Ian slowed the "hog," as he called it. "Must we stop so soon?" Tee'ah pleaded. "Can we not ride for a bit more?"

He laughed with abandon. "I think you know the answer to that question, Miss Tee." The nickname gave her an incredible rush of pleasure.

Ian leaned forward as they accelerated away from the market, taking a left turn onto a narrower road she didn't know existed. It headed out toward an area where an old forest fire had turned the woods into grassland that reminded her poignantly of her home, Mistraal. But her homesickness soon dissolved in the sheer joy of the ride.

He was a strong, athletic cyclist. When he leaned into a turn, she moved with him, awkwardly at first, and then with increasing confidence. Now she understood why he often left the ship at dawn to experience this. It was like flying. No, better than flying—it was as if she'd soared skyward and became part of the wind itself. She whooped in joy.

The rush of air drowned out her voice. But Ian's gloved hand found her thigh and gave her a gentle squeeze. *I feel the same.* As sure as she breathed, she knew he'd spoken those words with his touch. She wanted to cover his fingers with hers, hand over glove, but she didn't dare let go of his waist to do so.

As they came around a wide bend in the road, a herd of Tromjha steers ambled off a pasture and into their path. Ian slowed, but kept driving forward. The mass of hulking bodies continued to spill onto the road, passing left to right.

Breathless, she warned, "Ian, watch out for the cattle."

"You, who flew through an asteroid field—by hand—are concerned about a few furry steers?"

She risked letting go to raise her visor, grabbing hold of his jacket with her other hand. "We're not going to ride through the herd . . . are we?"

"Don't you like moo-moos?"

"Moo-moos?"

He chuckled. "That's what we call them on Earth. *Cows.* They look almost the same. Watch out, moo-moos," he called. "Or my accomplice here will buy one of you for our dinner."

As they neared the trihorned cattle, dust rose, obliterating the path ahead. "How can you see?" Tee'ah demanded, then shrieked when they narrowly missed a pair of the beasts. "You *can't* see!"

"Who says I need to see? I can tell by your tugs on my jacket whether I'm going to crash into something. Now hang on," he said, mimicking the warning she'd uttered the day they had lost the autoflier.

She half screamed, half laughed as Ian expertly wove in and out of the bulky white and brown bodies. Finally they cleared the herd.

"That was some kind of driving," she said, mimicking his Earth-accented Basic.

"The appropriate response would be, It was nothing."

She didn't have to see his face to know he was grinning.

They left the musty scent of dust and manure behind them. Ian leaned forward, accelerating faster than before. Her hair fluttered in the wind as Ian careened around a dizzying curve, blurring the agrarian landscape. Exhilarated, she threw her head back and laughed with abandon. The scenery, Ian's company, and her freedom made it easy to believe that she'd escaped her old life for good.

A particularly pretty meadow appeared in the distance. Ian slowed and veered off the road. With a hissing spray of gravel he came to a halt. At first all she heard was the ringing in her ears when he cut off the engine. Then the chirps of crick-burrs and the drowsy buzzing of insects punctuated the silence. At the far end of the meadow a pond sparkled in the light of Grüma's white-dwarf sun.

She followed Ian's lead and tugged off her helmet. A faint breeze teased the fuzzy, overprocessed ends of her hair, reddish gold roots deepening to brown-green ends. She ran her fingers through her locks, too invigorated to care if they stood on end. She felt *alive*, almost painfully so, as if every neuron in her body had wrenched free of a lifelong slumber. *You've waited your entire life for this.*

She wasn't a loner at heart; her dreams of freedom always included an imagined future in which she shared adventures with a man she loved. Now she wondered if that man might turn out to be Ian Stone.

He dismounted and held out his hands. She grabbed them and swung her leg over the seat. Legs trembling, she gazed up at him. "You enjoyed the ride," he said, his eyes sparkling.

She sighed. "Very much."

He pulled his hands from hers reluctantly, as if he craved physical contact as much as she did, but wanted to hold back from engaging in it. In fact, most of the time he avoided being alone with her. He was worried about the repercussions of having a relationship with an employee, she reasoned. But surely such liaisons happened all the time in the frontier. Nothing need hold them apart here.

Her heart thudded in her throat as she raised both hands, flattening them on his chest. "That was wonderful, glorious; I can't begin to describe it." She took a step forward. He stepped back, as if trying to preserve the distance between them, but his boot heel caught on the thick, damp grass, and he stumbled backward. Momentum carried her forward and she landed on top of him, one knee wedged between his legs, his chest cushioning her breasts.

Damp, fragrant grass formed a green halo around them, muting the sunshine and accentuating the knowledge that she and Ian were completely alone in an isolated meadow. The awareness of his muscular body, pressed so firmly to hers, took her breath away. But it was the astonishment and shared wonder in his beautiful eyes that captured her heart. With a soft sigh, she leaned over him to claim the kiss denied her since that magical night in the woods.

Closing her eyes, she buried her fingers in his silky hair. His lips were closed but, when she ran her tongue along the seam between them, they parted. Uncertainly, then with increasing eagerness, she stroked his tongue with hers.

He didn't respond for several shocked seconds. Then, as if something inside him gave way, he made a needy groan and splayed one hand behind her head, pressing her close to him. He kissed her deeply, hungrily, his fervor matching her own. She abandoned herself to pure sensation: his scent, his hot, slick mouth, the flexing of his firm, muscled legs twined with hers, and his warm fingertips subtly exploring her body. The feelings he evoked in her were powerfully erotic, but the pulsing heat between her thighs reminded her that she wanted more from him, much more.

As if he'd heard her silent wish he rolled her onto her back in the soft grass. Passion scorched through her as his palm glided up her hip to her ribs, stopping frustratingly short of caressing her breast. With mere kisses, the pleasure he gave her was incredible, nothing like what she'd imagined from all she'd read and had been told by the sophisticated instructors who'd seen to her explicit, *Vash Nadah*–required sexual education. But whatever she might lack in actual application skills, she was determined to make up for with sheer enthusiasm.

Eagerly she reached for the zipper on Ian's coat and yanked it down to his waist.

Chapter Thirteen

Two small, strong hands sliding under his leather jacket jolted Ian back to reality. What the hell was he doing? *Exactly what you swore you wouldn't.* But what had he thought would happen if he stopped in an isolated meadow that screamed of picnics-for-two and romantic interludes, with a fun, sexy woman who was not only a fantastic pilot, but gorgeous, too, despite her totally bizarre hair?

He tore his mouth from hers. Hands flat on the cool grass, he raised himself over her. Her eyes were heavy-lidded, her flushed face alive with passion as she grabbed his collar, tugging him back down to her. As their lips met, white-hot desire blazed through him. Ian tried to fight back. He wanted her, but without the possibility of a future together, he couldn't have Tee. He would not repeat the sins of his father: physical intimacy without emotional loyalty. The only solution was to demonstrate the restraint expected of a *Vash* prince.

But damn if she didn't blow apart his best intentions.

The wet pointed tip of her tongue was teasing, tempting. "Come on, Ian," she coaxed, her fingers playing in his hair. "Kiss me again." She seemed so different . . . so carefree out here, alone with him.

It's *only* kissing, he reasoned, using logic he didn't want to examine too closely. They could kiss, but no more. Call it a line in the sand, he thought. One he simply wouldn't cross . . .

Hungrily, he took her mouth. She uttered a muffled cry and locked her hands behind his head, kissing him back with an indescribable mix of eagerness and uncertainty, knowledge and unpracticed innocence. She felt good. *Too good.* He wanted to touch her, to taste her everywhere; he wanted to feel the tight, liquid heat of being inside her. But when her splayed hands slid from his chest to his abs and under the waistband of his jeans, he broke off the embrace with an effort that nearly killed him.

The line . . . don't cross it.

Tee regarded him with perceptive golden eyes. "Well?" she asked breathlessly.

He exhaled. "Wow."

Her low, husky laugh revealed her pleasure at his comment. "Better than the Harley ride, yes?"

"No contest." He closed his eyes as she swept kisses along his jaw. "But we can't do this."

"Really?" Her attention lazily shifted from his eyes to his mouth. "What do you call that, then—what we just did?"

"Playing with fire." He pushed himself up, leaving Tee lying on the trampled grass. Sitting next to her, he drew one leg up to his chest and balanced a forearm on his knee. "Which everyone knows is not a good idea."

"I see." She rolled onto her side, suddenly engrossed in a blade of grass which she twirled between her slender fingers. "You have a woman, then. I should have—"

"No, Tee, it's not that. There's no one else."

She dropped the blade of grass, came up on her knees, and flung her arms over his shoulders. "Good," she said against his lips. "I could not tolerate anyone who was unfaithful to a mate. Now, where were we?" she asked, tracing her fingertip over his mouth. He caught her hand and pressed his lips to her damp palm, then pulled her into his lap. She shifted in his arms, her supple body molding to his.

He needed to stop this. Now. Get up and walk back to the Harley. But Tee was to his soul like an open window was to a long-sealed musty room. The lightness of spirit she evoked in him was addictive. As a boy, he'd taken it upon himself to make his mother's life as easy as possible, to compensate for the pain his father had caused her. No one had asked him to; he'd simply acted out of an inner, driving sense of decency. Consequently, his life for so long had been serious, heavily laden with responsibility, self-imposed and otherwise.

And his future promised more of the same. But this wasn't a crime, doing something for the fun and the pleasure of it! He might as well while he still could. And she definitely seemed to want it as much as he did.

It's only kissing.

"We were doing *this*," he said and rolled her beneath him. He nuzzled her ear, nibbled the velvety lobe. She smelled like green grass and soap. They kissed again, sweet and light, caressing each other for what seemed like hours. The affection between them flowed so easily, so naturally. It was as if they'd known each other all their lives. How was that possible? he found himself wondering.

"Quin's going to wonder where we went," he murmured finally, touching his lips to the tip of her nose.

Softly she laughed. "Let him."

He tightened his arms around her. His kisses turned deep, wet, and hot, the way he longed to make love to her. Her impassioned response nearly spun him into oblivion, almost made him forget all the reasons he shouldn't be with her: they had no hope for a future; she lacked the holy bloodlines required of the proper wife he must marry in order to placate the *Vash Nadah* council; the rest.

From inside his jeans pocket, the comm crackled.

"*Sun Devil* to Captain Stone." Muffin's muffled deep voice emanated from somewhere near Ian's crotch, which happened to be nestled deliciously between Tee's thighs.

He pushed up on his arms, and his pants "spoke" again. "Captain, what is your status?"

Their faces inches apart, he and Tee burst into breathless laughter. Then they sat up, brushing torn grass from their clothing.

"Shall we tell him?" Tee asked impishly.

Ian pulled the comm from his pocket and offered it to her. "Go ahead."

"Is that a dare?"

"Interpret it any way you want, pixie."

She grabbed the comm. "This is Tee. Go ahead."

There was a moment of silence, then: "It's been two hours since you two left. Everything under control?"

"Well, it is now." She winked at Ian. "For a while there I wasn't quite sure. But I tweaked the captain and I think he'll be fine now."

Ian gave a bark of laughter.

"Hmm. Sounds like a maintenance problem to me," Muffin said. "I'll give you to Quin."

Without seeing Muffin's face, Ian found it hard to tell if the man was pulling his leg.

Quin came on the comm next. His voice was an octave higher than usual. "What's the problem? Do you need me or Push to come out there?"

"No!"

211

Ian snatched the comm from her. "Everything's
fine. We took the hog out for a spin and went farther than I'd planned." To his amusement, Tee
blushed. "We're headed to the market now. Give us
a standard hour. Captain Stone out."

They stood, brushing themselves off as they
walked back to the Harley. There Ian pocketed the
comm. "I can't believe you said that."

Her face fell. "Ah! What was I thinking?"

"Tee, I was only teasing. I thought it was funny."

"Oh." She lowered her hands and managed an
embarrassed smile. "All my life I've been told I'm
too brash, and too forward. So, I assumed—" She
shrugged. "Well, I do ramble on sometimes."

"Hey. I happen to like your 'rambling.' "

Her eyes glittered. With happiness? With tears?
Before he could decipher her strangely emotional
re- action to his simple comment, she folded her
arms atop her head and turned in a slow circle, her
face tilted into the sunshine. "Oh, Ian. The ride . . .
this . . . it's wonderful." She lowered her arms, sighing in pure pleasure. "I never really felt part of the
events and people around me. I thought I must be
defective in some way, because I felt as if I were
living my life inside a bubble. But not anymore."
Her mouth twisted in a slow, shy smile. "Did you
ever just dare yourself to leave behind what was safe
and familiar, so you could finally experience what it
was like to be alive—crazily, utterly alive?" Her
voice faltered and became husky. "Then did you

ever get so frightened by what you'd done that you could hardly breathe?"

The back of his neck tingled. *The moment our lips met, I felt all those things.*

"Yes," he said carefully. "I have." He kept his expression neutral as he helped her climb onto his Harley. Not for the first time, he contemplated the enormous responsibilities that went along with his new role as heir to the galaxy. Obligation, sacrifice— they were what gave his life meaning, and he couldn't picture living without a defined sense of purpose. Only now, in an instant, he couldn't picture living without Tee. With no apparent effort, she'd taken his just-fine-the-way-it-was, black-and-white existence and blasted it into sense-wrenching color. He fought a sharp sense of loss, envisioning the day they would have no choice but to go their separate ways.

He zipped his jacket to his chin, turned up his collar, and lowered his helmet visor. The last thing he wanted was for Tee to witness his inner battle; it would only complicate what was to come.

At the market, Tee'ah recognized admittedly exotic versions of many ingredients she'd seen presented at meals on Mistraal. Although she had never visited the kitchens, she'd often strolled through the shady, peaceful orchards and humidity-laden vegetable gardens in the vast greenhouses on her homeworld. Fresh produce made the best meals, in her opinion, and she decided to prepare dinner from as many fresh ingredients as she could gather, mentally recalling the myriad dishes she'd admired and consumed over the years.

After the purchases were made, she and Ian walked back to his Harley, which was secured beyond several trees. "I suppose we do have to go back now," Tee'ah said. "The crew will be wanting their dinner."

"We can always go on another ride some other time." He regarded her for a moment, an affectionate smile playing around his lips. "I've been thinking about what you said earlier . . . how you feel alive now, but you didn't before. I can't imagine you any different from how you are now."

As they stood in front of the motorcycle, Tee'ah shifted her weight from one foot to the other. He was making an obvious attempt to get to know her better. She relented and took the first step; someday, if things progressed as part of her hoped, there would be no more secrets between them. "I had a very comfortable life, actually. I should have been content, happy, satisfied, all those things. But I wasn't. I loved my family. I still do. But if I'd done what they wanted, if I'd married, I would have died a little more every day, until my spirit, the part in here"—she tapped her chest with her right hand—"that's *me* drained away."

She dropped her hand. "But I don't expect people to understand why I was so miserable in what others would consider extremely pleasant surroundings."

"Not everyone has the strength to fight what is expected of them, Tee. If you ask me, it takes more guts to leave a nice life because you're supposed to be happy. If you're not, it's easy to blame it on yourself. What you did took courage," he said admiringly. "So many people never go after what they truly want out of life. You did. Be proud."

His comprehension took her breath away. They stood there, a few feet apart, more passing between them with a simple gaze than what a thousand words could convey.

"You speak as if from experience," she managed finally.

"It was my mother's experience, not mine. Her story is a lot like yours. It took her years to work up the courage to change her life, but she did, and now she's married again and happier than I've ever seen her." His mouth tightened and he jerked on his gloves, one finger at a time. "My father had other women. It hurt her. But she held the marriage together for the sake of my twin sister and me. When we were teenagers, my parents separated and my father remarried a much younger woman, and he had a kid with her. They're divorced, too, now." His mouth twisted bitterly. "But I digress. What I'm trying to say is that after the marriage ended, my mother had friends, a career she was passionate about . . . a perfectly nice life. But not contentment, not happiness. She felt that with all she had, she had

215

no right to complain or to crave more."

Tee'ah felt a shudder ripple through her. Ian's description of his mother's quandary was so close to her own experience. It was reassuring to learn that others felt as she did. Which didn't take away her guilt over leaving home, but it made it easier to bear.

Ian pulled on his helmet. "You'd have thought a woman who flew jets wouldn't have been afraid to break out of a rut," he said, lowering his visor. "But she was."

Tee'ah felt the blood drain from her head. "She—she flew jets?" Her world tilted, and she clutched the Harley's seat to keep her balance. Jas Hamilton B'kah was a pilot. She was also Rom B'kah's queen and—

The crown prince's mother. Had she been right before? Had she simply been avoiding what she didn't want to be?

Numb, she prayed Ian would again offer her something, anything, to indicate he was not Ian Hamilton, the prince admired for his faultless adherence to *Vash Nadah* tradition. She couldn't fathom what he'd be doing in the frontier, without luxuries, without the trappings of power. Was this a way to prove himself to those who doubted his ability to rule?

Perhaps. But what good did it do to show he could live without riches, without protection, when he'd never be asked to?

Ian spoke as he tightened her helmet's chinstrap.

The dark visor hid the panic in her eyes. "Yes," he said. "She's a pilot. A good one, too. Like you."

Her dry lips formed a hoarse. "Thank you."

He patted the seat. "Let's head home before Quin has a heart attack."

Or before *she* did. Shakily, she mounted the two-wheeled transport and balanced herself on the seat. Despite the crisp air, a droplet of perspiration trickled down her temple. She pondered the physical resemblance between Ian and Jas. They shared the same lovely shade of greenish gray eyes, accentuated by dark lashes and brows, but that was all. Yet when she added in Ian's knowledge and grasp of galactic politics, his scandalized reaction to the conditions on Barésh, and his quickness to defend the *Vash*, her throat tightened until she could barely swallow. Sweet heaven, what was she going to do?

"Hey." Ian pressed a gloved hand onto her shoulder. His expression was unreadable behind his tinted visor. "Why so quiet all of a sudden?"

She drew on all her strength to stay calm. There was no use fretting until she was certain of Ian's identity. And she had yet to figure out how she might become so. "I'm thinking of dreams," she said softly. "And how badly I want to hold on to mine."

"Go for them, Tee. Don't let anyone stop you."

You wouldn't say that if you knew who I was. Woodenly, she replied, "I won't."

For no reason at all she felt like weeping, and she didn't understand the reaction. She ought to be terrified at the possibility that she sat inches away from a paragon of *Vash* virtue. Instead, she regretted that she might never again experience the heart-pounding joy of a Harley ride. Or Ian's kisses.

If he was the crown prince . . .

Ian threw his leg over the seat and let the engine warm up before rolling the motorcycle forward over the bumpy dirt to the road. As they raced back to the *Sun Devil*, Tee'ah couldn't help but wonder if the handsome Earth dweller would prove to be her liberation or her doom.

She waited until she was alone in the galley before she fell apart. With the hatch shut against curious visitors and potential crown princes, she leaned over the counter, head bowed, unable to catch her breath. Ian could end her newfound freedom with one call to the palace on Mistraal. Dar security would be dispatched immediately. She wouldn't elude them this time; they'd know exactly who and where she was.

Where is your courage, Tee'ah?

Powerful, impossible ancient, the voice echoed in the silent, inner passages of her mind. The voice of her ancestors: the founders of the *Vash Nadah*. Generations ago, those eight warriors saved the galaxy from annihilation. But there were many demoralizing defeats before they finally achieved that victory. Her own setbacks were minuscule in comparison.

What would her heroic ancestors think if they saw her cowering this way?

Hadn't she escaped her home and come so far already? The quivering in her arms stilled. The roiling of her stomach eased. Eyes closed, she worked on her breathing until it slowed. Then, deliberately, she raised her head. In her moment of crisis she'd instinctively drawn strength and guidance from her noble legacy. With sudden insight she understood that no matter how far she traveled from her roots, no matter how rebelliously she shunned the beliefs she was brought up with, she would always carry the essence of those ancient heroes in her soul. It was an inborn sense of pride no one could erase. It was an odd feeling to take strength from all she'd abandoned, but it brought her calm; she would survive, no matter what.

She went to work cleaning the fruits and vegetables she'd purchased at the market. Then she attempted to carve them into the ornate designs created by her father's palace chefs. Dish after dish was assembled and put aside. As she worked, her thoughts circled back to Ian.

His mother flew Earth jets.

Viciously, she shoved her knife into a crispy, bulbous vegetable, twisted until it split in two. Then she hacked it into quarters. Throwing down the blade, she grimaced and pressed the heel of her palm to her forehead. She'd lost her starspeeder, staggered out of bars, gotten drunk, purchased birth control, admonished her almost-brother-in-law in a virtual reality arcade, and, if all that wasn't enough, she'd just now practically raped her employer, a man who could very well represent everything she'd tried to escape!

Tee'ah picked up the knife again and stabbed it deep into another fibrous root—one that rather reminded her of Klark Vedla. She remained uncertain why he hadn't upheld tradition and attempted to bring her home. Certainly the B'kah heir would have. How often had her father remarked that Ian Hamilton had to be more than perfect if he hoped to gain the trust of the Great Council?

And now she was on his ship. Or might be.

Her anxious chopping had turned the root to pulp. Unwilling to waste the vegetable, she slapped it into a pasty pancake. Who would eat that? she wondered. Quin, maybe.

"From firing range to kitchen, eh?" Gredda sauntered into the galley. She picked up one of the berries Tee'ah had glazed with a sticky sweetener before piling them into a miniature conical mountains. "Fresh lalla-berries," she murmured as she popped it into her mouth. With a smile of amused approval, she inspected the fruit and vegetables Tee'ah had arranged on whatever trays and platters she had found.

Seeing Gredda reminded Tee'ah how fast she'd come to view the crew as a substitute family. But tonight she felt more like an outsider than ever.

Likely everyone knew who the captain was except for her. Obviously, despite what had happened between them, Ian didn't trust her yet.

Gredda sniffed, as if testing the air. Then she frowned. "Where is the meat?"

Tee'ah concerns swung back to a more immediate problem. She spread her sticky hands on the counter. "We're eating a vegetarian meal tonight."

"Vegetarian? Bah. We women need our protein."

Tee'ah stopped short of admitting that she'd be happy to oblige, if only she knew how long to cook the fowl, beef, or the savory sea serpent bundled in the giant chiller in the rear of the galley.

Gredda studied her, her eyes sympathetic as if she'd guessed the real reason for their meatless meal. But she didn't embarrass Tee'ah by saying so. "I know it is your night to cook, and I do not wish to intrude upon your preparation, but I'd be most pleased if you'd let me make Tromjha beef according to the Valkarian recipe—from my homeworld. These off-world men, they prefer their stew with their suitable-for-babies, cut-up bits of beef. But I say it's high time they learned to eat meat the way it was meant to be consumed. Are you with me, Tee?" she asked with a wink.

Tee'ah lifted her hands in surrender. "Show me what to do."

As evening fell, the crew gathered around the dining table. Ian inhaled deeply. "Something smells good."

"You will like it," Gredda said, her muscles flexing as she spread a napkin over her lap.

"Tee gave you an advance tasting?" Muffin asked sulkily. "She wouldn't let me in the galley."

"Me, either," Push said.

Tee emerged from the galley, a tray held proudly in her hands. As she walked to the table, her expression was pleasant, but infinitely unreadable. When Ian tried to make eye contact, she avoided looking at him. His mouth twisted in exasperation.

She hurried back to the galley for another tray, making several return visits until three heaping platters of what could only be called vegetable and fruit sculptures sat on the table. They were crooked and misshapen—one even crumbled as they watched it—but the effort that had gone into building each was obvious. No one quite knew what to say.

Finally, an awed Push tapped a hill of berries with his utensil. "Plain old stew would have been fine with us."

"Wait," Tee said. "There's more." She and Gredda shared a private glance. This time, when Tee disappeared into the galley, she returned with a heavy tray of meat.

"Valkarian steer," she announced breathlessly and plunked the tray onto the table. Juices ran from fork holes punched in the unevenly hacked-away flesh, filling the tray with a delicious-smelling gravy.

Quin gaped at the steaming hunk of meat. "The paw . . . it's still attached."

"The hoof," Gredda corrected, her eyes shining with a voracious glint. "The full leg always tastes best. Why you off-worlders mince up perfectly good hunks of meat, I don't know. On Valkar we rip the flesh from the bone with our teeth. Go on, eat your fill, mechanic." The hungry twinkle in her eyes turned suggestive. "A real man needs real meat."

Understanding suffused Quin's face. As the two crewmates considered each other in what appeared to be a new light, Tee'ah took her usual place next to Ian.

"Great dinner," he said in her ear, trying hard to forget it was the same sweet little lobe he'd nibbled before he'd almost devoured the rest of her.

She kept her attention trained on her empty dish. "Thank you." She pushed one of the fruit trays in his direction. "Eat, please."

"After you. You had quite a morning," he added playfully in hopes of coaxing her out of her obvious sudden shyness.

She blushed. Finally, he thought. A reaction.

"Some . . . carrot-flowers," he offered.

"P'wulla-squash florets," she corrected. "Just one, please." Again she fell silent.

He sighed. "We're going to talk about this later," he whispered.

"That's not necessary."

"I beg to differ." He hated to lose their spirited rapport all because they'd made out in a meadow. Yet when his mind fast-forwarded to his future, to

223

the enormous responsibilities he'd undertaken and the promises he'd made, he knew it was the best thing for them both.

Yeah, he thought. *And lima beans are supposed to be good for you, too.*

After dinner, Tee'ah loaded dirty dishes into the sterilizer and wiped the counter clean of seeds, bark and vegetable scrapings. Next she prepared a tray of *tock* and coffee.

The laughter and conversation of her cheery, well-fed crewmates rolled through the hatch from the dining room. If circumstances forced her to leave the ship, she'd miss them terribly. Worse yet, she couldn't bear the thought of leaving Ian. His quiet concern at her silence had only endeared him to her further, but the only way she'd hold on to her new life was to avoid her old one. There was no escaping that.

She threw her cloth into the sterilizer, grabbed the tray and mugs—among them her favorites: the round-eared rodent Ian called "Mickey Mouse," and another emblazoned with an impossible starship and the Earth runes BEAM ME UP, SCOTTY!—and walked through the hatch.

Over the *tock* and coffee, Ian set out the evening's plans. "Since we haven't made much headway with our daytime watch for Randall's comings and goings, I thought we'd head into town tonight and see if we can find him at one of those restaurants."

"We'll go back to that bar," Gredda proposed. "And you can sing us a song, Captain."

"We can go to that bar"—Ian grimaced behind his mug of coffee—"but don't expect me to provide the entertainment."

Muffin asked, "Whose turn is it for watch?"

Tee'ah almost raised her hand. The idea of watching Ian sing, albeit badly, was more than she could bear right now.

"Mine again," Push spoke up glumly. "I guess you'll have to have fun without me." The cargo handler's shoulders drooped.

Tee'ah found herself thinking how unfair it was. Why should he be forced to stand watch when the very last thing she felt like doing was merrymaking? "No, Push. I'll stay."

Everyone glanced her way.

"I feel sick." At least that was the truth, she thought. Besides, no one should care which crewmember stayed aboard the *Sun Devil*, as long as one did.

Ian appeared more than worried; he looked downright guilty. Had he figured her out? "How sick?" he asked.

"Just . . . sick." She managed a wan smile.

"All right," he said resignedly. "Push goes. You stay."

Rising Gredda mumbled something affectionate about Tee'ah needing more meat in her diet. One by one, the rest of the crew stood. They wished Tee a speedy recovery, then followed the brawny woman into the corridor to don coats for the walk into town.

Ian remained behind.

Moving his chair closer, he leaned toward Tee'ah. "Now we can talk." He radiated heat, the fragrance of soap, and his own unique scent, making her again acutely aware of the hard, finely toned body he hid beneath his clothing. "What happened between us today bothered you, didn't it?"

No. The secrets between us do.

"You have every right to be upset," he continued. "I took things too far. I apologize."

His acute self-consciousness surprised and charmed her. "You're forgetting that I started it all!" she said.

"You may have started it, but I sure didn't fight too hard."

"No"—she smiled—"you didn't."

He frowned. "It was unprofessional. It won't happen again."

Despite her worries about his identity, despite her fears of losing her freedom, Tee'ah's disappointment rushed to the surface before she could stop it. Or analyze it. And the gleam in his eyes told her that he had seen. Heat flooded her face. She masked her embarrassment with a blasé and—she hoped—worldly explanation. "Even if it does, don't be concerned. Casual, uncomplicated liaisons are what I prefer. No need to make more of that kiss than what it was."

A mixture of astonishment, disappointment, and relief flickered across his expressive face. "Well," he said slowly. "I'm glad we got that cleared up."

"Captain," Muffin's voice rumbled from down the corridor. "We're ready."

Ian pushed his chair backward. All business again, he told her, "Activate the security locks on the hatches. Then you won't have to stand watch if you don't feel well. Let the computer do the baby-sitting."

She snorted. "Like when I flew through the asteroids? No thanks."

"Quin says the computer checks out fine. I believe him, or I wouldn't leave you here alone." He stood. "Get some sleep."

She doubted she would.

Quietly, she walked with him to the cockpit. From there, she watched him depart with the rest of the crew. Even after all five of their shadows vanished into the ink-black woods, she continued staring out into the night, listening to the sound of her breathing in the silent, empty ship.

"Computer—play 'Melody of Cyrrian Flutes,' " she said, settling into the pilot's chair. Soft music filled the ship. She propped her boots on the navigation console and tried to keep her mind off who Ian was—or who he was not.

As long as he doesn't know who you are, you're safe.

Yes. Surely she was safer now than ever before. The crown prince's ship was the last place anyone would expect to find her.

A brisk scrabbling noise from outside invaded her thoughts. She dropped her feet and sat up, cocking her head. Grüma was home to a variety of wild creatures, but like the traders who frequented the local bars, they were mostly harmless. Mainly they participated in long, active nights of foraging and caterwauling. Likely the lingering scent from their dinner of roasted meat had brought a few of the animals closer than usual.

She fetched her pistol from the storage drawer at her station and turned up the ship's exterior lights. Two muffled thumps emanated from the hull, as if the sudden illumination had startled whatever was out there. Her heartbeat picked up. If it was a marauding, carnivorous beast, it was a large one.

She scanned the exterior of the ship using an infrared, heat-seeking enhancement that displayed objects according to temperature. The scanner showed a few small life-forms in the darkness beyond the fringe of light ringing the *Sun Devil*. Several animals foraged closer to the ship—rodents, or something similar. She kept searching.

Grüma was filled to the brim with people of all backgrounds. She'd heard Quin and Gredda talk about some of the more unsavory merchants whom they said preyed on empty ships, stealing parts for sale on the black market. But someone might want to do harm to the *Sun Devil* for other, far darker reasons, someone who didn't want them following the Earth-Senator Randall—a target who took on an entirely new and fascinating significance now that she suspected the crown prince himself was spying on him.

She cursed her habit of concocting elaborate schemes of intrigue, a consequence of growing up among *Vash* royalty. She had no reason to believe that anyone was plotting anything. Nonetheless, if Ian was who she thought he was, his position made him a natural target for assassination—especially given his non-*Vash* heritage. And while she doubted anyone would make an open attempt on his life in the central part of the galaxy, making his death look like an accident in the frontier might be feasible. Even those who loved Rom B'kah might not investigate too thoroughly the mistaken death of his improper heir. Then a "proper" prince could assume the throne—a prince like Ché Vedla, the man she would have married.

Foreboding chilled her. No wonder Ian was keeping a low profile.

Another thump jolted her attention to the ship's engine-status display. A green rectangle representing the main access panel to the number-one engine thruster went from green, to blinking amber, to steady red, telling her the panel was now ajar. Had she not seen the undeniable evidence displayed on the schematic, she wouldn't have believed it—or the equally shocking image on the infrared scanner. A human-sized shape crouched near the thruster. Someone *was* trying to damage the ship!

She reached for the main comm at the same instant the interior of the ship went dark. False lights sparked in her eyes with each thud of her heart, which sounded like it was about to explode. "Captain, this is the *Sun Devil*; do you read?"

There was no answer.

She tried again. "Return to the *Sun Devil*—immediately."

The comm was dead. All power to the ship must have been cut off, the security locks included, she realized with a disconcerting sense of vulnerability. Luckily the hatches locked mechanically upon total power loss and couldn't be opened from the outside without dismantling the hatch itself. But if the trespasser wanted to, he certainly could force his way inside given enough time.

He wasn't going to have that time; she'd make sure of it.

She grabbed her pistol and an auxiliary flashlight. Then she released the manual door lock to the main entry hatch. It lifted with an overly loud hiss. Frigid air hit her like a slap in the face. The temperature outside was far colder than she'd expected. As she stepped out, a twig snapped beneath her boots. She winced. Then, shivering without her jacket, she inched forward, peering around the fuselage to the aft part of the ship.

She aimed the flashlight and her weapon into the darkness, bracing herself. "Who goes there? Identify yourself," she called. The beam of her light illuminated a cloaked intruder—and the pistol he aimed at her head.

A blazing streak of light whizzed past. She dove toward the ship, seeking cover. The air crackled. The ground nearby exploded and burned where her opponent's shots grazed the dirt. Heavens, she was in a gun battle! Unless people made easier targets than produce boxes, she was in deep trouble.

There were more shots. Her ears were ringing. She peeked around the fuselage and tried to see her attacker. He fired and almost hit her. She retaliated blindly, fearing that if she stopped firing, his next volley would kill her. But her shots went wild. There was an answering burst of light inches from her shoulder, raising the hairs on the back of her neck. Then the intruder bolted into the woods.

She chose a tree and fired above his head, thinking she could stop him by dropping a tree limb on his head. A crisp beam of green-tinged red streamed out from her pistol. With an ear-splitting crack, the smoldering branch crashed to the ground, barely missing her fleeing assailant.

Full of adrenaline, she jumped after him. Startled birds, woken from their slumber, took to the sky as her attacker crashed through the trees. Then, just before he disappeared, he cast a glance over his shoulder. Her heart stopped, and so did she. She knew those eyes, so like her own. And that face; it was imprinted in her memory.

"Klark!" she screamed after him. She reeled with fury. A primitive, bloodthirsty urge to finish the kill urged her to again give chase, but common sense held her back. Gulping air, she lowered her pistol and sagged with spent terror against the *Sun Devil's* fuselage. The acrid odor of hot metal and charred wood stung her nostrils.

She'd hoped she'd seen the last of Klark, that he'd satisfied his need for vengeance by humiliating her in the arcade. But he was back and he'd almost killed her. What did he want—her very life for spurning his brother? That was insane.

When her legs stopped quivering, she jogged around to the thruster. She found the cowling hanging open and the torn-apart innards of the engine exposed. Clutching the fabric of her flightsuit to her chest, she squeezed her eyes shut. In the arcade Klark had said this wasn't about her, but she hadn't believed him. Now she understood.

He wanted to destroy Ian.

Chapter Fourteen

Fists deep in his pockets to fight the effects of the cold night air, Ian walked alongside Muffin, half-listening to Push, Gredda, and Quin's humorous reminiscences as they all tromped back through the woods.

After a drink in the nearest bar and a sweep through town looking for Randall, in which they came up empty-handed, they'd unanimously called off the evening early. Randall was obviously holed up back at his ship.

It was just as well—Ian wanted more time to work on his proposal. He knew that his detractors expected him, as an Earth dweller and frontiersman, to be incapable of holding his own in serious negotiations, but they were wrong. When he confronted the senator, he would have several coherent, well researched plans—or at least the bare bones of them. That

233

had always been his strength: forethought and discipline.

A shot rang out in the distance. Screeching birds exploded out of the trees nearby, but an intense exchange of pistol-fire drowned out cries.

Muffin threw his arm in front of Ian, the instinctive gesture of a man protecting his leader, at the same time Ian reached for his gun with adrenalized speed.

More laser-fire ended in an explosive crack of splitting wood that echoed through the forest. Then a woman screamed.

Tee!

Ian broke into a run. "To the ship!" he called.

Branches clawed at his face. Breathless, he burst from the treeline, skidding to halt at their ship's landing pad. Right on his heels, Quin stumbled to a stop and aimed his flashlight at the *Sun Devil*.

Chest heaving, Tee squinted back into the beam, her eyes wild. From one hand dangled a smoking pistol; clutched in her other was a flashlight. Blood glistened on her forehead.

"Push," Ian shouted. "Check the perimeter for intruders. Gredda, get the medical kit." His crew took off in opposite directions.

As Muffin guided Tee away from the ship and sat her on the ground, Quin said, "I'll get the auxiliary generator online—the one that should have come on automatically."

"Why didn't it?" Ian demanded. He'd left Tee

alone with a faulty security system and told her to sleep? The deed was criminal, especially knowing that someone might be after him.

"Hell if I know, Captain. But I intend to find out." Swearing at the ship's computer the mechanic jogged to the entry ramp and, after a few false starts, manually started the generator. The exterior and interior lights came on bright.

Mollified, Ian walked to where Tee sat with her long legs sprawled out on the dirt. As he crouched in front of her, she gazed up at him with a slightly dazed expression. Something inside him gave way as an elemental need to hold her, to care for her, dwarfed anything he'd felt before. But instead of pulling her into his arms, he cursed the circumstances that kept them apart. "Gredda will fix you up," he said gently.

"I'm injured?" She lifted a shaking hand to her head.

Ian snatched her fingers. "Don't."

"Something must have ricocheted and hit me," she said. "I didn't feel it." She looked herself over. "I'm not shot, am I?"

Smiling, he took off his jacket and draped it over her shoulders. "Not that I can tell. Thank God."

"Good. Now I can kill him." Her mouth contorted with rage. "Preferably with my bare hands so that I can feel him suffer."

"Kill him? Kill who? Tee, what the hell happened?"

"Someone tried to sabotage the ship."

Stepping away from the thruster, Quin shoved his hands in his pockets. "Someone *did* sabotage the ship."

Ian's neck tingled. He took his comm out of his pocket. "See anything, Push?"

"No, sir. Not yet."

Quin interjected, "I think I can have it fixed by mid-morning," with grudging acknowledgment he added, "Tee chased whoever it was off before he did any real damage."

Ian sighed. "Take what time you need to do the repairs right. When Randall leaves for Earth, I want us to be on his tail. I don't want there to be any reason for us to be left behind, especially not sitting here nursing a busted ship."

Gredda returned with the medical kit and Tee's coat.

Tee winced as the big Valkarian tended to the wound on her scalp. "The power went off—the security locks, too," she said. "I saw what looked like a person near the thruster, so I went outside to scare him off."

"You shouldn't have gone out alone," Ian told her.

His concern sprang from his frustration at not being there to protect her, but she took it as an insult. "I quite understood the risk. I considered the situation desperate enough to warrant it. It was a decision that probably saved your ship."

"And almost cost you your life," he snapped. "You blindly charged into action. You should always think things through, make a plan."

Her nostrils flared. "In other words, I didn't handle this the right way."

"The safe way, Tee," he amended.

"*Your way*, you mean."

They glared at each other. Prudence versus pluck, he thought.

Her tone softened—only a fraction, but enough to tell him she'd finally recognized the worry in his tone. "I tried to reach you, Ian. The power went off before the call went through. My personal comm was in my quarters, and in the dark I didn't think I had enough time to get it and save the ship. When he saw me come out, he started firing. I fired back. Then he ran into the woods. I nearly put that tree branch on his head."

In unison, the crew's eyes veered to a huge smoldering branch crushing a grove of wet fern-like plants.

Tee growled, "I wish I had."

"Practice will make perfect," Gredda said from beside her. The big woman was concentrating on her ministrations, covering Tee's abrasion with healer-film. Then she ruffled Tee's hair. The short green-brown locks on her forehead sprang straight up and stayed there. "There. You'll live."

Tee climbed to her feet. Ian tried to assist her, but she pushed away, clutching his jacket around her. Her pale eyes blazed with indignation. "I want some clarification about this job of mine, and I want it now. The same cargo that was in the hold the day I came aboard this ship is still there. We haven't made a single act of trade in the entire time I've worked for you. You say we're checking out your competitor, but we've been following an Earth senator. Come on, Ian. How stupid do you think I am?"

Quin coughed. Gredda fiddled with a loose stud on her vest, and Muffin whistled silently, drumming his fingers on his upper arms. "I'd better check the perimeter again," Push said and made an abrupt about-face.

Ian couldn't think of anything to say. With her aptitude for galactic politics, it had been inevitable that Tee would guess his identity before long.

The young woman drew herself up to her full height. "I've worked hard for you, Earth dweller. I've *risked my life* for you. Not because I had to, but because I wanted to. Yet still you don't trust me. What more do I have to do to prove my loyalty to you and this crew?"

"Nothing, Tee. You have a right to know everything."

Her voice lost its edge. "You're not a trader, are you?"

"No," he said quietly. "I'm not."

She let out a quick, harsh breath.

"My name is Ian Hamilton. I'm the heir to the Trade Federation and crown prince of the *Vash* empire. I haven't broadcast that fact because I wanted to keep a low profile. I wouldn't have been able to learn what I have otherwise."

Shivering, Tee dabbed her nose with the back of her hand. For the first time since he'd met her, she looked truly afraid. "You have enemies, Ian," she said finally.

"I get that feeling."

"It's time you found out who they are. I—I don't want anything to happen to you."

He shifted his weight. "Nothing's going to happen to me."

"You don't know who you're up against." Something in her tone struck him.

"Do *you?*" he asked.

Her breath formed clouds in the chill air as she squeezed her hands together, a gesture he'd come to associate with her tension. The entire crew gathered around them, listening intently. "There was a man at the market the day you and Muffin took me shopping. He was staring at me from across the street, so openly that the merchant noticed and called my attention to it. He was wearing a cloak and hood so I couldn't see his face, but as he turned away I was able to see his eyes." The flicker of true fear—was it for him?—that crossed her face vanished so fast that he wasn't sure he'd seen it. "Ian, he was *Vash Nadah.*"

"A *Vash?* Here?" His blood surged. That truly was

suspicious. His stepfather's people infrequently left the interior of the galaxy.

Tee continued, "Because I didn't know who you were, then, I didn't say anything. It doesn't excuse my negligence, but I was so focused on self-preservation that I didn't stop to think he might be a danger to you and the crew."

"After the near-miss with those Dars on Blunder, I can see why," he acknowledged.

"Then, on Barésh, when we got separated, I was followed. It was the cloaked Vash again, and this time we talked. He let it slip that he was on Don-avan's Blunder."

Ian thought of the loony bartender and his warn-ing. *Watch your back.* "Who was he, Tee? Did he say?"

"Klark Vedla." A muscle jumped in her cheek, and her face gleamed with perspiration despite the frosty air. "You know him, yes?"

"Yes." He was more familiar with the prince's older brother. Ché had been first in line for the throne until Ian entered the picture.

"Klark was here, Ian. Tonight. *He* damaged your ship."

Her statement hit him like a two-by-four between the eyes. A surge of fury rolled through him. "To heck with the ship; he almost killed you!" He'd hoped his dedication to the *Vash*, his participation in the Great Council, his work to become the per-fect *Vash* prince, would have reassured anyone who disagreed with his selection as Rom's heir. But now it was clear that any such optimism was premature. The *Vash Nadah* were pacifists on a galactic scale, but what about on a more personal level? It wasn't like them to resort to violence, but what if they saw him as a threat to their cherished age-old bloodlines? How far were they willing to go to keep one of their own on the throne? And now that he suspected foul play, how should he handle it? The execution would be as critical as the resolution.

Ian returned his attention to Tee. "Tell me exactly what happened in the arcade. What did this *Vash* do? What did he say to you?"

"He made me sit with him and share a drink. I didn't want to stay there, of course, so he got angry and began ranting. He blurted that he thought his older brother deserved more power than what the king was willing to give him." She shifted from foot to foot uneasily, and Ian found himself thinking that either she was scared or she was holding something back. After a moment she added, "The entire episode was very odd. It seemed all he wanted me to do was have a drink."

"How many did you have?"

"Only the barest taste of one," she shot back defensively.

"One taste?" he repeated.

There was dead silence. Even the night creatures hushed as an almost eerie calm invaded him. "You could barely walk out of that bar. Didn't you wonder about that?"

"I blamed it on my low tolerance to alcohol and the strength of what I drank . . ." Her eyes widened with understanding. "You think it's more than that."

"Vedla's been poisoning our pilots. *All along*." Ian let out a quick pained laugh and raised his hands. "And here I thought you were all alcoholics."

Tee grimaced. "The pilot that came before me, he killed him?"

"Deliberately—or accidentally through overdose," Muffin agreed. "If he wanted to slow us down and keep us from catching up with Randall, it worked. At first."

The crew grumbled with more observations and suppositions.

Ian struggled to control his rage. "But I didn't fire you for drunkenness like he hoped, so now he's after the ship. We've had more than our share of maintenance problems, Quin. Do you see any connection to Klark?"

The mechanic shook his head. "The malfunctions are too random. Different systems break down each time, and they're systems he couldn't get to. I wish he *was* the answer, Captain, because I'm damned tired of trying to fix our rotten luck."

"And I'm damned tired of being a fool." With his hand on his holster, Ian walked toward a thicket of trees a dozen yards away. "Go on inside, everyone. We've done all we can tonight. I recommend you get your sleep while you can. We'll take care of Klark soon enough!" His proclamation worked; the crew left in higher spirits, mumbling about how the *Vash* saboteur was about to get his due.

"*Hot damn!*" Ian could hear his sister saying. "*Ian Hamilton's going to kick some ass.*" Yeah, that's what Ilana would like—a good old-fashioned ass kicking— and Tee would too, by the sound of it earlier. But that's not how he operated. He'd taken all those years of Tae Kwon do on Earth so that he wouldn't ever have to fight—and it had worked. He'd always been able to use his brains and his mouth to get out of every situation.

Vigilant for unusual sounds or movement in the woods, he tipped his head back and stared at the stars, but their stark beauty was lost on him tonight. If what the pixie said was true, Klark had been interfering with his mission from nearly the beginning.

Twigs crackled behind him. He didn't have to see who it was; he felt Tee's presence on a plane that went beyond the physical: affinity of thought. This must be what the *Vash* meant when they spoke of it.

"It's cold, Ian."

He took his jacket from her, and she donned her own coat. "If he'd wanted to assassinate me, I'd be dead already," was all he said.

Her tone revealed her abhorrence of the subject. "Yes. I think so, too."

He rolled his shoulders to ease the tightness in his neck. "If you take assassination out of the equation, every act he perpetrates appears calculated to keep me away from Randall. But why?"

"The answers lay inside you," Rom would say. *"Listen to your senses Ian, Trust them."*

Closing his eyes, Ian recalled, word by word, nuance by nuance, everything Rom had taught him about heeding his senses and taking his precognition to a higher level. The *Vash Nadah* valued the importance of intuition, over the centuries had raised its cultivation to an art form, but was he ready to do so himself?

His instincts had always been good. He'd inherited that ability from his mother and in recent years learned to hone it, thanks to Rom's patience and expert instruction. *Guide me . . .*

Tee's voice broke his concentration. "The more I ponder this, the more I think Klark *wanted* us to come after him. Tonight. Why else would he have let himself be seen?"

Ian opened one eye. "Yes! That's exactly it. A diversion—he wants to deflect my attention from Randall. He has to." Euphoria made him forget his exhaustion. He let out a whoop, then laughed at Tee's surprise. "Don't you see? Klark is Randall's associate!"

"Sweet heaven." Tee breathed.

"He's the one who told Randall about Barésh.

244

He's the one who showed him the fringe worlds." It was the perfect conspiracy—A *Vash* royal facilitating interaction between troubled frontier worlds and Earth, encouraging a powerful Earth politician's views of a self-ruling frontier, raising the specter of future galactic volatility the Great Council would insist only a full-blooded *Vash* king could handle.

"An unstable frontier would leave my stepfather no choice but to pick a *Vash* successor," Ian speculated aloud.

Tee's lips compressed. "Someone like Klark's older brother."

"And that's exactly why I'm not going after Klark." *Remember your mission.* "Klark's the distraction. Randall's the focus." His gut told him so.

Ian flattened his hand on the small of Tee's back and urged her toward the ship. "Randall's getting ready to leave for Earth, and soon—I *feel* it. And Klark's dangling himself as bait to keep me from going after him." More supposition, he thought. Another guess. Did he dare risk letting Klark run amok while he concentrated on wooing Randall? What if his interpretation of Klark's plan was faulty?

But time was running out. He had to trust his instincts, to believe in himself.

Ian's eyes sought the stars once more. Each twinkle was a world he'd someday rule. But wasn't that presumption, too, based only on a hunch—Rom's premonition that his ascension to the throne would restore freshness to a stagnating society and unity to a galaxy on the brink of revolution?

A tremor ran through him. His destiny had its merits, he supposed, but it was clear that a serene and peaceful life wasn't going to be one of them.

"At first light, I'm going to Randall's ship," he said.

"You said your proposal wasn't ready."

"We're out of time, Tee; Randall's leaving. I have to reassure him about Barésh . . . and about me, before he passes on his one-sided observations to Earth." They stopped at the bottom of the entry ramp. "Besides, I have a few hours," he added, then cracked a smile. "Who needs sleep anyway?"

"I'll help you," she offered.

Ian gazed down at his pilot. His fingers throbbed from the cold. Slipping his hands in his jacket pockets he said, "You have no obligation to do so, Tee."

"I know I wasn't part of your original crew, but I believe in you and what you're doing. You care a great deal for Barésh and the worlds like it. You want to help them while also convincing Earth to stay in the Federation. I admire that . . . how you want to balance the needs of your home with the galaxy's future." Her gold eyes glinted strangely. In a tight voice she added, "You'll make a fine king."

The inevitability of their eventual separation sat heavy in his chest. And hers, too, if he was reading her right. She, like him, realized that they could never be together. And she too must be trying hard to pretend the ache wasn't there.

He brought his hand to her cheek. This sweet-faced quick-talking pixie was trouble incarnate for him—a smart, irrepressible woman with *Vash* eyes and a questionable past. She kept him wondering what it'd be like to make love to her though his mind belonged somewhere else—*anywhere* else—and the need to touch her was so close to overpowering his better judgment.

"Please," she said. "Let me help. I have . . . a yen for politics."

"I noticed."

"Then let me be a part of it all. Let me help."

The years spent submerged in *Vash* culture had urged him to trust his senses, and those senses told him to take the assistance she offered. He trusted her. "Okay," he said, unable to shake the feeling that in joining forces with Tee, he'd just spun his destiny into a sharp left turn.

Her face glowed. Smiling, he brushed his open hand over her hair, savoring the silkiness of the shorn ends against his palm. "Ah, pixie," he said. "You wear your heart on your sleeve."

She laced her fingers with his and brought his knuckles to her cheek. "What does that mean?"

"It's what we say on Earth when someone's feelings are easy to read. Yours are to me . . . even when you think you're hiding them." He paused. "You still have secrets, though. Big ones. In time I'll know what they are."

He hadn't meant to sound threating, but her mouth tightened in alarm. She dipped her head, obviously trying to hide her eyes now that he'd told her how easily he could read her.

He tucked his thumb under her chin and tilted her face up to his. "As soon as you're ready to tell me," he reassured her, his voice soft.

She gave him the barest of nods. "Know this, Ian. When I was with you this morning"—her cheeks colored—"in the meadow, I still thought of you as Ian Stone."

"A simple black-market trader," he said, moving closer.

"To me, that's who you'll always be."

"Ah, Pixie . . . "

Their breath mingled, and his thumb stroked her lower lip. Then he dipped his head and kissed her.

After a brief hesitation, she slipped her arms around his waist. He remembered her eager determination in the meadow, but this was different. She kissed him with a soft, almost loving tenderness he found moved him even more. He smoothed his palms over her hips and sweet backside, pressing her closer. Sighing, she melted against him, her fingers tangling in the hair at the nape of his neck, sending shivers down his spine.

It's only kissing.

No. It's more than that. You'd be crazy to deny it.

A sound from inside the ship reminded him where he was and what he was doing. Breaking off their kiss he hugged Tee to his chest, afraid to let her see his face before he got himself under control. She'd claimed she preferred uncomplicated liaisons. *Right.* There was nothing uncomplicated about this woman.

"Get a little sleep," he whispered into her ear. "I want you at least semi-conscious when you play the part of Randall while I practice what I'm going to tell him."

She hunched her shoulders, reacting to his warm breath on her skin with a shudder. Sliding her hands from around his waist, she stepped out of his arms, her expression impish. "I will . . . because of all we have ahead tomorrow." She backed away, but before she disappeared into the ship, she glanced over her shoulder. "There will come a night, though, Captain, when I won't be so easily dismissed."

The look she gave him promised things he wasn't supposed to be thinking about. It was deep into the night before he finally pushed them from his mind.

"Woo-hoo, Gann! I've got your quarry in my crosshairs!"

Lara breezed into the *Quillie*'s cockpit, bending to give the ketta-cat a cautious pat on the head before she stopped in front of Gann.

He put aside the palmtop he'd been using to re-

249

view data they'd collected so far on the Dars' runaway daughter. "I take it you had a fruitful afternoon in Padma City?"

Her eyes lit up with triumph. "I found her."

"Here? Oh Padma?" *The mission is complete; Lara Ros will be out of your hair and your life will go back to the way it was before.* Odd, but the realization didn't quite bring the cheer he had expected.

The tracker took off her jacket and tossed it over the back of her pilot's chair. "No, not here. She's on Grüma."

"Grüma's known for its trade in illegal goods, is it not?"

"The black market, yes. Hmmm." She smiled. "I wonder what our spoiled heiress is selling. On the other hand, perhaps someone is selling *her*."

Gann's gut clenched at the thought. The princess was an innocent in so many ways. What if the darker elements in the frontier got to her before he could bring her to safety?

Lara rolled her eyes. "I'm joking," she said.

He sat back in his chair, a smile of surprise curving his lips. Although the thought of the princess in illicit flesh trade was horrible, even a jest in poor taste was a breakthrough for Lara Ros. He said, "Oh. This is a memorable day, then—in more ways than one."

Incredibly, she gifted him with her first genuine smile. He hadn't made any headway in coaxing a kiss out of her, but then his quest had been subtle. Too subtle, he thought with an inner grin. Now that he'd gotten the first good smile out of her, perhaps it was time to make his intentions clear. A night of pleasure was definitely what they both needed.

Had he ever gone so long without me?

"I questioned a few merchants just in from Grüma," she was explaining. "They say there's an Earth dweller with a small crew there. He has two women in with him. One's a Valkarian. The other is tall, thin, and a bit unusual-looking."

"In what way?"

"Her hair is shorn off."

Gann leaned forward, taking the bait. "Go on."

"She wears an Earth-dweller cap most of the time to cover it. But one gentleman got a glimpse of what's underneath. It's green."

"Green!" Gann exclaimed.

"Well, brownish green. But it looks really green in certain light, they say. One of the merchants remarked that it was a shame she had such awful hair, because she had the face of an angel. A purebred *Vash Nadah* angel."

"That's her. It has to be. You say the captain's an Earth dweller?"

"Yes." Lara plopped into the chair next to his. "Which means they might at any time head back to Earth."

"Or any number of planets in between," Gann speculated, frowning.

The silver bracelets on Lara's wrist tinkled as she

called up Grüma's coordinates on the nav computer. "I can get us there in precisely"—she studied the data—"two-point-four standard days."

Satisfaction swelled inside him. Lacing his fingers over his stomach, he reclined in his chair. "I'm in your hands, Lara. Let's go get her."

Instead of taking her seat, the tracker tucked the ketta-cat under one arm and mounted the ladder leading down from the cockpit.

Gann raised a brow. "What in blazes are you doing?"

"Putting the cat out," she said and ducked out of sight.

By the time he caught up to the woman, she was standing at the top of the exit ramp, nudging the ketta-cat with her boot.

"I said, go on. Shoo." The creature butted its head against Lara's calves repeatedly until she finally relented and patted its back. Gurgling softly, it brushed at her trousers with one velvety paw. Lara plunked her hands on her hips. "It won't leave."

Gann smiled. "Apparently not."

"I'll bring it to the freighter next door. Surely its crew can use a ketta-cat to reduce the vermin population in their cargo holds." But when she reached for the cat, it rolled onto its back. Clearly at a loss, Lara sighed.

"She wants you to rub her belly," Gann said. He crouched down and stroked his hand up and over the animal's warm, silky stomach. The cat writhed, wanting more. "Ah, here, too, eh?" he murmured, rubbing his thumb under its chin. The ketta-cat's head tipped back and its purrs turned to snorts.

Gann said pointedly, "Notice that even this small creature knows that pleasure is heaven's gift, a treasure to be shared and savored. See how she tells me just how to please her? I do like that."

Lara made a small sound in her throat.

He glanced sideways. Her attention was glued to his hands. Her reaction pleased him; he enjoyed having discovered a way to circumvent her self-protective barrier.

He rolled the ketta-cat over and traced the bumps of its spine with his fingertips. Spreading the toes of its front paws, it arched into his hand, tilting its pelvis toward him.

He noticed Lara shut her eyes, color rising in her cheeks. "We have to leave," she said. "Put it outside."

All innocence, he asked, "Why? By now she considers herself part of the crew."

Lara snatched the animal away and marched with it down the ramp. She lowered the ketta-cat to the ground. "Take advice from someone who's been around the frontier awhile; you're better off on your own." She gave it a firm push, then she wiped her hands and walked up the ramp.

Mewing, it trotted after her. "What is wrong with it?" She snatched the ketta-cat up off the ground, holding it in midair, inches from her face. "You know nothing about me. Yes, today I fed you. Tomorrow I might sell your mangy hide to a coat factory!"

The ketta-cat told her what it thought of her threat by rubbing its whiskered face against her smooth cheek.

"Bring her along," he said. "How much trouble can one ketta-cat be?"

She glared at him. "This is *your* fault. The blasted thing's become attached. I told you this would happen."

"That's what pets are supposed to do. Become attached." He gentled his tone as he added, "People, too."

Fire flashed in her eyes. "Attachment means dependence." She spat the last word as if it were a filthy epithet. "Dependence is dangerous."

She apparently remembered she was holding the animal. Shoving it at Gann she growled, "Get rid of it. I've got a preflight checklist to run," then stormed back to the cockpit.

Gann shook his head at the ketta-cat. "She sure can be endearing at times, can't she?" Apparently in agreement, the little creature darted up the ramp after her.

Lara waited until after they'd launched and were established in the space lanes before she turned in her chair to glower first at the ketta-cat, eating from a bowl on the floor, and then Gann. "You never listen to what I say."

"I listen, Lara. But perhaps what I hear is the essence, the feelings behind your words."

She made a sound of disgust. "Here we go. You *Vash* and your thinky-feely, listen-to-your-senses crap." The ketta-cat jumped onto her lap. She sighed. "Now you've gotten its hopes up. It'll think it's found a home."

"Hope. Another concept that you find dangerous. Like dependence?"

Her jaw tightened. "Gann," she said past clenched teeth. "This discussion is not covered—"

"In your contract," he finished for her. "Yes, I know. Regardless, I'd like to continue—off the official record."

He stepped closer until he stood directly before her. "I suppose that if you expect the worst from others, then no one can disappoint you. Insulate yourself from disappointment and you don't get hurt. Right, Lara? Is that your credo?"

She made a strangled sound in her throat, then she brought her fists to her eyes. His heartbeat faster; blood rushed through his veins. He sensed he was close to breaking through the mighty wall she'd erected, and he did not want to back down until he did. "I am curious," he persisted. "Are your expectations of others as low? Or do you simply have none at all?"

With that, she slammed her fists onto her thighs. "Gann, you are a *pain in the ass*."

Her directness delighted him. But the torment in

her eyes emptied him of that amusement quicker than mog-melon wine from an upended uncorked flask.

"Lara," he said quietly, surprised. "Your hands are shaking."

She made a choking noise. "What's your game, *Vash*? Do you want to know more about me? Is that what this is all about?"

"Yes." He placed his hands over her cold, bloodless fists, warming them. "You knock me off-balance continually. I like returning the favor." His fingers fanned out over her fists. "That, and I know you're not what you appear to be."

Whatever she was trying to say to him appeared to be a struggle. Finally she mumbled, "You're not always what you appear to be, either."

He smiled ruefully. "No, Lara. I'm not."

She stared at their linked hands. On her face curiosity battled with constraint. Then, abruptly, she yanked her fingers out from under his. "I grew up on Barésh, a wretched, filthy place. I don't suppose you've heard of it."

Gann searched his knowledge of the frontier. "It's an asteroid. The Baréshti mines are located there."

"That's correct. It's a place right out of the Dark Years. Centuries and centuries of backbreaking labor, isolation, and boredom have bred the Baréshtis into a population of cooperative drudges—except during their time off. For that, we have the virtual reality arcades ... and the usual hallucinogenic drugs to heighten the experience. Of course some prefer the real thing; dangerous activities, near-death experiences." Her mouth twisted bitterly. "Nothing like a little self-inflicted or dished-out pain to remind you that you're not already dead."

Her eyes hardened. "My father lost a leg in a mining accident. My mother took his place because they wouldn't let him back into the caverns and we had to eat. A few years later, she was killed. A gas explosion, we were told."

For a heartbeat Lara's voice lost its hard edge, then her tone iced over again. "My father said he'd find me a cabin position on an intersystem cargo freighter. The salary I'd send back home would make up for the loss of my mother's. I was drunk with anticipation."

She pushed herself to her feet and walked to the sweeping forward viewscreen. "I'd always dreamed of flying, and he knew it. We Baréshtis worshipped the starpilots like gods. They were gods, I suppose, to us—we, who could never leave. But my father and I both understood that without money or influence to get me into flight school I'd have to start at the bottom and work my way up. I started at the bottom, all right. On a bed beneath a filthy swindler's sweaty body."

She halted, faced him, her mouth twisting bitterly. "My father sold me into sexual servitude. I was thirteen."

It felt as if the floor dropped out from beneath him. He reached for her. "Lara . . ."

Her hand shot out, stopping him. She swallowed, twice. "I spent my teenage years as a receptacle for a man's depraved fantasies. At mealtimes, the pig chained me to the leg of the table. *Naked.*" She searched his face for a reaction. "With a collar around my neck."

He stood there, too stunned to move.

"One night he choked to death on a piece of meat," she said breezily, a tone at odds with the rigid way she held her body. "After he tumbled off his chair, I used his key to unlock my collar. Then I helped myself to his ship and made it mine."

She attempted to maintain the lighthearted tone, but it sounded false. "I learned to fly from what I'd read, watched, and heard. It wasn't pretty, and I think I was in love with the autoflyer. And I didn't attempt a landing for months. Finally, when supplies ran low, I learned to dock—fast."

"I imagine you did. And then picked yourself up, dusted yourself off, and became the best blasted tracker I've seen in years."

She shrugged, suddenly awkward. Gann sensed that she'd at first told her story wanting to shock him, but she'd finished craving the solace she hated to admit she needed.

He opened his arms. "All I want is to comfort you," he explained, seeing her dismay.

"I don't know, Gann." She wrapped her arms over her small breasts. The bracelets adorning her wrists glinted in the starlight streaming across the cockpit viewscreen. "I don't think I can respond in kind. Should you need me to." Helplessly she added, "Should *anyone* need me to."

"Of course you can." He hadn't realized before what he was up against. Now that he did, his heart went out to her.

"No. I'm . . . too closed up inside." She pressed her fingers to her lips.

His insides twisted. "Lara, you are so full of fire, so full of life. Let yourself feel, let yourself *heal*. Otherwise you're condemning yourself to a lifetime of loneliness."

The moment dragged out, tense yet tender. Then, miraculously, her arms lifted. He captured her fingers and drew her close. Strangely, his need to hold Lara went beyond wanting to console her; they had shared something, something he struggled to define. Sure of only one thing he bent his head to taste her lips, but she stopped him.

"He never kissed me," she said.

Of course the creature hadn't kissed her, Gann thought, feeling ill. "But, afterward, after you'd escaped, didn't you . . . Haven't you . . ."

"Once. Years later. He was a trader. . . . I think. We went straight from the bar to bed, and I was so drunk he got right to business." She shrugged. "After that, I thought, why bother?"

He'd been raised to celebrate lovemaking and the relations between the sexes. Lara's outlook and experience were at utter odds with what he knew to be true. He pondered that, and the way she wore her mistrust of the *Vash* like a coat of armor. *Great Mother.* "He was *Vash*, wasn't he?" he practically growled. "Your 'keeper.' "

"Yes, a *Vash*." Her mouth dipped in a sneer. "Raised to follow the Treatise of Trade, and to *respect and revere* women."

"The man who abused you was an aberration, Lara. A monster. Sexual slavery is banned. It has been since the Great War."

"Don't be naïve. It still exists. Granted, perhaps only here and there in the frontier, a place you *Vash* somehow manage to exploit without involving yourselves in our welfare."

Gann spread his hands on top of the narrow briefing table next to her, his mind wracked with dark images of Lara abused by a *Vash* whom he prayed would suffer for all eternity to pay for his cruelty.

A place you Vash somehow manage to exploit without involving yourselves.

Her accusation rang with a truth he couldn't deny. "But the lawlessness and lower standard of living in the frontier stems from neglect, not malevolence," he defended. "Rom B'kah, our new king, once described the *Vash* federation as an old quilt— the center tight, the edges frayed. He wants badly to bring the frontier into the fold. He's been working to do so. . . ."

"How?" she demanded.

The Star Prince

Ian. The answer came to Gann in a rush: Rom's stepson, a frontiersman himself. In choosing the young, contested heir, Rom had proven brilliantly his commitment to the peoples of the outer reaches. Ian would be the first ruler with blood ties to both the frontier and the Great Council. People on both sides would look to him for leadership. And once Ian was well established, no man would be better suited to lead the Federation into a new era where the quality of life in the farthest corners of the galaxy equaled that enjoyed in the central regions. Earth was the newest upcoming power in the area, and to right the wrongs in the frontier, the Federation needed that planet's help.

"I'm deeply ashamed, Lara. You have suffered because of the Federation's shortcomings. But with Rom's son-by-marriage as the crown prince, I believe we can change what is wrong."

She assumed her familiar, defiant stance. "The fact he's not *Vash Nadah* makes me more inclined to believe it."

Gann suppressed a smile. He supposed that was as close as he'd get to an "I think you may be right." He also had the feeling he'd come as close as he was going to get for a kiss. But there were two-point-four days left to remedy that. He was more attracted to Lara than ever before.

He glanced over at a furry lump curled in her chair. "Look. Cat's helped herself to our ship."

Lara surprised him with a pleased, throaty laugh,

261

clearly recognizing his reference to her earlier comment. "*Your* ship, *Vash*. My ship's impounded. Thanks to my idiot associate, Eston."

She sauntered to her seat and buckled in. "That's the only reason I'm traipsing around the frontier, looking for a spoiled girl too half-witted to recognize how good she had it at home. Someone should tell her."

Gann winced. Poor Tee'ah Dar. The soon-to-be-rescued princess had no idea what she was be in for once she met Lara, master tracker, face to face.

Chapter Fifteen

Outside the ship, a slow rosy Grüman dawn melted away the shadows. Inside the *Sun Devil*, the day was well underway. Tee'ah returned to Ian's quarters with *tock* and coffee, though, at that point, having been up most of the night, she was certain she was well beyond the benefits of stimulating beverages.

"It is Tee," she said at the door. The hatch slid open with a soft hiss, revealing his uncluttered, ship-shape bedchamber. The few pieces of furniture were simple and masculine, and the fabrics covering the bed and floor cushions were dyed in desert tones of ocher, russet, and light brown. But just as she learned that Ian was not as he first appeared, so the room's neutral hues were unexpectedly spiked with brilliant colors: a pillow of pure turquoise, a yellow bowl, an old-fashioned wax candle in bright red. In fact, she found the effect extremely pleasing.

She stepped around a lumpy piece of metal that looked like it belonged to the Harley. Next to it was a neatly folded polishing rag. A razor and the barest of toiletries were stuck to the magnetic shelf above Ian's sink. Nothing in the chamber indicated that Ian would, upon Rom's retirement to the Great Council of Elders, ascend to the most powerful ruling position in the galaxy.

But Ian looked every inch a leader—especially as he, Quin, and Muffin huddled around a holographic map of Grüma. She poured the hot drinks, looking up to find Ian's eyes seeking hers. His smile made her heart do a little flip-flop.

He doesn't know who you are. For the hundredth time since discovering who Ian was, she reassured herself of that fact.

His face taut with tension, he reiterated the day's plans with his men. "With the very good chance that Klark will make another attempt at sabotage, I'm separating the two main elements I'll need to fly off-planet—the *Sun Devil* and Tee. She'll come with me. Muffin, you have the ship; and Quin, keep plugging away repairing the thruster. Gredda and Push will be stationed downtown, looking for any sign of Klark—or Randall, should he not be at his ship. Everyone remains in comm contact at all times, with check-ins every hour."

Despite the grim silence, knowing looks broadcast the men's approval of the plan.

Ian reached for the holographic map. "Display

sector 3-A." A tiny, forested ridge appeared in front of them, a replica of the green-blue hills above downtown Grüma. "This morning Tee and I will do surveillance from the ridge above the fortress where Randall landed his ship. This afternoon, if all checks out okay, I'll head down there.

"Have you loaded the food and water onto the Harley?" Ian asked Tee'ah, closing the holo-map.

"Yes. Everything is ready," she said, wondering if he'd given any thought to what happened when they'd last ridden together.

Muffin and Quin departed for their assigned duties, and Ian unlocked a safe, out of which he plucked a smallish brown box. Open, the box emitted the pungent sweetness of fragrant wood. Carefully he spilled the contents onto the desktop: unfamiliar coins and a thick roll of green-and-white old-fashioned paper credits—Earth money, she guessed—and a leather pouch.

He explained in a quiet voice, "I suppose if labels and titles define a person, then these would be me."

She could hardly breathe as she watched him take a long beaded chain with a curious golden charm—a cross with a tiny man pinned to it—from the pouch and set it aside. "Rosary beads. I was raised Catholic," he explained, translating the English words into Basic with some apparent difficulty. Next, he laid out two gold rings. One carved band had a blue gem and the Earth runes A.S.U. "My class ring. I graduated with a Bachelor of Science degree in finance."

The study of money and trade, she gathered, although again she suspected that several words didn't translate exactly.

He placed the second gold band in her hand. "This is what I will be wearing when I see Randall." The ring was weighty and ornately forged with etched runes far more familiar to her than those on the other. *Fealty, fidelity, family*, it said. The triad comprised the ancient code of the *Vash* warrior, one that stressed the control and self-discipline, that underpinned her entire civilization.

But this wasn't just any *Vash Nadah* signet ring. Age-old Siennan symbols indicated that it was of the house of B'kah, a ring only the galactic crown prince could wear.

Hearing Ian's declaration of his identity was one thing; seeing the proof sitting in her palm was another. She met his gaze with her most stoic face—one that she'd learned in her years at her father's court—and hoped that she could conceal her inner turmoil.

"Thank you for letting me see your personal things," she said, handing the ring back to him. He slipped it on his finger.

As long as he doesn't know who you are, you're safe, she reminded herself as they walked into the corridor. In fact, none of her plans needed to change—from her goal to save money and pay for her own starship to any of her other hopes. Especially her most personal quest to lose her virginity. Wasn't giving her innocence to the man of her choice the ultimate physical expression of her liberation? And could she imagine a man she would choose more readily than Ian Hamilton?

And yet, in doing so, she'd forever close the door to returning home. The thought exacerbated an ache that hadn't yet disappeared for good. *Vash Nadah* men were subject to far fewer restrictions than their female counterparts. While Ian was unmarried, he might make love to her and suffer none of the far-reaching consequences she herself would endure. If she made love to him, she could never go back.

Ian waited for her to climb down the gangway to the exit hatch before he followed. His Earth jeans stretched deliciously tight across his toned, muscular buttocks. Fastening her coat all the way up to her neck, she bit back a sigh. Oddly, the image that filled her mind was not of Ian making love to her, but of her giving him the gift of pleasure . . . of watching his expression as she wrapped the waistband of his jeans around her knuckles and eased his pants lower. Desire would make her eager, and eagerness would make her tremble as her breath whispered over his bare, sensitive skin. At first only her fingertips would stroke his hardened flesh: then, as she'd been taught in countless readings, she'd take him into her mouth loving him with her lips, her teeth, her tongue, until . . .

"Are you all right?" Ian gave her a funny look.

Tee'ah's skin felt oddly warm all over, and her

pulse echoed in the most intimate places. "Yes, fine; a little sleep deprivation, is all."

"You'll have time to rest later."

Would she? Her hot little fantasy was disconcerting to say the least, but it had also provided her with an intriguing inspiration.

On the outskirts of the planetary system that included Grüma, the *Quillie* left cruising speed. "Decelerating," Lara confirmed.

"Ah. I don't think there's a sweeter sounding word."

From where she sat at the controls of the craft, she glanced over her shoulder. "Why? Because you know the unprotected and frightened Dar princess is awaiting your rescuing arms?"

"Something like that."

One corner of her mouth quirked. "I knew it."

He found himself mildly annoyed. "Why would you ridicule the idea of a man coming to the aid of a distressed female? I find the concept inherently romantic."

"I think it's the act of saving that you're in love with. The princess . . . the ketta-cat—though it's debatable as to whether you really 'saved' it . . . and then, of course, there's me." As if in agreement, the ketta-cat in her lap blinked sleepily over at him.

Gann didn't know how to respond. He acknowledged that she was right in that he hoped to rescue her in some sense. But wasn't that what he wanted for himself, as well? Rescue from his two-dimensional existence as an instrument of his king? He'd long-imagined himself in his older years finding a trusted companion with whom he could share his life . . . and perhaps come to love, but that had eluded him for most of his adult life. Of course, he'd managed to keep himself relatively well satisfied when it came to physical concerns—at least until now. Never had his plans to take a woman to bed been so delayed. Not that he'd ever wanted anyone else as much as he did Lara.

She turned away with a satisfied smirk. "I didn't think you'd want to answer that one, *Vash*. Besides, I don't need rescuing, so stop trying. What would you do with me, anyhow, once you'd saved me?"

I'd make love to you until we were both too exhausted for anything but sleep and too sated to care, he almost said. But her shadowed eyes and sad little mouth pricked his protective instincts instead. "I'd pamper you, as you deserve to be. I'd treat you like a princess, because you'd be one to me," he said with simple frankness.

She'd turned, so he couldn't see her face. But her hunched shoulders told him she heard every word.

"But I honestly wonder, Lara, if you'd ever view my efforts as anything other than sympathy."

After what seemed like eternity, she answered him. "It depends how you define it. Feeling sorry for oneself is pity. When you feel sorry for another, then, yes, it's sympathy. But if the sympathy is mutual, that would be commiseration, I think."

"You . . . feel sorry for me?"

She looked at him as if he hadn't an atom of self-awareness. "You're as lonely as I am. More, maybe."

He fell back in his chair. He *was* lonely, a lonesome and sometimes melancholy old warrior who missed the excitement of the old days. Only it was disconcerting hearing the diagnosis from Lara.

She shifted so that he could see her profile. "No, I wouldn't call what we feel toward each other sympathy. Maybe . . . compassion, reciprocated." Then she grimaced. "Gah! Did I just say that? It sounds like something you'd come up with."

He laughed. "So it does."

As always, silence fell between them. Only this time it was different. Something had eased, although he couldn't define what it was. Instead of trying, he kept quiet and watched her fly as she resumed her preparations for entry into Grüma's crowded space lanes.

The rumbling of the ship's massive star-drive shook the floor beneath his boots. They dropped out of light speed, the stars outside shrinking from elongated streamers to pinpricks of light. One of those lights was Grüma.

Tee's arms tightened around Ian's waist as he maneuvered the Harley away from the landing pad, bouncing along the dirt path until they reached Grüma's version of a highway. No speed limits here, he thought. Accelerating, he lowered his body into the wind and gave in to the addictive freedom of riding, a rush of sensation made more powerful by the necessity to see Randall before the senator left for Earth.

Downtown Grüma and its surrounding forest faded to a hazy smear in his rear-view mirrors. The road narrowed and climbed higher into pristine tree- and-boulder-strewn hills. *Watch your back*. He put his senses on full alert, scanning the landscape ahead and behind. So charged were his muscles that, when one of Tee's hands crept from his waist down to his thigh, he almost swerved the Harley onto the shoulder.

Her thumb began moving back and forth along the crease where his leg met his hip. He slapped his gloved hand over hers and squashed the subtle movement of her fingers. Then he pointedly placed her hand back on his waist and silently thanked her for keeping it there.

Road signs in block-like Basic runes pointed toward the area of the ancient ruins where Randall was based. The road grew steeper and narrower as they progressed. When they finally reached the summit of the ridge overlooking the fortress, he veered off the pavement and killed the engine.

A vast unspoiled forest spread out before them, green-blue under a lavender sky. To the east, the remains of an ancient wall snaked along the tops of distant hills, reminding him of when he'd visited the

271

Great Wall of China in the outskirts of Beijing. Far below was a group of ancient sprawling buildings, most of them crumbling stone.

He raised his binoculars and studied the ruins. On a landing pad sat a workhorse of a starship, no sleek lines or graceful delta shape, only a blunt fuselage and short, blocky wings meant for long-term deep-space travel. Most importantly, the ship wasn't issuing the telltale signs of being readied for launch. "Where are you, Randall?"

Tee lowered her own binoculars. "It doesn't look like anyone is home."

"They could be inside."

"Shall we check?" she asked somewhat uneasily.

"Not yet. It's early. He hasn't started his day. When he does, I want to see where he goes and what he does."

"So we wait then? We might as well enjoy the scenery." She walked to the edge of the ridge, and he watched the gentle sway of her backside and the way her pants clung to her long legs. His body reacted instantly. "It's incredible, is it not?" she called over her shoulder.

"Very." *Discipline*. He opened one of the saddlebags and moved to hand her a membrane filled with water. She tipped her head back and drank with lusty, unselfconscious enjoyment.

He chuckled. "You appreciate the simple pleasures, do you?"

She contemplated him as she dabbed the back of

her hand to her mouth. "And the not-so-simple ones too, Ian." Her eyes downright scorched him.

He pretended he hadn't heard the implicit invitation. "Well." He cleared his throat. "I'll put some oil in the hog. You can rest."

She followed him back to the Harley. "We've worked nonstop for weeks now. I say we've both earned a little rest," she said. A reasonable argument, he thought . . . until her fingers closed on either side of his jaw.

She turned his head, forcefully, then pressed her soft lips to his. "Is this not relaxing?" she murmured against his mouth.

It was anything but. "Tee," he mumbled.

"Shush, Earth dweller." Her fingertips slid into his damp hair. Closing his eyes, he savored her sweet touch. Fighting his physical reaction to her had been a struggle since the beginning. Now he was battling against an intellectual and emotional response, too. Plain old lust he could handle, because he refused to be the man his father was. But *this*—it was crazy. In an amazingly short time, she'd become a part of his life that he didn't want to give up, and that turned their flirtation into a personal risk he really couldn't afford.

His spread hands hovered by her head, reflecting his evaporating restraint as she pressed her lips to his mouth, his chin, his forehead. But when she opened her mouth over his and slipped her tongue inside, her enthusiasm couldn't quite cover her awkwardness.

The combination boggled his senses. He'd thought she was experienced.

"Casual, uncomplicated liaisons are what I prefer."

So what if she wasn't as knowledgeable as she claimed? he thought.

All the more reason to stop what they were doing.

She began suckling his tongue, and his thoughts went blank. The sound he made in his throat was one of desperation. His hands landed on her head, and he dragged her to him, guiding her into a long, lush, open-mouthed kiss. His resistance was fading.

Don't cross the line.

Groaning, he thrust her to arm's-length, holding her there. "Tee, we can't."

A determined smile played across her lips. "You have a terrible habit of ending kisses just when they are getting good," she complained, then splayed one hand on his chest and marched him backward. "I must train you not to do that."

He warned, "I'm not free to be with you."

"I know." The sorrow that clouded her eyes vanished in an instant. "I'm not free to be with you either. This is all I want." His back bumped flat against a tree trunk. "Pleasure," she breathed, coming up on her toes. "Accept this gift I offer you. It will do us both a world of good."

Not only did she look like a *Vash*, she thought like a *Vash*. "Tee—"

She rolled her eyes. "Must you always argue?" Then she cut off his answer by covering his mouth with hers and yanked his T-shirt out of his jeans.

He framed her sweet, flushed face in his hands. "Pixie. What are you doing?"

She snatched his hands and pointedly placed them by his hips. "Relax. You will enjoy this."

His laugh was cut short as she unzipped his jeans.

He couldn't believe it. The woman who fired his fantasies night after night had thrown him against a tree and was demanding he let her have her way with him? Only the cool air washing over his bare thighs warned him it wasn't a dream. But when she gathered the waistband of his boxers in her hands and lowered them, he didn't stop her. He'd always followed the rules. *Until Tee, sweet, wild Tee.*

Her hot hand cupped him intimately, and the back of his head slammed into the tree. Bark pattered onto his face. "Dear heaven, you're beautiful," he heard her say.

He was so hard, so sensitive, that he nearly exploded with those first, exploratory touches. She must have realized, because she circled her fingers around him, squeezing but not stroking. Just as he gained control, she took him fully into her mouth.

He sucked in a breath at the gentle scrape of her teeth, the circling of her tongue, and tried to keep his knees from buckling. When she began an erotic rhythmic suction, he wanted to explode. He groaned, trying not to make fists in her short silky hair. "Ah,

Tee," he managed to blurt out. "You're . . . incredible." *Indescribable*. He wanted to give this pleasure back to her—a thousand times over.

But she wasn't close to done with him. She paced her movements, building him slowly with a growing confidence he sensed hadn't been there at first. Her palms followed the contours of his stomach, her fingers splayed. Then her nails traced a light path down his bare thighs, sliding around to his behind. Gripping him firmly, she took him deeper inside her hot, wet mouth.

He bucked forward, his breath hissing. "Tee," he gasped. Then her tongue did something incredible and he exploded, his entire body shuddering in a release that was almost painful in its intensity.

When at last he opened his eyes again, it seemed the sun was higher in the sky, warming his neck and shoulders. All was silent but for the music of the wilderness: insects clicking, creatures chirping, the breeze swishing in the treetops.

He was still standing, at least. So was the tree. Then he realized that Tee's arms were wrapped around his waist, her warm head tucked under his chin. He hugged her close, circling his palm soothingly over her back. He still throbbed, pulses of pleasure arcing up through his stomach. But the surge of tenderness he felt for the woman in his arms was far more powerful.

"*Sweetheart*," he murmured.

She tipped her head up. "An Earth endearment?"

she asked, giving him a smile that made his chest tighten.

"Yeah. An Earth endearment." He tucked his thumb under her chin and kissed her gently, lovingly, and tasted himself on her lips. The intimacy of it threw him. Why had she come into his life at all if he couldn't be with her? This had to be some kind of cruel test. "What am I going to do about you?" he whispered.

She covered a fleeting pensive expression with a mischievous smile. "Perhaps the better question is: what are you going to do *to me?*"

He chuckled, zipping up his jeans. There was nothing wrong with a little foreplay, he reasoned, as long as there was no *after*play. Abruptly he spun her around and backed her into the tree. "Good question." With his forearm propped on the bark over her head, he leaned his weight against the trunk. His voice was low and thick. "I think you'll like the answer." Her stomach muscles contracted and her breaths quickened as he curved his hand between her thighs.

A distant rumbling interrupted the forest's serenity. Tee went rigid. "Someone's coming."

He tucked in his shirt. Tee snatched their binoculars from the Harley, and they bolted through the trees and shrubs toward the road. "Talk about lousy timing," he said with an apologetic smile.

"It's not as bad as it could have been." The know-

ing twinkle in her eyes brought him damned close
to blushing.

They hunkered down behind some shrubbery that
hid them from the road. The noise grew louder. A
flash of sunlight glinted off metal, and Randall's jeep
raced past with a whoosh of gasoline-scented wind.
It was headed toward the fortress.

The vehicle carried four passengers: the senator,
his two companions Ian had met in the bar, and
another man. Ian lifted his binoculars to his eyes.

The wind played with the stranger's hood, lifting
it just far enough to reveal his face . . . and the trademark coppery gold hair of a highborn *Vash Nadah*.

"This traffic is ridiculous," Lara said over her shoulder to Gann. "I'll take a shortcut." Grabbing hold
of the control yoke she banked the *Quillie* to the left
and careened across Grüma's heavily traveled space
lanes.

Gann uncrossed his legs and dropped his feet to
the floor. The navigation viewscreen grew cluttered
with symbols denoting other vessels. Then the ship's
proximity siren sounded, alerting them to oncoming
traffic.

Gann clenched his thigh muscles, bracing himself.
"Watch it!" he shouted.

Lara jerked the ship to the right, but not quickly
enough. A glowing fuselage whooshed past the front
viewscreen close enough for Gann to count every
porthole, whether he'd wanted to or not.

"Didn't you see that ship?" he demanded. Outside the *Quillie*'s viewscreen the stars glowed sweetly, as if they hadn't just witnessed his near-death.

"Of course," Lara shot back. "They saw us too."

"At that distance, we'd have been hard to miss. You cut that awfully close, Miss Sunshine."

Lara appeared startled by his use of the nickname he'd until now only used inside his head.

"I may have cut it close," she said in a somewhat more conciliatory tone. "But I don't cut corners. I knew what I was doing."

"Which was?"

"Getting us to Grüma—quickly. We've your *Vash* damsel-in-distress waiting there, no doubt wishing we'd arrived yesterday."

He sauntered over to her chair, leaned against her worktable, crossing his arms over his chest. "It's a rush for you, isn't it? The risk-taking."

She swallowed, re-establishing them in the space lanes. For a moment, she appeared as if she'd challenge him, but she relented. "It once was," she admitted. "Danger reminded me that I wasn't dead. Now"—she searched his face, a smile playing gently around her lips—"it seems your badgering does a far more effective job."

At first silence hovered between them, then Gann reached out and smoothed his hand over her tawny hair and then her cheek. She shuddered and shut her eyes. "I want to do more than badger you, Lara," he whispered. And he did. Never had he so wanted to make love to a woman.

Her eyelids twitched but remained closed. He brought his other hand to her face, framing her jaw, tipping up her chin as he bent toward her. Their breath mingled. Then she stretched upward and touched her lips to his.

He tasted her, moving his mouth over hers lightly, savoring the feel. It was the gentlest of kisses, an invitation. A promise, he hoped, of more, of better. "Sweet sunshine," he murmured.

He thought he heard her sigh as he pulled away, but he wasn't sure. Nonetheless, he gave her his most irresistible smile. "So, my badgering is effective, eh? You may regret revealing that little discovery."

She gave a small smile, then said, "For once I'd say the gamble is worth the risk." Then she turned her back to him and went to work getting them when they needed to go, one hand resting on the ketta cat's bony back.

There was a spring in his step as Gann returned to his seat. As soon as the Princess Tee'ah was safely onboard his ship, he planned to show Lara exactly what she'd just wagered, one exquisite, pleasure-filled step at a time.

Chapter Sixteen

Tee'ah's heart lurched. *Crat*. "That's Klark Vedla in Randall's jeep."

"So, it is," Ian said, his tone ominous.

The bliss left from her moments alone with Ian vanished as quickly as the dust settling in the jeep's wake. Her first impulse was to run in the opposite direction. But she shoved aside her self-indulgent, self-centered fear, as she'd failed to do on Barésh. Klark's interference in frontier politics could have disastrous consequences. Although living within the confines of its culture was impossible, she was proud of her *Vash Nadah* heritage and she didn't want to see all her people had accomplished ruined by bigotry and the Vedlas' ambition. Her status as a fugitive didn't allow her to expose the danger of Klark's interference to the Great Council; but, by the heavens, it didn't mean she couldn't help Ian do exactly that.

"It's as you said." Ian lowered his binoculars. "*Vash* are involved in Randall's campaign."

"But do you think he understands who Klark is?"

He considered her question. "Randall resents the Federation. I can't imagine him agreeing to a *Vash* using him so blatantly to keep me off the throne, just so they might install one of their own." Ian's expression turned dark. "Ché . . . I've met him. I liked him, too. I thought it was mutual." His frown deepened, making it obvious he felt betrayed.

A muscle in his jaw pulsed as he peered through the binoculars to where the road crested the ridge and descended to the ruins, a group of ancient sprawling buildings made of crumbling stone. Tiny now, the jeep was parked next to a sleek hovercar in front of the buildings where the men had disembarked.

"Let's go," Ian said.

"To the fortress?" She was instantly lightheaded. "Klark's there."

"He's a coward. He won't do anything in front of the senator." Ian touched his laser pistol. "I guarantee it."

It wasn't what he'd do that worried her, but what he might reveal about her. *Be brave. You carry the blood of the ancient warriors.* She mounted the Harley and tried not to contemplate the unpleasantness surely to come of the reunion with her ex-fiancé's brother.

They headed downhill toward the ruins. Klark emerged from Randall's starship. He stopped, looked up the road. To her horror, he dashed across the clearing to the hovercar and closed the hatch.

It glided onto the road.

Tee'ah pounded her fists against Ian's hips. "He's coming this way," she yelled.

Ian slowed the Harley and veered closer to the shoulder. So did the hovercar.

"Ian—watch out!"

The shriek of turbofan engines drowned out her scream. Sleek and gray, the hovercar bore down on them.

Ian threw his arms around her and shoved her off the Harley. They fell onto the grass, tumbling, arms and legs flying. Klark's car roared past. Whipped into a maelstrom, pebbles and thorny pine needles struck the exposed skin on her neck and wrists.

"You bastard!" Ian whipped out his pistol and took aim at the vehicle as it continued up the road. Then he swore, lowering the weapon. "With my luck he'd crash into a tree and kill himself," he told her. "Although right now I can't say I'd mind, I imagine the Great Council might." He pocketed his weapon and whipped out his comm. "*Sun Devil*, Ian here."

Muffin answered so quickly Tee'ah was certain the big man had been waiting for that very call, his thick finger hovering over the message button. "Acknowledged."

"Klark's headed your way in a hovercar—Expedition model, I believe. Metallic gray. Find him, detain him until I get back."

"You got it, Captain," Muffin said and went offline.

Ian pulled Tee'ah to her feet. "You okay?" he asked, squeezing her gloved hand.

From below, a hiss escaped the docked starship. "They're doing a preflight checklist," Tee'ah said urgently. "Your senator's getting ready to depart."

The late model hovercar glided along the docks. When it finally settled in front of an unmarked starspeeder, three members of the *Sun Devil*'s crew were waiting.

Muffin opened the door, reached inside and pulled Klark out. The toes of the *Vash*'s immaculate boots scrubbed over the pavement.

The startled prince fought back. He was tall, athletic, but no match for Muffin's bulk. The bodyguard marched him away from the car like a recalcitrant child.

"What do you want with me?" he demanded.

"You have an audience with the crown prince. I'm making sure you get there." There was more tussling.

Quin walked alongside. "You've caused us a lot of trouble, my lord."

"The crown prince is not happy," Gredda threw in. "I suppose you'll have some explaining to do."

Outrage tightened Klark's aristocratic features, and he reached inside his cloak. Gredda shoved the heel of her boot behind his knee. Klark stumbled forward and his dagger skittered over the pavement. Quin snatched it away, shocked. The mechanic started sputtering.

Klark regained his footing, but Muffin seized him from behind. "Frisk him, Gredda."

She gave Klark a slow smile. "My pleasure."

The prince fought in vain to free his arms from Quin and Muffin. Gasping, he sneered at her as she patted her hands over his body. "I hear you Valkarian women sodomize each other because your men won't touch you. Is that true, you cow?"

Gredda grabbed his groin and squeezed. "You tell me, Lord Vedla."

Grimacing, Klark wrenched free and struck out with his right fist. The men were back on him so fast that it took them a moment to realize what he was shouting as he tried theatrically to struggle away.

"Help! Please, help me! Pickpockets. *Thieves!*"

A crowd gathered. "Aw, bite my butt," Muffin said glumly. Two eager-to-help, armed trade police were pushing their way past the spectators.

Tee'ah and Ian strode to the senator's ship. Randall and his guard Lucarelli met them at the bottom of

the gangway. Recognition flared in the Earth senator's eyes. "Why, it's Stone," he said in English.
"From the karaoke bar. I apologize, but I won't have
time for that drink I promised you. I'm heading
home."

"Stone is an alias, sir. My real name is Ian Hamilton. I'm here on a mission critical to maintaining
galactic peace, on behalf of Romlijhian B'kah, ruler
of the *Vash Nadah* Trade Federation." He'd spoken
in Basic—for her, Tee'ah realized with a surge of
feeling that was disturbingly more than affection.
"We need to talk, senator. Now. Here or in private."

Randall ignored the overture to hold the conversation in Basic. "Run a digital ID," he ordered Lucarelli in English.

"I consent to a retinal scan, too," Ian told them.

Tee'ah reached into her thigh pocket for her
wafer-thin Basic-to-English translator, Muffin's gift
to her weeks ago.

Lucarelli disappeared inside the ship and returned
with a device that he held to Ian's right eye. The
man then aimed the device's infrared beam at his
gauntlet computer. No one spoke as the two pro-
cessors communicated. After thirty seconds or so,
Lucarelli glanced up. Astonishment tinged his voice.
"It's him, sir."

Randall's expression reflected both curiosity and
cynicism—and a good deal of mistrust. Nonetheless,
he extended his hand. "It's about time we met."

"I say so, too, senator." They shook warily.

Rumbling erupted from underneath the starship as mechanical components needed for its long space journey were bought online. Tee'ah was still so unsettled by the near miss with Klark's hovercar that she jumped back. Resting her hand on her pistol, she watched the road for Klark's return.

"Senator, hold off showing your footage of the fringe worlds to the president."

Randall lifted a silver brow. "Why?"

"Because if you don't, you'll open a rift between Earth and the Federation. Yes, we need to help Barésh and the worlds like it—immediately—but alone Earth doesn't have the technology to rebuild entire planets. You know that. We have to work together with the Federation. I'm in a once-in-a-lifetime— maybe a *once-in-history* position to be that mediator, to make Earth a vital and important member of the Federation. But if the situation at home worsens and Earth declares independence, the *Vash* will never agree to me becoming king, and you'll have lost the best chance, maybe the last chance, to play a positive role in the galaxy's future."

Randall took a couple of steps back from the small group, then he folded his arms over his chest and walked forward. Broken flagstones crackled under his shoes. "How do I know if you're not asking me to behave just so you won't lose the crown?"

A muscle jumped in Ian's jaw. "You don't. You also don't know that a *Vash Nadah* prince is using you as an instrument in a conspiracy to keep me from being confirmed as Rom B'kah's successor."

Randall exchanged bewildered glances with Lucarelli and the other man just joining them, Gruber, whom Tee'ah remembered from the bar.

"In fact, he did his best just now to run me down in his hovercar."

The senator gave him a funny look. "Do you mean Kip?"

"His name is Klark, Klark Vedla. He's a full-blooded *Vash* prince, the second-born son of the Vedlas, one of the eight royal *Vash Nadah* families."

"Son, you're mistaken. He's no more *Vash* than your companion is. They owe their appearances to mixed blood."

Tee'ah read her translator and grimaced. If Ian only knew . . .

"Kip's from a wealthy family," Randall insisted. "But he's an avenger of sorts. He does what he can to help the downtrodden peoples of the galaxy."

"The only thing he's avenging is Rom B'kah's choice in heirs," Ian argued. "He showed you the worst conditions in the galaxy not because he cares about its victims, but because he recognizes your sense of honor and your ability as a leader and he's using them to further his own interests."

"Which are?"

"Making sure his eldest brother succeeds Rom B'kah and not me." As Ian explained Randall's un-witting role in Klark's plan to destabilize the frontier, the senator listened first with irritation, then denial, and finally dismay. "If he succeeds," Ian said, "I won't be confirmed as Rom's heir, and Earth will lose out. You speak highly of the home team. I was born in Arizona, senator. If that's not the 'home team,' I don't know what is. Earth stands to benefit hugely if I take the throne."

Gruber, the commerce secretary spoke up. "Benefit? I don't see how. If you'd just once publicly offered assurance that Earth would gain influence with such a move up, maybe I'd feel differently. But you haven't been home—that I know of—in five years. *Five years.*"

"I have to agree with Mike," Randall said. "By all appearances, you're more like them than you are like us."

Ian let out a breath. "No, sir," he said firmly. He turned his eyes to Gruber. "I've made several trips home, low-key, private trips, to see family and friends. I didn't think to schedule public appearances or speaking engagements. All my energy was devoted to gaining the trust of the *Vash Nadah*. I assumed Earth's trust would be automatic. Now I know that was a serious mistake. I focused on wooing the *Vash* at the expense of my homeworld." Ian lifted his hands. "I stumbled badly, senator."

The three men appeared taken aback, as if they'd expected a different response, perhaps aggressive denial or an angry offensive.

"I immersed myself in the *Vash* culture out of re-

Susan Grant

spect and love for my stepfather," Ian acknowledged. "I didn't expect him to name me as his successor, and it's made for some intense years at the palace. Still, some members of the Great Council don't think an Earth guy can do the job. I think they're wrong."

Randall rubbed his chin. "I didn't know what kind of man you'd be," he said as if thinking aloud. "But I imagine you must be a fish out of water among all those *Vash*."

Ian responded with a self-deprecating smile. "Yeah. I'm sometimes out of my league. But I've always liked being the underdog."

"So have I," the senator said in a quiet voice.

Tee'ah didn't have to consult her translator to understand that the dynamics of the interaction had shifted. As the two men sized each other up, shivery bumps prickled her skin. Charlie Randall and Ian Hamilton held the power to change the course of history. And she, a once hidden-in-the-shadows princess, had been instrumental in bringing them together on this tiny, far-flung world, with the hope that they might solve their differences with words, not weapons. Her role as a royal *Vash* woman hadn't made a direct role in politics a possibility, but now that she was free, someday, somewhere like Earth, she could go after that dream.

"Work with me," Ian said. "Let's bring Earth the future it deserves."

Regret shadowed Randall's sharp features, and

that made Tee'ah's pulse race. "In my absence, the Earth-First movement has taken on a life of its own. They're protesting in all the major cities of the world. The United Nations is overwhelmed. They're considering a move to immediately rescind the decision to join the Federation."

"Can you keep the footage of those fringe worlds from them until I get there?"

"I . . . don't know."

Ian glanced at her, and Tee'ah caught the frustration in his eyes. "Sweet heaven," she whispered. He had to, or Klark would succeed in his efforts and Ian's entire mission would be for naught.

"Son, I sent what I recorded on ahead a few minutes before you showed up. At Kip's urging," Randall added with an uneasy expression. "For safe-keeping, in case something happened to my ship. It's in the president's hands now. I can ask him to wait until we arrive before he shows it to anyone else, maybe."

Ian swore. "Do it. I want to speak to him first."

"All right. Meet me in Washington. I'll arrange everything."

Randall gave him his contact information and instructions. "But don't delay. After meeting the president, go to the world leaders next. Whether or not you wanted the job, you're heir to an empire. It's time to act the part."

Ian extended his arm, and the two men clasped hands, first in the manner of Earth dwellers, then in the hearty, forearm-gripping fashion of the *Vash Nadah*.

"Muffin to Hamilton." A familiar deep voice blasted out of Tee'ah's trouser pocket. She grabbed her comm at the same time Ian snatched his.

Ian answered. "Go ahead."

"We have a problem, Captain," Muffin said. "I'm in jail."

The main office of Grüma's detention center was a small room filled with viewscreens and the smell of stale *tock*. An open door let in cold, fresh air, reminding Ian that Randall was about to launch, if he hadn't already.

He paced in front of a pursed-lipped police officer. "Let me see if I heard you right. My crew is charged with *disrupting the flow of trade?*" He'd expected something more colorful, like beating the crap out of an asshole.

The women touched her fingertip to the row of golden triangles she wore vertically down the bridge of her nose. It was a gesture he'd noted she fell back on when speaking to him. "Yes, that is the charge. The café owner and several witnesses said the hovercar and resulting disturbance blocked the entrance to his establishment. Thus the more serious charge of disrupting the flow of trade applies."

Ian worked to calm himself. "Why didn't you arrest the driver, too?"

Tee stared at her boots. He had no doubt her

mind was full of images of Klark in various forms of misery.

"Your crewmen were the aggressors, sir," the officer explained. "But, as I said, all charges will be dropped with your generous contribution to the local economy."

Meaning a sizable bribe. Furious, Ian handed over the credits necessary to secure the crew's release. Then he smiled tightly. "Now may I escort my crew from your facility?"

"I can arrange an appearance before the magistrate tomorrow," the police officer said, studying her viewscreen.

Tee blurted out, "Tomorrow?"

Ian flattened his hands on the desk and leaned toward the woman. "I thought the fine—"

"The contribution," the officer corrected, rubbing her nose.

"Yes, the contribution," Ian said with deadly calm. "It cleared their records of any charges. Or am I mistaken?"

"No, sir. That's correct. After the appearance they'll be released."

"Tomorrow."

"Yes. Tomorrow."

He pushed away from the desk. He didn't have until tomorrow. If the tapes got into the U.N.'s hands before he got there, Klark would succeed. Not for the first time, he almost told the officer who he was. He'd follow up with a few hints that things would go badly for her if she and her comrades didn't release his crew. But if he hoped to be the mediator for this region contemplating sovereignty, he couldn't afford word getting out that the galactic crown prince simply threatened local trade police who didn't do his bidding. No, he had to play by the rules, now more than ever, or he risked being thrown out of the game.

He conceded defeat with a charming smile. In response, the officer simply rubbed her skin jewelry faster.

"Let's go," he said to Tee.

Invisible barriers blocked the entrances to the cells. Muffin and Quin were in one, and Gredda in another. Ian stood with Tee in the area between.

"Greetings, Captain." Muffin rolled up his sleeves, revealing massive forearms. Though the air was cool, his skin gleamed. But his sheepish grin shattered the image of a merciless warrior. "We got in a bit of trouble."

"They tell me you were the aggressors." Ian's voice held a certain approval, despite their now compromised position.

"I might have been a little rough with him," the big man admitted readily, "but he deserves much more."

"Aggressors, bah." Quin's face contorted in the grumpy scowl he'd once reserved only for Tee. "Pretty boy got off lucky. Just a bruised chin and a good scare."

"Wish they'd have let me finish with him," Gredda said. "He wouldn't have been so pretty . . . in the end."

"All right, listen up," Ian snapped. "The good news is that the charges will be dropped. I made a generous contribution to the local economy."

Tee snorted. "A sizable bribe, he means."

"What's the bad news?" Muffin asked warily.

"They won't release you until you appear before the magistrate tomorrow morning. I guess we'll leave after that."

"No, Captain." Muffin stood so close to the invisible barrier that the air rippled like a layer of phosphorescent film. "Don't wait. Take Tee and go. The ship's mostly repaired. Randall's on his way home, and you have to go after him."

"I understand that. But it doesn't mean I'll desert my crew."

"With all due respect, sir, Gredda, Quin, and I have more time in space than you've been alive," Muffin said. "We'll be fine."

"Listen to him, Ian," Tee urged. "Push is on the *Sun Devil*. He'll stay here when we leave. He'll take care of the crew."

"He'd have to secure lodging," Ian said thoughtfully.

"You bet, Captain," Quin piped in. "For as many days as we need before we get transportation off-planet."

Ian massaged the back of his neck. He didn't like

295

being forced into making a decision before he could give it proper consideration. But what choice did he have? His homeworld was descending into chaos stirred up by a man who'd like to see him dead.

Tee came to rest on his arm. "Your crew will be fine, but if we wait another day Earth won't." Her gold eyes glinted strangely. "The needs of the many outweigh those of the few," she whispered.

He searched her ardent face, drawing strength from her certainty; her faith in him. *The needs of the many outweigh those of the few*—a passage from the Treatise of Trade, the holiest document of the *Vash* people and the foundation of their society. His mother and stepfather had drawn strength from that particular quote through some rough times. Sometimes Ian felt as if he lived and died by its close cousin: *The welfare of the group comes before the desires of an individual*. From both passages, he now drew the confidence to finish what he'd started.

Chapter Seventeen

By the time Push arrived at the jail, allowing Tee'ah and Ian to depart, the main road out of town was deserted. Where the sun had set, the sky was soaked with shades of purple, indigo, and streaks of pink. Tee'ah leaned forward, as if she could somehow make the Harley fly swifter than it already was toward the *Sun Devil*. And, ultimately, to Earth.

Lately it felt as if her life was speeding by faster than any motorcycle, sweeping her with dizzying speed from one adventure after another, an existence as volatile as her days at the palace had been predictable and dull.

As Ian brought the Harley to a stop, she pressed her cheek to his strong back and briefly closed her eyes. A poignant pleasure, she thought, for each heart-pounding minute brought her closer to the day that she and Ian would have to go their separate ways.

"Get her up and going as fast as you safely can," Ian said as they climbed off the bike.

"You got it, Captain." The words seemed so horribly formal after their intimacy hours earlier. She turned to the gangway, but he caught her arm.

"I just wanted to say . . . thanks for this morning."

Her cheeks warmed. She'd been so awkward, so unskilled. "You don't have to say that. I'm sure the palace courtesans are far better—"

"No, Tee." His mouth tightened, as if she'd insulted him. "They wouldn't even come close. No one does."

His esteem for her as an individual was an aphrodisiac like no other, and her sexual awareness of him skyrocketed. His intense gaze told her he felt the pull between them as strongly as she did. Smiling sadly, she touched her fingertip to the dark prickles of his beard, scratchy on his upper lip and cheeks. He looked so wild, so exotic. How could he truly be the rule-abiding prince she knew him to be?

But he was. And soon he'd return to the very life she'd fled.

She dropped her hand and left him standing at the bottom of the gangway. All through her preflight preparations, she remained focused on her tasks. But as the *Sun Devil* launched, thundering up and away from the forest, she couldn't help wondering what level fate destiny hid beyond the cloak of the night sky.

Onboard the *Sun Devil*, Ian closed the instrument panel on his desk, then stood and stretched. He joined Tee in the forward section of the cockpit, where she sat at her flight station, waiting until they cleared the space lanes before taking the ship to light speed. "I heard you talking," she said.

"I sent one-way encrypted messages to Rom B'kah and my evil twin, Ilana. Now they'll know I'm coming to Earth."

She raised a brow. "Evil twin?"

"Yeah. Black and white. Yin and yang."

"Am I going to have to fetch the translator?" she asked dryly.

He laughed. "No. I call Ilana my evil twin, and she calls me Goody-two-shoes. Which isn't fair, of course," he added quickly. "But we have different outlooks."

"How?"

"I like to think things through. She rushes into action headfirst. She also doesn't care much for rules, and she has no discipline." He chuckled. "She'd make a terrible *Vash*. And that's fine by her."

Tee was listening intently. "I believe I would like this woman," she said slowly.

The lights flickered and went out. The emergency lights came on but the thrust levers flew back, all on their own. The sudden deceleration threw Ian to the floor, but by some miracle he floated away from what would have been a bone-crushing encounter with the flight console.

"Gravity generator failure," called the flight system computer.

"No kidding," he muttered.

Tee worked at putting the thrust levers back where they belonged. "For the love of heaven, Ian! Are you all right?"

"Yes." He floated like a kite above the empty chair. "Just relocated."

He tugged himself into his chair, buckled in, and inventoried his body parts. What ached from ricocheting off the floor didn't appear to be broken. Amazingly, his pulse had barely jumped. It meant he was getting used to the almost surreal, 007-like quality of his new existence. Though he couldn't decide if that was a good thing or bad. "What the hell happened?"

"I show multiple systems failures." Her green-brown, red-gold hair floated around her face. "*Crat!* Systems are dropping off-line faster than the ship can put them back on. And now the computer's not giving me the backups."

"Do it manually!"

"I am!"

The lights went out, and the auxiliary lights kicked on, dim and tinted amber.

"ELECTRICAL FAILURE, UPPER DECK," droned the computer's voice.

His stomach dropped with a wave of nausea, and he felt suddenly heavy in his seat. He swallowed convulsively, cold sweat prickling his forehead.

"I got the gravity generator back on-line," Tee shouted.

There was a jolt and the ship went silent. It took him a few seconds to realize that the ever-present sound of the air-recyclers was gone.

"PRIMARY LIFE-SUPPORT SYSTEM FAILURE. BACKUP SYSTEM UNAVAILABLE," the computer reported.

"There goes our air." Ian unstrapped. "We're out of here."

Tee slammed her hands onto her desk. "Great Mother, I don't show any pressure change on the status instruments. It's got to be a computer malfunction."

"We don't know that," he shouted back.

A klaxon blared. "ABANDON SHIP. ABANDON SHIP."

"Abandon ship?" Tee gaped at him. "How are we going to do that?"

"The external maintenance pod will do," he said as the thought occurred to him. It was a chamber of about three hundred square feet, little more than a launching point for space walks when needed for outside repairs. "We can detach it, then drift away from the ship."

"HULL BREACH DETECTED. FIVE MINUTES UNTIL STRUCTURAL FAILURE."

301

"Let's go!" He unbuckled her harness even as she battled to throw more failing systems on-line. Dying he could handle, if he had to, but he couldn't wrap his mind around the possibility of losing Tee. "Computer!" he commanded. "Transmit mayday message: 'Situation desperate, need immediate assistance.'"

Tee smacked her open hand on a red disc on the comm panel, activating a distress signal. Then she had the presence of mind to dislodge a portable emergency beacon to bring with them to the pod, to guide a rescuer to their location in case they drifted too far from the *Sun Devil*.

No doubt about it: the pixie was clearheaded in a crisis.

They stumbled out of the cockpit. Pushing her ahead of him along the gangway, he scrambled after her and they sprinted down the corridor.

"Something's affected the ship's warning software," she speculated, gasping as they ran. "It's disabled the alerts that were supposed to tell us something was wrong. Now the computer *thinks* we have massive failures."

"THREE MINUTES UNTIL STRUCTURAL FAILURE. ABANDON SHIP. ABANDON SHIP."

"Or," she shouted above the klaxon, "we really *do* have massive failures and we're about to depressurize."

He swore. "Now's not the time to turn pessimistic."

Ahead was the hatch to the external pod. It looked like a golf ball with a white padded interior. He shoved her inside and pushed the heavy hatch closed, but it jammed a finger's width from sealing.

"SIXTY SECONDS UNTIL STRUCTURAL FAILURE."

He cursed viciously past his clenched teeth. If he couldn't get the hatch closed and the ship in fact depressurized, they'd lose all the air in the pod, with little time to grasp the thought before their lungs exploded and their blood boiled.

"FIFTEEN SECONDS UNTIL STRUC-TURAL FAILURE."

"Kick the door shut!" he shouted. They rolled on their backs, pounding their boots against the jammed hatch. *Close, damn it, close.*

"STRUCTURAL FAILURE. ABANDON SHIP."

Tee made a strangled scream and rammed the bottoms of her feet on the door. "No!"

"ABANDON SHIP. ABANDON SHIP."

The hatch sealed shut with an ear-popping hiss, and the life-support system inside the pod took over. The air was dry and stale-smelling. Ian sucked in huge, lung-filling gulps. "By your right arm—the manual release—*pull it!*"

Tee yanked the release handle.

His heart pounded like a sledgehammer.

The pod detached with a jolt and floated free, bobbing in space like a fishing lure in a rippling pond.

"This thing has propulsion jets. Somewhere." His fingers searched an unfamiliar control panel. The manufacturer had familiarized him with the pod's operation once, on the starship's maiden voyage. "There." He activated the nozzles and used a tiny joystick to back away from the *Sun Devil*—even at full speed, maybe too slowly to save them, should the ship blow.

Tee must have read his thoughts. "At least this way we have a chance," she insisted. "On the ship we'd have none."

They braced themselves for the explosion, huddled together, eyes shielded. But all that thundered around them was their labored breathing.

The *Sun Devil* held together.

"Well," he said. "It looks like we're still in the game."

She huffed. "You'd better believe we are. We're going to get back in that ship and start her up. I'll have you on Earth before Randall's engines grow cold."

He didn't know whether to shout a war cry or kiss her senseless. "Let's do it."

They fell away from each other and went to work. Ian fired the steering jets rearward, stopping their backward movement. Holding the joystick, he tapped the steering jets, expelling just enough force to start the pod moving toward the ship. Tee crouched by the porthole to offer additional visual guidance. It was a fair distance to the ship, and there was no guarantee they'd make it; the little pod wasn't designed to fly long through open space.

"We're not getting any closer," Tee observed, frowning.

He gave the jets more fuel. But the *Sun Devil* maintained its position relative to the pod.

"We need more," she said.

"Fuel's almost gone."

"Already?"

"We traveled a good distance, though it doesn't look like it."

She stared outside, her expression grim. "The *Sun Devil* is drifting away from us at a greater velocity than this pod can manage."

If they didn't catch up with the ship, they'd be stranded in the pod that, unlike the *Sun Devil*, held a very finite volume of air. "How much time do we have if we're stuck in here?"

Tee held her palmtop with trembling hands that revealed the truth about her outwardly cool and calm demeanor. "Approximately five standard galactic hours."

Five hours. The clock was ticking.

He gave the jets another spurt of propellant.

"Low fuel," cautioned the onboard computer in a soft, feminine voice.

"We're gaining on her now," Tee said excitedly.

Ian manipulated the joystick. "I played a lot of Nintendo as a kid." he said. He sent more propellant into the jets. *Come on, come on.*

Adjacent to his joystick, a red light blinked in warning. "Jesus, not yet."

The jets drained the last of the fuel. Ian threw up his hands. "That's it," he said.

"Fuel depleted," agreed the pod's computer. Though it did no good, the voice sounded ever so sorry.

On Grüma, Lara emerged from a café wearing an expression of triumph. Her delicate silver jewelry sparkled in the moonlight. "They tell me the princess' crew is staying at that inn"—she beckoned with her chin—"across the street."

"That's odd." Gann walked alongside her. "Why aren't they on their ship?"

Her breath misting in the chill predawn stillness, she said, "Well, according to that man in the café, these folks just got out of jail. They were released only an hour or so ago. Perhaps their ship is impounded, like mine."

He gave her a small smile. "By the looks of it, yours will soon be back in your hands."

Once they reached it, Gann banged his fist on the door to a guest room within which the man in charge of the crew supposedly slumbered. He hoped, for Tee'ah's parents' sake, that the gentleman in question wasn't at that moment sharing his bed with the princess. *Vash* royal women were expected to be virgins when they married. But then, *Vash* royal women were expected to stay home, too.

He knocked again. Sounds rustled from inside the

door. Then a deep and very irritated voice called out, "Coming."

Armed and ready for trouble, Lara stood a few paces behind him, her collar turned up to ward off the chill. There were a few more thumps. "You Grümans don't let up, do you?" the man grumbled from inside. "This had better be good." The door slid open.

For a heartbeat Gann lost his vision in the bright light spilling out from the room. Then a shadow loomed in the doorway. Gann blinked, squinting at the giant towering above him. "Great Mother, Muffin! What in the blazes are *you* doing here?"

In the pod, Tee sat back on her haunches, her expression one of utter disbelief. "We're out of fuel?"

"We even used up the fumes." *Think*. There had to be another way out.

"I don't believe this," she said. "The ship is right there"—she slammed her open hand on the porthole—"full of air. And we're here."

Four hours and forty-one minutes. The air-remaining readout was extrapolated out to the ten-thousandth place. The speed-blurred descending digits were a taunt, a challenge. *What are you going to do now?* He dug through boxes, storage lockers, lifted the padded flooring and peered underneath. There was a solution hidden, somewhere. There had to be. The thought of passively waiting for rescue revolted him on the most basic level.

Tee's hand rolled into a fist. "It's the computer. It did this to us." Her knuckles turned white, and she let out what sounded suspiciously like a growl. "I swear to you, Ian, if I ever get my hands on the manufacturer, I'll wring his neck." She gave a wan, crooked smile. "Pilot, negotiator, cook . . . murderer—look at all I'll have on my resume after this stint. Oh, and marksman. We mustn't forget about that."

Her attempt at humor coupled with her obvious apprehension drove a stake through his heart. He thought of her jump-in-feet-first enthusiasm, her desire to make the most of each moment. The likelihood now loomed that her life would be stolen from her, too soon and unfairly.

"I shouldn't have dragged you into this mess," he said. "I'm sorry I ever offered you a job that day on Donavan's Blunder."

"No, you aren't." She crawled to where he sat and placed one hand on his raised knee. "And neither am I. No regrets—do you hear me, Earth dweller?" Her chest rose and fell, and her eyes grew strangely bright. "These past few weeks have been the most glorious time of my life."

Her confession drove home the sacrifice he'd made when he'd put aside his personal wishes for the good of the *Vash* Empire. He wanted Tee as his wife, though reason told him a future with her was as frustratingly out of reach as the ship floating outside the porthole. In a quiet voice, he admitted, "I feel the same."

She sighed, and he pulled her close. For long moments they stayed like that, cheek to cheek, breathing in unison. Succor and sexual arousal mingled as naturally as scent and smoke from burning incense.

Four hours and twenty-seven minutes.

"Hold me tight," she whispered. Their arms came around each other, their legs tangling. As the contours of their bodies fitted together, their lips met in a kiss—soft, warm, and loving. She clung to him as he buried his face in her hair and, before he had the chance to analyze all the reasons he shouldn't, he murmured, "I love you."

She threw her head back, bewilderment, fear, and joy filling her wide golden eyes. The mental and emotional affinity he'd felt with her since the day they met surged, combining in a powerful physical attraction.

In wonder, she touched her fingertips to his mouth. "I know we can't be together, but—"

"Don't give up on us so easily." He wanted her, damn the consequences.

The welfare of all outweighs the desires of an individual. Hastily he summoned the *Vash* teaching that was supposed to remind him of his duty and make him feel better about falling in love with the wrong woman.

It didn't.

Softly, she said, "We might die."

"We're not going to die," he ground out. He shot another glance around the pod, looking for an answer, anything to fix this mess. "We'll find something. We always do."

"But if we don't . . ." Her hands smoothed over his thighs. His muscles bunched under her palms. Ian, "I don't want to die not knowing what it was like to . . . make love with you."

He grabbed her fingers and squeezed. She winced, and he relieved the pressure. "I see. We make love, because we don't have to worry about consequences. Nothing matters anymore, right? But it does, Tee. It does to me. Yes, we might die. But I'd never do it for that reason alone. I've wanted you forever. I've wanted this consummation, too."

Tears filled her eyes, the first he'd seen in the entire time they'd been together.

He brought his forehead to hers. Their damp skin heated, their breath mingled. "It's been almost five years."

He felt her tense with surprise. "Without love-making? Are there no palace courtesans on Sienna?"

"I chose not to visit them. Sexual intimacy means nothing to me without emotional commitment."

She searched his face. Then, so matter-of-factly, she unearthed the doubt that underlay every relationship he'd ever had. "Because of your father? Because you fear that having many women will prove you and he are alike?"

His gut knotted up. "I've thought of that once or twice."

"You *aren't* him," she said with conviction. "And you never will be. Your heart is far too big, and your willingness to sacrifice is far too great. That is exactly why Rom B'kah chose you to succeed him as king; he saw in you a man of principle and devotion if not ancestry and experience."

Ian simply said, "I hope so."

"You aren't your father," Tee repeated. "You have extraordinary self-discipline." Their lips were almost touching. "Not just in your abstinence, but in all things, everyday. Except, perhaps, when riding your Harley," she murmured against his mouth.

"I found something I like much better than the Harley." He rubbed his thumb over the swell of her breast, and she arched against him. "You," he whispered in her ear.

Her moan of pleasure, his pent-up longing, and the uncertainty of the next few hours blew apart the last of his resistance. He opened the front of her flightsuit, freed her full, soft breasts. He'd already lost his battle to keep his distance, now he lost himself in her.

Four hours and two minutes.

Sensation drowned him: the heat of her skin, her scent, her taste. He returned to her mouth, kissing her hot and hard. He cupped her buttocks, lifting and holding her as he slowly rolled his hips against

Susan Grant

her. If it weren't for the fabric of their clothes, he'd be inside her.

Her hands fluttered over his back, then came to rest uncertainly on his shoulders. It was more than the awkwardness he'd felt in their first few kisses; she seemed indecisive, almost scared, a turnaround from their previous encounters.

He pulled away. "What is it, sweet pixie?"

She blushed. "I wasn't going to say anything. . . ."

He kissed the tip of her nose. "To say what?"

"Okay, the truth." She cleared her throat, then spoke in a rush. "I'm *Vash*. I couldn't abide by the restrictions placed on women. I left my homeworld for a new life, my *own* life."

He smiled, pleased by the information. "I thought you looked a little too pure to have mixed blood."

She regarded him, plainly self-conscious. "Maybe so. But I'm rather certain you didn't know you're about to make love to a virgin."

Chapter Eighteen

Once Gann and Lara talked to Muffin, it hadn't taken them long to figure out that Ian was the Earth dweller who'd hired Tee'ah. In possession of Ian's jump coordinates, the crew members were eager to reunite with their captain.

The crew had been waiting for passage on a ship to Earth, but when Gann showed up, their problem was solved. They'd rushed to his ship.

By the time he, Muffin, and the rest of Ian's crew climbed the gangway into the *Quillie*, Gann was ready for a hot shower and a few hours in the bunk. But, rest wouldn't come until he'd caught up with Ian.

In the cockpit, Lara waited in her pilot's chair. Propping her elbow on the flight table, she rested her jaw on her thumb and forefinger and examined the motley group filing in. When she spied Gredda, her mild disdain changed to respectful curiosity. "You're Valkarian," she said.

The muscular woman answered with a friendly nod. "And you?"

Lara's eyes flicked to Gann, then back to Gredda. "I don't claim any world as home." She turned back to her flight panel. After a moment's hesitation she added, "But I was born on Barésh."

Gann smiled gently at the back of her head. *That took a lot, Sunshine*, he thought. Admitting to a birthplace, the memories of which caused her pain, told him that she was making an effort to come to terms with her past.

As Muffin lumbered to an empty seat between the thin young man called Push, and Quin, their stocky, grim-faced mechanic, the launch clearance came through.

"We're off," Lara said triumphantly.

Once clear of the space lanes, she loaded the jump coordinates Muffin had given her into the computer. Her lips pursed as her fingers skimmed over the icons on her navigation display. "Odd. When I enter the coordinates, the location comes up as not applicable."

Quin groaned. "They haven't made the jump yet. We've had maintenance problems since day one. If I had to guess, I'd say that thruster we told you about balked at light speed." He exchanged glances with Muffin. "Delayed again. The captain's not going to be a happy man."

"What do you think, Lara?" Gann asked. "With their coordinates, we can find them; correct?"

She gave a smug laugh. "At sublightspeed they're practically lying in our path." She pushed the thrust levers forward. "Get ready to meet me, Princess."

Push's eyes took on a faraway look. "I still can't believe it. Tee. A princess."

"Tee'ah," Gredda corrected.

Quin snorted. "No wonder she couldn't hold her liquor. Remember that time—"

"*Stop!*" Gann held up his hands. "I don't want to know more"—than he already did, that was. What he'd heard so far of Tee'ah Dar's escapades would age her parents several decades. Fortunately his worries were over. The virtuous young princess was safely in the crown prince's capable hands.

"You're a virgin?" Ian blurted. "But you have a birth-blocker patch on."

"I . . . thought I'd plan ahead." Tee'ah hoped he'd still want to make love with her now that he'd learned she knew nothing about the act of sexual consummation—other than what she'd read and heard . . . and dreamed.

He absorbed what she'd told him. When he spoke, his voice was gentler. "Look where we are." He swept his hand over her hair. "For your first time, is this what you want?"

315

Am I who you want? he asked with his eyes.

Her heart swelled. "When the man is special, I imagine most women would agree that the setting doesn't matter."

"A *Vash Nadah* woman's first time is a holy, religious act," he said.

"Yes," she said on a breath. If she thought she'd left that notion behind with her old life, she was wrong. She craved the customs and rituals she was raised to associate with this milestone in her life. It didn't matter that Ian hadn't the required incense and scented oils at his disposal, or perhaps even *Vash* training in the sexual arts. It mattered only that he *knew*. And now he did.

Three hours and thirty-one minutes.

She sighed and pulled him down on top of her. He settled his strong body against hers, supporting his weight on his elbows and knees as he bowed his head to brush a kiss over her lips. Where their thighs were tangled, she felt him, hard and thick. Fully aroused. But his manner reflected the extent of his control.

He gazed down at her, his eyes radiating a heart-stopping combination of heat and affection. Then, with reverence worthy of the moment, he recited the formal verses used, and more appropriate for, a *Vash Nadah* couple's wedding night. " 'In this we begin our life. In this we form a blessed bond not to be broken. In this *inajh d'anah*, two shall become one. . . .' "

Tingles cascaded down her spine. "Thank you.

For saying the words." *Inajh d'anah*: flesh of my flesh.

"I wasn't sure I'd remember them—I've had to do a lifetime of memorizing in a very short time." He smiled. "That passage didn't mean much before." He touched his finger to her lips. "Now it does."

His gaze was so steeped in sexuality it made her toes curl. She took his fingertip into her mouth and suckled gently. His eyes darkened and a soft groan escaped his locked jaw. Abruptly, he rose to his knees, crossed his arms, and pulled his T-shirt over his head. She hadn't seen a man as masculine and sexy in all her life. His well-toned stomach muscles flexed, and the thin gold chain he always wore lay against a chest lightly but evenly coated with dark brown hair. Fascinating. *Vash* males had little body hair, and certainly none on their chests. Her fingers twitched, aching to touch him there . . . everywhere.

He tossed the rest of his clothes onto the floor and bent over her. The necklace dangled, tickling her jaw. He whispered in her ear as he undressed her, his breath as fiery as his intimate compliments and erotic promises.

When she was bared to him, he told her how beautiful she was, how much he desired her. With wide, callused palms, he explored the most sensitive places on her body, refusing to take her, he said, until he'd "made her crazy." That's when she felt the nubs of his beard prick her inner thighs.

Sweet heaven. She inhaled a long, shuddering

317

breath. Having pleasured herself from time to time over the years, she was no stranger to the intimate areas of her body. But nothing she'd felt before came close to the carnal delight of Ian's tongue and fingers.

He took his time with her, learning what pleased her as *she* learned what pleased her. When the desire for completion swamped all else, she grabbed his wrist. "Please, Ian."

But he wouldn't succumb to her pleading.

His tongue flicked; his fingers circled. Her body tensed, tightened. "Ian . . ." She moaned, her hands fisting in his wavy hair.

"Sweetheart," he said in a thick voice. "Come for me . . ." His fingers slipped deep inside her. Her hips jerked, and she heard herself cry out. "That's it," he coaxed. "Now let yourself go."

He touched her once more and she climaxed, pushing hard against his hand. Squeezing her inner muscles, she prolonged the throbbing pleasure, as Ian rubbed his other hand, fingers splayed, over her lower belly.

Before she had the chance to float down from her peak, he covered her with his body. The heat of his bare skin astonished her. "Tee," he said with a harsh breath. "I'll go as slow as I can. Tell me if I hurt you."

Her heart sped up, this time from nerves instead of passion. The start of his penetration stretched her. Instinctively she raised her thighs to hasten his slow and careful entrance. There was a sharp twinge. She sucked in a breath and held it until the stinging faded.

Fully inside her, Ian cradled her face in his palms. *"You okay, baby?"*

She didn't understand the Earth words, but the meaning was clear. "Yes. It's done," she whispered.

One corner of his mouth lifted. "Oh, it's not done, pixie. It's just starting."

He cupped her bottom, lifting her. She closed her eyes as his hips began a slow, undulating motion, sending thick, aching pleasure radiating outward. She didn't know whether to sigh, groan, or laugh with the joy.

He rocked slowly, deeply. "Move with me," he whispered in her ear. She lifted her hips, and his breath caught. "Yes, like that." After a bit, they found their rhythm. She locked her legs behind him, clutching his shoulders: rigid muscles beneath smooth skin. He encouraged her, guided her, breathed beautiful and erotic words that described how it felt making love to her. They swayed together, their skin glistening with sweat, their scents mingling. Gradually, she lost her apprehension, her self-consciousness, and gave in to pure sensation.

But Ian's pleasure had built far more swiftly. She sensed he was close to the edge, and he would not be able to take her with him. It didn't matter. That she could bring him such pleasure did.

Her hands covered his buttocks and urged him

toward his release. His neck corded, his breaths came faster, harsher. Still he struggled, she knew, not to thrust too hard and hurt her in the face of her newly lost innocence.

With this act, she might have forever lost the chance to go home, but the choice had allowed her to give herself to the one man who held her heart. "I love you, Earth dweller," she said, a fervent whisper in his ear.

He expelled an explosive breath, threw back his head, and found release deep inside her body. His peak was unbridled and prolonged. Closing her eyes, wrapping her arms around his heaving body, Tee'ah took his essence into her soul.

Two had become one.

"There they are, Gann." Lara poked her finger at her viewscreen.

Gann came up behind her. "Where?"

"Right where we thought they'd be. The *Sun Devil*. At the threshold of the jump they never made."

Gann folded his arms over his chest. "Contact them on the comm."

"*Sun Devil*, this is the *Quillie*."

Silence met the request.

Lara upped the signal strength. "Try again."

"*Sun Devil*, this is the *Quillie*; how do you read?" Unease prickled the back of his neck. The ship was there; he could "see" it on the viewscreen. Why wasn't Ian answering?

"How long until we reach them?" he asked Lara.

She checked the computer. "A standard hour, max. I'll try reaching them again in a few minutes." A jaunty little melody slipped from her lips.

He leaned over her shoulder. "Are you actually humming?"

She gave him a winning smile. "I'll soon have my ship back. And my life, too."

Roused by Lara's uncharacteristic cheer, the ketta-cat unfurled its thin body and stood, stretching up on its toes, its tail quivering. It yawned broadly, then touched the tip of its nose to Lara's.

"It's been a long time since we served together on the *Quillie*."

Gann turned to find Muffin towering over him, years of memories in his gaze. "Yes. This reminds me of the old times . . . the good times."

"They were good," the big man acknowledged. He frowned, stroking his chin with his thick fingers. "I don't know if she'll want to go with you. She wants her freedom."

Gann beckoned him out of Lara's earshot, surprised by his friend's perceptiveness. "I know," he said under his breath. "All she talks about is her ship, what it looks like, how it flies." He rolled his eyes. "It's not easy competing with a hunk of trillidium. It's impounded, you know. That ship of hers. As soon as I have the princess, she'll be paid—money she'll use to reclaim her ship. As soon as that happens, I have the feeling she's out of my life for good.

321

Though sometimes I don't think that would be a bad idea. . . ." He sighed. "You always had a way with the ladies, Muff. What should I do?"

The bodyguard appeared bemused. "I meant Tee'ah, the princess."

"Ah." Gann tried to appear casual. Then it hit him what Muffin had said. "Why wouldn't the princess come with us? Surely she's had her fill of frontier life by now."

"Not Tee. She's thrived out here. That is, when she wasn't drinking," the big man joked.

Gann's hand shot up. "Don't want to know about it."

Muffin said in a quieter tone, "Ian doesn't know who Tee is, though he did suspect she was *Vash* and was hiding it. And the looks they've been giving each other lately . . ." He cracked a smile. "Makes me wonder what's developed between them."

"We don't want that. She's not yet promised to the Vedla heir, but she will be when we get her home." Gann rubbed his chin. "Ian's not been matched yet, though, has he?"

Muffin shook his shaggy head. "I hope it happens soon, his promise ceremony. The last thing the lad needs is scandal. And that's what will happen if he steals Tee'ah away."

"I trust Ian will do what is right. He always has."

Muffin shrugged. Then his attention shifted to Lara. "You want my opinion with her? Ask for flying lessons."

"I know how to fly."

Muffin rolled his eyes. "Ask for a refresher course—on her rig. How and why do you think I learned to fly all those years ago, a skill I haven't used since?" The bodyguard's face creased into a smile. "Trust me, my friend; it was a venture well worth the trouble."

Chuckling, a rich and deep sound, Muffin left Gann standing there, pondering the possibilities.

Thirty-three minutes.

On the pod, the temperature climbed as the air quality spiraled slowly downward. Curled on her side on the padded floor, Tee woke from a fitful doze.

Ian stroked her tousled bangs off her forehead. "Hey, pixie."

She pressed her hands together, palm to palm, and wedged them under her cheek. "Anyone call while I was out?"

He tightened his jaw and shifted his gaze outside. "No." But nonetheless they waited, fully dressed, for some rescue he now doubted would get to them in time.

She sat up. He rubbed her back. "Sore?"

"A little." She smiled shyly. "But it was well worth it."

Ian drew her snugly against his chest and touched his lips to her hair. "Come back with me," he said. "To Sienna."

Susan Grant

She gave a mournful laugh. "Can you imagine the uproar that would cause?"

"We'll make it work," he said firmly, though there was too little time remaining to figure out how.

She sighed. "When I told you I was *Vash Nadah*, I didn't tell you everything. But now . . . I don't want any secrets between us."

He stroked her damp, close-cropped hair. "After the past few hours, I can't imagine we have any secrets left."

"Well, there's one. A rather big one."

He moved her back.

She tipped her chin up. "You know your cousin Tee'ah?"

While he tried and failed to picture the woman, she said, "Well, I'm her. Princess Tee'ah, daughter of the Dars."

"You're . . . Tee'ah?" He prayed it was a bad joke brought on by their impending asphyxiation.

"Yes. That's how I knew who Klark was. That's how I eventually figured out who you were." Quieter, she said, "That's why everything you're trying to accomplish in the frontier means so much to me."

Speechless, he stared into her pale gold eyes, the eyes of a *Vash Nadah* princess, a princess he'd just deflowered out of wedlock, going against every law the *Vash* had in place. He felt lightheaded, and not from lack of air. "The way I treated you . . . The places I took you—"

"Overprotection was why I left home. With you

324

I found everything I'd always dreamed of."

And hadn't he, too?

Twenty-eight minutes.

He glanced at the air-remaining readout and grimaced. Strangely, he wasn't afraid of dying; just incredibly pissed. But if he was going to go out, he was going to do it right. He took hold of Tee's hands. "This a little after the fact, but considering the circumstances, I ask that you bear with me." He brought her knuckles to his lips. " 'My love, I give you my heart, my allegiance, my promise of fidelity and protection . . .' "

"The promise ceremony," she whispered.

"Yes," he said, and finished reciting the passages that dated back to the birth of the Treatise of Trade.

Tee's chest rose and fell, faster now. She squeezed his hands, her expression a heart-wrenching blend of grief and joy. " 'My love, I take your promise. In return, I give you my heart, my devotion, my promise of—' "

His personal comm crackled. It used a discreet frequency, known only by his crew, but someone, or something, had just tried to reach him on it.

For a few shocked seconds he and Tee'ah stared at each other. Momentum had carried them toward death and desperate, last-minute pledges. Now rescue had arrived. Unexpectedly. Dazed, they had to shift gears.

Tee stumbled to her feet. "Look! Ships! Two— no three of them."

Ian cupped his hands around his eyes and peered into the blackness of space. The *Sun Devil* had long dwindled into a speck of light. But the dark form of another starship coasted past at close range. Two more hovered beyond, maneuvering around the pod.

The stuffy air and warm temperature dulled his senses, but the likelihood of rescue dragged him to full alertness. Ian brought his comm to his mouth. "Mayday, mayday. Survivors in pod. Mayday, mayday. Twenty minutes of air remaining. I repeat: twenty minutes of air."

Muffin's voice blared loud and clear. "Captain, we've got you in sight. I copy the minutes left. We'll have you onboard in five. Standby for emergency tow."

Their pod was equipped with minimal communication equipment, making it impossible to hear all the transmissions between the ship Muffin was on and the other two, but after a few moments the other pair of would-be rescuers wheeled around and accelerated away.

Muffin's ship closed on their pod, using valuable minutes to decelerate sufficiently to allow the delicate task of pod retrieval to take place.

Ian asked, "Is the rest of the crew with you?"

Muffin replied, "They're on the *Sun Devil*."

"The *Sun Devil*? The computer's gone crazy."

"We know. When we got there, the computer claimed the ship no longer existed. Quin, Gredda, and Push boarded in life support suits."

Quin's voice chimed in. "You ever hear of nano-machines, Captain?"

"Microscopic computers?"

"Someone got them in our computer. Early in the mission, I'd say."

"Klark?" Tee speculated.

"Likely. High-tech terrorism at its worst. He turned our computer into an unwitting traitor. Any one of the spare parts we bought could have carried the invaders. Over time, and unknown to us, a battle's been going inside the ship's computer between the ship's backup and warning system, and the rudimentary artificial intelligence sent in to destroy it. It's an easy fix, though. Now that the *Quillie*'s computer pointed out the little saboteurs."

Ian exchanged glances with Tee. "That explains all the problems we've been having," she said.

He nodded grimly. Klark's malevolence proved his willingness to kill. How he'd bring Klark to justice would take some thought, though. Ian was still, in many ways, an outsider. Rushing to the Great Council with the accusation that one of their princes had tried to assassinate him would be as ill thought out as slalom skiing on his Harley.

On the side of the rescue ship, clamshell doors opened to a maw revealing an empty cargo bay.

"Prepare to be swallowed whole," Tee said.

He laid his arm over her shoulders. "I am." In more ways than he ever imagined.

A claw-arm extended from the bay, reminding Ian

of a tongue. With a thunk, it grabbed hold of the pod, tossing he and Tee to the padded floor. Then it slowly, deliberately drew them inside the ship.

As soon as the gigantic outer door closed behind them, Muffin's voice blasted through the comm. "The bay's pressurized."

Ian cracked the hatch open. Cold, dry air rushed inside. He and Tee filled their lungs with it. Sitting together on the floor, they felt the ship accelerate.

After a short flight a vibration rumbled through the vessel, indicating a docking maneuver was underway.

"The ship we're on is docked with the *Sun Devil*," Muffin said finally. "I'll come down to get you. Wait until you see who brought me here."

Muffin escorted Ian and Tee'ah out of the cargo bay. Ian climbed the gangway leading to the main deck of the rescuing ship. Tee'ah grabbed hold of the first rung, but Muffin stopped her with a firm hand on her shoulder. His voice was urgent and low. "Gann is here. He's come to bring you home."

"What?" she asked. Her stomach plummeted. *Home?* It looked as if her family had finally caught up to her. Only this time there was no place to run. "Gann . . . who?"

"Gann Truelénne, Rom B'kah's loyal warrior." The big man appeared apologetic. "And my good friend."

Her hands tightened on the rung. Gann. She tried to picture him and couldn't, but the name was familiar. Her parents must have contacted Rom for help and he'd chosen Gann for the mission.

"I thank you for telling me. I wouldn't have wanted to be caught unawares."

"I know," the big man said with surprising empathy. "I figured all along that if you'd wanted to go home, you'd have told us who you were."

"You knew who I was? All along?"

He grinned. "It's been seven years, but I never forget a face."

"Why didn't you say anything? Why didn't you tell Ian?"

"It was never my destiny to change yours," he replied cryptically. *Go*, he said with his eyes, *and don't let on to a soul what I just told you.*

At the top of the gangway a tall, handsome *Vash* gentleman embraced Ian. They pounded each other on the back and appeared genuinely excited by the reunion.

"Ah. The pampered one returns," said a woman standing behind them. Her eyes were so jaded and cool that Tee'ah didn't give her the pleasure of a reaction. The lovely dangling silver earrings of the same length as her hair suggested delicacy, but the woman appeared as hard as any ship's trillidium hull.

Ian stepped away from Gann. "Don't tell me you just happened to be in the area."

Gann laughed. "We've been tracking you for

329

weeks, only I had no idea it was your trail we were on. Rom sent me." He shifted his eyes to Tee'ah. If her odd-colored shorn hair shocked him, he did an excellent job of hiding it. His eyes reflected curiosity, but his smile was cordial, revealing his respect of the social distance between them and little of the true man behind it. The palace dwellers had smiled at her like that all her life. She'd thought she'd escaped it. "My mission," he said, "was to find your cousin, Princess Tee'ah. Welcome to the *Quillie*, honored lady."

"Thank you." She avoided meeting Ian's eyes.

As a group, they moved into the cockpit. Quin was there, wiping his hands on a rag. "Princess." He made a fist over his barrel chest and bowed.

She sighed through her nose. Never had she thought she'd long for the mechanic's overbearing know-it-all manner.

A chime sounded, indicating an incoming priority message. "Lara, would you get that?" Gann asked the woman with the cold eyes. Interesting, but when she looked at Gann her gaze thawed.

Lara took the call as everyone milled about, exchanging stories of what had happened in the last hellish days. Almost sheepish, Tee'ah and Ian stood next to each other. They'd just tied their hearts to each other in what they'd thought was the hour of their death. Now they'd have to endure the awkwardness of knowing they'd made promises they'd never be able to keep.

"It sounds like we'll be able to continue our mission without much delay," she told him lightly. "At least this time we'll have the whole crew with us."

Ian looked appalled. "You're a *Vash Nadah* princess."

"So it seems," she agreed dryly.

He lowered his voice to a private tone. "You've been sheltered all your life. You can't work on the *Sun Devil* anymore."

"So. I'm fired?"

"You'll get yourself killed."

"Please, Ian. As if working for you wasn't dangerous this morning, or in all the weeks before—" She stopped herself, trying desperately to forgive his lack of logic; he was as rattled as she was.

"You don't belong in the frontier." He spread his hands. "You're *a princess*."

"So, where do good little princesses go, hmm? Home?"

He grabbed her arm and pulled her close to whisper in her ear. Blast it; his warm breath still gave her tingles. "But you can't go home in this . . . condition."

"You mean independent? Free? *Happy?* Yes, you're quite right."

"I gave my promise to you. I intend to follow through. We'll . . . work out the details. After Earth."

She had no doubt that the by-the-books, do-right crown prince would fulfill any promise he'd made

Susan Grant

out of principle and his driving sense of accountability. But the last thing she'd let herself do was to become another one of Ian's "obligations."

"No," she said sharply under her breath. "I'll not ruin your chances for the throne. You need a marriage chosen by your stepfather. And you have to convince Earth to stay in the Federation. Those are the only ways you'll end the Great Council's doubts about you once and for all."

"A promise is a promise."

"It wasn't binding, Ian."

Either relief or hurt crossed his face. She wasn't sure. But both were equally painful to contemplate. She yanked her arm free, cringing inside. "I want my freedom," she whispered fervently. Marrying her was the honorable choice, and Ian was an honorable man. She'd expected nothing less from him. Only she hadn't expected that her own refusal would hurt so much. Or his rightfully choosing duty over her.

"The message is for the princess," Lara announced. "It's her father." Tee'ah's stomach muscles cramped. The cold-eyed woman pointed to a console at the far end of the cockpit. "If you wish, you can use that chair for privacy."

Tee'ah's throat was so tight, she could hardly breathe, much less talk. "I would," she managed to squeeze out. "Thank you."

Alone at the comm station she opened a viewscreen. "Greetings, Father."

Joren Dar's golden eyes reflected both sharp relief

and angry disapproval. Tee'ah fought a watery feeling in the pit of her stomach.

"Daughter . . ." It seemed her appearance had momentarily stolen his ability to speak. The last time he'd seen her, her hair was coppery dark blond and reached past her hips.

He recovered quickly, unfortunately. "The crew of the *Quillie* will accompany you home."

She squeezed her clasped hands together until blood throbbed in her fingertips. "I can't come home."

His expression sharpened. "I've . . . changed," she said and glanced away. She felt an echoing twinge in the part of her anatomy in question.

He slammed his hand down. "Who was it? Who were you with? Ian Hamilton? I thought he was a man of honor! If he thinks this is the way to become the—"

Hastily, she lowered the volume on the viewscreen. "He *is* a man of honor." More than anyone imagined.

"You were with him for weeks without chaperones."

"I was with a number of his crewmembers."

He sputtered in shock.

"Not in that way, father," she put in before he choked to death.

He exhaled. "I am relieved to hear it."

Clearly, he thought she meant that she hadn't been with Ian in "that way," either. She didn't cor-

rect him. More than any other prince, Ian needed
an unsullied reputation. He'd admit to sleeping with
her if he thought it would protect her, but she
wouldn't give him that chance. She loved him; she
would not ruin him.

"Everything's at stake, Tee'ah. I have no choice
but to publicly state that you've undergone the test
of purity."

The blood drained from her head. The rite was
an ancient, rarely used determination of virginity.
Appalled, she stared at her father. If she refused to
go through with the test, it would cast doubt on Ian.

"I won't actually have you checked," her father
assured her. "That would be too barbaric. But we
must go through the motions to appease the Great
Council. And the Vedlas."

"Yes, father." Sweet heaven. The Vedla family
knew. What would stop Ché—or Klark—from demanding that their physicians perform the actual ex-
amination?

She touched trembling fingers to the viewscreen.

"Your mother and I miss you," he said finally.

Her throat constricted. "Me, too."

Then the viewscreen went blank. Her mind raced
through all the choices spread before her. They
were fewer now, but crucial all: Return home for
the test and save everyone from scandal? But, in doing so, she'd risk having to take the test itself and
have the news of her impure state announced
through the *Vash* Empire. Could she avoid it alto-

gether by accepting Ian's promise of marriage? Unfortunately, both of those choices required that she return to the life she'd fled. What she needed was a safe haven away from everyone who had her "best interests" at heart. Earth came to mind, but she'd be so easy to find there.

Exhaustion, both mental and physical, overtook her. Unsteadily, she stood. Ian was waiting as the rest of the two crews pretended to go about their duties. No one had missed their first impassioned, whispered argument, and they were no doubt expecting another.

Ian searched her face, and his own fell. "He wants you to go home," he said.

"Yes."

"Are you?"

"I think it's best right now."

"But it's not what you want."

"Life's that way, it seems," she said crisply.

"Wait there for me. Wait until I'm finished on Earth. We'll put our heads together and figure something out. The way we always do."

"No. I have my duty. And you, sir, have yours."

Her soul wrenched with the look of disbelief that crossed his face. She took a step backward, as if putting distance between them physically would help her do so emotionally.

"You're right," he said after a moment, coldly. "I do."

Her chest was so tight that it hurt. She hurried

335

off before she did something irreparable, like throw herself into his arms.

In the main area of the cockpit she addressed the cold-eyed woman named Lara. "Would you please show me where I might bathe?"

The woman nodded curtly and led her into the corridor. Part of her expected Ian to come after her, to fight for her, to rail at her, refusing to listen to her reasoning why they couldn't be together. But he didn't. Nor did she look back.

It was done.

Chapter Nineteen

"You sure don't look like a princess." Seemingly unaware of the skinny ketta-cat sleeping in her lap, Lara slouched in a chair in her quarters on the *Quillie* as she waited for Tee'ah to finish dressing.

Tee'ah didn't bristle at Lara's brusque, derisive manner. In fact, she preferred it to the careful courtesy and sympathy now displayed by the rest of the crew. She put on a fresh flightsuit and took a quick peek at her reflection in the mirror as she combed her wet hair off her forehead. In the overhead illumination, red-gold roots glinted. The person she once was, she thought, trying to push free. "To be honest, I don't *feel* much like a princess anymore."

"The men trying to save you don't seem to mind."

Tee'ah made a face. "I've never asked anyone to coddle me. But everyone does." She thought of Ian. "As soon as they find out I'm a princess."

"So many heroes willing to help. They'll have you back in your sumptuous palace before you know it. All your beautiful gowns will be waiting, cleaned and pressed."

Tee'ah shuddered at an image of the bedchamber. "My gilded cage. No, thank you."

"I will never understand how people who have luxuries don't appreciate them."

Tee'ah gave her left sleeve a too-sharp yank. "That's because people like you only see what I had, not what I didn't."

"Poor princess. What didn't you have?"

"Freedom." Her voice thickened with bitterness. "All the personal decisions you take for granted were made for me. Everything; relentlessly, every day, since the day I was born and likely before that. I was told how to style my hair, how to walk, how to talk. When my parents found out I was learning to fly— my only true act of rebellion in twenty-three standard years—they forbid me to continue. Even the selection of the man I was to marry was out of my hands." She sighed. "Have you any idea what it's like to have no say in any aspect of your life?"

Clearly taken aback, Lara stared at her and said nothing.

"I don't care how many glittering gowns hang in my closet, I'm not going back to that life. I'm going to Earth, actually." *Her safe haven.* "They have a non-extradition policy for all races, human and *Vash*."

Lara gave her a funny look. "How do you know?"

"I looked it up a short while ago. I wanted to make sure it wouldn't cause any political fallout when I ask for asylum and my family demands my return."

"You're really serious about this."

She gazed out the viewscreen at a panorama of deep, cold, space. "It's not only for me. I can aid Ian in his efforts. I *want* to. I believe in his cause."

And if she had to see Ian from time to time in so doing, so be it, she thought desolately. They were both adults. In time, the hurt feelings and awkwardness between them would pass.

She turned to Lara. "I'll become involved in politics on Earth. The more people learn about the *Vash*, those of us who are progressive and who care about the frontier, the less uneasy they'll be about staying part of the Federation. I'll study the languages, so I can become a bridge of sorts between their politicians and ours." She tapped her chin. "I'll stay with Ian's twin sister, Ilana, if she'll have me. Ian told me quite clearly that she doesn't care for rules." Tee'ah hoped that meant propriety wasn't important to her, either, and that she wouldn't mind harboring a soiled, odd-looking, runaway princess. "It will be a start, at least, until I'm settled enough to move on." Her skin tingled. "Earth is my destiny, Lara. I truly believe that."

Frozen in place, Lara looked like she'd swallowed an oster egg.

Tee'ah wondered if she'd done the right thing by trusting this woman with her plans. "What is it?"

"Blast it all to hell. Those damned *Vash*." The pilot glanced up sharply. "No offense, but I thought I was helping retrieve a spoiled, impetuous royal— Not forcing a woman back to a life she doesn't want." A look of profound pain constricted Lara's features, as if she were fighting a tremendous inner battle. "No," she said. "I won't do it. I won't steal your choices . . . the way mine were stolen, long ago."

Tee'ah placed a comforting hand on her shoulder. "You understand?"

Lara's lips thinned. "Too well." She thought for a moment. "If I offered you a way to get to Earth, would you take it?"

Tee'ah's heart sped up. "Yes. Yes, I would."

Lara stood, spilling the ketta-cat out of her lap. "Let's go, princess." She took her by the arm and dragged her into the corridor. "I'm flying you to Earth. But if you want half a chance at succeeding, we'll have to do it before the men get back."

Ian strode through the *Sun Devil* in one last inspection of the repaired spacecraft. Gann followed, his hands clasped behind his back. Muffin brought up the rear, while Quin wrapped up last-minute details in the cockpit and Gredda and Push secured the air-depleted maintenance pod in the cargo bay.

Ian forcibly dragged his mind away from what had

happened in it. He'd chosen galactic peace over his own personal desires. It was the responsible thing to do, so why did he feel like such a jerk? *You slept with her. And then you let her go.* Part of him wished she had been willing to fight harder to keep what they had. But she hadn't, and she was right.

The good of the many outweighs the needs of the few.

The passage that had always guided his actions now left a bitter taste in his mouth. But it would get him through the next few days.

It had to.

"Captain!" Quin caught up to them. "There's a call for you. It's the king."

"Ah, good." He'd been trying to contact his stepfather all day, but Rom hadn't replied. Unusual for him not to do so, but then the man had his other responsibilities.

Ian took the call in the cockpit. Rom's face was already framed in the main communications viewscreen. "Ah, Ian." A small scar on his stepfather's upper lip stretched thin. "Greetings."

Something was off, but Ian couldn't tell what it was. He nodded uneasily. "Greetings, my lord. I need to bring you up to date on what's happened."

"I imagine you do." Rom pressed his splayed fingertips together. "You changed the encryption codes on your comm. I couldn't reach you."

Something was *definitely* off. "I intended to brief you fully, as I will now. But at the time, I didn't want to risk broadcasting the details of my mission

Susan Grant

before I had the chance to determine Senator Randall's intentions."

Rom's voice rose. "Your mission is over."

"My lord?"

"I can't have you complicating the matter more so than it is already. My senior trade minister tells me the situation on Earth is near collapse."

"Help's on the way. I'm meeting with Randall and the president of the United States two days after I arrive. I forwarded you the information on the fringe worlds. Randall's ready to work with me on all counts. I believe I'm in a unique position to bring both sides together."

"No," Rom said bluntly. "The problem needs to be addressed in the Great Council first. We will debate the issues, agree on a course of action and proceed."

Ian didn't know how to respond. Rom was telling him one thing, but his gut was telling him another. Calling off the mission now smacked of recklessness and arrogance, not the prudence the Federation was renowned for. "Rom. By the time the Great Council makes a decision, it'll be too late—"

"I have too many fires to put out, Ian. I don't need you lighting any more. The frontier is more in danger of splitting apart than ever before. And on the home front, I have the Dars on one side, demanding to know what their daughter was doing on your ship, and on the other, the Vedlas are in an uproar, and understandably so."

342

Ian almost brought up Klark and his accusations against the prince. But he sensed that now wasn't the time. Instead he cleared his throat and said, "About the princess . . ."

"Joren says you stole her away."

"No, sir. She has higher principles than that. Higher than her father or anyone else, it seems, is willing to acknowledge."

"Higher than her own obligations, it appears."

"She didn't want to marry Ché. The family tried to force her—and they still might. It's barbaric. I thought we wanted to lose the outdated traditions." In your private life *you* don't observe them, he wanted to argue. But he was already walking the fine line between honesty and disrespect, and so he pulled back. "If they try to force her again, we need to step in."

The muscles in Rom's jaw flexed, as if he was clenching his teeth. "I'm willing to discuss any aspect of your relationship with her, *except* you continuing it."

"Well, she was a damned good starpilot and an indispensable member of my crew. She'll be missed."

"Just make sure she gets home." Rom regarded him stonily. "I will see you at the palace." The viewscreen went blank.

Ian gripped his armrests. He felt like a ship ripped from its mooring line in a class-five hurricane. In all his dealings with the *Vash Nadah*, the Great Council, the other royals, one thing he'd always had, and had learned to count on, was Rom's encouragement and support. With the extensive information he'd compiled and had now sent on to Rom, he couldn't fathom his stepfather ordering him to come home. Not now, not when he was so close. But obviously Rom thought he'd screwed up. Worse, the king had summoned him to Sienna to keep him from mucking up anything else.

Wearily, Ian stood. Muffin and Gann were staring at him in shock. He jerked his hands in the air. "What?"

Muffin shook his head. "You've really done it now, Captain."

"I'll say." Gann scratched his fingers through his hair. "In thirty years working with the man, I've never seen him that angry."

Muffin let out a half-nervous, half glad-it-wasn't-me chuckle.

Ian glared at them. "Nothing like a supportive crew in times of trial." He rubbed his hands over his face and walked to the gangway. "We're aborting the mission. Prepare to depart for Sienna," he said bitterly. As he hoisted himself to the first rung, a vibration rumbled through the *Sun Devil*, then a jolt followed by ominous silence.

Gann, Muffin, and Ian exchanged disbelieving glances. "They wouldn't," Ian said.

Gann swore under his breath. "Normally, I'd agree with you. With *her* I'm not so sure."

They bolted up the gangway and down the corridor to the portal where the *Quillie* had been docked. What had been an open passageway leading to Gann's ship was now a closed airlock. In front of the hatch the ketta-cat sat, lonely and forlorn, mewing its heart out.

Damn it all to hell. The women had taken the *Quillie* and left.

"Grab their jump coordinates," Ian ordered from where he paced in front of the huge, curved forward viewscreen in the cockpit.

"They didn't transmit any."

And why would they? They didn't want to be followed, obviously. Ian placed his hands behind his back and scowled. "Then input our coordinates for Sienna." When he arrived at the palace, he was going to have to explain a lot more than his handling of the frontier, now that it looked like Tee had taken her freedom.

Good for you, *pixie*, part of him thought. She'd fought for what she wanted, and hadn't given up until she'd got what she was after. Unlike him, trudging home to the barn like an obedient cow.

"Coordinates for Sienna are in," Gann said. "I'm ready when you are."

Ian lifted his hand to give the order. But he hesitated.

The crew watched him curiously.

If he returned to Sienna, it would underscore

Randall's original doubts about him, that he put the needs of the Federation over his homeworld. Then the footage of Barésh would make it to the United Nations, who were spring-loaded to sever ties to the *Vash*. And they had every right, if this is the way the *Vash Nadah* dealt with the frontier, treating its peoples' concerns like nuisance administrative issues that could be discussed at their leisure. They were wrong in this. Rom was wrong. And if the frontier split from the Federation, the galaxy would lurch toward years of unrest that would end in another devastating war.

The way out of that future rested on his shoulders.

His hand became a fist. "Your orders have changed. Cancel the coordinates for Sienna and set a course for Earth."

"Sir?" Gann exchanged glances with Muffin.

"I'm not calling off the mission. Set a course for Earth, Mr. Truelénne."

"The king asked us to return."

"He didn't ask us," Ian informed him. "He ordered us. And I'm countermanding that order. I may be new at this game, but I know what's right. Turning tail and running is wrong. I'm the only one who can resolve the situation on Earth. And I intend to—with or without *Vash* backing. You can't follow the rules all the time."

The crew considered him with a strange mix of

shock and curiosity, as if they'd opened a box and found something they hadn't expected.

"Are you with me?" he asked them.

Gredda raised her hand. "I am."

"Count me in," Muffin said. "And us," Quin and Push chimed in.

For Gann, though, the decision appeared to be a struggle. He'd followed Rom to hell and back, and his loyalty had never wavered.

"You can leave once we get to Earth," Ian told him. "I understand."

Gann glanced up. "No, Ian; you have my support in this mission. I believe you can bring both sides together. It's Rom I can't understand." His lips thinned. "Just as he might not understand when I explain that I did this for him." He spread his hands on the desk in front of him. "I await your order, Captain."

Ian lowered his fist in one sweeping motion. "Take us to Earth. Maximum speed."

At the outer reaches of the solar system, the *Sun Devil* dropped out of hyperspace and raced toward Earth. Ian stood at the helm and gazed at his planet's sun, at this distance still tiny and cold. *It is time*, he thought determinedly. Time to prove his theory that Earth would stay in the Federation if they were given a tangible reason to do so, and if they felt they could play an important role within an established civilization so vast that it boggled the mind. Once in Washington, his greatest challenge would be presenting the image of capable leadership, despite his lack of *Vash* support. He had to come across as a levelheaded crusader, a man willing to stand up for the rights of his people. And he had to do this without antagonizing the Federation. Then, he hoped, he could begin the long process of bridging his two worlds without sacrificing the needs of either.

The way you sacrificed Tee.

He winced. He'd let her turn him down. He'd watched her walk out of his life. He'd made a mistake.

"I've got the *Quillie*!" Gann shouted.

Ian spun around. "Where?"

"Twelve o'clock, and no more than a standard hour ahead."

"They must have flown straight here. And at breakneck speed, too." The discovery told him two things: Tee knew exactly where she wanted to go. And she didn't want to be followed.

Ian strode to where Gann sat: the pilot chair that had once been Tee's. "Contact them," he ordered. A triangular symbol on Gann's instrument panel represented the *Quillie*.

"*Quillie*, this is the *Sun Devil*." Gann had to repeat the call several times before the women answered.

"*Quillie* here. Go ahead." At Lara's voice the ketta-cat let out an indescribable sound that was half gurgle, half howl, and ran to the speaker. It circled in frustration, trying to get at the voice inside.

"I know how you feel, cat," Gann grumbled.

Ian demanded, "Tee, what the hell are you doing?"

"This is Lara. Tee'ah asked me to speak in her place. She's commandeered the *Quillie*. That's all I'm allowed to say ... and that we're both fine. Don't forget to feed Cat, Gann. *Quillie*, out."

"Wait!" Ian shouted. But the channel was already closed. "We're both at sub-light speed. Download their route. I want to know where they're going."

"They're headed for ... *Loss Ahn-gelleez*," Gann said, reading his viewscreen.

"Los Angeles?" His first thought was of Ilana. Tee had been intrigued by his description of his sister. He bet she was headed to L.A. thinking she'd found a kindred spirit. He was afraid she was right.

He scrutinized the triangular symbol denoting Tee's ship. It was comprised of colors and numbers, two-dimensional, the opposite of the real woman, who was warm and loving, unpredictable and stubborn, the only person who'd ever made him feel like he was living life, not watching it happen all around him. *Grab happiness when it dangles in front of you*, his mother often told him. *You don't always get a second chance*. His neck tingled, and he closed his eyes, letting his mother's voice guide him.

"With all due respect, Ian," Gann interrupted quietly from beside him. "A chance at happiness missed is an opportunity perhaps never repeated."

Ian's eyes jolted open. Rom had once said Gann's

349

senses were turned to an almost impossible level, but he hadn't said anything about the man being a mind reader. "Were you referring to yourself?" Ian asked as he turned around. "Or me?"

Gann looked every inch the travel-weary space captain with too many solitary nights logged in. "Both."

Ian studied him. Gann mourned the chances he'd never taken, regretting all he'd missed.

What if they stopped missing chances? he thought suddenly. Then there wouldn't be any reason for regret, would there? Thoughtfully, Ian rubbed his chin. "I don't have to be in Washington until the day after tomorrow. There's a little time to play with."

Gann's mouth quirked. "I await your orders," he said as he moved and his finger hovered over the destination icon for Los Angeles.

Ian turned to the crew. "Anyone opposed to a little detour?"

"No, sir," they chorused heartily.

Ian's blood surged. He'd fix the problem on Earth, but first he'd fix the mistake he'd made with Tee. He was going to win her back.

Moments later, they were on their way to Los Angeles. Ahead, the *Quillie* breezed past Interstellar customs with a thumbs-up from the infant agency Earth System Patrol and Customs, known as ES-PAC. But when the *Sun Devil* arrived at the checkpoint, the patrol ships denied them entry.

Gann swore. "I don't believe this. Two women in a stolen ship breeze past ESPAC with a wink and a kiss, and *we* get pulled over?"

"Bad luck again," Quin grumbled.

"No," Ian said firmly. Everything he'd once taken for granted was up in the air, putting everything he cared about at risk. "From here on out, we're making our own luck."

An ESPAC customs agent transmitted first in English and then in Basic. "Decelerate and prepare for boarding."

"Yes, ma'am," Ian replied with a dangerous smile. The official had no idea what she was in for. This time he was pulling rank.

Chapter Twenty

With newly bought eye-shaders hiding their eyes, Tee'ah and Lara hurried through what the Earth dwellers called Los Angeles International Airport. The landing fee was exorbitant, explaining why there were no other merchant-class starships in residence, but Lara had paid the bill with funds borrowed from Gann's supply of credits. "He owes me more than that," she said matter-of-factly. "I was hired to find you and bring you home. The way I see it, I'm doing what I was paid."

Tee'ah squeezed her arm. Lara gave her a small grin then glanced away. No matter how hard she tried, Tee'ah doubted she'd ever be able to fully express how much this woman's help meant to her. This no-nonsense pilot from Barésh had aided her at the risk of losing her reputation and her starship, a craft Tee'ah sensed was the center of Lara's fierce independence. "I pray this doesn't keep you from retrieving your ship."

Lara's mouth turned down. "Princess, some risks are worth the trouble and some aren't. Let's leave it at that."

A man thrust a piece of paper into Lara's hands and walked away, speaking in English as he passed papers to others. "What does it say?" Lara asked. She handed the sheet to Tee'ah who input the runes into her hand-held translator.

"Earth First," she read. "Boycott *Vash*-made goods." Uneasily, she glanced around the airport. Posters in store windows proclaimed, "Earth First." Some were racist in nature, portraying highborn *Vash* with exaggerated characteristics—amber-gold hair and skin, high cheekbones, long straight noses, and pale gold eyes. Some had whips in their hands, subjugating an unwilling human population.

Anti-Federation sentiment had taken hold. For Ian's sake, Tee'ah hoped that it hadn't yet rooted too deep. Nonetheless, as a precaution, they didn't pause to look around, as much as Tee'ah would have liked.

They approached a bank of comm boxes with viewscreens, from one of which Tee planned to contact Ilana. Reading English phonetically presented in Basic runes displayed on her translator, she chose one and told it, "Connect me to Ilana Hamilton." Nothing happened. She tried again, but the screen remained blank. Sighing, she sidestepped to the next comm box.

A man using the comm device next to them leaned over. "These new picture phones are confusing if you've never used one before." He had black hair and almost black eyes, and his smile was brilliant against his smooth brown skin. They stared at him, enthralled.

Preening slightly, he asked, "Just in from overseas?"

Lara followed Tee'ah's lead and nodded eagerly.

"Welcome to the country, ladies." He pointed to the device he held pressed to his ear. Then, with his thumb and forefinger, he gestured to the receptacle where they were to insert the Earth credits they'd bought upon arriving. "First insert your cash card. Then lift the receiver."

Tee'ah nodded and smiled, then did as the man indicated. This time her transmission went through. She clutched her translator and waited.

"What listing, please?" asked a female voice.

Tee'ah replied haltingly. The business of waiting for the translation, and then reading it was awkward. "Ilana Hamilton."

"I have an I. Hamilton in Santa Monica."

Tee'ah waited. Lara whispered, "I think she wants you to answer her."

"What do I say?"

"I don't know! Say . . . yes."

"Yes." Tee'ah pinched the bridge of her nose. Exhaustion had set in, making her head throb and her eyes hurt. How long had it been since she'd last had more than a few hours' sleep? She'd lost count of the days. All she wanted was a soft bed, a full night's rest, and—

"Hello?"

A young woman appeared onscreen, her hands over her head as she pulled an untamed mane of hair through a circlet of the same light blue as her eyes. The roots of her hair were almost as dark as Ian's, but the rest of the strands were infused with many lighter shades, from dark blond to nearly silver. *Clay-roll*, Tee'ah thought with an approving smile. "Ilana," she said.

The woman dropped her hands, and her plume of hair flipped jauntily around her shoulders. "Yes? Who is it?"

Using the translator, Tee'ah recited, "I am Tee'ah Dar. Your cousin-by-marriage." She took off her eye-shaders to prove her assertion. "I am in the Los Angeles . . . International . . . Airport."

Ilana's mouth fell open, and she leaned forward. "Omigosh. Tee'ah. What are you doing here? Wait. It's late. Do you have a place to stay? Can I come get you?"

Upon reading the words, Tee'ah let the sweet warmth of relief fill her. "Yes," she whispered. "Yes to all."

*   *   *

The chaos Tee'ah was beginning to see characterized Ilana's house resumed at dawn the next morning when Ilana poked her head into the small bedchamber Tee'ah had shared with Lara. "Time to get up, girls," she said in heavily accented Basic. "We're leaving in an hour."

After being tracked down on every planet she'd visited, Tee'ah didn't have high hopes of escaping notice on Earth. "I must disguise myself."

"I'll take care of that," Ilana assured her, her arms full of clothes and hats. "I have to work, but I'm taking you both with me. There's a major shoot on-location downtown—movie-making, Earth entertainment—and I'm filming the filming. Confusing, I know, but it's Hunter Holt's first film out of rehab." She flashed an apologetic look at Tee'ah's translator and enunciated: "A famous actor consumed too many mind-bending substances. I'm shooting a documentary about his road to recovery."

She blew her messy hair off her forehead. "I want you to come. You'll safe with me . . . though maybe not with a few of my more Neanderthal planetmates." She glanced at Tee'ah's translator. "Did that thing translate Neanderthal? I'm all for freedom of expression, for presenting opposing points of view, but these Earth-Firsters are ignorant, and in their ignorance they could easily screw up all my stepfather's good work."

Ilana sighed as she draped the dresses over a bedside chair. "But that's politics, and I try to leave that up to the rest of my family."

She left them to their hasty preparations.

After using the shower, Tee'ah and Lara dressed in their borrowed clothes, straw hats and gauzy dresses decorated with Earth blossoms, loose-fitting enough to accommodate their varying shapes.

While Lara fastened her boots, Tee'ah stepped onto the veranda to view the ocean. Ilana's residence was on the second floor of a building separated from the beach by a busy road for ground cars. Until last night, she'd never personally seen an ocean that wasn't computer generated. The reality was staggeringly beautiful. In the early morning light, the sea was as smooth and deeply hued as a bolt of blue-gray Nandan silk.

The dress Ilana lent her was flimsy and low cut— likely by her own prim standards, though, and not by Ilana's or any other Earthwoman's. She raised her arms above her head and let the wind brush across the indecent garment, but the breeze was a poor substitute for Ian's caresses. The mere thought of his skillful hands and hot mouth on her body brought her pulse throbbing to life between her thighs.

But he had his duty, and she had her dreams. Those things would forever keep them apart.

"You're thinking about him again."

Tee'ah whirled around. Lara stood in the doorway, watching her with ancient eyes. "It hurts," she admitted to the pilot. "It will for some time, I think."

"I wouldn't know."

"Haven't you ever been in love?"

Lara glanced away. A muscle in her jaw jumped. "No," she said softly. "Never."

"I'm no expert," Tee'ah quickly told her. "There was only Ian, and no one else. But I know in my heart that someday the right man will treasure you and respect you. You are beautiful and precious, inside and out. Any man who does not see that does not deserve you."

Lara compressed her lips and stared at the sea. "That's what he told me . . . this man. He sees in me what I don't. Or didn't." Her face took on a look of innocence, or perhaps wonder, then the look was gone just as fast. She cracked a smile. "Perhaps *he* deserves me, yes?"

Tee'ah smiled back. "Find him and see."

Thoughtful, Lara considered. "Perhaps . . ."

Together they walked inside, where Ilana met them. "Tee'ah," Ian's sister said. "We have to talk." The Earth girl took her aside, leaving Lara to eat the morning meal with Linda Hurst, a perky, middle-aged red-haired "film-assistant" who had accompanied Ilana to the airport the evening before.

Ilana's comm device—ringing constantly, it seemed—trilled again. She glanced at the incoming call and switched it off. "My latest ex," she explained. At Tee'ah's obvious bafflement, she tried again in careful Basic.

"A man-friend whom I no longer wish to see."

Awed, Tee'ah gazed at her. "You have many lovers then?"

At first, Ilana appeared startled. Then she laughed. "Always. And I make it a point to leave while the bed's still warm."

Tee'ah sensed pain behind that cheerful declaration. She wondered if Ilana's parade of lovers was a consequence of her father's infidelity, just as Ian's celibacy was.

Ilana's sky-blue eyes searched Tee'ah's face. "Now make sure you use that translator of yours. I'm going to speak in English because my Basic stinks and I have some things to say." When Tee'ah had complied, she said, "You're in love with my brother."

Tee'ah's pulse pounded in her throat. "Ian . . . is a man-friend I no longer wish to see."

"Ha!"

"I'll ruin his reputation."

"Promise?"

Tee'ah sighed. "Even if that did not matter, I can't return to that life."

"I understand. But Ian would never make you live in the traditional way. My mother doesn't."

"Rom B'kah is a hero, Ilana. He can live as he likes. Ian is being scrutinized—and challenged. It would be unfair to make him choose between me and what the *Vash Nadah* consider proper behavior. I won't do it. I won't jeopardize his bid for the throne."

"If Ian succeeds on Earth, he'll be a hero, too. Now that I've met you, I have even more reason to hope he does. Frankly, I think you're exactly what my geek of a brother needs. Okay, so he's a hunky geek. And a very honorable geek, too. Much, much better behaved than me, let me tell you. But then he's older than me by four minutes." Ilana laughed. "I'm getting ahead of myself here. Rewind."

Tee'ah's head spun from the string of untranslatable words.

"You've turned his perfectly ordered existence upside-down. This is good. The last thing I want to do is tell you how to run your life, but I'd love to see you unbutton his stuffy shirt and show him how to live."

A shiver ran down Tee'ah's spine. "Ian showed *me* how to live."

Ilana's gaze warmed with affection. "Then I hope you two come to your senses." She used a hand mirror to apply black liquid to her long lashes. "Anyway, Ian knows you're here."

Tee'ah almost dropped the translator.

"Probably from Rom, who got my secured comm message that you were safe. He really wants to talk to you."

"Ian? He called? Here?"

"Three times."

"What did he sound like?" Tee'ah blurted without intending to.

Ilana grinned. "Angry. Desperate." Her tone softened a fraction. "Sorry."

"Did you speak to him?"

"Hell, no," Ilana answered breezily. "Let him worry some more. I want him to believe he's lost you."

"He has," Tee'ah whispered, her heart wrenching.

"Please, Tee'ah. You're such a terrible liar." She pushed the makeup wand back in its little tube and steered a befuddled Tee'ah back to the table where Lara was reading a palmtop under Linda's pleased gaze.

"The publishers are putting out novels in Basic now," Linda explained, peering over the primitive eye-magnifiers perched on her nose. "I'm a book reviewer on the side. Cach, Ragan, and Asaro, too— must-read classics. I recommend them highly."

"Talk books in the car, Linda, or we'll be late." Ilana gave Tee'ah a sealed mug and piece of bread shaped like a wheel. "Breakfast on the run," she explained and herded everyone out the front door.

Tee'ah hurried along beside her, envisioning Ian desperate and sorry, all the while struggling to stay afloat in the torrent of energy that was his sister.

The in-dash satellite navigation in the shiny black electric car Ian had rented guided him from LAX to his sister's place in Santa Monica. Gann sat next to him, Muffin was hunched over in the back seat, and the rest of the crew had stayed behind on the *Sun Devil*.

Ian parked behind Ilana's house. He glanced at his reflection in the rearview mirror and ran a hand over his stubble. "Muffin, toss me my shaver." Looking like an escaped convict wasn't going to help his standing with Tee.

Muffin unzipped Ian's duffel bag. There was an ear-ripping shriek, and the big man's head bounced off the car's ceiling with a muffled thud.

Gann twisted around. "What in blazes is the ketta-cat doing here?"

Muffin rubbed his head. "Hell if I know!"

Ian killed the engine. "Whatever you do, don't let anyone see it. Animals are quarantined state to state. This one's from across the galaxy."

Gann reached around his seat and pushed Lara's pet into the duffel. It gave a muffled yowl in protest. "I miss her, too," he said under his breath, zipping the bag nine-tenths shut. "But you're a trouble-maker, just like she is."

He hooked the bag over his shoulder and exited the vehicle, then followed Ian up an outside flight of stairs to the second floor. A piece of paper taped to Ilana's door fluttered in a strengthening breeze coming off the Pacific. Ian tore the note off the wood. "They're not here."

Muffin accepted the news with professional calm,

but Gann didn't try to hide his concern. "Where are they?"

Ian struggled to make out his twin sister's scrawled handwriting. "Ilana's working . . . downtown LA . . . on the roof of the Court Tower. It's the tallest building in the city." He folded the note. "She's got both Tee'ah and Lara with her. Let's go."

They hustled back down the stairs and into the car. Ian merged into traffic on a street busy with summer visitors, then he accelerated onto a high-speed lane reserved for electric vehicles leading directly downtown.

Gann's hands flew to the dashboard. "Great Mother."

"What's wrong?"

"The other ground cars"—he swallowed—"they're too close."

Ian tried not to laugh. "They're supposed to be."

"I journeyed in a similar vehicle, years ago, with Rom. But we never reached this velocity."

"On an electric speedway it's perfectly legal; trust me." He pictured Tee, wondering what she thought of Earth, or driving on the highway. Or seeing the ocean for the first time. There were so many places he wanted to show her, so many things he wanted to experience with her, not the least of which was more incredible lovemaking.

She left you.

The gnawing worry that Tee wanted nothing more to do with him sharpened into impatience to make things right between them. Their futures were intertwined. He was prepared for every conceivable argument to the contrary; he wasn't about to let her go.

He flipped on the vehicle's digital entertainment system. The images of *Vash* representatives and Earth's statesmen clashing in public and private forums didn't lighten his mood. "The Senior Galactic Trade Minister is camped out outside the U.S. president's office," he muttered. His friends' command of English was weak, and Ian found himself translating the news as it unfolded. "I'd guess he's awaiting word from Rom on how to proceed."

Ian wondered what Rom would tell the minister now that he thought he'd recalled Ian. Earth would never cooperate as long as they believed there was little hope of a true partnership with the Federation.

Find Tee, his instincts told him. *Everything else will fall into place.*

Still, no matter what his instincts said, reuniting with Tee in the middle of L.A. was going to be anything but simple.

From the top of the Court Tower, Tee'ah viewed the entire city of Los Angeles, glittering in the hazy, muted light of Earth's star. The wide rooftop was windswept and seemed to touch the sky. Her skirt whipped around her bare legs as she gazed all around her. Glassy buildings nearby rivaled the dizzying height of the one she was on; chaotic roads below were busy with ground cars; huge white runes glowed on a distant hill: Hollywood.

She turned her attention back to the Earth dwellers working on the rooftop. Ilana radiated pure pleasure as she used her *Sony* to capture images. It was a gift, being free to practice a vocation she so enjoyed; Tee'ah hoped Ian's sister understood her good fortune.

Perhaps succumbing to the urge to draw Lara out of her shell, Ilana had asked the woman for assistance. Now Lara stood among those who were filming, holding a "boom mike," pointing it up and outward to capture sound while Ilana's assistant, Linda, coordinated with the other Earth dwellers. Chaos reigned, yet there was a simmering energy given off by the Earthers which Tee'ah found fascinating. With such dash inherent in their culture, no wonder they were balking at the idea of being submerged in a galaxy-wide federation in which they played a minor role.

More Earth dwellers arrived: KCAL-TV news, their equipment stated. As a crisply dressed woman narrated, her companion filmed Ilana filming the Earth dwellers who were filming the actor, a man whom Tee'ah considered nowhere near as compelling as Ian, yet who was inexplicably the focus of so much interest.

Sudden movement dragged Tee'ah's attention to the onlookers milling behind a row of barriers set up around the activity.

Crat. Flanked by Muffin and Gann, Ian jostled his way through the crowd.

Ilana's assistant's eyes widened. "Who's *that?*"

"Buy new glasses, Linda," Ilana said. "It's Ian."

"No, the big blond hulk—I mean hunk."

"His name's Muffin. He's my stepfather's bodyguard."

"Muffin." Linda's mouth curved in a hungry smile. "Darn. There goes my diet."

Tee'ah had no tolerance for such lighthearted conversation. "What is Ian doing here? He's supposed to be in Washington." Her heart wrenched. His mission was critical to galactic peace. How dare he flirt with the controversy she would undoubtedly bring him?

Part of her hoped he was here to see his sister, but the instant his gray-green eyes found her, he left his escorts behind. His expression was resolute, his strides long. His glossy, windblown hair and black leather jacket were more suited to a rebel trader than a galactic crown prince, but he commanded no less respect for it.

The crowd parted, allowing him past. As he closed on her, the world seemed to fall away. Conversation grew distant, the people around her blurred. All she felt was the wind tossing her hair, her dress fluttering against her bare skin, and her love for Ian, giving her a sense of time standing still.

She forcibly looked away, breaking the spell. "Why did you come?" she demanded when he stopped in front of her. "We're over," she said in English—one of his sister's expressions. "You know that."

"I made a mistake, pixie."

"Yes, you did. By coming here. Look around you. Earth dwellers are taking pictures. You can't afford to be seen with me—"

He pulled her into a fierce and possessive kiss. Then he slowly moved her back. "How's that for being seen with me?"

Breathless, she touched her fingertips to her lips. "What are you doing?"

"Breaking the rules." He gripped her shoulders, moving her back. "Come to Washington. Then, after that, we'll work with the Great Council on the subject of you and me."

"No. The timing is wrong. You have to concentrate on your future."

"*Our* future," he reminded her. "We're a team, sweetheart, a great one. Haven't you figured that out yet?"

She hugged her arms to her ribcage. "Don't do this, Ian."

"Sorry, but I'm going to try my damnedest to win you back. We belong together." He tucked a stray lock of hair behind her ear. Tingles spread from where his thumb stroked her cheek. "I know you know it, too. You wear your heart on your sleeve, remember?"

She made a sound of anguished exasperation and twisted out of his grasp. Ian went after her.

Lara grabbed Ilana's hand and pointed after Tee'ah and Ian. She said in Basic, "You want to give Earth a reason to stay in the Federation? Film *them*."

Ilana's face lit up. "Lara, you're brilliant." She tapped her finger against her cheek. Then she turned to the reporter nearby. "You network signatories have an agreement, right? That any breaking news of world significance can be spontaneously pooled at the authority of the net on the scene?"

"That's right." The reporter studied her. "Why?"

"The crown prince of the galaxy is about to choose his future queen. Right here. *Right now!*"

The reporter's eyes veered toward Tee'ah and Ian, arguing passionately in hushed voices.

"He could very well be the next king of the galaxy," Ilana said, "*if* he's approved, and if we Earth-types support him. Just think, a hometown boy in charge. As Rom B'kah's stepdaughter, I can provide the insider narration, if you want: Ladies and gentlemen, watch as we establish—today, right before your eyes—a thrilling new star-spanning dynasty in which *we*—Earth—play a crucial role!"

"I'll call my producer." The reporter pressed her cell phone to her ear.

Ilana paced in short, tense bursts. Lara bit the inside of her lip, opening and closing her fists. The transaction seemed to take forever.

Finally, the reporter lowered her cell phone. "We got it!"

"Yes!" Ilana gave Lara a high-five.

The reporter shouted to her cameraman, "Pool it, global!" and she gestured frantically for him to start filming.

Around the globe, televisions and computers flicked on to catch the breaking story. Satellite coverage shared by the different nets around the world began a simultaneous feed. Then, with just a two-second lag, the image of Tee'ah and Ian began popping on screens from Kalamazoo to Karachi to Kazakhstan.

Ian caught up with Tee on a windswept helipad commanding a spectacular view of the city and a hazy glimpse of the ocean beyond. "Maybe I'm not being clear. I want to marry you, Tee."

She spun around, her eyes anguished, her hair wild. "*No.* I'll not ruin your chance for the throne!"

He advanced on her. "That's why you left, isn't it? You feel you need to protect me—from you."

Her expressive face gave him his answer. He reached for her. She backed away. "You need a traditional wife. I can't be that woman. Royal life suffocates me. I want to fly, to make my own choices."

"Why would I stop you? I don't support the old traditions, you know that."

"That's what you say now, but you'll change," she said with conviction.

369

"I won't!"

"You already have. On the *Quillie* you told me that I could no longer work for you, that the job was too dangerous. Those were your exact words." Her hand crept to her chest and balled into a fist. "I know," she whispered. "I felt every one."

"It was a knee-jerk reaction. I didn't mean you couldn't . . . that I'd . . ." He exhaled. "I was caught off guard, Tee. I reacted badly, and I apologize. I won't change into a traditionalist; I promise you. You know *Vash* custom, we have to be promised for a year before we can get married, time to get to know each other, to see what we're really like. And at the end of that year . . . you'll be free to walk away."

She gave him a grudging nod that told him she didn't believe he wouldn't ultimately go back to the *Vash* way of thinking. Or maybe she was still worried their engagement would keep him from becoming Rom's heir.

"A lot happened over the past few days, Tee, life-changing things."

Now she looked worried. "What, Ian?"

"Rom didn't care for the way I was handling the frontier situation. He ordered me back to Sienna." He lowered his voice. "I didn't go."

"He did?" Her voice rose. "You disobeyed the king?" She grew as pale as a *Vash* could get. "Is that what you meant when you said you broke the rules?"

"You can't follow them all the time, pixie. You

taught me that. The right path isn't always the one everyone uses. Sometimes you've got to go your own way." He took her hands in his. "You have to believe me, Tee, when I say I won't make you live in the traditional way. Isolation should be a choice, not a law. I'm American; I've always felt that way. Being the crown prince won't change that, or how I feel about Earth and my family. Or you, sweet pixie."

Fascinated, Earth's population watched the exchange—in pubs, in cars and shopping malls. In the Oval Office where a weary president argued with an incensed senior *Vash* trade minister, Senator Charlie Randall rose to his feet.

"I don't believe it," he said, pointing to a television mounted on the wall. "There's our boy."

Ian pulled her snug against him. Cheek to cheek, breathing in unison, he rocked her back and forth. "So, what do you say?"

"Don't do this," Tee said in a tight whisper.

"Give me one reason why not."

" 'The welfare of all comes before the desires of the few.' "

"Who's to say this isn't for the good of the many? I'm from the frontier. You're from one of the eight original families. Yeah, things are going to be a little touchy until the Great Council finds a wife for Ché, but it'll settle down. Come on; I love you, Tee. And you love me. Let's get married. To hell with what anyone thinks!"

From nearby came the sound of a crowd whooping and whistling.

Ian lifted his head and glanced over his shoulder. *Holy Toledo.* His sister, the news crew, *everyone*, had formed a half-ring around the helipad.

Ilana's finger came up against her lips. She shook her head, her eyes urging him not to say anything. *Keep going*, she mouthed. *You're doing great.*

Ian was at a loss. Should he capitalize on this fortuitous impromptu forum, allowing the world to eavesdrop on a conversation that should have been private, so he could show Earth that he was human, fallible, and on their side? The day he said he'd be Rom's heir, he'd agreed tacitly to a public life. But this was crazy.

"Say yes! Say yes!" The chant started with a whisper from Ilana's lips. Then Lara took up the chorus, followed by the others on the rooftop.

Ian realized that they were urging Tee to accept his proposal. But she'd shut her eyes. What looked like a prayer formed on her lips. She was going to turn him down, he thought with gloomy certainty.

"Say yes! Say yes!" The cheer spread quickly. Images of the events taking place on a rooftop in Los Angeles streamed into deep space, destined for planets all over the civilized galaxy.

Her eyes opened and she swore.

Ian's mouth quirked. "That's not exactly the answer I was after."

"No." She pointed into the crowd. "I thought I was imagining it. But *look*."

Ian squinted past the lights aimed at him. A pair of newcomers walked toward them. They had smooth amber skin and coppery-blond hair. Both were tall and broad shouldered, with eyes as pale and aristocratic as Tee's.

"It's Klark," Tee whispered. "On the right."

Ian's voice was low and lethal. "I can't believe he had the balls to hunt me down on my home planet." Was Klark so completely evil, or was he just stupid? The man on the left raised his hand in greeting. Every muscle in Ian's body tensed. Klark had brought his older brother, Ché—the man who had every right to claim Tee as his own.

Chapter Twenty-one

Ian set his jaw and met the gold, coolly rational eyes of his unexpected adversary. Ché carried himself with the inbred insolence so characteristic of royal *Vash Nadah* men. And why not? Ché held all the cards—on his own homeworld and here on Ian's. All the prince had to do was imply Tee was by rights his, and it would hurl everything into chaos.

Ian glanced at Tee. She looked stricken. He wanted to reach for her, to hold her tight. *One last time.* He doubted she'd marry Ché. More likely, she'd run deeper into the frontier to "save him from ruin" and pick up the reins of her original plan. He'd lose her either way.

Ché and Klark stopped in front of him, both a full head taller than he. Ché's regal, deep-green cloak swirled around his boots as he dropped to his knees. "Greetings, my prince," he said, bowing his head.

The show of respect threw Ian. "Rise," he said, and extended his hand.

Klark made a hissing noise. "Ché, what are you doing?"

Ché took Ian's wrist in the traditional *Vash* handshake, gripping his arm with passion not evident in his composed expression. Then Ché nodded in Tee's direction. "My lady."

"My lord," she replied softly.

They held each other's gazes for a few moments longer than what made Ian comfortable. Both had been children when they'd first met. Neither could have imagined the consequences of their doomed arranged union. When Ché finally spoke, Ian realized he'd been holding his breath. "I am experiencing a family crisis that disturbs me greatly," he said with a glance at Klark. "I ask for your guidance in choosing the best way to proceed."

"Go on," Ian said carefully.

Klark grabbed Ché's arm. "This is not what we planned! You were to challenge him."

"No," said Ché. "That's the old way. Rom is correct. We're the generation who can ensure a future of peace—but only if we adapt as times change." He waved his hand at Ian and the crowd surrounding them. "Times have changed."

"You would give the reins of our kingdom to this barbarian?"

The crowd sensed something had gone wrong. Their cheers turned to boos. Ian glanced from brother to brother. "What's going on?"

"We formally challenge your claim to the throne," Klark declared. "It's a ritual fight of ancient origins, fought without weapons and not to the death." He paused. "Though at times that happens."

Ian wracked his brain, thinking of all the readings he'd studied, and came up empty-handed. "I've never heard of a ritual challenge."

Ché scowled at his brother. "My brother makes it sound common. In fact, it has never once been enacted, and it won't be now."

Klark threw off his cloak. "If you won't do what is right, I will." Klark's hate-filled gaze settled on Ian. "I hereby challenge you, Earth dweller, in the name of my brother, Prince Ché, firstborn son of the Vedlas, the rightful heir to the throne."

Ian's neck muscles tightened. Though it was tempting, he wouldn't stoop down to Klark's level. Always the best way around a racist's ignorance was a thoughtful, non-threatening approach. "It's obvious we're in disagreement here. We can solve our differences without violence. By talking—"

Klark's fist came out of nowhere and caught him in the jaw. He staggered backward, his eyes watering from the knifelike pain. Tee's cry carried above roar of the crowd. Her fear for him invaded his psyche.

376

"Coward. Unschooled savage." Klark swung at him again. This time Ian blocked his fist, absorbing the shock with his open hand. The impact sent him to his knees, and Klark's boot arced toward his face. But because of his Tae kwon do training, his hands were already there. He hooked Klark's leg by the ankle and swept the prince onto his back.

Around the globe, outrage reigned. In the United Nations, talks between diplomats and the *Vash* chief envoy broke down. In a bar in Sydney, Australia, the patrons turned angry eyes toward a lone *Vash* tourist.

"Hey, mate. You're not welcome here." In a commotion of fists and jeers, he found himself tumbling over the sidewalk. Soaked with beer, he landed in a heap by a parked car.

In the White House, the president bellowed, "This is the man you want to bring to the negotiation table, Randall? Our cool-headed mediator?"

"What would you have him do, Mr. President, put his tail between his legs and run?" The senator exchanged glances with Rom's trade minister. "My money's on Hamilton," he drawled. "How about yours, *Vash?*"

Sprawled on his back, Klark groaned.

Ian had spent his teenage years practicing martial arts, earning his black belt. But fighting on pavement was a lot more serious—and painful—than landing on mats. Rubbing his throbbing hand, Ian stood over his opponent. "Klark, you made your point. Now let's work things out. This isn't what Rom would want." Not that he had any right to say what the king wanted or didn't, seeing that he was here against the man's orders. "I'll help you up."

The prince nodded humbly and raised his arm. Their hands clasped. Then Klark yanked him off balance and hurled him over his head.

The world spun, and Ian landed hard. The impact knocked the wind out of him. Choking, tasting blood, he writhed over the cement, his neck and back burning with pain. He was vaguely aware of the shouting crowd, his sister and Tee trying to reach him but being held back. He tried to get up, but almost passed out. He couldn't see, and his ears rang so loudly he couldn't hear anything else. All he'd ever believed in was solving conflict through reason. Now, ironically, he stood to lose everything he valued on the outcome of what was nothing more than a street fight.

Klark's boots crunched back and forth on the pavement. Bitterness spewed out of him. "Is this the man you want as king?" he called. "Look at him, squirming on the ground like an unearthed invertebrate. He wants to talk, eh? It's because he can't fight."

"Enough," Ché told his brother.

"Enough, is right. If he can't stand up for what he believes in, how is he supposed to defend the galaxy?" Klark's laughter echoed across the rooftop.

Ian growled. Now he was starting to get pissed. *Hot damn! Ian Hamilton's going to kick some butt. Tae kwon do.* His sister's words the day he'd learned Randall was coming to the frontier came back to haunt him. "You prefer the thinking man's approach," she'd teased. "Diplomacy is paramount; 'make love not war,' the *Vash Nadah* creed. Hey, it worked for most of eleven thousand years, right? But sometimes, you just have to kick a little ass."

Klark loomed over him. "Are we finished already, Earth dweller? Are you ready to relinquish your claim to the throne and hand it over to a real man?" Grabbing Ian's hand, the *Vash* prince yanked him to his feet with one hand and hurled a punch with his other.

Ian blocked the strike and hit Klark in the chin. A roundhouse kick sent the stunned prince to the ground. "Actually, I'm going to kick your butt."

The crowd went wild. Klark rose and came at him again, albeit wobbly. Ian blocked his kicks, sent him sprawling again. Clearly enraged, blood dribbling from his split chin, the *Vash* climbed unsteadily to his feet and threw another punch. Ian ducked. Instantly he had Klark in a choke hold.

Ian's breaths hissed in and out as he ratcheted his arm tighter. "What do you think, Klark? Is this man enough for you?"

Klark struggled, wheezing. "Barbarian."

"You say the word like there's something wrong with it."

Ilana whooped, and Ché regarded her with a bemused expression.

Ian yanked Klark's pants and took him down, holding him flat on the cement with an arm bar, a clamp he made even more painful for Klark each time the man attempted to move. With the prince immobile, he pressed his thumb and finger into his neck. Klark's face turned purple. "Can we safely say this is over now?"

Klark squeezed out, "You'll have to kill me."

He compressed Klark's pinned arm. The prince bared his teeth in pain.

"Leadership is about making choices, Klark. I don't have to kill you." He pressed his fingers into the man's throat until his legs convulsed. "However, that doesn't mean I won't."

Klark's gold eyes met his. In their depths perhaps the beginning of respect glimmered. Not the respect that came from admiration, though, but the wrong kind: respect born of fear. It's not what Ian wanted, yet it was a start. "Today we'll end this battle this way," he said. He released Klark. "Inflexibility almost caused the Federation to fall seven years ago— to a cult leader, a mere religious fanatic. All because, after eleven thousand years of peace, they didn't believe he could start a war. But he did. And it cost you tens of thousands of lives. It might have been millions if Rom B'kah hadn't had the vision to act in time."

He sought Tee's gaze. "It's time for change," he said quietly. "I will set the example in my home, and with my wife."

Her slow, proud smile gave him hope. Maybe he still had a chance with her.

With the fight over, Gann pushed his way through the onlookers to Lara. "Commandeered, my eye," he muttered upon reaching her. "You brought Tee'ah here voluntarily."

"I brought her home. That's what I was paid to do. You never specified where home was."

"You helped her," he argued. "At the high probability of forfeiting the money you need to retrieve your ship."

"Yeah, well . . ." She averted her gaze.

He cupped her chin between his thumb and index finger and forced her to look at him. "You have a generous and loving heart, Lara. Not the black hole you think is in there." Her shocked eyes grew moist. "And if you ever again say otherwise, I'll . . . I'll . . ." Blast, he didn't know what he'd do. He swept her into his arms instead.

Her free hand flattened against his chest. "Gann—"

"I want flying lessons," he declared.

She looked at him as if he'd grown another head. "You do?"

"Teach me how to fly. You know, on that amazing ship of yours . . . as soon as we"—he paused to enunciate the words—"get it out of impoundment."

Joy lit up her face. Then her eyes narrowed. "Hey. You know how to fly."

He framed her face in his hands. "Ah, Sunshine, not high enough." Hesitantly at first, her arms slid around his waist. "No, not high enough," he murmured and brushed his lips over hers.

They didn't see the ketta-cat wriggling free of the duffel bag until it was too late. Before Gann could stop it, the creature bolted under and between legs, darting away until it became lost in the crowd.

"Cat!" Lara yelled. Together they ran after her runaway pet.

The unmistakable meow of a ketta-cat caught Ian's attention. Gann looked almost comical as he bent his muscular warrior's body to the task of trying to retrieve the animal.

"Cat," Lara crooned. "Here, cat."

The next thing he knew, Tee was hunched over, making kissing noises.

Ian sighed and met Ché's equally disbelieving gaze. Why had he ever convinced Gann to bring the animal, when it could have stayed in the car, cooking nicely as the interior hit one-hundred and twenty degrees in the sun?

Gann made another swipe at the ketta-cat and missed. It brushed against Ian's leg then padded over to Klark. The crouching man and the animal considered each other. Then the ketta-cat squatted, its tail stiff and upright, and a puddle of bright yellow urine trickled over Klark's boot.

Eyes watering, Lara snatched the animal and hurried away. Gann gave Ian a two-fingered salute and went after her.

Klark glowered at the droplets glittering on his boots. "I rescind the challenge," he managed past gritted teeth.

"I hope so." Tee made her way to the sullen prince. Ian let her pass by. More than anyone, she deserved her piece of Klark. "And an apology is forthcoming, too, I hope. Because of you, one of Ian Hamilton's pilots drank himself to death, and you almost killed his entire crew by tampering with his ship. You humiliated me where no one could see, and you almost killed me that night in the woods. You never challenged us outright, always from the shadows, where you were certain you wouldn't be caught. You're a cowardly, meddling bastard, Klark. Men like you give us *Vash* a bad name in the frontier. If you weren't already crouched there bleeding, I'd kick the stuffing out of you. Now do what is right and show your respect for your future king."

Klark's hunched shoulders and lowered eyes gave the impression of humble repentance. But as he crouched before them, his forearm balanced on one upright knee, Ian saw disdain flicker in his eyes, at odds with his outward compunction.

His hand curled into a fist. "This was not the out-come I'd conceived. But you were the clear victor, Ian." His knuckles turned white. "Perhaps, today, I have learned something about Earth dwellers."

Ian replied, "And I've learned some things about the *Vash*. Some traditions don't translate well into our changing society—the old treatment of the frontier, the enforced isolation of royal women, this sort of bloodletting," he added, tasting the salty tang in his mouth. "But I don't want to alienate the sup-porters of the old ways. We can work together on the subject, Klark, you and me, when we feel more like speaking to rather than thrashing each other."

Klark's mouth almost curved. "Yes; when we're ready, my lord." He exhaled. "Now, I await your judgment."

Ian turned and said to the elder Vedla prince, "Your brother committed several very serious crimes. He needs to be punished."

"Agreed," said Ché.

"Determine what that punishment will entail. Then brief me on what you decide. We need to all work together in fairness and forgiveness for a better galaxy."

Gratitude and respect flashed in Ché's eyes. Ian's spine tingled as he once more glimpsed the future. Not only had he made an ally today, he'd formed a friendship—one he sensed would become indispen-sable in the years to come.

Tee's hand came to rest on Ian's arm. "You say

we're a team. Why, then, have we not fought as hard for us as we have against Klark?"

He ran his hand over her hair. "I don't know," he said wearily. "But I say we start."

Her gaze shifted to Ché, the man she was supposed to marry. Ian braced himself. In a quiet, respectful tone, Ché said, "Princess Tee'ah, even if we had been officially promised, I would release you."

Ian knew Tee'ah struggled to tamp down on what would be a tactless show of joy and relief. "I thank you," she said in a hushed voice.

Exultation surged through Ian. He grabbed her hands. "We'll bring together the old and the new, the Federation and the frontier. Your blood and mine." He listened to himself in amazement. He was sounding more *Vash* by the minute.

The crowd didn't seem to mind. Again, they began to chant, "Say yes, say yes!"

In the dead of night, on a harsh desert world, a signal left an ancient palace and began a long, silent journey through the lonely reaches of space. Made possible by paradoxical technology, whose origins were lost in history, the stream of data made its way toward Earth, finding its final target with a little help from Ilana Hamilton and a KCAL-TV news crew. When the slightly larger-than-life-sized, three-dimensional holographic image of the galaxy's king appeared on the L.A. rooftop, awe silenced the crowd.

Luminous radiance flickered like St. Elmo's fire over Romlijhian B'kah's projected deep-blue, floor length cape. Stony faced, he stood before them, his arms folded over his chest. His features were rugged, resolute, and when he cast his unflinching gaze around the roof, as if searching for someone, most fought the urge to duck. But not Ian, Tee'ah thought, who clasped her hand in a warm, reassuring grip and led her across the windy helipad to meet the king.

The lights and cameras followed them. Her neck tingled. She knew the events transpiring today would echo through the years, and that her children would want to hear of them again and again.

They stopped in front of the radiant image. Rom's expression remained unchanged.

She'd expected Ian to bring up Earth, or even Klark, but he began with a matter of the heart. If she'd ever doubted she'd come first with this man of honor, her reservations were erased in that glorious and frightening moment.

"You don't approve of my relationship with Tee'ah. Nor does the Great Council."

Nor my father, she thought.

"But whether or not you give us your blessing, I want to marry Tee'ah—if she'll have me."

She squeezed his hand. Why couldn't two people who were in love defy the galaxy?

She forced her chin up a notch. She'd hijacked a starspeeder, cruised through asteroid fields, shot at intruders, yet she was terrified of speaking to the king. "My lord, I love Ian. I want to spend my life with him, whether or not my father approves— though I do regret it if he does not. I love my family and miss them, but if tradition is more important to them than my happiness, I'm prepared to live with the consequences of my actions."

"And you, sir," Ian said, "are going to have to do something about the frontier. Have you read my report on the conditions on Barésh and the worlds like it? The situation is contemptible. How could the *Vash* not know? It's inexcusable. We ought to be ashamed. The abuse of the frontier must stop."

"You're right," Rom said.

Ian's hand clamped over hers. "My lord?"

"We have not given the frontier the attention it requires," Rom went on, seemingly oblivious to their shock. "And so over the years, as we've added many more worlds, things slipped through the cracks. I never would have allowed such suffering to continue had I known about it. That I wasn't aware of the problem tells me that our management of the region must change. I hereby assign Earth as the sovereign administrator of the frontier. This is more power than any planet other than a *Vash* homeworld has ever held. But the situation requires it. Perhaps you and Tee'ah will opt to live there part of the year, in the tradition of a typical *Vash* homeworld. How the particulars will work, regarding Earth's reporting to the Trade Federation, you may discuss in your upcoming meetings in Washington. Until then, I offer Earth and the worlds of the frontier my official apology."

This was not what Tee'ah had expected. Nor had Ian, judging by the expression of disbelief on his face. She wondered if Rom had been testing them all along. If so, she hoped they'd passed.

Tenderly, she touched her fingertips to Ian's bruised jaw. "Now everything you came here to achieve has come to pass," she whispered.

His smile turned sly. "Not yet." *Wait*, his eyes told her.

Ian dropped to one knee. Tee'ah knelt beside him.

" 'My loyalty for life,' " Ian told Rom and pressed his fist over his heart.

"A *Vash* princess deserves no less," Rom said in a quiet voice. "Nor do you, Ian, from your future wife. Yes, of course, you'll marry Tee'ah. I never meant for anything else since you first mentioned her. Show the galaxy that you feel as I do—as your mother and I do. Bring us together; unite us in peace."

Fingers linked, they rose. Then, with billions, perhaps trillions looking on, Ian took Tee'ah's shaking hands in his. "Rom B'kah chose me to carry on his legacy," he said. "Never will I forsake the man who sacrificed so much to bring the galaxy peace. Nor, my love, will I ever forsake you." He squeezed her hands. "I ask for your promise of marriage."

The cry "Say yes" rose once more into a thunderous chant.

Tee'ah wound her arms over his shoulders. "Yes, Earth dweller. *Yes.*"

"Now everything I've wanted has come to pass," he murmured in her ear.

Tears in her eyes, she kissed him enthusiastically on the mouth.

Around the globe cheers erupted. In the United Nations, diplomats applauded, and the *Vash* chief envoy embraced a thoroughly bemused female Secretary General.

In Sydney, a bedraggled *Vash* tourist was dragged back into the bar, where he was offered more foaming glasses of beer than he'd be able to drink in a lifetime. But it would be said, much later, that he put forth his best effort for galactic peace.

In the Oval Office, the President of the United States uncorked a bottle of champagne. "Our future and the Federation's is looking better all the time," he said to Senator Randall and the now smiling *Vash* trade minister. "This calls for a toast." He raised his crystal flute. "To peace."

The minister winked. "To profit, too."

"And to underdogs that become champions," Randall said and tipped his glass in Ian's direction.

Onboard the *Sun Devil*, Gredda smiled and nodded. "The captain is a lucky man."

"*She* is a lucky woman," Quin argued.

And much later, thousands of light years away, in an age-old palace on the B'kah homeworld—Sienna—Jas and Rom smiled with pride as Ian and their niece enchanted a jaded galaxy.

Chapter Twenty-two

Exactly one standard year had passed since Ian had last visited, but nothing much had changed: Donavan's Blunder was still the sorriest stopover in the frontier.

At old Garjha's bar, Ian sipped his *tock* and studied the woman next to him. "Just think; two more months of being single, then you'll be shackled to me for life."

"I know," Tee said in lousy imitation of acting glum. She plunked her elbows on the bar. Her almost shoulder-length hair curled in the humid evening air, the color evened out thanks to a bottle of Clairol's Desert Sunrise. Affection swelled in his chest, and he stroked his hand over the silky strands.

She smiled and propped her cheek on the knuckles of her clasped hands. "Buy you another *tock*, bad boy?" she asked in heavily accented English.

"No. I think your last trip to Donavan's Blunder as a single woman calls for something stronger." He pounded his fist on the counter. "Bartender—Mandarian whiskey!"

Garjha perked up. Mumbling to himself, the man reached under the bar for a dusty red bottle. Uncorking it with steady hands, he filled two glasses.

Tee'ah waved her hands. "Oh, no. Not that stuff."

Ian smiled innocently. "Why? Have fun. You'll soon be a quiet, compliant wife."

She snorted. "Right."

He took one of the glasses, distracting her with conversation while he slipped an extra ingredient into the pungent smelling whiskey. "Don't forget, we're taking Lara's cloaker friend Eston out to dinner. We can ply him with food and alcohol and make him tell us what Gann and Lara have been up to."

"Gann and Lara. I can't wait to see if they arrive at the wedding together or separate." She laughed. "Together is my wager, but we'll have plenty of entertainment either way."

Vash weddings lasted six days. There were feasts, parties, and ceremonies, making it clear why couples were required to wait a year after taking the promise vows. Otherwise, there wouldn't be enough time to memorize the required passages from Treatise of Trade and the rituals they'd have to perform. Tee'ah had worked closely with her mother through all the arrangements, helping to heal her relationship with her family.

"Entertainment," he said, cradling the glass of whiskey in his hands. "You wouldn't mean Ché and my sister, would you?"

"They won't admit it, but they're boozers about each other."

He laughed. "That's bonkers, pixie."

She pursed her lips. "I don't speak English like an Earth dweller, but I'm getting close, yes?"

He leaned closer, his fingers sliding up her thigh. Her eyes darkened and her muscles bunched under his hand. "Drink up, Miss Tee," he said and handed her the glass.

She tried to force it back into his hands. Whiskey splashed onto their jeans. He crossed his arms over his stomach and leaned back on his stool.

Her mouth twisted. "I cannot believe you really want me to—" She noticed something glinting on the bottom of the glass and fished it out with two fingers. A small sound of pleasure escaped her. Staring at the dripping diamond ring cupped in her palm, she bit her lower lip. "Ian . . ."

"An engagement ring. It's time to do this right."

Her nostrils flared with emotion. She gazed down at the ring, her fingertip making tiny loving circles around the radius of the platinum band.

Quietly he explained, "I wanted to do this before we headed back for the wedding, and since this is the one-year anniversary of our first meeting, I thought the timing was right."

Her lips curved in a soft smile. "It is," she whispered.

He took her hands in his. "I always thought, deep inside, that we were meant to be together. But only recently did I find out how true that was."

Her brows drew together.

"My stepfather married my mother the night he left for the battle of Balkanor. It was a rushed ceremony, and painful. They figured they'd never see each other again. A very old woman married them, a seer. Afterward, she told them that they'd have good futures, long lives." He searched Tee'ah's face and smiled. "And many descendants. 'Your progeny will travel to many worlds,' she told them."

He took the ring from Tee's hand. "Naturally my mother didn't believe her. Even if Rom survived, he couldn't father children. But now we know what that old woman meant. Us, Tee. Jas's son, Rom's niece."

Tee's face was luminescent with love. "Our children will be a part of them both."

His back tingled—destiny looking over his shoulder, he thought. Swallowing, he crouched on one knee. "Some things have to be done the old-fashioned Earth way," he explained. Then he took a deep breath. "Tee'ah Dar, will you marry me?"

"Ah, Ian." She leaned forward. "I will."

He slipped the ring on her finger. They kissed and slowly moved apart.

Then he led her away from the bar to where the lights of the town didn't reach. He murmured into her hair, "Once I wondered if I'd ever be up to the task of taking Rom's place."

"We're a team," she said. "We'll go the distance together."

And so they stood before a sea of stars, and a future that was finally theirs.

THE
STAR

SUSAN GRANT

Careening out of control in her fighter jet is only the start of the wildest ride of Jasmine's life; spinning wildly in an airplane is nothing like the loss of equilibrium she feels when she lands. There, in a half-dream, Jas sees a man more powerfully compelling than any she's ever encountered. Though his words are foreign, his touch is familiar, baffling her mind even as he touches her soul. But who is he? Is he, too, a downed pilot? Is that why he lies in the desert sand beneath a starry Arabian sky? The answers burn in his mysterious golden eyes, in his thoughts that become hers as he holds out his hand and requests her aid. This man has crossed many miles to find her, to offer her a heaven that she might otherwise never know, and love is only one of the many gifts of . . . the Star King.

___52413-9 $5.50 US/$6.50 CAN

Dorchester Publishing Co., Inc.
P.O. Box 6640
Wayne, PA 19087-8640

Please add $2.50 for shipping and handling for the first book and $.75 for each book thereafter. NY, NYC, and PA residents, please add appropriate sales tax. No cash, stamps, or C.O.D.s. All orders shipped within 6 weeks via postal service book rate. Canadian orders require $2.00 extra postage and must be paid in U.S. dollars through a U.S. banking facility.

Name_____
Address_____
City_____ State_____ Zip_____
I have enclosed $_____in payment for the checked book(s).
Payment <u>must</u> accompany all orders.☐Please send a free catalog.
CHECK OUT OUR WEBSITE! www.dorchesterpub.com

Shamara
Catherine Spangler

In a universe of darkness and depravity, the Shielders battle to stay one step ahead of the vengeful Controllers, who seek the destruction of their race. Survival depends upon the quest of one man. Jarek san Ranul has found evidence of a wormhole, a vortex to another galaxy; an escape. But when his search produces the most intriguing woman he's ever met, he finds he wants something more than duty and honor.

On the run from a mighty warlord, Eirene Kane has to protect her identity as an Enhancer, one of a genetic few with a powerful gift. Then her flight hurls her into the arms of Jarek, a man who steals her heart and uncovers her perilous secret—and though she knows she should flee, Eirene finds herself yearning for both the man and the one thing he claims will free them forever.

___52452-X $5.50 US/$6.50 CAN

Dorchester Publishing Co., Inc.
P.O. Box 6640
Wayne, PA 19087-8640

Catherine Spangler

SHADOWER

Sabin has been in every hellhole in the galaxy. In his line of work, hives of scum and villainy are nothing to fear. But Giza's is different, and the bronze-haired beauty at the bar is something special. Not only can she sweep a man off his feet, she can break his legs—and steal his heart. And though Moriah isn't what Sabin had come for, she is suddenly all he desires.

The man is a menace, what with his dark good looks and overwhelming masculinity. Worse, Sabin is a shadower, a bounty hunter, which means he is only one step removed from the law. He is dangerous to a smuggler like Moriah, to her freedom. Yet he draws her as a moth to a flame, and even as she pledges to stay cool, her senses catch fire. Then, in his arms, Moriah realizes that this bounty hunter is different. His touch is gentle, and his kiss sweet. And his love leads to a fantastic freedom she's never known.

___52424-4 $5.50 US/$6.50 CAN

Shielder

Catherine Spangler

Unjustly shunned by her people, Nessa dan Ranul knows she is unlovable—so when an opportunity arises for her to save her world, she leaps at the chance. Setting out for the farthest reaches of the galaxy, she has one goal: to elude capture and deliver her race from destruction. But then she finds herself at the questionable mercy of Chase McKnight, a handsome bounty hunter. Suddenly, Nessa finds that escape is the last thing she wants. In Chase's passionate embrace she finds a nirvana of which she never dared dream—with a man she never dared trust. But as her identity remains a secret and her mission incomplete, each passing day brings her nearer to oblivion.

___52304-3 $5.50 US/$6.50 CAN

Dorchester Publishing Co., Inc.
P.O. Box 6640
Wayne, PA 19087-8640

Please add $1.75 for shipping and handling for the first book and $.50 for each book thereafter. NY, NYC, and PA residents, please add appropriate sales tax. No cash, stamps, or C.O.D.s. All orders shipped within 6 weeks via postal service book rate. Canadian orders require $2.00 extra postage and must be paid in U.S. dollars through a U.S. banking facility.

Name_____
Address_____
City_____State_____Zip_____
I have enclosed $_____ in payment for the checked book(s).
Payment <u>must</u> accompany all orders. ❑ Please send a free catalog.
    CHECK OUT OUR WEBSITE! www.dorchesterpub.com